GREAT STORIES OF THE
American West

GREAT STORIES OF THE
American West

STORIES BY

John Jakes, Elmore Leonard,
Marcia Muller, John D. MacDonald
and many others

EDITED BY

Martin H. Greenberg

DONALD I. FINE, INC.
New York

Library of Congress Catalogue Card Number: 94-071113
ISBN: 1-55611-417-6

Manufactured in the United States of America

10 9 8 7 6 5 4 3 2 1

Designed by Irving Perkins Associates

This novel is a work of fiction. Names, characters, places and incidents are either the product of the author's imagination or are used fictitiously. Any resemblance to actual events, locales, organizations or persons, living or dead, is entirely coincidental and beyond the intent of either the author or publisher.

Author
Notes

Loren D. Estleman is the best western writer of the under-fifty generation. He has brought poetry, historical truth and great wisdom to the genre. While it's difficult to cite only a few of his novels, *This Old Bill* and *Bloody Season* are especially notable.

Though Brian Garfield has written many westerns, he's probably best known for such major historical novels as *Wild Times*. The trouble with this assessment is that it overlooks some equally fine work he did with the traditional western in the early seventies, *Sliphammer* and *Gun Down* being particularly effective.

Donald Hamilton is best known as the creator of the Matt Helm books, which many believe is the best espionage series ever written by an American. But early in his career, Hamilton wrote a number of excellent traditional westerns as well, including such titles as *Mad River* and *The Two-Shoot Gun*.

Elmer Kelton is a major and widely respected name in modern western fiction. His work, which includes such novels as *The Man Who Rode Midnight* and *The Good Old Boys* are modern benchmarks of western fiction.

Dorothy M. Johnson wrote one of the great tales of all time, "The Man Who Shot Liberty Valance." Notice we didn't say "western" tales. Johnson's work often transcended genre limitations. She was pure storyteller, plucky and profound by turns.

Louis L'Amour was the most successful western writer of all time. He wrote the kind of action fiction beloved by so many generations of Americans. And yet, often overlooked in all his success, was the gentler and more philosophic side of L'Amour, as demonstrated in this wonderful story.

JOHN JAKES is one of America's best-selling authors. He modernized the historical novel and made it popular again with millions of Americans. But he is also a major western author, as he shows us here in this early and very well-written story.

ELMORE LEONARD has written what a number of critics feel is the single best western of our time, *Valdez Is Coming*. Though widely known as a crime writer, Leonard's westerns are considered by many to be at least as good as his suspense novels.

EVAN HUNTER is one of popular fiction's modern masters. As Ed McBain, he created the 87th Precinct, one of the most popular mystery series of all time; and as Hunter he's written many novels that captured wide public acclaim, including *The Blackboard Jungle* and *Last Summer*. Early in his career he wrote some western stories, and some very good ones, too.

JOHN D. MACDONALD was perhaps the best suspense writer of his time. All one needs to say is "Travis McGee" and any argument is pretty much settled. MacDonald started out in the pulps, writing everything from sports stories to war tales. He even had time for a few westerns. Consider this an homage to the action-packed pulps.

MARCIA MULLER has become one of the preeminent suspense writers of our time, a fact that overshadows her small but powerful body of work in the western field. Muller brings the same style and insight to the classic western as she does to the classic suspense story. This is a particularly memorable story.

DWIGHT V. SWAIN was another pulp writer who eventually made the transition to paperbacks. He was also a teacher and a fine student of writing, turning his observations into three first-rate books on the subject. Here's one of his pulp westerns for your enjoyment.

H. A. DEROSSO was a dark and lonely man who lived a brief life which ended by his own hand. He wrote brilliantly bitter western stories quite unlike anything else in the genre. The pain was real and he captured it with angry ferocity.

BILL PRONZINI has written important stories in virtually all genres but he's probably best known for creating one of the landmark detective series, the Nameless novels, and for contributing a steady supply of first-rate fiction to a variety of markets. Pronzini is one of the great popular writers of our time and it's way past time that that fact be acknowledged.

PEGGY S. CURRY wrote the kind of quiet western stories that escaped the attention of all but a few practiced eyes. This is probably her masterpiece, as good a story as any in this book, and a piece that shows how serious and well-wrought western fiction can be in capable hands.

BILL CRIDER is known for his wry suspense novels about modern-day Texas. But he's also a fine western stylist, bringing the same gifts—great characterization, skilled plotting and a real feel for mood—to his westerns as well. *A Time For Hanging* is especially notable.

AL SARRANTONIO is a fantasist of the Ray Bradbury school. And a damned fine detective-story writer. And a damned fine western writer, too. In this story, you'll see glimpses of all his skills at work.

JAMES M. REASONER has written several novels under pen names and at least one (a mystery called *Texas Wind*) that is one of the most sought-after paperback originals of all time. Reasoner's got his own slant on things and it's always a pleasure to read him.

"This is a western for grown-ups, written in a lean, hard-boiled style that should appeal to 'readers who don't (usually) read westerns.'" So said *Publishers Weekly* when *Death Ground* first appeared. ED GORMAN's work has won the Spur once and been acclaimed as "some of the best western fiction of our time" by the Rocky Mountain *News*. *Death Ground* is presently under option and may become a cable movie within the next two TV seasons.

Contents

Introduction

We ARE AN outlaw nation. Born in the Caesarean throes of revolution, America has throughout its history established itself from ambush.

Excepting *Moby Dick* and the compositions of George and Ira Gershwin, our only unique contributions to world culture have been the shady art forms of jazz, rock 'n' roll, the detective story, and the western. All have at one time or another been branded subversive; yet they are the first things that come to the minds of Europeans and Asians whenever the subject of America is discussed.

Not long ago, the western short story was ubiquitous. Fiction magazines bound in four-color covers depicting savage Indians and bullet-belching gunmen dominated drugstore racks and provided the storylines for Hollywood's most enduring classics: *Stagecoach, High Noon, A Man Called Horse,* and scores of other feature films began as thirty-minute reads in the pages of the great pulp magazines of the past. As late as 1990, Orion Pictures found enough meat in Michael Blake's novella *Dances with Wolves* to sustain three blockbuster hours starring Kevin Costner.

There is hope, then, despite a trend toward five-pound tomes on the New York *Times* list of bestsellers, that the lean, no-detours approach to frontier storytelling associated with Dorothy Johnson and the early Louis L'Amour is still with us and will prosper.

The stories in this collection represent the best of the best from our love affair with our own wide-open spaces. Some of the names—Leonard, MacDonald, and L'Amour—are legend. Others—Hamilton, Swain, and Muller—are cult heroes. Still others are less well known than their writing, and the remainder are new. All share the power of a form that could only have come from a place so vast that Thomas Jefferson predicted it would not be settled in five hundred years.

No less confidently—but I hope with greater accuracy—I predict that the reader who picks up this volume will set it down with the same sense of discovery that our pioneering ancestors knew when they broke with their European traditions to venture into the sunset for the very first time.

—LOREN D. ESTLEMAN

The Bandit

LOREN D. ESTLEMAN

THEY CUT HIM loose a day early.

It worried him a little, and when the night captain on his block brought him a suit of clothes and a cardboard suitcase containing a toothbrush and a change of shirts, he considered bringing it up, but in that moment he suddenly couldn't stand it there another hour. So he put on the suit and accompanied the guard to the administration building, where the assistant warden made a speech, grasped his hand, and presented him with a check for $1,508. At the gate he shook hands with the guard, although the man was new to his section and he didn't know him, then stepped out into the gray autumn late afternoon. Not counting incarceration time before and during his trial, he had been behind bars twenty-eight years, eleven months, and twenty-nine days.

While he was standing there, blinking rapidly in diffused sunlight that was surely brighter than that on the other side of the wall, a leather-bonneted assembly of steel and inflated rubber came ticking past on the street with a goggled and dustered operator at the controls. He watched it go by towing a plume of dust and blue smoke and said, "Oldsmobile."

He had always been first in line when magazines donated by the DAR came into the library, and while his fellow inmates were busy snatching up the new catalogs and finding the pages containing pictures of women in corsets and camisoles torn out, he was paging through the proliferating motoring journals, admiring the photographs and studying the technical illustrations of motors and transmissions. Gadgets had enchanted him since he saw his first steam engine aboard a Missouri River launch at age ten, and he had a fair idea of how automobiles worked. However, aside from one heart-thudding glimpse of the warden's new Locomobile parked inside the gates before the prison board decided its presence stirred unhealthy ambitions among the general population, this was his

1

first exposure to the belching, clattering reality. He felt like a wolf whelp looking on the harsh glitter of the big world outside its parents' den for the first time.

After the machine had gone, he put down the suitcase to collect his bearings. In the gone days he had enjoyed an instinct for directions, but it had been replaced by other, more immediate survival mechanisms inside. Also, an overgrown village that had stood only two stories high on dirt streets as wide as pastures when he first came to it had broken out in brick towers and macadam and climbed the hills across the river, where an electrified trolley raced through a former cornfield clanging its bell like a mad mother cow. He wasn't sure if the train station would be where he left it in 1878.

He considered banging on the gate and asking the guard, but the thought of turning around now made him pick up his suitcase and start across the street at double-quick step, the mess-hall march. "The wrong way beats no way," Micah used to put it.

It was only a fifteen-minute walk, but for an old man who had stopped pacing his cell in 1881 and stretched his legs for only five of the twenty minutes allotted daily in the exercise yard, it was a hike. He had never liked walking anyway, had reached his majority breaking mixed-blood stallions that had run wild from December to March on the old Box W. and had done some of his best thinking and fighting with a horse under him. So when at last he reached the station, dodging more motorcars—the novelty of that wore off the first time—and trying not to look to passersby like a convict in his tight suit swinging a dollar suitcase, he was sweating and blowing like a wind-broke mare.

The station had a water closet—a closet indeed, with a gravity toilet and a mirror in need of resilvering over a white enamel basin, but a distinct improvement over the stinking bucket he had had to carry down three tiers of cells and dump into the cistern every morning for twenty-nine years. He placed the suitcase on the toilet seat, hung up his hat and soaked coat, unhooked his spectacles, turned back his cuffs, ran cold water into the basin, and splashed his face. Mopping himself dry on a comparatively clean section of roller towel, he looked at an old man's unfamiliar reflection, then put on his glasses to study it closer. But for the mirror in the warden's office it was the first one he'd seen since his trial; mirrors were made of glass, and glass was good for cutting wrists and throats. What hair remained on his scalp had gone dirty-gray. The flesh of his face was sagging, pulling away from the bone, and so pale he took a moment locating the bullet-crease on his forehead from Liberty. His beard was yellowed white, like stove grime. (All the men inside wore beards. It was easier than trying to shave without mirrors.) It was his grandfather's face.

Emerging from the water closet, he read the train schedule on the blackboard next to the ticket booth and checked it against his coin-battered old turnip watch, wound and set for the first time in half his lifetime. A train to Huntsford was pulling out in forty minutes.

He was alone at his end of the station with the ticket agent and a lanky young man in a baggy checked suit slouched on one of the varnished benches with his long legs canted out in front of him and his hands in his pockets. Conscious that the young man was watching him, but accustomed to being watched, he walked up to the booth and set down the suitcase. "Train to Huntsford on schedule?"

"Was last wire." Perched on a stool behind the window, the agent looked at him over the top of his *Overland Monthly* without seeing him. He had bright predatory eyes in a narrow face that had foiled an attempt to square it off with thick burnsides.

"How much to Huntsford?"

"Four dollars."

He unfolded the check for $1,508 and smoothed it out on the ledge under the glass.

"I can't cash that," said the agent. "You'll have to go to the bank."

"Where's the bank?"

"Well, there's one on Treelawn and another on Cross. But they're closed till Monday."

"I ain't got cash on me."

"Well, the railroad don't offer credit."

While the agent resumed reading, he unclipped the big watch from its steel chain and placed it on top of the check. "How much you allow me on that?"

The agent glanced at it, then returned to his magazine.

"This is a railroad station, not a jeweler's. I got a watch."

He popped open the lid and pointed out the engraving. "See that J.B.H.? That stands for James Butler Hickok. Wild Bill himself gave it to me when he was sheriff in Hays."

"Mister, I got a scar on my behind I can say I got from Calamity Jane, but I'd still need four dollars to ride to Huntsford. Not that I'd want to."

"Problem, Ike?"

The drawled question startled old eardrums thickened to approaching footsteps. The young man in the checked suit was at his side, a head taller and smelling faintly of lilac water.

"Just another convict looking to wrestle himself a free ride off the C. H. & H.," the agent said. "Nothing I don't handle twice a month."

"What's the fare?"

The agent told him. The man in the checked suit produced a bent brown wallet off his right hip and counted four bills onto the window ledge.

"Hold up there. I never took a thing free off nobody that wasn't my idea to start."

"Well, give me the watch."

"This watch is worth sixty dollars."

"You were willing to trade it for a railroad ticket."

"I was not. I asked him what he'd give me on it."

"Sixty dollars for a gunmetal watch that looks like it's been through a thresher?"

"It keeps good time. You see that J.B.H.?"

"Wild Bill. I heard." The man in the checked suit counted the bills remaining in his wallet. "I've got just ten on me."

He closed the watch and held it out. "I'll give you my sister's address in Huntsford. You send me the rest there."

"You're trusting me? How long did you serve?"

"He's got a check drawn on the state bank for fifteen hundred," said the agent, separating a ticket from the perforated sheet.

The man in the checked suit pursed his lips. "Mister, you must've gone in there with some valuables. Last I knew, prison wages still came to a dollar a week."

"They ain't changed since I went in."

Both the ticket agent and the man in the checked suit were staring at him now. "Mister, you keep your watch. You've earned that break."

"It ain't broke, just dented some. Anyway, I said before I don't take charity."

"Let's let the four dollars ride for now. Your train's not due for a half hour. If I'm not satisfied with our talk at the end of that time, you give me it to hold and I'll send it on later, as a deposit against the four dollars."

"Folks paying for talking now?"

"They do when they've met someone who's been in prison since Hayes was President and all they've had to talk to today is a retiring conductor and a miner's daughter on her way to a finishing school in Chicago." The man in the checked suit offered his hand. "Arthur Brundage. I write for the *New Democrat*. It's a newspaper, since your time."

"I saw it inside." He grasped the hand tentatively, plainly surprising its owner with his grip. "I got to tell you, son, I ain't much for talking to the papers. Less people know your name, the less hold they got on you, Micah always said."

"Micah?"

He hesitated. "Hell, he's been dead better than twenty-five years, I don't reckon I can hurt him. Micah Hale. Maybe the name don't mean nothing now."

"These old cons, they'll tell you they knew John Wilkes Booth and Henry the Eighth if you don't shut them up." The ticket agent skidded the ticket across the ledge.

But Brundage was peering into his face now, a man trying to make out the details in a portrait fogged and darkened with years.

"You're Jubal Steadman."

"I was when I went in. I been called Dad so long I don't rightly answer to nothing else."

"Jubal Steadman." It was an incantation. "If I didn't fall in sheep dip and come up dripping double eagles. Let's go find a bench." Brundage seized the suitcase before its owner could get his hands on it and put a palm on his back, steering him toward the seat he himself had just vacated.

"The Hale-Steadman Gang," he said, when they were seated. "Floyd and Micah Hale and the Steadman brothers and Kid Stone. When I was ten, my mother found a copy of the *New York Detective Monthly* under my bed. It had Floyd Hale on the cover, blazing away from horseback with a six-shooter in each hand at a posse chasing him. I had to stay indoors for a week and memorize a different Bible verse every day."

Jubal smiled. His teeth were only a year old and he was just a few months past grinning like an ape all the time. "Then dime writers made out like Floyd ran the match, but that was just because the Pinkertons found out his name first and told the papers. We all called him Doc on account of he was always full of no-good clabber and he claimed to study eye doctoring back East for a year, when everyone knew he was in the Detroit House of Corrections for stealing a mail sack off a railroad hook. He told me I'd never need glasses." He took his off to polish them with a coarse handkerchief.

Brundage had a long notepad open on his knee. He stopped writing. "I guess I should have accepted that watch when you offered it."

"It ain't worth no sixty dollars. I got it off a fireman on the Katy Flyer when we hit it outside Choctaw in '73."

"You mean that was a story about Wild Bill?"

"Never met him. I had them initials put in it and made up the rest. It pulled me through some skinny times. Folks appreciated a good lie then, not like now."

"Readers of the *New Democrat* are interested in the truth."

He put his spectacles back on and peered at the journalist over the rims. But Brundage was writing again and missed it.

"Anyway, if there was someone we all looked to when things went sore, it was Doc's brother Micah. I reckon he was the smartest man I ever knew or ever will. That's why they took him alive and Doc let himself get shot in the back of the head by Kid Stone."

"I always wondered if he really did that just for the reward."

"I reckon. He was always spending his cut on yellow silk vests and gold hatbands. I was in prison two years when it happened so I can't say was that it. That blood money busted up all the good bunches. The Pinks spent years trying to undercut us with the hill folk, but it was the rewards done it in the end."

"The Kid died of pneumonia three or four years ago in New Jersey. He put together his own moving picture outfit after they let him go. He was playing Doc Holliday when he took sick."

"Josh always said Virge was a born actor. Virgil, that was the Kid's right name."

"I forget if Joshua was your older or your younger brother."

"Older. Billy Tom Mulligan stabbed him with a busted toothbrush first year we was inside. They hung him for it. Josh played the Jew's harp. He was playing it when they jumped us after Liberty."

"What really happened in Liberty?"

Jubal pulled a face. "Doc's idea. We was to hit the ten-twelve from Kansas City when it stopped to water and take on passengers, and the bank in town at the same time. We recruited a half dozen more men for the job: Creek Eddie, Charley MacDonald, Bart and Barney Dee, and two fellows named Bob and Bill, I never got their last names and couldn't tell which was which. Me and Josh and my kid brother Judah went with Micah and Charley MacDonald on the bank run and the rest took the train. Bart and Barney was to ride it in from Kansas City and sit on the conductor and porters while Doc and them threw down on the engineer and fireman and blew open the express car with powder. Doc said they wouldn't be expecting us to try it in town. He was dead-right there. No one thought we was that stupid."

"What made Micah go along with it?"

"Fambly bliss. Doc was threatening to take Kid Stone and start his own bunch because no one ever listened to them good plans he was coming up with all the time, like kidnapping the Governor of Missouri and holding him for ransom. Creek Eddie learned his trade in the Nations, so when we heard he was available, Micah figured he'd be a good influence on Doc. Meantime Creek Eddie thought the train thing was a harebrained plan but figured if Micah was saying yes to it, it must be all right." He showed his store teeth. "You see, I had twenty-nine years to work this all out, and if I knew it then—well, I wouldn't of had the twenty-nine years to work it all out.

"Micah and Charley and Josh and Judah and me, we slid through that bank like a grease fire and come out with seven thousand in greenbacks and another four or five thousand in securities. *And* the bank president and his tellers and two customers hollering for help on the wrong side of the vault door on a five-minute time lock. We never made a better or a quieter job. That was when we heard the shooting down at the station."

"A railroad employee fired the first shot, if I remember my reading."

"It don't matter who fired it. Bart and Barney Dee missed the train in Kansas City, and the conductor and a porter or two was armed and free when Doc and the rest walked in thinking the opposite. Creek Eddie got it in the back of the neck and hit the ground dead. Then everybody opened up, and by the time we showed with the horses, the smoke was all mixed up with steam from the boiler. Well, you could see your hand in front of your face, but not to shoot at. That didn't stop us, though.

"Reason was, right about then that time lock let loose of them folks we left in the bank, and when they hit the street yammering like bitch dogs, that whole town turned vigilante in a hot St. Louis minute. They opened up the gun shop and filled their pockets with cartridges and it was like Independence Day. I think as many of them fell in their own cross-fire as what we shot.

"Even so, only six men was killed in that spree. If you was there trying to hold down your mount with one hand and twisting back and forth like a steam governor to fire on both sides of its neck and dodging all that lead clanging off the engine, you'd swear it was a hundred. I seen Charley take a spill and get dragged by his paint for twenty feet before he cleared his boot of the stirrup, and Judah got his jaw took off by a bullet, though he lived another eight or nine hours. Engineer was killed, and one rubbernecker standing around waiting to board the train, and two of them damn-fool townies playing Kit Carson on the street. I don't know how many of them was wounded; likely not as many as are still walking around showing off their old gallbladder scars as bullet-creases. I still got a ball in my back that tells me when it's fixing to rain, but that didn't give me as much trouble at the time as this here cut that kept dumping blood into my eyes." He pointed out the white mark where his hairline used to be. "Micah took one through the meat on his upper arm, and my brother Josh got it in the hip and lost a finger, and they shot the Kid and took him prisoner and arrested Charley, who broke his ankle getting loose of that stirrup. Doc was the only one of us that come away clean.

"Judah, his jaw was just hanging on by a piece of gristle. I tied it up with his bandanna, and Josh and me got him over one of the horses and we got mounted and took off one way while Doc and Micah and that Bill and Bob went the other. We met up at this empty farmhouse six miles north of town that we lit on before the job in case we got separated, all but that Bill and Bob. Them two just kept riding. We buried Judah that night."

"The posse caught up with you at the farmhouse?" asked Brundage, after a judicious pause.

"No, they surprised Josh and me in camp two nights later. We'd split with the Hales before then. Micah wasn't as bad wounded as Josh and we was slowing them down, Doc said. Josh could play that Jew's harp of his, though. Posse come on afoot, using the sound of it for a mark. They threw down on us. We gave in without a shot."

"That was the end of the Hale-Steadman Gang?"

A hoarse stridency shivered the air. In its echo, Jubal consulted his watch. "Trains still run on time. Nice to know some things stay the same. Yeah, the Pinks picked up Micah posing as a cattle-buyer in Denver a few months later. I heard he died of scarlatina inside. Charley MacDonald got himself shot to pieces escaping with Kid Stone and some others, but the Kid got clear and him and Doc put together a bunch and robbed a train or two and some banks until the Kid shot him. I reckon I'm what's left."

"I guess you can tell readers of the *New Democrat* there's no profit in crime."

"Well, there's profit and profit." He stood up, working the stiffness out of his joints, and lifted the suitcase.

Brundage hesitated in the midst of closing his notebook. "Twenty-nine years of your life a fair trade for a few months of excitement?"

"I don't reckon there's much in life you'd trade half of it to have. But in them days a man either broke his back and his heart plowing rocks under in some field or shook his brains loose putting some red-eyed horse to leather or rotted behind some counter in some town. I don't reckon I'm any older now than I would of been if I done any of them things to live. And I wouldn't have no youngster like you hanging on my every word neither. Them things become important when you get up around my age."

"I won't get that past my editor. He'll want a moral lesson."

"Put one in, then. It don't . . . ." His voice trailed off.

The journalist looked up. The train was sliding to a stop inside the vaulted station, black and oily and leaking steam out of a hundred joints. But the old man was looking at the pair of men coming in the station entrance. One, sandy-haired and approaching middle age in a suit too heavy for Indian summer, his cherry face glistening, was the assistant warden at the prison. His companion was a city police officer in uniform. At sight of Jubal, relief blossomed over the assistant warden's features.

"Steadman, I was afraid you'd left."

Jubal said, "I knew it."

As the officer stepped to the old man's side, the assistant warden said, "I'm very sorry. There's been a clerical error. You'll have to come back with us."

"I was starting to think you was going to let me have that extra day after all."

"Day?" The assistant warden was mopping his face with a lawn handkerchief. "I was getting set to close your file. I don't know how I overlooked that other charge."

Jubal felt a clammy fist clench inside his chest. "Other charge?"

"For the train robbery. In Liberty. The twenty-nine years was for robbing the bank and for your part in the killings afterward. You were convicted also of accessory in the raid on the train. You have seventeen years to serve on that conviction, Steadman. I'm sorry."

He took the suitcase while the officer manacled one of the old man's wrists. Brundage left the bench.

"Jubal—"

He shook his head. "My sister's coming in on the morning train from Huntsford tomorrow. Meet it, will you? Tell her."

"This isn't the end of it. My paper has a circulation of thirty thousand. When our readers learn of this injustice—"

"They'll howl and stomp and write letters to their congressmen, just like in '78."

The journalist turned to the man in uniform. "He's sixty years old. Do you have to chain him like a maniac?"

"Regulations." He clamped the other manacle around his own wrist.

Jubal held out his free hand. "I got to go home now. Thanks for keeping an old man company for an hour."

After a moment Brundage took it. Then the officer touched the old man's arm and he blinked behind his spectacles and turned and left the station with the officer on one side and the assistant warden on the other. The door swung shut behind them.

As the train pulled out without Jubal, Brundage timed it absently against the dented watch in his hand.

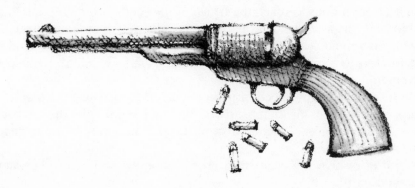

At Yuma Crossing

BRIAN GARFIELD

THE GRINGO CAME out of the desert on foot, carrying a dragoon pistol at one hip and a Texas knife at the other. A Colt rifle dangled in his right hand, a canteen in his left by the strap: by the way the wind moved it back and forth it was evident the canteen was empty.

From a hilltop he had his first view of the groined rivers flowing together; he paused there, half a mile above the rivers, for breath. The tongue came out of his mouth and scraped across dry-split lips.

The sun had both feet on his shoulders. Behind him the desert winked and glittered with particles of mica and pyrites; heat haze undulated in torpor above the withered land. His own tracks went back into it along an unsteady line. In front of him the long slope went down to dust-dry reed bottoms and the river, a shining muddy flow rushing through the sands. A single wagon stood sagging on the near bank of the Colorado just below the junction of rivers.

The Gringo started forward. He put each foot down with the flat-footed carelessness of exhaustion. Half a mile was, just then, a formidable distance to him. His boots stirred little clouds of powder dust. It took him a quarter of an hour to reach the fringe of the reed bottoms, and here he had to push his way through the dry stalks like a man walking through a crowded cornfield. The effort of it sapped him halfway to the river and he had to stop to gather energy; and that was when he heard a rustle of movement.

With the unthinking speed of practiced habit the rifle came up and lay across his left hand; his thumb curled over the hammer and drew it back. He went down on one knee and swept the dry undergrowth in a steady arc with his eyes.

A flutter of brown movement drew his attention to the left. His hand whitened on the rifle.

10

A ragged small figure emerged from the reeds, staring at him with large grave eyes: a dark little girl in a filthy sack of clothes.

She spoke to the Gringo in Spanish, in a piping high voice: "Who are you?" And she came toward him without fear.

The Gringo lowered the hammer of the rifle. His voice was hoarse with the desert-thickness of tongue. "You come from that wagon. How many of you are there?" His Spanish came without hesitation.

"There is just me," the little girl said. "And then there are the Mexicans."

"How many?"

"Who are you?" she said again.

"Corazón," he said very dryly, "I do not have time to fool with you. How many are the Mexicans?"

"The old man and the woman, that's all." She stood back some paces away, held there by a stiff reserve; her eyes were big and bottomless and held distrust, perhaps contempt, but not fear. Her skin was the color of old copper. She had a narrow triangular face and black hair tangled with burrs that fell below her shoulders. She seemed very thin. She might have been anywhere from nine to thirteen. The Gringo said, "You're Indian."

"I am Yaqui."

"All right." He had a stubble of beard and a cruel mouth; his face was like a mountain crag—rocky, broken, ungiving: it appeared as though it needed sorting out.

"You are a *ladrón,"* she told him. "You look like a *ladrón.* Like the man Glanton."

"Who?"

"The Mojaves killed him."

"John Glanton?"

"I do not know—what are names? You are a *ladrón,* a thief, an outlaw —is it not so?" For the first time she grinned.

"Get out of my way," the Gringo said. He tramped toward the river.

The little girl buzzed around him like a horsefly. The Gringo knelt by the bank and put his rifle down on the earth beside him; then his flat gray eyes touched on the girl, and he put his hand on the rifle and held it there while he crouched over the river and drank. He put one foot on the rifle and used both hands to scoop water, splashing it into his face. With his hat off he displayed a head of dark, filthy straw-colored hair, bleached yellow about the edges where the sun had reached it below his hat brim.

He stood up gaunt and tall, hefting the rifle in the circle of his fist. He said, "You look like a stinking Gypsy to me."

"I am Yaqui," she said angrily. "Who are you to say I lie? Ask the Mexicans. They know what I am."

"Get away from me," he told her. But she kept worrying about his heels while he walked along the bank toward the wagon. Once he stopped short and wheeled; he put his hand on her bony shoulder and pushed her away. "Don't dog me," he said in grating English, and went on. Behind him the little girl's voice piped defiantly:

"I do not speak that tongue. You must speak to me in Spanish."

"Ve," he snapped, and gestured with the rifle.

The little girl shrugged. She did not move. "I do not belong to you. Why should I obey a *ladrón?* Have you killed many men?"

The Gringo walked to the wagon. The old man and the woman sat in its narrow band of shade and the old man had a Spanish percussion rifle aimed at the Gringo. The Gringo walked up within two paces and stopped, and spat. "Put your rifle down, old man."

"You do not address me in that way, Gringo. Put your own weapons down and then I shall do the same."

The woman was dried up and fat; the old man looked sick, his cheeks were hollow; his eyes had an unnatural shine. He was lying still but his chest heaved up and down with his breathing. His face was lined as though he had slept with it pressed against a rabbit-wire screen.

The Gringo looked at both of them and then he kicked the rifle out of the old man's hand. It had not been cocked and it did not go off. The Gringo pushed it away with his foot. "I want food, old man."

The woman kept staring, saying nothing. The Gringo reached down and picked up the old man's rifle, and said, "This is not loaded."

"We have no ammunition left," said the old man. "There is little food but I suppose you must eat. Lupe."

The old woman stirred. She sat up and brushed strings of hair away from her eyes; her face was round and pouched. *"Niña,"* she said to the little girl, "build up the fire. Bring wood."

"For him?" the little girl demanded.

"You will obey or go without supper," said the fat woman.

"On the run," the Gringo said, and met the little girl's angry glance. The little girl screwed up her lip and then went away to gather reeds for the fire.

The old man had not moved; he lay with his head on a bundle of cloth. Soon the sun would reach its midpoint and either the old man would have to suffer its rays or move underneath the wagon. Now and then the Gringo saw the old man droop. His eyes closed slowly and popped open again. He wore dust-coated remnants of expensive clothing, the ornate costume of a don, but old, now: worn thin and patched.

The Gringo squatted in the shade with his back against the front wheel. Its iron rim was hot. "What happened to your mules?"

"Two Mojaves came here the night before last night. They ate our meal with us and then stole our mules and our cow."

"No mules," the Gringo said, and cursed in English, and said, "How do you expect to get anywhere without mules, you old fool?" The old man's eyelids had sagged. The Gringo wiped a forearm across his face and looked at the river. The ferry landing was there, empty; the ferry was tied up on the far side of the Colorado. It all looked deserted. The little Indian girl brought an armload of reeds and banked the fire against the wind that came damp and sultry off the river. The fat woman sighed and heaved to her feet; she brought a slab of smoked meat out of the wagon and put it on the fire. The Gringo watched it hungrily.

The old woman said, "The Indians cut the rope for the ferry when they killed the boatmen. There is no way to bring the ferry here except to swim across with a rope. The old man is sick and I cannot swim."

The Gringo didn't seem to pay any attention to her. After a while, with the smell of singeing meat in his nostrils, he said, "The Mojaves killed Glanton?"

"And all his friends. That is what the two Mojaves told us before they stole our animals. They were very pleased but I think it was not the Mojaves but the Yumas who did the killing. It does not matter, of course. Glanton is dead and his men are dead and the rope is cut, and the ferry is over there. That is what matters. Can you swim, Gringo?"

"I can swim." Unable to restrain himself, the Gringo turned to the fire and took the meat and gnawed at it half-raw. The old woman, having got started, seemed unable to stop talking.

"We had a servant, the Yaqui girl's mother, but she died on the desert and we buried her. We have seen much misfortune. The revolution has robbed my husband of his properties that were granted to his ancestors by the king two hundred years ago and now we are poor, and my husband, as you see, is ill. We must go to my uncle in California, in the county of Tuolumne."

The Gringo spoke around a mouthful of meat. "That's where they've found gold."

"Yes, I suppose it would be so. My husband is very ill and we must get him across the river, for he wishes to die in a house with a roof over him and a family around him. This desert is not a good place for a proud man to die. You see that, do you not?"

The Gringo made no answer of any kind. He finished eating and scraped a palm across his mouth; he took his rifle and walked down to the ferryboat landing and stared across the river. It was wide and there was a powerful rush to the current, swollen by melting snows in the faraway mountains. The little girl darted down to the dock and said, "How many men have you killed?" And he ignored her, finally turning to go back up to the wagon. Its stripe of shade was very thin now. The fat woman said, "Will you help me get him under the wagon?"

"To hell with him," said the Gringo, and sat down frowning at the river crossing. The old woman struggled with the old man's weight, pulling him under the wagon. The old man tried to help but he seemed weak to the point of helplessness. It was curious he had been able to hold a rifle.

The little girl stared down at the Gringo and said, "You were a friend of the *ladrón* Glanton."

"Ve, ve," he told her irritably.

The old woman crawled out from beneath the wagon and spoke sharply to the little girl. "Get away from him, little savage."

"I am better than you," the little girl shouted. "My father was a warrior."

"Your father is dead a long time," the old woman said wearily. "And now your mother too. You are an Indian and you had better learn what that means. Go away and leave the Gringo. He does not want you troubling him."

The little girl spat dry. "He is a *ladrón*. He takes your food and does nothing for you, but you take his side against me because I am Indian."

"Go," the old woman said. The little girl wheeled and darted into the reeds. There was a great crashing around which presently subsided.

The old woman sat down by the Gringo. "The *ladrón* Glanton and his friends stole the ferry from another Gringo. They charged much money for ferry passage and then they robbed many passengers afterward. No one is sorry the Indians have killed them. It was Glanton who sold Mexican scalps as Apache, for the bounty in Sonora. If he had stayed we would have killed him there. And you—you are a friend of Glanton?"

"I am a friend of no one," said the Gringo.

"Then you are a fool."

"You talk a lot, old woman."

"You came here because you heard that your *amigo* Glanton was making much money by robbing travelers—and all travelers must come by here. You expected to join the *ladrones*. But now Glanton is dead and there are no *ladrones* except yourself, and no one to rob except ourselves, and we are poor; it would not be worth your trouble. You must either go back or swim across to California. But you cannot go back, for you have no horse. What happened to your horse?"

"Broke a leg. You will hurt yourself talking so much."

"I have nothing to do but talk," she said, "and you have little else to do but listen. You cannot return across the desert without a horse because by yourself you cannot carry enough water. You must swim across. You will rest today, and tomorrow you will swim across."

"There's gold in California," he said.

"And rich men for you to rob."

"You have a loose tongue. What if I am not a robber?"

"Do you deny you are a robber?"

The Gringo said, *"Señora,* I would deny anything if the denial served me. The last time I told the truth when I knew it might hurt me was when I was the *niña*'s age. They sent me to the county farm."

"It was not the truth that hurt you."

"Be quiet, old woman."

"You must swim across tomorrow," she said. "I only ask that you carry the end of the rope and tie it at the ferry landing. When the rope is up we can pull the ferry across by its pulley."

The Gringo brooded upon the river. "Old woman, a rope is a heavy thing and when it is soaked with water it is heavier still. To build the ferry they used oxen to swim across with the rope."

"A strong man can do it."

"Old woman, you can die without my help." The Gringo got up and went down to the dock and sat there, taking off his boots and soaking his feet in the river. Today he was too tired; tomorrow he would take their food, as much of it as he could carry, and he would cross the river and leave them. All of them knew that much.

In time, travelers would come to the crossing. If they were soon enough, they would help the old man dying and the fat woman and the Indian girl; if they were not soon enough, they would bury the three.

The Gringo studied the brown flow with hooded eyes. After a while in the sun he climbed down underneath the dock, took off his clothes and buried himself in the shallow eddies under the dock. The flies were numerous but he paid them no mind.

When the little girl came down to the dock he reached out his hand and laid it upon his rifle and locked glances with her, and said, "You're a witch. Get away."

The little girl said, "The old man does not notice me. The woman keeps me because I can do work, but they hate me because I am Yaqui and they know the Yaqui is better than they are. You are a *ladrón,* you can understand. My father was a warrior and he killed many of them."

"And they killed him, didn't they."

It was sudden: she turned her head away from him, she put her back to him; her shoulders lifted. The Gringo said, "Yaquis are not supposed to cry. You are no Yaqui."

The little girl ran away.

After the Gringo dressed he picked up his rifle and went back to the wagon; he was hungry again and he took the last biscuit from the box. The old woman stared at him without expression. The old man was awake, breathing heavily beneath the wagon, a flush of heat on his cheeks. The little girl sat across the camp, staring with hate at all of them; presently she went into the reeds, and when she was gone the fat woman said, "The truth is that the *niña*'s mother was not a Yaqui and that the *niña* never met her father. He was a mountain thief." The woman shrugged her fat shoulders. "You know the Yaqui, how they are. *Ladrones.* The little girl is arrogant and thinks herself better than the rest of us because she believes her father died gallantly."

"Your mouth flaps," the Gringo told her.

The old woman grinned at him. Her teeth were gapped and yellow. She said, "Would you shoot me for that, tough one?"

"Aagh," the Gringo said in disgust.

"You will not shoot, but you will leave us to die. Is there a difference? It would be kinder to shoot us all."

"Old woman, I have trouble enough of my own."

In the late afternoon the Gringo was lying on his back in the shade of a reed clump; he had one knee bent and his rifle across his stomach, and the hat tipped forward over his face. The little girl came forward in her bare feet and kicked at the sole of his boot and laughed at him. The Gringo said, "Maybe I ought to shoot you."

"Your talk is very tough, *ladrón.*"

"*Ve.*"

The old woman was calling for the girl; it was time to build the fire. The girl squatted by the Gringo and said, "If we go to California the old man will die and the woman will have her family. They will have no use for me."

"Then you will have to learn to make your own way."

"I am a clumsy thief. What else can I do?"

"Work," said the Gringo, with a brief smile that fled quickly.

"What would you know of work? Who would give work to an Indian girl?"

He sat up angrily. "Why do you bring your problems to me? *Ve—ve!*"

Her eyes were moist. The old woman was calling in a strident voice. Her heavy footfalls sounded and she came to stand ponderously above the little girl. "The fire is waiting."

"Make your own fire," the girl said.

"Then you will have no supper."

"I will steal food when you are asleep."

"Urchin! Build the fire or I'll whip you."

"You cannot run fast enough," the little girl said, taking a step backward.

The old woman said, "You will not build a fire—why? Because you are too good for it? Because you are the daughter of a Yaqui? Let me tell you, little *ladrón,* your father was an ordinary thief—he died with his hands in another Yaqui's pocket. He was killed by his own people. That is your proud *padre.* Now build the fire."

"You are a liar!" the little girl screamed, and ran off into the bottoms.

The old woman sighed. "I hope she does not come back. She is an unpleasant mouth to feed. But now I must build my own fire. Will you break wood for it?"

"I'm hungry," the Gringo said. "I'll bring the wood."

The old woman propped the old man against the wagon wheel. When they were half through their meal the little girl came reluctantly out of the dusk and stood across the fire staring; and the old woman said, "All right, eat—but if you eat our food, you must do our work."

"You lied about my father."

"No," said the old woman, "I did not lie. It is time you know."

"I will eat."

The little girl sat a little distance away from them and ate her supper. The food was meager.

After dark the Gringo picked a spot away from the wagon and lay down with his hand on the warm metal of the rifle cylinder. The little girl came up and the Gringo looked at her out of one eye. "Go away—go to sleep."

"I will sleep here," she said, and dropped prone with a blanket which she wrapped around herself.

"Am I to feel honored?"

"I have no father," the little girl said. "I am the child of a thief. I will sleep with a thief."

"I'm not a thief."

"I don't believe you."

"Believe what you want," said the Gringo, and closed his eye.

The little girl said, "How can you swim across the river with the big pistol and the rifle?"

"I'll manage it."

"Your powder will all get wet. I have been thinking about it. If you swim across with the rope you can bring the ferry back and take your rifle and pistol over on the ferry. It will keep them dry."

"You think too much for a little girl," he said. "Go to sleep."

"You could also take the old man and the woman on the ferry."

He opened his eye. "Why should you care what happens to them?"

The little girl was watching him; she did not speak.

The Gringo said irritably, "The old man is too weak to travel. What purpose would it serve to get him across the river? That side is no better than this side."

"But the old woman would be alone on this side."

"Alone?"

"I will follow you," said the little girl. "I will not stay with them."

"Go away and sleep by yourself."

"I can swim," she said.

"The current is swift. You would drown."

"I will try," said the little girl. "It will make no difference to you if I drown."

"That's right."

In the morning the Gringo awoke and stretched. The little girl had a fire going and the old woman was grinding knuckles into her eye sockets. The old man lay under the wagon breathing shallowly, his mouth open and slack; his eyes were half-lidded but did not appear to see. The Gringo took his breakfast and then went down to consider the river. The flow was steady and strong.

He heard the old woman yelling at the girl, and in a moment the girl came running down the slope to him. The Gringo said, "You run away too much. If you want her food, stay and fight her."

The little girl said nothing; the Gringo said, "Why do you come to me?"

"I will swim across with you."

"The devil you will," he said in English.

"What is that?"

"Stay here," he told her, but he made no motion toward the water, and in a moment the girl said,

"You are afraid of the river."

"Why not?"

"I am not afraid of it."

"Then you're stupid."

"I know how to swim," she said proudly.

The old woman came down to the dock and said, "The rope is here," and pointed to where the hemp line lay coiled.

"Forget that," said the Gringo.

"The old man will die."

"He will die anyway, old woman." The Gringo kept frowning at the river, looking at neither the woman nor the rope.

The woman said, "Perhaps we could bring help for him. Warner's Ranch is not too far. But it is on the other side."

"Two days' walk, maybe more. The old man would be dead before you got back. Leave me alone, old woman."

The woman barked at the little girl and turned slowly to plod uphill. The little girl said to the Gringo, "If you are still tired today, you can wait and swim across tomorrow."

When there was no answer she moved closer to him and threw her head back to look at his face. "If I swim across with you and I do not drown, will you take me with you?"

"Where?"

"Where you go."

"*Ve,*" he told her. "*Ve allí.*" He waved an arm toward the reed bottoms. "Leave me alone."

"Do you hate everyone?" Her head was cocked to one side.

The Gringo looked at her with his eyebrows drawn together. When he drew the back of his hand across his face it scraped on the abrasiveness of his jaw. The girl said, "Will you stay today?"

"Why should I?"

"If you are tired," she said. "Will you stay and talk to me? You are a thief and—"

"Damn, I am not a thief."

"And I am a thief and we should talk together." She brought a strip of dried beef out from beneath her clothes. "You see? I have stolen this today from the old woman. We are thieves together." She regarded him gravely and began to chew on the string of meat.

The Gringo sat down on the riverbank and toyed with the frayed end of the rope coil. The sun, climbing notch by notch, blasted his back.

The little girl moved around him, stood beside him and said, "I have no father and no mother." The Gringo looked at her. She said, "I must go with my own kind. We are both thieves. You see, I have stolen the meat. I am a thief. You can trust me."

For a moment the Gringo appeared on the verge of laughter; but his face turned sour. Heat glistened on the muddy surface of the Colorado and the water made a steady slap-slap against the banks.

The old woman came down the hill and said, "He is dead."

The Gringo looked up at her. As if he had been released, he stood up and said, "I'll bury him."

"There is no shovel."

"I'll scoop a grave with sticks."

"It is kind."

The Gringo shook his head and went up toward the wagon. He scratched a shallow grave and they wrapped the old man in a blanket and buried him; the old woman mumbled words and the Gringo filled in the hole and tamped it down with his boots. The old woman said, "That has given you something to do for an hour or two, but now you are not better off than you were. There are still the three of us."

"No," said the Gringo. "There are two of you and then there is me."

"And we are not three? You have no arithmetic?"

"I have no ties," the Gringo said.

He went back to the dock and stood on the end of it where the water was deep; he looked across toward the ferry, tied up and swaying slightly with the ebb and flow of the current.

He protested, "The rope will be too heavy."

The old woman's slow smile crawled across her face but then the Gringo said, "No, I'm a goddamn fool. You can get across the river by yourself; the old man did."

"And now you are a philosopher?"

"I have wasted too much time here," said the Gringo.

The little girl said, "If there are two and one, it is not as you have divided it."

"Then we are one and one and one," said the Gringo. "You are not mine, *niña.*"

"Nor mine," said the old woman coolly; she went back toward the shade of the wagon with a slow stride of resignation. The little girl said, "She will sit in the shade and die. Don't you care?"

The Gringo said, "She doesn't care about you. Why think about her?"

"She does. She is only gruff."

"I thought you hated her."

"I do," said the little girl. "Maybe she does not care about me. Maybe I do not care about her."

"Make up your mind."

"What are you going to do?"

The Gringo said, "I will swim across the river." He stripped off his hat and boots and after a moment's consideration his gunbelt; together with his rifle he laid them in a neat pile on the dock and took off his shirt as well, and his trousers; he stood pale in his faded red trapdoors and put his troubled gaze on the river. Then he reached down and tied his shirt and pants into a bundle, which he wrapped around his waist and knotted by the shirt-arms. The boots he laced together and hung around his neck. He considered the gunbelt and rifle, and sat down to stuff the rolled gunbelt and pistol into his hat, which he then grasped in one hand.

The little girl said, "You cannot take the rifle."

"I'll have to do without it. If you have a use for it, you can have it."

"It is not a gift if you abandon it."

"Who said it was a gift?" Balancing the hat, he walked back to the bank and turned toward the river so that he could walk into it.

The little girl followed him and stood in water up to her knees. Up above, the old woman was sitting in the shade of the wagon fanning herself with the dead man's hat. The Gringo stopped and turned his head and looked at her over his shoulder, and then at the little girl who had no father and no mother and who was a thief.

The Gringo felt water lapping around his calves and felt the suck of the mud bottom. He turned and faced the little girl. She lifted her hand toward him.

The sun was very hot on his bare flesh. He wiped his mouth and turned to the dock beside him, and put his hat on the dock with the gunbelt and pistol; he untied the shirt-sleeves and laid that bundle and his boots with the hat.

The girl had taken a step closer to him, and when he turned again, her hand was still lifted, and he reached out to grasp it and walked with her toward the coil of rope.

The old woman waddled down and said, "If you walk upstream to the limit of the rope, it will be easier to swim across in an arc. The current will help you."

The little girl clung to the Gringo's hand and the Gringo said, "Let go of me, damn it." He picked up the rope and tied a small loop in the end of it, and inspected the dock cleat to make certain the rope was secured.

When he dragged the rope out to its full length, moving upstream along the bank, the little girl walked with him. He pulled the rope taut and stepped into the river, and found it warm and rushing. The little girl said, "I am a Yaqui and you are a Yaqui too."

"I guess maybe I am," the Gringo said in English, and struck out with the rope into the current.

The Guns of William Longley

DONALD HAMILTON

WE'D BEEN UP north delivering a herd for Old Man Butcher the summer I'm telling about. I was nineteen at the time. I was young and big, and I was plenty tough, or thought I was, which amounts to the same thing up to a point. Maybe I was making up for all the years of being that nice Anderson boy, back in Willow Fork, Texas. When your dad wears a badge, you're kind of obliged to behave yourself around home so as not to shame him. But Pop was dead now, and this wasn't Texas.

Anyway, I was tough enough that we had to leave Dodge City in something of a hurry after I got into an argument with a fellow who, it turned out, wasn't nearly as handy with a gun as he claimed to be. I'd never killed a man before. It made me feel kind of funny for a couple of days, but like I say, I was young and tough then, and I'd seen men I really cared for trampled in stampedes and drowned in rivers on the way north. I wasn't going to grieve long over one belligerent stranger.

It was on the long trail home that I first saw the guns one evening by the fire. We had a blanket spread on the ground, and we were playing cards for what was left of our pay—what we hadn't already spent on girls and liquor and general hell-raising. My luck was in, and one by one the others dropped out, all but Waco Smith, who got stubborn and went over to his bedroll and hauled out the guns.

"I got them in Dodge," he said. "Pretty, ain't they? Fellow I bought them from claimed they belonged to Bill Longley."

"Is that a fact?" I said, like I wasn't much impressed. "Who's Longley?"

I knew who Bill Longley was, all right, but a man's got a right to dicker a bit, and besides, I couldn't help deviling Waco now and then. I liked him all right, but he was one of those cocky little fellows who ask for it. You know the kind. They always know everything.

22

I sat there while he told me about Bill Longley, the giant from Texas with thirty-two killings to his credit, the man who was hanged twice. A bunch of vigilantes strung him up once for horse-stealing he hadn't done, but the rope broke after they'd ridden off and he dropped to the ground, kind of short of breath but alive and kicking.

Then he was tried and hanged for a murder he had done, some years later in Giddings, Texas. He was so big that the rope gave way again and he landed on his feet under the trap, making six-inch-deep footprints in the hard ground—they're still there in Giddings to be seen, Waco said, Bill Longley's footprints—but it broke his neck this time and they buried him nearby. At least a funeral service was held, but some say there's just an empty coffin in the grave.

I said, "This Longley gent can't have been so much, to let folks keep stringing him up that way."

That set Waco off again, while I toyed with the guns. They were pretty, all right, in a big carved belt with two carved holsters, but I wasn't much interested in leatherwork. It was the weapons themselves that took my fancy. They'd been used but someone had looked after them well. They were handsome pieces, smooth-working, and they had a good feel to them. You know how it is when a firearm feels just right. A fellow with hands the size of mine doesn't often find guns to fit him like that.

"How much do you figure they're worth?" I asked, when Waco stopped for breath.

"Well, now," he said, getting a sharp look on his face, and I came home to Willow Fork with the Longley guns strapped around me. If that's what they were.

I got a room and cleaned up at the hotel. I didn't much feel like riding clear out to the ranch and seeing what it looked like with Ma and Pa gone two years and nobody looking after things. Well, I'd put the place on its feet again one of these days, as soon as I'd had a little fun and saved a little money. I'd buckle right down to it, I told myself, as soon as Junellen set the date, which I'd been after her to do since before my folks died. She couldn't keep saying forever we were too young.

I got into my good clothes and went to see her. I won't say she'd been on my mind all the way up the trail and back again, because it wouldn't be true. A lot of the time I'd been too busy or tired for dreaming, and in Dodge City I'd done my best *not* to think of her, if you know what I mean. It did seem like a young fellow engaged to a beautiful girl like Junellen Barr could have behaved himself better up there, but it had been a long dusty drive and you know how it is.

But now I was home and it seemed like I'd been missing Junellen every minute since I left, and I couldn't wait to see her. I walked along the street in the hot sunshine feeling light and happy. Maybe my leaving my guns at the hotel had something to do with the light feeling, but the happiness was all for Junellen, and I ran up the steps to the house and knocked on the door. She'd have heard we were back and she'd be waiting to greet me, I was sure.

I knocked again and the door opened and I stepped forward eagerly. "Junellen—" I said, and stopped foolishly.

"Come in, Jim," said her father, a little turkey of a man who owned the drygoods store in town. He went on smoothly: "I understand you had quite an eventful journey. We are waiting to hear all about it."

He was being sarcastic, but that was his way, and I couldn't be bothered with trying to figure what he was driving at. I'd already stepped into the room, and there was Junellen with her mother standing close as if to protect her, which seemed kind of funny. There was a man in the room, too, Mr. Carmichael from the bank, who'd fought with Pa in the war. He was tall and handsome as always, a little heavy nowadays but still dressed like a fashion plate. I couldn't figure what he was doing there.

It wasn't going at all the way I'd hoped, my reunion with Junellen, and I stopped, looking at her.

"So you're back, Jim," she said. "I heard you had a real exciting time. Dodge City must be quite a place."

There was a funny hard note in her voice. She held herself very straight, standing there by her mother, in a blue-flowered dress that matched her eyes. She was a real little lady, Junellen. She made kind of a point of it, in fact, and Martha Butcher, Old Man Butcher's kid, used to say about Junellen Barr that butter wouldn't melt in her mouth, but that always seemed like a silly saying to me, and who was Martha Butcher anyway, just because her daddy owned a lot of cows?

Martha'd also remarked about girls who had to drive two front names in harness as if one wasn't good enough, and I'd told her it surely wasn't if it was a name like Martha, and she'd kicked me on the shin. But that was a long time ago when we were all kids.

Junellen's mother broke the silence, in her nervous way: "Dear, hadn't you better tell Jim the news?" She turned to Mr. Carmichael. "Howard, perhaps you should—"

Mr. Carmichael came forward and took Junellen's hand. "Miss Barr has done me the honor to promise to be my wife," he said.

I said, "But she can't. She's engaged to me."

Junellen's mother said quickly, "It was just a childish thing, not to be taken seriously."

I said, "Well, I took it seriously!"

Junellen looked up at me. "Did you, Jim? In Dodge City, did you?" I didn't say anything. She said breathlessly, "It doesn't matter. I suppose I could forgive . . . But you have killed a man. I could never love a man who has taken a human life."

Anyway, she said something like that. I had a funny feeling in my stomach and a roaring sound in my ears. They talk about your heart breaking, but that's where it hit me, the stomach and the ears. So I can't tell you exactly what she said, but it was something like that.

I heard myself say, "Mr. Carmichael spent the war peppering Yanks with a peashooter, I take it."

"That's different—"

Mr. Carmichael spoke quickly. "What Miss Barr means is that there's a difference between a battle and a drunken brawl, Jim. I am glad your father did not live to see his son wearing two big guns and shooting men down in the street. He was a fine man and a good sheriff for this county. It was only for his memory's sake that I agreed to let Miss Barr break the news to you in person. From what we hear of your exploits up north, you have certainly forfeited all right to consideration from her."

There was something in what he said, but I couldn't see that it was his place to say it. "You agreed?" I said. "That was mighty kind of you, sir, I'm sure." I looked away from him. "Junellen—"

Mr. Carmichael interrupted. "I do not wish my fiancée to be distressed by a continuation of this painful scene. I must ask you to leave, Jim."

I ignored him. "Junellen," I said, "is this what you really—"

Mr. Carmichael took me by the arm. I turned my head to look at him again. I looked at the hand with which he was holding me. I waited. He didn't let go. I hit him and he went back across the room and kind of fell into a chair. The chair broke under him. Junellen's father ran over to help him up. Mr. Carmichael's mouth was bloody. He wiped it with a handkerchief.

I said, "You shouldn't have put your hand on me, sir."

"Note the pride," Mr. Carmichael said, dabbing at his cut lip. "Note the vicious, twisted pride. They all have it, all these young toughs. You are too big for me to box, Jim, and it is an undignified thing anyway. I have worn a sidearm in my time. I will go to the bank and get it, while you arm yourself."

"I will meet you in front of the hotel, sir," I said, "if that is agreeable to you."

"It is agreeable," he said, and went out.

I followed him without looking back. I think Junellen was crying, and I know her parents were saying one thing and another in high, indignant voices, but the funny roaring was in my ears and I didn't pay too much attention. The sun was very bright outside. As I started for the hotel, somebody ran up to me.

"Here you are, Jim." It was Waco, holding out the Longley guns in their carved holsters. "I heard what happened. Don't take any chances with the old fool."

I looked down at him and asked, "How did Junellen and her folks learn about what happened in Dodge?"

He said, "It's a small town, Jim, and all the boys have been drinking and talking, glad to get home."

"Sure," I said, buckling on the guns. "Sure."

It didn't matter. It would have got around sooner or later, and I wouldn't have lied about it if asked. We walked slowly toward the hotel.

"Dutch LeBaron is hiding out back in the hills with a dozen men," Waco said. "I heard it from a man in a bar."

"Who's Dutch LeBaron?" I asked. I didn't care, but it was something to talk about as we walked.

"Dutch?" Waco said. "Why, Dutch is wanted in five states and a couple of territories. Hell, the price on his head is so high now even Fenn is after him."

"Fenn?" I said. He sure knew a lot of names. "Who's Fenn?"

"You've heard of Old Joe Fenn, the bounty hunter. Well, if he comes after Dutch, he's asking for it. Dutch can take care of himself."

"Is that a fact?" I said, and then I saw Mr. Carmichael coming, but he was a ways off yet and I said, "You sound like this Dutch fellow was a friend of yours—"

But Waco wasn't there anymore. I had the street to myself, except for Mr. Carmichael, who had a gun strapped on outside his fine coat. It was an army gun in a black army holster with a flap, worn cavalry style on the right side, butt forward. They wear them like that to make room for the saber on the left, but it makes a clumsy rig.

I walked forward to meet Mr. Carmichael, and I knew I would have to let him shoot once. He was a popular man and a rich man and he would have to draw first and shoot first or I would be in serious trouble. I figured it all out very coldly, as if I had been killing men all my life. We stopped, and Mr. Carmichael undid the flap of the army holster and pulled out the big cavalry pistol awkwardly and fired and missed, as I had known, somehow, that he would.

Then I drew the right-hand gun, and as I did so I realized that I didn't particularly want to kill Mr. Carmichael. I mean, he was a brave man coming here with his old cap-and-ball pistol, knowing all the time that I could outdraw and outshoot him with my eyes closed. But I didn't want to be killed, either, and he had the piece cocked and was about to fire again. I tried to aim for a place that wouldn't kill him, or cripple him too badly, and the gun wouldn't do it.

I mean, it was a frightening thing. It was like I was fighting the Longley gun for Mr. Carmichael's life. The old army revolver fired once more and something rapped my left arm lightly. The Longley gun went off at last, and Mr. Carmichael spun around and fell on his face in the street. There was a cry, and Junellen came running and went to her knees beside him.

"You murderer!" she screamed at me. "You hateful murderer!"

It showed how she felt about him, that she would kneel in the dust like that in her blue-flowered dress. Junellen was always very careful of her pretty clothes. I punched out the empty and replaced it. Dr. Sims came up and examined Mr. Carmichael and said he was shot in the leg, which I already knew, being the one who had shot him there. Dr. Sims said he was going to be all right, God willing.

Having heard this, I went over to another part of town and tried to get drunk. I didn't have much luck at it, so I went into the place next to the hotel for a cup of coffee. There wasn't anybody in the place but a skinny girl with an apron on.

I said, "I'd like a cup of coffee, ma'am," and sat down.

She said, coming over, "Jim Anderson, you're drunk. At least you smell like it."

I looked up and saw that it was Martha Butcher. She set a cup down in front of me. I asked, "What are you doing here waiting tables?"

She said, "I had a fight with Dad about . . . well, never mind what it was about. Anyway, I told him I was old enough to run my own life and if he didn't stop trying to boss me around like I was one of the hands, I'd pack up and leave. And he laughed and asked what I'd do for money, away from home, and I said I'd earn it, so here I am."

It was just like Martha Butcher, and I saw no reason to make a fuss over it like she probably wanted me to.

"Seems like you are," I agreed. "Do I get sugar, too, or does that cost extra?"

She laughed and set a bowl in front of me. "Did you have a good time in Dodge?" she asked.

"Fine," I said. "Good liquor. Fast games. Pretty girls. Real pretty girls."

"Fiddlesticks," she said. "I know what you think is pretty. Blond and simpering. You big fool. If you'd killed him over her they'd have put you in jail, at the very least. And just what are you planning to use for an arm when that one gets rotten and falls off? Sit still."

She got some water and cloth and fixed up my arm where Mr. Carmichael's bullet had nicked it.

"Have you been out to your place yet?" she asked.

I shook my head. "Figure there can't be much out there by now. I'll get after it one of these days."

"One of these days!" she said. "You mean when you get tired of strutting around with those big guns and acting dangerous—" She stopped abruptly.

I looked around, and got to my feet. Waco was there in the doorway, and with him was a big man, not as tall as I was, but wider. He was a real whiskery gent, with a mat of black beard you could have used for stuffing a mattress. He wore two gunbelts, crossed, kind of sagging low at the hips.

Waco said, "You're a fool to sit with your back to the door, Jim. That's the mistake Hickok made, remember? If instead of us it had been somebody like Jack McCall—"

"Who's Jack McCall?" I asked innocently.

"Why, he's the fellow shot Wild Bill in the back . . ." Waco's face reddened. "All right, all right. Always kidding me. Dutch, this big joker is my partner, Jim Anderson. Jim, Dutch LeBaron. He's got a proposition for us."

I tried to think back to where Waco and I had decided to become partners, and couldn't remember the occasion. Well, maybe it happens like that, but it seemed like I should have had some say in it.

"Your partner tells me you're pretty handy with those guns," LeBaron said, after Martha'd moved off across the room. "I can use a man like that."

"For what?" I asked.

"For making some quick money over in New Mexico Territory," he said.

I didn't ask any fool questions, like whether the money was to be made legally or illegally. "I'll think about it," I said.

Waco caught my arm. "What's to think about? We'll be rich, Jim!"

I said, "I'll think about it, Waco."

LeBaron said, "What's the matter, sonny, are you scared?"

I turned to look at him. He was grinning at me, but his eyes weren't grinning, and his hands weren't too far from those low-slung guns.

I said, "Try me and see."

I waited a little. Nothing happened. I walked out of there and got my pony and rode out to the ranch, reaching the place about dawn. I opened the door and stood there, surprised. It looked just about the way it had when the folks were alive, and I half expected to hear Ma yelling at me to beat the dust off outside and not bring it into the house. Somebody had cleaned the place up for me, and I thought I knew who. Well, it certainly was neighborly of her, I told myself. It was nice to have somebody show a sign they were glad to have me home, even if it was only Martha Butcher.

I spent a couple of days out there, resting up and riding around. I didn't find much stock. It was going to take money to make a going ranch of it again, and I didn't figure my credit at Mr. Carmichael's bank was anything to count on. I couldn't help giving some thought to Waco and LeBaron and the proposition they'd put before me. It was funny, I'd think about it most when I had the guns on. I was out back practicing with them one day when the stranger rode up.

He was a little, dry, elderly man on a sad-looking white horse he must have hired at the livery stable for not very much, and he wore his gun in front of his left hip with the butt to the right for a cross draw. He didn't make any noise coming up. I'd fired a couple of times before I realized he was there.

"Not bad," he said when he saw me looking at him. "Do you know a man named LeBaron, son?"

"I've met him," I said.

"Is he here?"

"Why should he be here?"

"A bartender in town told me he'd heard you and your sidekick, Smith, had joined up with LeBaron, so I thought you might have given him the use of your place. It would be more comfortable for him than hiding out in the hills."

"He isn't here," I said. The stranger glanced toward the house. I started to get mad, but shrugged instead. "Look around if you want to."

"In that case," he said, "I don't figure I want to." He glanced toward the target I'd been shooting at, and back to me. "Killed a man in Dodge, didn't you, son? And then stood real calm and let a fellow here in town fire three shots at you, after which you laughed and pinked him neatly in the leg."

"I don't recall laughing," I said. "And it was two shots, not three."

"It makes a good story, however," he said. "And it is spreading. You have a reputation already, did you know that, Anderson? I didn't come here just to look for LeBaron. I figured I'd like to have a look at you, too. I always like to look up fellows I might have business with later."

"Business?" I said, and then I saw that he'd taken a tarnished old badge out of his pocket and was pinning it on his shirt. "Have you a warrant, sir?" I asked.

"Not for you," he said. "Not yet."

He swung the old white horse around and rode off. When he was out of sight, I got my pony out of the corral. It was time I had a talk with Waco. Maybe I was going to join LeBaron and maybe I wasn't, but I didn't much like his spreading it around before it was true.

I didn't have to look for him in town. He came riding to meet me with three companions, all hard ones if I ever saw any.

"Did you see Fenn?" he shouted as he came up. "Did he come this way?"

"A little old fellow with some kind of a badge?" I said. "Was that Fenn? He headed back to town, about ten minutes ahead of me. He didn't look like much."

"Neither does the devil when he's on business," Waco said. "Come on, we'd better warn Dutch before he rides into town."

I rode along with them, and we tried to catch LeBaron on the trail, but he'd already passed with a couple of men. We saw their dust ahead and chased it, but they made it before us, and Fenn was waiting in front of the cantina that was LeBaron's hangout when he was in town.

We saw it all as we came pounding after LeBaron, who dismounted and started into the place, but Fenn came forward, looking small and inoffensive. He was saying something and holding out his hand. LeBaron stopped and shook hands with him, and the little man held on to LeBaron's hand, took a step to the side, and pulled his gun out of that cross-draw holster left-handed, with a kind of twisting motion.

Before LeBaron could do anything with his free hand, the little old man had brought the pistol barrel down across his head. It was as neat and cold-blooded a thing as you'd care to see. In an instant, LeBaron was unconscious on the ground, and Old Joe Fenn was covering the two men who'd been riding with him.

Waco Smith, riding beside me, made a sort of moaning sound as if he'd been clubbed himself. "Get him!" he shouted, drawing his gun. "Get the dirty sneaking bounty hunter!"

I saw the little man throw a look over his shoulder, but there wasn't much he could do about us with those other two to handle. I guess he hadn't figured us for reinforcements riding in. Waco fired and missed. He never could shoot much, particularly from horseback. I reached out with one of the guns and hit him over the head before he could shoot again. He spilled from the saddle.

I didn't have it all figured out. Certainly it wasn't a very nice thing Mr. Fenn had done, first taking a man's hand in friendship and then knocking him unconscious. Still, I didn't figure LeBaron had ever been one for giving anybody a break; and there was something about the old fellow standing there with his tarnished old badge that reminded me of Pa, who'd died wearing a similar piece of tin on his chest. Anyway, there comes a time in a man's life when he's got to make a choice, and that's the way I made mine.

Waco and I had been riding ahead of the others. I turned my pony fast and covered them with the guns as they came charging up—as well as you can cover anybody from a plunging horse. One of them had his pistol aimed to shoot. The left-hand Longley gun went off, and he fell to the ground. I was kind of surprised. I'd never been much at shooting left-handed. The other two riders veered off and headed out of town.

By the time I got my pony quieted down from having that gun go off in his ear, everything was pretty much under control. Waco had disappeared, so I figured he couldn't be hurt much; and the new sheriff was there, old drunken Billy Bates, who'd been elected after Pa's death by the gambling element in town, who hadn't liked the strict way Pa ran things.

"I suppose it's legal," Old Billy was saying grudgingly. "But I don't take it kindly, Marshal, your coming here to serve a warrant without letting me know."

"My apologies, Sheriff," Fenn said smoothly. "An oversight, I assure you. Now, I'd like a wagon. He's worth seven hundred and fifty dollars over in New Mexico Territory."

"No decent person would want that kind of money," Old Billy said sourly, swaying on his feet.

"There's only one kind of money," Fenn said. "Just as there's only one kind of law, even though there's different kinds of men enforcing it." He looked at me as I came up. "Much obliged, son."

"Por nada," I said. "You get in certain habits when you've had a badge in the family. My daddy was sheriff here once."

"So? I didn't know that." Fenn looked at me sharply. "Don't look like you're making any plans to follow in his footsteps. That's hardly a lawman's rig you're wearing."

I said, "Maybe, but I never yet beat a man over the head while I was shaking his hand, Marshal."

"Son," he said, "my job is to enforce the law and maybe make a small profit on the side, not to play games with fair and unfair." He looked at me for a moment longer. "Well, maybe we'll meet again. It depends."

"On what?" I asked.

"On the price," he said. "The price on your head."

"But I haven't got—"

"Not now," he said. "But you will, wearing those guns. I know the signs. I've seen them before, too many times. Don't count on having me under obligation to you, when your time comes. I never let personal feelings interfere with business . . . Easy, now," he said to a couple of fellows who were lifting LeBaron, bound hand and foot, into the wagon that somebody had driven up. "Easy. Don't damage the merchandise. I take pride in delivering them in good shape for standing trial, whenever possible."

I decided I needed a drink, and then I changed my mind in favor of a cup of coffee. As I walked down the street, leaving my pony at the rail back there, the wagon rolled past and went out of town ahead of me. I was still watching it, for no special reason, when Waco stepped from the alley behind me.

"Jim!" he said. "Turn around, Jim!"

I turned slowly. He was a little unsteady on his feet, standing there, maybe from my hitting him, maybe from drinking. I thought it was drinking. I hadn't hit him very hard. He'd had time for a couple of quick ones, and liquor always got to him fast.

"You sold us out, you damn traitor!" he cried. "You took sides with the law!"

"I never was against it," I said. "Not really."

"After everything I've done for you!" he said thickly. "I was going to make you a great man, Jim, greater than Longley or Hardin or Hickok or any of them. With my brains and your size and speed, nothing could have stopped us! But you turned on me! Do you think you can do it alone? Is that what you're figuring, to leave me behind now that I've built you up to be somebody?"

"Waco," I said, "I never had any ambitions to be—"

"You and your medicine guns!" he sneered. "Let me tell you something. Those old guns are just something I picked up in a pawnshop. I spun a good yarn about them to give you confidence. You were on the edge, you needed a push in the right direction, and I knew once you started wearing a flashy rig like that, with one killing under your belt already, somebody'd be bound to try you again, and we'd be on our way to fame. But as for their being Bill Longley's guns, don't make me laugh!"

I said, "Waco—"

"They's just metal and wood like any other guns!" he said. "And I'm going to prove it to you right now! I don't need you, Jim! I'm as good a man as you, even if you laugh at me and make jokes at my expense . . . *Are you ready, Jim?*"

He was crouching, and I looked at him, Waco Smith, with whom I'd ridden up the trail and back. I saw that he was no good and I saw that he was dead. It didn't matter whose guns I was wearing, and all he'd really said was that he didn't know whose guns they were. But it didn't matter, they were my guns now, and he was just a little runt who never could shoot for shucks, anyway. He was dead, and so were the others, the ones who'd come after him, because they'd come, I knew that.

I saw them come to try me, one after the other, and I saw them go down before the big black guns, all except the last, the one I couldn't quite make out. Maybe it was Fenn and maybe it wasn't . . .

I said, "To hell with you, Waco. I've got nothing against you, and I'm not going to fight you. Tonight or any other time."

I turned and walked away. I heard the sound of his gun behind me an instant before the bullet hit me. Then I wasn't hearing anything for a while. When I came to, I was in bed, and Martha Butcher was there.

"Jim!" she breathed. "Oh, Jim . . . !"

She looked real worried, and kind of pretty, I thought, but of course I was half out of my head. She looked even prettier the day I asked her to marry me, some months later, but maybe I was a little out of my head that day, too. Old Man Butcher didn't like it a bit. It seems his fight with Martha had been about her cleaning up my place, and his ordering her to quit and stay away from that young troublemaker, as he'd called me after getting word of all the hell we'd raised up north after delivering his cattle.

He didn't like it, but he offered me a job, I suppose for Martha's sake. I thanked him and told him I was much obliged but I'd just accepted an appointment as Deputy U.S. Marshal. Seems like somebody had recommended me for the job, maybe Old Joe Fenn, maybe not. I got my old gun out of my bedroll and wore it tucked inside my belt when I thought I might need it. It was a funny thing how seldom I had any use for it, even wearing a badge. With that job, I was the first in the neighborhood to hear about Waco Smith. The news came from New Mexico Territory. Waco and a bunch had pulled a job over there, and a posse had trapped them in a box canyon and shot them to pieces.

I never wore the other guns again. After we moved into the old place, I hung them on the wall. It was right after I'd run against Billy Bates for sheriff and won that I came home to find them gone. Martha looked surprised when I asked about them.

"Why," she said, "I gave them to your friend, Mr. Williams. He said you'd sold them to him. Here's the money."

I counted the money, and it was a fair enough price for a pair of secondhand guns and holsters, but I hadn't met any Mr. Williams.

I started to say so, but Martha was still talking. She said, "He certainly had an odd first name, didn't he? Who'd christen anybody Long Williams? Not that he wasn't big enough. I guess he'd be as tall as you, wouldn't he, if he didn't have that trouble with his neck?"

"His neck?" I said.

"Why, yes," she said. "Didn't you notice when you talked to him, the way he kept his head cocked to the side? Like this."

She showed me how Long Williams had kept his head cocked to the side. She looked real pretty doing it, and I couldn't figure how I'd ever thought her plain, but maybe she'd changed. Or maybe I had. I kissed her and gave her back the gun money to buy something for herself, and went outside to think. Long Williams, William Longley. A man with a wry neck and a man who was hanged twice. It was kind of strange, to be sure, but after a time I decided it was just a coincidence. Some drifter riding by just saw the guns through the window and took a fancy to them.

I mean, if it had really been Bill Longley, if he was alive and had his guns back, we'd surely have heard of him by now down at the sheriff's office, and we never have.

The Debt of Hardy Buckelew

ELMER KELTON

I GUESS YOU'D call him crazy. We did, that spring of '78 when old man Hardy Buckelew set out to square his account against the Red River.

That was my third year to help graze the Box H steer herd from South Texas up the Western Trail toward Dodge. The first year I had just been the wrangler, bringing up the *remuda* to keep the riders in fresh mounts. A button job, was all. The second year they promoted me. Didn't matter that they put me back at the dusty tail end of the herd to push up the drags. It was a cowboy job, and I was drawing a man's wages, pretty near.

Old Hardy Buckelew had only one son—a big, rawboned, overgrown kid by the name of Jim, wilder than a Spanish pony. They used to say there was nothing Jim Buckelew couldn't whip, and if anything ever did show up, old man Hardy would whip it for him. That's the way the Buckelews were.

I never did see but one thing Jim couldn't whip, but we'll get to that directly.

Jim was only nineteen first time I saw him. That young, he wasn't supposed to be going in saloons and suchlike. He did anyway; he was so big for his age that nobody paid him much mind. Or, if they did notice him, maybe they knew they'd have to throw him out to get rid of him. That wouldn't have been much fun.

One time in San Antonio he fell into a card game with a pair of sharpers, and naturally they fleeced him. He raised a ruckus, so the two of them throwed together and lit into him. They never would have whipped him if the bartender in cahoots with them hadn't busted a bottle over Jim's head.

Now, a man who ever saw old Hardy Buckelew get mad would never forget it as long as he lived. He was one of those old-time Texas cowmen —the likes of which the later generations never saw. He stood six feet tall in his brush-scarred boots. He had a hide as tough as the mesquite land he rode in and a heart as stout as a black Mexican bull. When he hollered at a man, his voice would carry a way yonder, and you could bet the last dollar you owned that whoever he hollered at would come a-running, too.

Old Hardy got plenty mad that time, when Jim came limping in broke and bruised and bloody. The old man took him way off to one side for a private lecture, but we could hear Hardy Buckelew's bull voice as far as we could see him.

Next day he gathered up every man he could spare, me included, and we all rode a-horseback to San Antonio. We marched into the saloon where the fight had taken place and marched everybody else out—everybody but the bartender and the two gamblers. They were talking big, but their faces were white as clabber. Old Hardy busted a bottle over the bartender's head and laid him out colder than a wedge. Then he switched those fiery eyes of his to Jim Buckelew and jabbed his stubby thumb in the direction of the gamblers.

"Now this time," he said, "do the job right!"

Jim did. When we left there, three men lay sprawled in the wet sawdust. Jim Buckelew was grinning at us, showing a chipped front tooth like it was a medal from Jeff Davis himself. His knuckles were torn and redsmeared as he counted out the money he had taken back from the gamblers' pockets.

Old man Hardy's voice was rough, but you couldn't miss the edging of pride in it. "From now on, Jimbo, whether it's a man or a job, don't you ever take a whippin' and quit. No matter how many times it takes, a Buckelew keeps on comin' till he's won."

Now then, to the debt of Hardy Buckelew.

Late in the summer of '77 we finished a cow hunt and threw together a herd of Box H steers to take to Kansas and the railroad before winter set in. Hardy Buckelew never made the trip himself anymore—too many years had stacked up on him. For a long time now, Will Peril had been his trail boss. Will was a man a cowboy liked to follow—a graying, medium-sized man with the years just commencing to put a slump in his shoulders. His voice was as soft as the hide of a baby calf, and he had a gentle way with horses and cattle. Where most of us might tear up enough ground to plant a potato patch, Will Peril could make livestock do what he wanted them to without ever raising the dust.

He handled men the same way.

This time, though, Hardy Buckelew slipped a joker in the deck.

"Will," Hardy said, "it's time Jimbo took on a man's responsibilities. He's twenty-one now, so I'm puttin' him in charge of this trail herd. I just want you to go along and kind of keep an eye on him. You know, give him his head, but keep one hand on the reins, just in case."

Will Peril frowned, twisting his mule-hide gloves and looking off to where the cook was loading the chuck wagon. "Some men take longer growin' up than others do, Hardy. You really think he's ready?"

"You want to teach a boy to swim, you throw him in where the water's deep. Sure, he'll make some mistakes, but the education he gets'll be worth the price."

So we pointed them north with a new trail boss in charge. Now, Jim was a good cowboy, make no mistake about that; he was just a shade wild, is all. He pushed too fast and didn't give the cattle time enough to graze along and put on weight as they walked. He was reckless, too, in the way he rode, in the way he tried to curb the stampedes we had before we got the cattle trail-broke. He swung in front of the bunch one night, spurring for all he was worth. His horse stepped in a hole and snapped its leg with a sound like a pistol shot. For a minute there, we thought Jim was a goner. But more often than not a running herd will split around a man on foot. They did this time. Jim just walked away laughing. He'd have spit in the devil's eye.

All in all, though, Jim did a better job than most of us hands thought he would. That is, till we got to the Red River.

It had been raining off and on for three days when we bunched the cattle on the south bank of the Red. The river was rolling strong, all foamy and so muddy you could almost walk on it. You could hear the roar a long time before you got there.

The trail had been used a lot that year, and the grass was grazed down short. Will Peril set out downriver to find feed enough that we could hold the cattle while we waited for the water to run down. He was barely out of sight when Jim Buckelew raised his hat and signaled for the point man to take cattle out into the river.

"You're crazy, Jim!" exclaimed the cook, a limping old Confederate veteran by the name of Few Lively. "A duck couldn't stay afloat in that water!"

But Jim might have had cotton in his ears for all the attention he paid. When the point man held back, Jim spurred his horse out into that roaring river with the same wild grin he had when he waded into those San Antonio gamblers. Him shaming us that way, there was nothing the rest of us could do but follow in behind him, pushing the cattle.

The steers didn't like that river. It was all we could do to force them into it. They bobbed up and down, their heads out of the water and their horns swaying back and forth like a thousand old-fashioned rocking chairs. The force of the current started pulling them downriver. Up at the point, Jim Buckelew was fighting along, keeping the leaders swimming, pushing them for the far bank.

For a while there it looked like we might make it. Then, better than halfway across, the lead steers began to tire out. They still had heart in them, but tired legs couldn't keep fighting that torrent. Jim Buckelew had a coiled rope in his hand, slapping at the steers' heads, his angry voice lost in the roar of the flood. It was no use; the river had them.

And somehow Jim Buckelew lost his seat. We saw him splash into the muddy water, so far out yonder that no one could reach him. We saw his arms waving, saw him go under. Then we lost sight of him out there in all that foam, among those drowning cattle.

The heart went out of all of us. The main part of the herd milled and swam back. It was all we could do to get ourselves and the cattle to the south bank. Not an animal made it to the far side.

It was all over by the time Will Peril returned. We spent the next day gathering cattle that had managed to climb out way yonder down the river. Along toward evening, as the Red dropped, we found Jim Buckelew's body where it had washed in with an uprooted tree. We wrapped him in his blankets and slicker and dug a grave for him. A gentle rain started again like a quiet benediction as Will Peril finished reading over him out of the chuck-box Bible.

The burial done, we stood there numb with shock and grief and chill. Will Peril stuck the Bible inside his shirt, beneath the slicker.

"We haven't got a man to spare," he said tightly, "but somebody's got to go back and tell Hardy."

His eyes fell on me.

It had been bad enough, watching Jim Buckelew die helpless in that boiling river. In a way it was even worse, I think, standing there on the gallery of the big house with my hat all wadded up in my hand, watching old Hardy Buckelew die inside.

He never swayed, never showed a sign of a tear in his gray eyes. But he seemed somehow to shrink up from his six feet. That square, leather face of his just seemed to come to pieces. His huge hands balled into fists, then loosened and began to tremble. He turned away from me, letting his gaze drift out across the sun-cured grass and the far-stretching tangle of thorny mesquite range that he had planned to pass down to Jim. When he turned back to me, he was an old man. An old, old man.

"The cattle," he whispered, "did Jim get them across?"

I shook my head. "No, sir, we lost a couple hundred head. The rest got back to the south bank."

"He never did quit, though, did he? Kept on tryin' all the way?"

"He never quit till he went under, Mister Buckelew."

That meant a lot to him, I could tell. He asked, "Think you could find Jimbo's grave for me?"

"Yes, sir, we marked it."

The old man's voice seemed a hundred miles away, and his mind, too. "Get some rest, then. We'll leave at daylight."

Using the buckboard, we followed the wide, tromped-out cattle trail all the way up to the Red River. We covered more ground in one day than the herd had moved in three or four. And one afternoon we stood beside Jim Buckelew's grave. The cowboys had put up a little brush fence around it to keep trail cattle from walking over it and knocking down the marker.

The old man stood there a long time with his hat in his hand as he looked at his son's resting place. Occasionally his eyes would lift to the river, three hundred yards away. The water had gone down now. The Red moved along sluggish and sleepy, innocent as could be. The dirty-water marks of silt and debris far up on the banks were all that showed for the violence we had seen there.

Then it was that I heard Hardy Buckelew speak in a voice that sent fingers of ice crawling up my spine. He wasn't talking to me.

"I'll be back, Jimbo. Nothin' has ever beat a Buckelew. We got a debt here, and it's goin' to be paid. You watch, Jimbo, I'll be back!"

I had never really been afraid of Hardy Buckelew before. But now I saw something in his face that made me afraid, a little bit.

He turned toward the buckboard. "Let's go home," he said.

All those days of traveling for that single hour beside the river. And now we were going home again.

The old man wasn't the same after that. He stayed to himself, getting grayer and thinner. When he rode out, he went alone and not with the boys. He spent a lot of his time just puttering around the big house or out at the barn, feeding and currying and petting a roan colt that had been Jim's favorite. He never came to the cook shack anymore. The ranch cook sent his meals up to the big house, and most of it would come back uneaten.

When the trail crew finally returned from Dodge City, old Hardy didn't even come out. Will Peril had to take his report and the bank draft up to the big house.

Will was shaking his head when he came to the cook shack for supper. There was worry in his eyes. "The thing's eatin' on him," he said, "turnin' him in on himself. I tell you, boys, if he don't get off of it, it'll drive him out of his mind."

Knowing how much Will loved that old cowman, I didn't feel like telling him what Hardy had said at the grave by the Red River. The way I saw it, Hardy Buckelew was pretty far gone already.

When winter came on, he just seemed to hole up in the big house. He didn't come out much, and when he did we wished we hadn't seen him. For a time there, we didn't expect him to live through the winter. But spring came and he was still with us. He began coming down to the cook shack sometimes, a living ghost who sat at the end of the long table, deaf and blind to what went on around him.

Time came for the spring cow hunt. Hardy delegated all of his responsibility to Will Peril, and the chuck wagon moved out.

"He won't live to see this roundup finished," Will said. You could see the tears start in his eyes. "One of these days we'll have to quit work to come in and bury him."

But Will was wrong. As the new grass rose, so did Hardy Buckelew. The life that stirred the prairies and brought green leaves to the mesquite brush seemed to touch the old man, too. You could see the change in him from one day to the next, almost. He strengthened up, the flesh coming back to his broad shoulders and his square face. He commenced visiting the wagon more and more often, until one day he brought out his bedroll and pitched it on the ground along with the rest of ours.

We thought then that we had him back—the same old Hardy Buckelew. But he wasn't the same. No, sir, he was another man.

The deep lines of grief that had etched into his face were still there, and we knew they would never fade. Some new fire smoldered in his eyes like camp coals banked for the night. There was a hatred in that fire, yet we saw nothing for him to hate. What had happened was nobody's fault.

As the strength came back he worked harder than any man in the outfit. Seemed like he never slept. More often than not, he was the one who woke up the cook of a morning and got the coffeepot on to boil. He was always on the go, wearing out horses almost as fast as we could bring them up for him.

"Tryin' to forget by drivin' himself into the grave," Will Peril said darkly. "I almost wish he was still mopin' around that ranchhouse."

So did some of the others. Hardy got so hard to follow that three of his cowboys quit. Two "reps" for other outfits left the Box H wagon and swore they wouldn't come back for anything less than his funeral. Hardy didn't even seem like he noticed.

We finished the regular spring works, and we had a sizable bunch of big steers thrown together for the trip up the trail to Dodge. For those of us who usually made the drive, it was a welcome time. We were tickled to death with the idea of getting away from Hardy Buckelew awhile. I think even Will Peril, much as he thought of the boss, was looking forward to a little breathing spell himself.

We spent several days getting the outfit ready. We put a fresh trail brand on the steers so that if they ever got mixed up with another bunch we could know them easy. We wouldn't have to stretch a bunch of them out with ropes and clip away the hair to find the brands.

You could tell the difference in the men as we got ready. There wasn't much cheer among those that were fixing to stay home, but the trail crew was walking around light as feathers. Trail driving being the hard, hot, dusty, sleepless and once-in-a-while dangerous work that it was, I don't know why anybody would look forward to it. But we did.

The night before we started, Hardy Buckelew dropped us the bad news. He was going, too.

Will Peril argued with him till he was blue in the face. "You know what it's like to go up that trail, Hardy—you've done it often enough. You're not in any condition to be makin' the trip."

Will Peril was the only man Hardy Buckelew ever let argue with him, and even Will didn't do it much.

"Who owns this outfit?" Hardy asked.

"You do," Will said.

"What part of this outfit is yours?"

"None of it," Will admitted.

"Then shut up about it. I'm goin', and if you don't like it you can stay home!"

Right about then I imagine Will was tempted to. But you could see the trouble in his eyes as he studied Hardy Buckelew. He wouldn't let the old man get off on that trail without being around someplace to watch out for him.

Hardy didn't bother anybody much the first few days. It was customary to drive the cattle hard the first week or so. Partly that was to get them off the range they were used to and reduce the temptation for them to stray back. Partly it was to keep them too tired to run at night till they were used to trail routine.

Hardy rode up at swing position, leaving everybody pretty much alone. Once in a while you would see him turn in the saddle and look back, but he didn't have anything to say. Seemed like everything suited him—at first.

But one morning after we had been on the trail a week he changed complexion. As we strung the cattle out off the bedgrounds Will Peril told the point man to slow it down. "We got them pretty well trail-broke," he said. "We'll let them start puttin' on a little weight now."

But Hardy Buckelew came riding up like a Mexican bull looking for a fight. "You don't do no such of a thing! We'll keep on pushin' them!"

Will couldn't have been more surprised if Hardy had set fire to the chuck wagon. "Hardy, we keep on like we started, they won't be nothin' but hide racks, time we get to Dodge."

Hardy Buckelew didn't bother to argue with him. He just straightened up and gave Will that "I'm the boss around here" look that not even Will would argue with. Hardy rode back to the drags and commenced pushing the slow ones.

From then on, Hardy took over the herd. The first couple of days Will Peril tried every way he could to slow things down. But Hardy would just run over him. Will finally gave up and took a place at swing, his shoulders slumped like he had been demoted to horse wrangler. In a way, I guess you might say he had.

Hardy Buckelew was as hard to get along with on the trail as he had been on the cow hunt—harder, maybe. He was up of a morning before first light, routing everybody out of bed. "Catch up on your sleep next winter," he would growl. And he wouldn't let the drive stop till it was too dark to see. I remember the afternoon early in the drive when Few Lively found a nice little creek and started setting up camp on it. It was about six o'clock when the point came even with the place. If Will had been bossing the outfit, right there's where we would have bedded the herd. But Hardy Buckelew rode up to the wagon in a lope, looking like he was fixing to fight somebody.

"What're you doin' here?" he demanded.

Few Lively swallowed about twice, wondering what he had done wrong. "I always camp here if we make it about this time of day. Good water, plenty of grass. Ain't nothin' ahead of us half as good."

Hardy's face was dark with anger. "There's two more hours of good daylight. Now you git that team hitched up and that camp moved a couple more miles up the trail."

As cook, and as one of the old men of the outfit, Few wasn't used to being talked to that way. "There's ain't no good water up there, Mister Buckelew."

"We'll drink what there is or do without. Now you git movin'!"

Hardy was like that, day in and day out. He would wear out four or five horses a day, just riding back and forth from drag up to the point and back again, stopping every little bit to cuss somebody out and tell him to push them harder. We rode from can-see to can't, Hardy's rough voice never very far away. Not able to fight Hardy Buckelew, and having to work it off someway, some of the boys took to fighting with one another. A couple of them just sneaked off one night while they were on night guard. Didn't ask for their time or anything. Didn't want to face Hardy Buckelew.

Time we got to the Red River, the whole outfit was about ready to bust up. I think if any one man had led off, the rest of us would have ridden out behind him, leaving Hardy Buckelew alone with all those steers. Oh, Will Peril probably would have stayed, but nobody else. That's the way it usually is, though. Everybody waits for somebody else to start, and nobody does.

Like the year before, it was raining when we got to the Red. The river was running a little bigger than usual when Will Peril rode up ahead to take a look at it. He came back and told the point man to keep on going till he reached the other side.

Hardy Buckelew had loped up right after Will Peril and took a long look at the river. He came back holding his hand up in the air, motioning the men to stop.

"We're goin' to camp right here."

Middle of the day, and Hardy Buckelew wanted to camp! We looked at each other like we couldn't believe it, and I think we all agreed on one thing. He'd finally gone crazy.

Will Peril said, "Hardy, that river's just right to cross now. Got just enough water runnin' to swim them and keep them out of the quicksand. Not enough current to give them a lot of trouble."

Hardy shrugged his shoulders as if he had already said all he wanted to about it. "We're goin' to camp—rest up these cattle."

Will was getting angry now, his face red and his fists clenched up. "Hardy, it's rainin'. If we don't get them across now, we're liable to have to wait for days."

Hardy just turned and gave him a look that would melt a bar of lead. "This is *my* herd, Will. I say we're goin' to rest these cattle."

And rest them we did, there on the south bank of the Red, with the rain falling and the river beginning to swell. Will Peril would go down by the river and pace awhile, then come back and try arguing again. He had just as well have sat down with the rest of us and kept dry under the big wagon sheet stretched out from the wagon. He couldn't have moved Hardy Buckelew with a team of horses.

We were camped close to Jim Buckelew's grave. Old Hardy rode off down there and spent awhile. He came back with his eyes aglow like they had been the fall before, when I had brought him here in the buckboard. He spent little time under the wagon sheet, in the dry. He would stand alone in the rain and stare at that mud-red river.

"He'll catch his death out there," Will Peril muttered, watching the old man like a mother hen watches a chick. But he didn't go out to get him.

The old man had never said a word to anybody about Jim. Still, we knew that was all he was thinking of. We could almost feel Jim right there in camp with us. It was an eerie thing, I'll tell you. I would be glad when we got out of that place.

The second day, after standing by the river a long time, Hardy walked in and spoke to Will Peril. "Is the river the way it was the day Jim drowned?"

Will's eyes were almost closed. "No, I'd say it was a little worse that day."

The old man went out in the rain and watched the river some more. It kept rising. He came back with the same question, and Will gave him the same answer. Now an alarm was starting in Will's face.

Finally the old man came back the third time. "Is it as big now as it was that day?"

Will Peril's cheekbones seemed to stand out as the skin drew tight in his whiskered face. "I reckon it is."

The look that came into the old man's gray eyes then was something I never saw before and have never seen again. He turned toward his horse. "All right, boys," he said evenly, "let's go now. We're puttin' them across!"

Talk about surprise, most of us stood there with our mouths open like we'd been hit in the head with the flat side of an ax. But not Will Peril. He must have sensed it coming on. He knew the old man better than anybody.

"You've waited too long, Hardy," he said. "Now it can't be done."

"We couldn't go across earlier," spoke Hardy. "We'd have been cheatin' Jimbo. No Buckelew ever started anything but what it got finished. We're goin' to finish this job for *him.*" Hardy shoved his left foot in the stirrup and started to swing into the saddle.

Will Peril took three long strides toward him. "Listen to me, Hardy, I'm goin' to tell it to you straight. Jim rode off into somethin' too big for him and knew it. He was playin' the fool. You've got no call to take it up for him."

Hardy's eyes blazed. If he had had a gun, I think he would have shot Will.

"He was my boy, Will. He was a Buckelew." Hardy's eyes left Will and settled on the rest of us. "How about it, you-all comin'?"

We all just stood there.

Hardy looked us over, one by one. We couldn't meet his eyes. "Then stay here," he said bitterly, swinging into the saddle. "I'll do it alone!"

Will Peril was close to him now. Will reached out and grabbed the reins. "No, Hardy. If you won't stop, I'll stop you!"

"Let go, Will!"

"Get down, Hardy!"

They stared hard at each other, neither man giving any ground. All of a sudden the old man swung down and waded into Will.

Will wasn't young but he was younger than Hardy Buckelew. Most of us thought it would be over with in a hurry. It was, but not the way we expected. Hardy was like a wild man, something driving him as we had never seen him driven before. He took Will by storm. His fists pounded

Will like mallets, the sound of them solid and hard, like the strike of an ax against a tree. Will tried, but he couldn't stand up under that. Hardy beat him back, and back, and finally down.

The old man stood over him, swaying as he tried for breath. His hands and face were bloody, his eyes afire. "How about it now?" he asked us again. "You comin'?" When we didn't, he just turned and went back to his horse.

You almost had to figure him crazy, the way he worked those cattle, getting them started, forcing the first of them off into the water. We stood around like snake-charmed rabbits, watching. We'd picked Will Peril up and dragged him under the wagon sheet, out of the rain. He sat on the muddy ground, shaking his head, his gaze following Hardy Buckelew.

"You tried," I told Will. "You can't blame yourself for what he does now."

Will could see that Hardy was going to take at least a few of those cattle out into the water, with or without us. The trail boss stood up shakily.

"You boys can do what you want to. I'll not let him fight it alone!"

We looked at Will, catching up his horse, then we looked at each other. In a minute we were all on horseback, following.

It was the same as it had been the last time, the water running bankwide and strong. It was a hard fight, just to get those cattle out into the river. They were smarter than us, maybe—they didn't want to go. I don't really know how we did it, but we got it done. Old Hardy Buckelew took the point, and we strung them out.

Time or two there, I saw the leaders begin to drift and I thought it was over for Hardy the way it had been for Jim. But Hardy Buckelew was fighting hard, and Will Peril moved up there to help him.

I can't rightly say what the difference was that we made it this time, and we hadn't the time before. Maybe it was the rest the cattle and horses had before they started across. Maybe they were tougher, too, the way they had been driven. But mostly I think it was that determined old man up there ahead of us, hollering and swinging his rope and raising hell. He was crazy for going, and we were crazy for following him.

But we made it.

It was a cold and hungry bunch of water-soaked cowboys that threw the herd together on the north bank of the Red. We couldn't get the chuck wagon across—didn't even try—so we went without supper that night and slept without blankets.

But I don't think anybody really minded it much, once it was over. There was the knowledge that we had taken the Red's challenge and made it across. Then, too, there was the satisfaction we got out of seeing peace come into Hardy Buckelew's face. We could tell by looking at him that he was one of us again, for the first time in nearly a year.

Next morning we got the wagon across and had a chance to fill our bellies with beef and beans and hot coffee. At Few Lively's fire, Hardy Buckelew looked at Will Peril and said:

"From here on, Will, I'm turnin' it back over to you. Run it the way you want to. I'm goin' home."

Surprised, Will said, "Home? Why?"

Hardy Buckelew smiled calmly. "You were right, Will, I'm too old for this foolishness. But I owed Jimbo a debt. And I'd say that you and me—all the boys in the outfit—have paid it in full."

Lost Sister

DOROTHY M. JOHNSON

OUR HOUSEHOLD WAS full of women, who overwhelmed my Uncle Charlie and sometimes confused me with their bustle and chatter. We were the only men on the place. I was nine years old when still another woman came—Aunt Bessie, who had been living with the Indians.

When my mother told me about her, I couldn't believe it. The savages had killed my father, a cavalry lieutenant, two years before. I hated Indians and looked forward to wiping them out when I got older. (But when I was grown, they were no menace anymore.)

"What did she live with the hostiles for?" I demanded.

"They captured her when she was a little girl," Ma said. "She was three years younger than you are. Now she's coming home."

High time she came home, I thought. I said so, promising, "If they was ever to get me, I wouldn't stay with 'em long."

Ma put her arms around me. "Don't talk like that. They won't get you. They'll never get you."

I was my mother's only real tie with her husband's family. She was not happy with those masterful women, my Aunts Margaret, Hannah and Sabina, but she would not go back East where she came from. Uncle Charlie managed the store the aunts owned, but he wasn't really a member of the family—he was just Aunt Margaret's husband. The only man who had belonged was my father, the aunts' younger brother. And I belonged, and someday the store would be mine. My mother stayed to protect my heritage.

None of the three sisters, my aunts, had ever seen Aunt Bessie. She had been taken by the Indians before they were born. Aunt Mary had known her—Aunt Mary was two years older—but she lived a thousand miles away now and was not well.

There was no picture of the little girl who had become a legend. When

46

the family had first settled here, there was enough struggle to feed and clothe the children without having pictures made of them.

Even after Army officers had come to our house several times and there had been many letters about Aunt Bessie's delivery from the savages, it was a long time before she came. Major Harris, who made the final arrangements, warned my aunts that they would have problems, that Aunt Bessie might not be able to settle down easily into family life.

This was only a challenge to Aunt Margaret, who welcomed challenges. "She's our own flesh and blood," Aunt Margaret trumpeted. "Of course she must come to us. My poor, dear sister Bessie, torn from her home forty years ago!"

The major was earnest but not tactful. "She's been with the savages all those years," he insisted. "And she was only a little girl when she was taken. I haven't seen her myself, but it's reasonable to assume that she'll be like an Indian woman."

My stately Aunt Margaret arose to show that the audience was ended. "Major Harris," she intoned, "I cannot permit anyone to criticize my own dear sister. She will live in my home, and if I do not receive official word that she is coming within a month, I shall take steps."

Aunt Bessie came before the month was up.

The aunts in residence made valiant preparations. They bustled and swept and mopped and polished. They moved me from my own room to my mother's—as she had been begging them to do because I was troubled with nightmares. They prepared my old room for Aunt Bessie with many small comforts—fresh doilies everywhere, hairpins, a matching pitcher and bowl, the best towels and two new nightgowns in case hers might be old. (The fact was that she didn't have any.)

"Perhaps we should have some dresses made," Hannah suggested. "We don't know what she'll have with her."

"We don't know what size she'll take, either," Margaret pointed out. "There'll be time enough for her to go to the store after she settles down and rests for a day or two. Then she can shop to her heart's content."

Ladies of the town came to call almost every afternoon while the preparations were going on. Margaret promised them that, as soon as Bessie had recovered sufficiently from her ordeal, they should all meet her at tea.

Margaret warned her anxious sisters. "Now, girls, we mustn't ask her too many questions at first. She must rest for a while. She's been through a terrible experience." Margaret's voice dropped way down with those last two words, as if only she could be expected to understand.

Indeed Bessie had been through a terrible experience, but it wasn't what the sisters thought. The experience from which she was suffering, when she arrived, was that she had been wrenched from her people, the

Indians, and turned over to strangers. She had not been freed. She had been made a captive.

Aunt Bessie came with Major Harris and an interpreter, a half-blood with greasy black hair hanging down to his shoulders. His costume was half Army and half primitive. Aunt Margaret swung the door open wide when she saw them coming. She ran out with her sisters following, while my mother and I watched from a window. Margaret's arms were outstretched, but when she saw the woman closer, her arms dropped and her glad cry died.

She did not cringe, my Aunt Bessie who had been an Indian for forty years, but she stopped walking and stood staring, helpless among her captors.

The sisters had described her often as a little girl. Not that they had ever seen her, but she was a legend, the captive child. Beautiful blonde curls, they said she had, and big blue eyes—she was a fairy child, a pale-haired little angel who ran on dancing feet.

The Bessie who came back was an aging woman who plodded in moccasins, whose dark dress did not belong on her bulging body. Her brown hair hung just below her ears. It was growing out; when she was first taken from the Indians, her hair had been cut short to clean out the vermin.

Aunt Margaret recovered herself and, instead of embracing this silent stolid woman, satisfied herself by patting an arm and crying, "Poor dear Bessie, I am your sister Margaret. And here are our sisters Hannah and Sabina. We do hope you're not all tired out from your journey!"

Aunt Margaret was all graciousness, because she had been assured beyond doubt that this was truly a member of the family. She must have believed—Aunt Margaret could believe anything—that all Bessie needed was to have a nice nap and wash her face. Then she would be as talkative as any of them.

The other aunts were quick-moving and sharp of tongue. But this one moved as if her sorrows were a burden on her bowed shoulders, and when she spoke briefly to answer to the interpreter, you could not understand a word of it.

Aunt Margaret ignored these peculiarities. She took the party into the front parlor—even the interpreter, when she understood there was no avoiding it. She might have gone on battling with the major about him, but she was in a hurry to talk to her lost sister.

"You won't be able to converse with her unless the interpreter is present," Major Harris said. "Not," he explained hastily, "because of any regulation, but because she has forgotten English."

Aunt Margaret gave the half-blood interpreter a look of frowning doubt and let him enter. She coaxed Bessie. "Come, dear, sit down."

The interpreter mumbled, and my Indian aunt sat cautiously on a needlepoint chair. For most of her life she had been living with people who sat comfortably on the ground.

The visit in the parlor was brief. Bessie had had her instructions before she came. But Major Harris had a few warnings for the family. "Technically, your sister is still a prisoner," he explained, ignoring Margaret's start of horror. "She will be in your custody. She may walk in your fenced yard, but she must not leave it without official permission.

"Mrs. Raleigh, this may be a heavy burden for you all. But she has been told all this and has expressed willingness to conform to these restrictions. I don't think you will have any trouble keeping her here." Major Harris hesitated, remembering that he was a soldier and a brave man, and added, "If I did, I wouldn't have brought her."

There was the making of a sharp little battle, but Aunt Margaret chose to overlook the challenge. She could not overlook the fact that Bessie was not what she had expected.

Bessie certainly knew that this was her lost white family, but she didn't seem to care. She was infinitely sad, infinitely removed. She asked one question: "Ma-ry?" and Aunt Margaret almost wept with joy.

"Sister Mary lives a long way from here," she explained, "and she isn't well, but she will come as soon as she's able. Dear sister Mary!"

The interpreter translated this, and Bessie had no more to say. That was the only understandable word she ever did say in our house, the remembered name of her older sister.

When the aunts, all chattering, took Bessie to her room, one of them asked, "But where are her things?"

Bessie had no things, no baggage. She had nothing at all but the clothes she stood in. While the sisters scurried to bring a comb and other oddments, she stood like a stooped monument, silent and watchful. This was her prison. Very well, she would endure it.

"Maybe tomorrow we can take her to the store and see what she would like," Aunt Hannah suggested.

"There's no hurry," Aunt Margaret declared thoughtfully. She was getting the idea that this sister was going to be a problem. But I don't think Aunt Margaret ever really stopped hoping that one day Bessie would cease to be different, that she would end her stubborn silence and begin to relate the events of her life among the savages, in the parlor over a cup of tea.

My Indian aunt accustomed herself, finally, to sitting on the chair in her room. She seldom came out, which was a relief to her sisters. She preferred to stand, hour after hour, looking out the window—which was open only about a foot, in spite of all Uncle Charlie's efforts to budge it higher. And she always wore moccasins. She never was able to wear shoes from the store, but seemed to treasure the shoes brought to her.

The aunts did not, of course, take her shopping after all. They made her a couple of dresses; and when they told her, with signs and voluble explanations, to change her dress, she did.

After I found that she was usually at the window, looking across the flat land to the blue mountains, I played in the yard so I could stare at her. She never smiled, as an aunt should, but she looked at me sometimes, thoughtfully, as if measuring my worth. By performing athletic feats, such as walking on my hands, I could get her attention. For some reason, I valued it.

She didn't often change expression, but twice I saw her scowl with disapproval. Once was when one of the aunts slapped me in a casual way. I had earned the slap, but the Indians did not punish children with blows. Aunt Bessie was shocked, I think, to see that white people did. The other time was when I talked back to someone with spoiled, small-boy insolence —and that time the scowl was for me.

The sisters and my mother took turns, as was their Christian duty, in visiting her for half an hour each day. Bessie didn't eat at the table with us—not after the first meal.

The first time my mother took her turn, it was under protest. "I'm afraid I'd start crying in front of her," she argued, but Aunt Margaret insisted.

I was lurking in the hall when Ma went in. Bessie said something, then said it again, peremptorily, until my mother guessed what she wanted. She called me and put her arm around me as I stood beside her chair. Aunt Bessie nodded, and that was all there was to it.

Afterward, my mother said, "She likes you. And so do I." She kissed me.

"I don't like her," I complained. "She's queer."

"She's a sad old lady," my mother explained. "She had a little boy once, you know."

"What happened to him?"

"He grew up and became a warrior. I suppose she was proud of him. Now the Army has him in prison somewhere. He's half Indian. He was a dangerous man."

He was indeed a dangerous man, and a proud man, a chief, a bird of prey whose wings the Army had clipped after bitter years of trying.

However, my mother and my Indian aunt had that one thing in common: they both had sons. The other aunts were childless.

There was a great to-do about having Aunt Bessie's photograph taken. The aunts, who were stubbornly and valiantly trying to make her one of the family, wanted a picture of her for the family album. The government wanted one too, for some reason—perhaps because someone realized that a thing of historic importance had been accomplished by recovering the captive child.

Major Harris sent a young lieutenant with the greasy-haired interpreter to discuss the matter in the parlor. (Margaret, with great foresight, put a clean towel on a chair and saw to it the interpreter sat there.) Bessie spoke very little during that meeting, and of course we understood only what the half-blood *said* she was saying.

No, she did not want her picture made. No.

But your son had his picture made. Do you want to see it? They teased her with that offer, and she nodded.

If we let you see his picture, then will you have yours made?

She nodded doubtfully. Then she demanded more than had been offered: If you let me keep his picture, then you can make mine.

No, you can only look at it. We have to keep his picture. It belongs to us.

My Indian aunt gambled for high stakes. She shrugged and spoke, and the interpreter said, "She not want to look. She will keep or nothing."

My mother shivered, understanding as the aunts could not understand what Bessie was gambling—all or nothing.

Bessie won. Perhaps they had intended that she should. She was allowed to keep the photograph that had been made of her son. It has been in history books many times—the half-white chief, the valiant leader who was not quite great enough to keep his Indian people free.

His photograph was taken after he was captured, but you would never guess it. His head is high, his eyes stare with boldness but not with scorn, his long hair is arranged with care—dark hair braided on one side and with a tendency to curl where the other side hangs loose—and his hands hold the pipe like a royal scepter.

That photograph of the captive but unconquered warrior had its effect on me. Remembering him, I began to control my temper and my tongue, to cultivate reserve as I grew older, to stare with boldness but not scorn at people who annoyed or offended me. I never met him, but I took silent pride in him—Eagle Head, my Indian cousin.

Bessie kept his picture on her dresser when she was not holding it in her hands. And she went like a docile, silent child to the photograph studio, in a carriage with Aunt Margaret early one morning, when there would be few people on the street to stare.

Bessie's photograph is not proud but pitiful. She looks out with no expression. There is no emotion there, no challenge, only the face of an aging woman with short hair, only endurance and patience. The aunts put a copy in the family album.

But they were nearing the end of their tether. The Indian aunt was a solid ghost in the house. She did nothing because there was nothing for her to do. Her gnarled hands must have been skilled at squaws' work, at butchering meat and scraping and tanning hides, at making tepees and beading ceremonial clothes. But her skills were useless and unwanted in a civilized home. She did not even sew when my mother gave her cloth and needles and thread. She kept the sewing things beside her son's picture.

She ate (in her room) and slept (on the floor) and stood looking out the window. That was all, and it could not go on. But it had to go on, at least until my sick Aunt Mary was well enough to travel—Aunt Mary who was her older sister, the only one who had known her when they were children.

The sisters' duty visits to Aunt Bessie became less and less visits and more and more duty. They settled into a bearable routine. Margaret had taken upon herself the responsibility of trying to make Bessie talk. Make, I said, not teach. She firmly believed that her stubborn and unfortunate sister needed only encouragement from a strong-willed person. So Margaret talked, as to a child, when she bustled in:

"Now there you stand, just looking, dear. What in the world is there to see out there? The birds—are you watching the birds? Why don't you try sewing? Or you could go for a little walk in the yard. Don't you want to go out for a nice little walk?"

Bessie listened and blinked.

Margaret could have understood an Indian woman's not being able to converse in a civilized tongue, but her own sister was not an Indian. Bessie was white, therefore she should talk the language her sisters did— the language she had not heard since early childhood.

Hannah, the put-upon aunt, talked to Bessie too, but she was delighted not to get any answers and not to be interrupted. She bent over her embroidery when it was her turn to sit with Bessie and told her troubles in an unending flow. Bessie stood looking out the window the whole time.

Sabina, who had just as many troubles, most of them emanating from Margaret and Hannah, went in like a martyr, firmly clutching her Bible, and read aloud from it until her time was up. She took a small clock along so that she would not, because of annoyance, be tempted to cheat.

After several weeks Aunt Mary came, white and trembling and exhausted from her illness and the long, hard journey. The sisters tried to get the interpreter in but were not successful. (Aunt Margaret took that failure pretty hard.) They briefed Aunt Mary, after she had rested, so the shock of seeing Bessie would not be too terrible. I saw them meet, those two.

Margaret went to the Indian woman's door and explained volubly who had come, a useless but brave attempt. Then she stood aside, and Aunt Mary was there, her lined white face aglow, her arms outstretched. "Bessie! Sister Bessie!" she cried.

And after one brief moment's hesitation, Bessie went into her arms and Mary kissed her sun-dark, weathered cheek. Bessie spoke. "Ma-ry," she said. "Ma-ry." She stood with tears running down her face and her mouth working. So much to tell, so much suffering and fear—and joy and triumph, too—and the sister there at last who might legitimately hear it all and understand.

But the only English word that Bessie remembered was "Mary," and she had not cared to learn any others. She turned to the dresser, took her son's picture in her work-hardened hands, reverently, and held it so her sister could see. Her eyes pleaded.

Mary looked on the calm, noble, savage face of her half-blood nephew and said the right thing: "My, isn't he handsome!" She put her head on one side and then the other. "A fine boy, sister," she approved. "You must"—she stopped, but she finished—"be awfully proud of him, dear!"

Bessie understood the tone if not the words. The tone was admiration. Her son was accepted by the sister who mattered. Bessie looked at the picture and nodded, murmuring. Then she put it back on the dresser.

Aunt Mary did not try to make Bessie talk. She sat with her every day for hours, and Bessie did talk—but not in English. They sat holding hands for mutual comfort while the captive child, grown old and a grandmother, told what had happened in forty years. Aunt Mary said that was what Bessie was talking about. But she didn't understand a word of it and didn't need to.

"There is time enough for her to learn English again," Aunt Mary said. "I think she understands more than she lets on. I asked her if she'd like to come and live with me, and she nodded. We'll have the rest of our lives for her to learn English. But what she has been telling me—she can't wait to tell that. About her life, and her son."

"Are you sure, Mary dear, that you should take the responsibility of having her?" Margaret asked dutifully, no doubt shaking in her shoes for fear Mary would change her mind now that deliverance was in sight. "I do believe she'd be happier with you, though we've done all we could."

Margaret and the other sisters would certainly be happier with Bessie somewhere else. And so, it developed, would the United States government.

Major Harris came with the interpreter to discuss details, and they told Bessie she could go, if she wished, to live with Mary a thousand miles away. Bessie was patient and willing, stolidly agreeable. She talked a great deal more to the interpreter than she had ever done before. He answered at length and then explained to the others that she had wanted to know how she and Mary would travel to this far country. It was hard, he said, for her to understand just how far they were going.

Later we knew that the interpreter and Bessie had talked about much more than that.

Next morning, when Sabina took breakfast to Bessie's room, we heard a cry of dismay. Sabina stood holding the tray, repeating, "She's gone out the window! She's gone out the window!"

And so she had. The window that had always stuck so that it would not raise more than a foot was open wider now. And the photograph of Bessie's son was gone from the dresser. Nothing else was missing except Bessie and the decent dark dress she had worn the day before.

My Uncle Charlie got no breakfast that morning. With Margaret shrieking orders, he leaped on a horse and rode to the telegraph station.

Before Major Harris got there with half a dozen cavalrymen, civilian scouts were out searching for the missing woman. They were expert trackers. Their lives had depended, at various times, on their ability to read the meaning of a turned stone, a broken twig, a bruised leaf. They found that Bessie had gone south. They tracked her for ten miles. And then they lost the trail, for Bessie was as skilled as they were. Her life had sometimes depended on leaving no stone or twig or leaf marked by her passage. She traveled fast at first. Then, with time to be careful, she evaded the followers she knew would come.

The aunts were stricken with grief—at least Aunt Mary was—and bowed with humiliation about what Bessie had done. The blinds were drawn, and voices were low in the house. We had been pitied because of Bessie's tragic folly in having let the Indians make a savage of her. But now we were traitors because we had let her get away.

Aunt Mary kept saying pitifully, "Oh, why did she go? I thought she would be contented with me!"

The others said that it was, perhaps, all for the best.

Aunt Margaret proclaimed, "She has gone back to her own." That was what they honestly believed, and so did Major Harris.

My mother told me why she had gone. "You know that picture she had of the Indian chief, her son? He's escaped from the jail he was in. The fort got word of it, and they think Bessie may be going to where he's hiding. That's why they're trying so hard to find her. They think," my mother explained, "that she knew of his escape before they did. They think the interpreter told her when he was here. There was no other way she could have found out."

They scoured the mountains to the south for Eagle Head and Bessie. They never found her, and they did not get him until a year later, far to the north. They could not capture him that time. He died fighting.

After I grew up, I operated the family store, disliking storekeeping a little more every day. When I was free to sell it, I did, and went to raising cattle. And one day, riding in a canyon after strayed steers, I found—I think—Aunt Bessie. A cowboy who worked for me was along, or I would never have let anybody know.

We found weathered bones near a little spring. They had a mystery on them, those nameless human bones suddenly come upon. I could feel old death brushing my back.

"Some prospector," suggested my riding partner.

I thought so too until I found, protected by a log, sodden scraps of fabric that might have been a dark, respectable dress. And wrapped in them was a sodden something that might have once been a picture.

The man with me was young, but he had heard the story of the captive child. He had been telling me about it, in fact. In the passing years it had acquired some details that surprised me. Aunt Bessie had become once more a fair-haired beauty, in this legend that he had heard, but utterly sad and silent. Well, sad and silent she really was.

I tried to push the sodden scrap of fabric back under the log, but he was too quick for me. "That ain't no shirt, that's a dress!" he announced. "This here was no prospector—it was a woman!" He paused and then announced with awe, "I bet you it was your Indian aunt!"

I scowled and said, "Nonsense. It could be anybody."

He got all worked up about it. "If it was *my* aunt," he declared, "I'd bury her in the family plot."

"No," I said, and shook my head.

We left the bones there in the canyon, where they had been for forty-odd years if they were Aunt Bessie's. And I think they were. But I would not make her a captive again. She's in the family album. She doesn't need to be in the family plot.

If my guess about why she left us is wrong, nobody can prove it. She never intended to join her son in hiding. She went in the opposite direction to lure pursuit away.

What happened to her in the canyon doesn't concern me, or anyone. My Aunt Bessie accomplished what she set out to do. It was not her life that mattered, but his. She bought him another year.

The Gift
of Cochise

LOUIS L'AMOUR

TENSE, AND WHITE to the lips, Angie Lowe stood in the door of her cabin with a double-barreled shotgun in her hands. Beside the door was a Winchester '73, and on the table inside the house were two Walker Colts.

Facing the cabin were twelve Apaches on ragged calico ponies, and one of the Indians had lifted his hand palm outward. The Apache sitting the white-splashed bay pony was Cochise.

Beside Angie were her seven-year-old son Jimmy and her five-year-old daughter Jane.

Cochise sat his pony in silence; his black, unreadable eyes studied the woman, the children, the cabin, and the small garden. He looked at the two ponies in the corral and the three cows. His eyes strayed to the small stack of hay cut from the meadow, and to the few steers farther up the canyon.

Three times the warriors of Cochise had attacked this solitary cabin and three times they had been turned back. In all, they had lost seven men, and three had been wounded. Four ponies had been killed. His braves reported that there was no man in the house, only a woman and two children, so Cochise had come to see for himself this woman who was so certain a shot with a rifle and who killed his fighting men.

These were some of the same fighting men who had outfought, outguessed and outrun the finest American army on record, an army outnumbering the Apaches by a hundred to one. Yet a lone woman with two small children had fought them off, and the woman was scarcely more than a girl. And she was prepared to fight now. There was a glint of admiration in the old eyes that appraised her. The Apache was a fighting man, and he respected fighting blood.

"Where is your man?"

"He has gone to El Paso." Angie's voice was steady, but she was frightened as she had never been before. She recognized Cochise from descriptions, and she knew that if he decided to kill or capture her it would be done. Until now, the sporadic attacks she had fought off had been those of casual bands of warriors who raided her in passing.

"He has been gone a long time. How long?"

Angie hesitated, but it was not in her to lie. "He has been gone four months."

Cochise considered that. No one but a fool would leave such a woman, or such fine children. Only one thing could have prevented his return. "Your man is dead," he said.

Angie waited, her heart pounding with heavy, measured beats. She had guessed long ago that Ed had been killed but the way Cochise spoke did not imply that Apaches had killed him, only that he must be dead or he would have returned.

"You fight well," Cochise said. "You have killed my young men."

"Your young men attacked me." She hesitated then added, "They stole my horses."

"Your man is gone. Why do you not leave?"

Angie looked at him with surprise. "Leave? Why, this is my home. This land is mine. This spring is mine. I shall not leave."

"This was an Apache spring," Cochise reminded her reasonably.

"The Apache lives in the mountains," Angie replied. "He does not need this spring. I have two children, and I do need it."

"But when the Apache comes this way, where shall he drink? His throat is dry and you keep him from water."

The very fact that Cochise was willing to talk raised her hopes. There had been a time when the Apache made no war on the white man. "Cochise speaks with a forked tongue," she said. "There is water yonder." She gestured toward the hills, where Ed had told her there were springs. "But if the people of Cochise come in peace they may drink at this spring."

The Apache leader smiled faintly. Such a woman would rear a nation of warriors. He nodded at Jimmy. "The small one—does he also shoot?"

"He does," Angie said proudly, "and well, too!" She pointed at an upthrust leaf of prickly pear. "Show them, Jimmy."

The prickly pear was an easy two hundred yards away, and the Winchester was long and heavy, but he lifted it eagerly and steadied it against the doorjamb as his father had taught him, held his sight an instant, then fired. The bud on top of the prickly pear disintegrated.

There were grunts of appreciation from the dark-faced warriors. Cochise chuckled.

"The little warrior shoots well. It is well you have no man. You might raise an army of little warriors to fight my people."

"I have no wish to fight your people," Angie said quietly. "Your people have your ways, and I have mine. I live in peace when I am left in peace. I did not think," she added with dignity, "that the great Cochise made war on women!"

The Apache looked at her, then turned his pony away. "My people will trouble you no longer," he said. "You are the mother of a strong son."

"What about my two ponies?" she called after him. "Your young men took them from me."

Cochise did not turn or look back, and the little cavalcade of riders followed him away. Angie stepped back into the cabin and closed the door. Then she sat down abruptly, her face white, the muscles in her legs trembling.

When morning came, she went cautiously to the spring for water. Her ponies were back in the corral. They had been returned during the night.

Slowly, the days drew on. Angie broke a small piece of the meadow and planted it. Alone, she cut hay in the meadow and built another stack. She saw Indians several times, but they did not bother her. One morning, when she opened the door, a quarter of antelope lay on the step, but no Indian was in sight. Several times, during the weeks that followed, she saw moccasin tracks near the spring.

Once, going out at daybreak, she saw an Indian girl dipping water from the spring. Angie called to her, and the girl turned quickly, facing her. Angie walked toward her, offering a bright red silk ribbon. Pleased at the gift, the Apache girl left.

And the following morning there was another quarter of antelope on her step—but she saw no Indian.

Ed Lowe had built the cabin in West Dog Canyon in the spring of 1871, but it was Angie who chose the spot, not Ed. In Santa Fe they would have told you that Ed Lowe was good-looking, shiftless and agreeable. He was, also, unfortunately handy with a pistol.

Angie's father had come from County Mayo to New York and from New York to the Mississippi, where he became a tough, brawling river boatman. In New Orleans, he met a beautiful Cajun girl and married her. Together, they started west for Santa Fe, and Angie was born en route. Both parents died of cholera when Angie was fourteen. She lived with an Irish family for the following three years, then married Ed Lowe when she was seventeen.

Santa Fe was not good for Ed, and Angie kept after him until they started south. It was Apache country, but they kept on until they reached the old Spanish ruin in West Dog. Here there were grass, water, and shelter from the wind.

There was fuel, and there were pinons and game. And Angie, with an Irish eye for the land, saw that it would grow crops.

The house itself was built on the ruins of the old Spanish building, using the thick walls and the floor. The location had been admirably chosen for defense. The house was built in a corner of the cliff, under the sheltering overhang, so that approach was possible from only two directions, both covered by an easy field of fire from the door and windows.

For seven months, Ed worked hard and steadily. He put in the first crop, he built the house, and proved himself a handy man with tools. He repaired the old plow they had bought, cleaned out the spring, and paved and walled it with slabs of stone. If he was lonely for the carefree companions of Santa Fe, he gave no indication of it. Provisions were low, and when he finally started off to the south, Angie watched him go with an ache in her heart.

She did not know whether she loved Ed. The first flush of enthusiasm had passed, and Ed Lowe had proved something less than she had believed. But he had tried, she admitted. And it had not been easy for him. He was an amiable soul, given to whittling and idle talk, all of which he missed in the loneliness of the Apache country. And when he rode away, she had no idea whether she would ever see him again. She never did.

Santa Fe was far and away to the north, but the growing village of El Paso was less than a hundred miles to the west, and it was there Ed Lowe rode for supplies and seed.

He had several drinks—his first in months—in one of the saloons. As the liquor warmed his stomach, Ed Lowe looked around agreeably. For a moment, his eyes clouded with worry as he thought of his wife and children back in Apache country, but it was not in Ed Lowe to worry for long. He had another drink and leaned on the bar, talking to the bartender. All Ed had ever asked of life was enough to eat, a horse to ride, an occasional drink, and companions to talk with. Not that he had anything important to say. He just liked to talk.

Suddenly a chair grated on the floor, and Ed turned. A lean, powerful man with a shock of uncut black hair and a torn, weather-faded shirt stood at bay. Facing him across the table were three hard-faced young men, obviously brothers.

Ches Lane did not notice Ed Lowe watching from the bar. He had eyes only for the men facing him. "You done that deliberate!" The statement was a challenge.

The broad-chested man on the left grinned through broken teeth. "That's right, Ches. I done it deliberate. You killed Dan Tolliver on the Brazos."

"He made the quarrel." Comprehension came to Ches. He was boxed, and by three of the fighting, blood-hungry Tollivers.

"Don't make no difference," the broad-chested Tolliver said. " 'Who sheds a Tolliver's blood, by a Tolliver's hand must die!' "

Ed Lowe moved suddenly from the bar. "Three to one is long odds," he said, his voice low and friendly. "If the gent in the corner is willin', I'll side him."

Two Tollivers turned toward him. Ed Lowe was smiling easily, his hand hovering near his gun. "You stay out of this!" one of the brothers said harshly.

"I'm in," Ed replied. "Why don't you boys light a shuck?"

"No, by—!" The man's hand dropped for his gun, and the room thundered with sound.

Ed was smiling easily, unworried as always. His gun flashed up. He felt it leap in his hand, saw the nearest Tolliver smashed back, and he shot him again as he dropped. He had only time to see Ches Lane with two guns out and another Tolliver down when something struck him through the stomach and he stepped back against the bar, suddenly sick.

The sound stopped, and the room was quiet, and there was the acrid smell of powder smoke. Three Tollivers were down and dead, and Ed Lowe was dying. Ches Lane crossed to him.

"We got 'em," Ed said, "we sure did. But they got me."

Suddenly his face changed. "Oh Lord in heaven, what'll Angie do?" And then he crumpled over on the floor and lay still, the blood staining his shirt and mingling with the sawdust.

Stiff-faced, Ches looked up. "Who was Angie?" he asked.

"His wife," the bartender told him. "She's up northeast somewhere, in Apache country. He was tellin' me about her. Two kids, too."

Ches Lane stared down at the crumpled, used-up body of Ed Lowe. The man had saved his life.

One he could have beaten, two he might have beaten; three would have killed him. Ed Lowe, stepping in when he did, had saved the life of Ches Lane.

"He didn't say where?"

"No."

Ches Lane shoved his hat back on his head. "What's northeast of here?"

The bartender rested his hands on the bar. "Cochise," he said. . . .

For more than three months, whenever he could rustle the grub, Ches Lane quartered the country over and back. The trouble was, he had no lead to the location of Ed Lowe's homestead. An examination of Ed's horse revealed nothing. Lowe had bought seed and ammunition, and the seed indicated a good water supply, and the ammunition implied trouble. But in the country there was always trouble.

A man had died to save his life, and Ches Lane had a deep sense of obligation. Somewhere that wife waited, if she was still alive, and it was up to him to find her and look out for her. He rode northeast, cutting for sign, but found none. Sandstorms had wiped out any hope of back-trailing Lowe. Actually, West Dog Canyon was more east than north, but this he had no way of knowing.

North he went, skirting the rugged San Andreas Mountains. Heat baked him hot, dry winds parched his skin. His hair grew dry and stiff and alkali-whitened. He rode north, and soon the Apaches knew of him. He fought them at a lonely water hole, and he fought them on the run. They killed his horse, and he switched his saddle to the spare and rode on. They cornered him in the rocks, and he killed two of them and escaped by night.

They trailed him through the White Sands, and he left two more for dead. He fought fiercely and bitterly, and would not be turned from his quest. He turned east through the lava beds and still more east to the Pecos. He saw only two white men, and neither knew of a white woman.

The bearded man laughed harshly. "A woman alone? She wouldn't last a month! By now the Apaches got her, or she's dead. Don't be a fool! Leave this country before you die here."

Lean, wind-whipped and savage, Ches Lane pushed on. The Mescaleros cornered him in Rawhide Draw and he fought them to a standstill. Grimly, the Apaches clung to his trail.

The sheer determination of the man fascinated them. Bred and born in a rugged and lonely land, the Apaches knew the difficulties of survival; they knew how a man could live, how he must live. Even as they tried to kill this man, they loved him, for he was one of their own.

Lane's jeans grew ragged. Two bullet holes were added to the old black hat. The slicker was torn; the saddle, so carefully kept until now, was scratched by gravel and brush. At night he cleaned his guns and by day he scouted the trails. Three times he found lonely ranch houses burned to the ground, the buzzard- and coyote-stripped bones of their owners lying nearby.

Once he found a covered wagon, its canvas flopping in the wind, a man lying sprawled on the seat with a pistol near his hand. He was dead and his wife was dead, and their canteens rattled like empty skulls.

Leaner every day, Ches Lane pushed on. He camped one night in a canyon near some white oaks. He heard a hoof click on stone and he backed away from his tiny fire, gun in hand.

The riders were white men, and there were two of them. Joe Tompkins and Wiley Lynn were headed west, and Ches Lane could have guessed why. They were men he had known before, and he told them what he was doing.

Lynn chuckled. He was a thin-faced man with lank yellow hair and dirty fingers. "Seems a mighty strange way to get a woman. There's some as comes easier."

"This ain't for fun," Ches replied shortly. "I got to find her."

Tompkins stared at him. "Ches, you're crazy! That gent declared himself in of his own wish and desire. Far's that goes, the gal's dead. No woman could last this long in Apache country."

At daylight, the two men headed west, and Ches Lane turned south.

Antelope and deer are curious creatures, often led to their death by curiosity. The longhorn, soon going wild on the plains, acquires the same characteristic. He is essentially curious. Any new thing or strange action will bring his head up and his ears alert. Often a longhorn, like a deer, can be lured within a stone's throw by some queer antic, by a handkerchief waving, by a man under a hide, by a man on foot.

This character of the wild things holds true of the Indian. The lonely rider who fought so desperately and knew the desert so well soon became a subject of gossip among the Apaches. Over the fires of many a rancheria they discussed this strange rider who seemed to be going nowhere, but always riding, like a lean wolf dog on a trail. He rode across the mesas and down the canyons; he studied sign at every water hole; he looked long from every ridge. It was obvious to the Indians that he searched for something—but what?

Cochise had come again to the cabin in West Dog Canyon. "Little warrior too small," he said, "too small for hunt. You join my people. Take Apache for man."

"No." Angie shook her head. "Apache ways are good for the Apache, and the white man's ways are good for white men—and women."

They rode away and said no more, but that night, as she had on many other nights after the children were asleep, Angie cried. She wept silently, her head pillowed on her arms. She was as pretty as ever, but her face was thin, showing the worry and struggle of the months gone by, the weeks and months without hope.

The crops were small but good. Little Jimmy worked beside her. At night, Angie sat alone on the steps and watched the shadows gather down the long canyon, listening to the coyotes yapping from the rim of the Guadalupes, hearing the horses blowing in the corral. She watched, still hopeful, but now she knew that Cochise was right: Ed would not return.

But even if she had been ready to give up this, the first home she had known, there could be no escape. Here she was protected by Cochise. Other Apaches from other tribes would not so willingly grant her peace.

At daylight she was up. The morning air was bright and balmy, but soon it would be hot again. Jimmy went to the spring for water, and when breakfast was over, the children played while Angie sat in the shade of a huge old cottonwood and sewed. It was a Sunday, warm and lovely. From time to time, she lifted her eyes to look down the canyon, half smiling at her own foolishness.

The hard-packed earth of the yard was swept clean of dust; the pans hanging on the kitchen wall were neat and shining. The children's hair had been clipped, and there was a small bouquet on the kitchen table.

After a while, Angie put aside her sewing and changed her dress. She did her hair carefully, and then, looking in her mirror, she reflected with sudden pain that she *was* pretty, and that she was only a girl.

Resolutely, she turned from the mirror and, taking up her Bible, went back to the seat under the cottonwood. The children left their playing and came to her, for this was a Sunday ritual, their only one. Opening the Bible, she read slowly,

". . . though I walk through the valley of the shadow of death, I will fear no evil; for thou art with me; thy rod and thy staff, they comfort me. Thou preparest a table before me in the presence of mine enemies: thou . . ."

"Mommy." Jimmy tugged at her sleeve. "Look!"

Ches Lane had reached a narrow canyon by midafternoon and decided to make camp. There was small possibility he would find another such spot, and he was dead tired, his muscles sodden with fatigue. The canyon was one of those unexpected gashes in the cap rock that gave no indication of its presence until you came right on it. After some searching, Ches found a route to the bottom and made camp under a wind-hollowed overhang. There was water, and there was a small patch of grass.

After his horse had a drink and a roll on the ground, it began cropping eagerly at the rich, green grass, and Ches built a smokeless fire of some ancient driftwood in the canyon bottom. It was his first hot meal in days, and when he had finished he put out his fire, rolled a smoke, and leaned back contentedly.

Before darkness settled, he climbed to the rim and looked over the country. The sun had gone down, and the shadows were growing long. After a half hour of study, he decided there was no living thing within miles, except for the usual desert life. Returning to the bottom, he moved his horse to fresh grass, then rolled in his blanket. For the first time in a month, he slept without fear.

He woke up suddenly in the broad daylight. The horse was listening to something, his head up. Swiftly, Ches went to the horse and led it back under the overhang. Then he drew on his boots, rolled his blankets, and saddled the horse. Still he heard no sound.

Climbing the rim again, he studied the desert and found nothing. Returning to his horse, he mounted up and rode down the canyon toward the flatland beyond. Coming out of the canyon mouth, he rode right into the middle of a war party of more than twenty Apaches—invisible until suddenly they stood up behind rocks, their rifles leveled. And he didn't have a chance.

Swiftly, they bound his wrists to the saddle horn and tied his feet. Only then did he see the man who led the party. It was Cochise.

He was a lean, wiry Indian of past fifty, his black hair streaked with gray, his features strong and clean-cut. He stared at Lane, and there was nothing in his face to reveal what he might be thinking.

Several of the younger warriors pushed forward, talking excitedly and waving their arms. Ches Lane understood some of it, but he sat straight in the saddle, his head up, waiting. Then Cochise spoke and the party turned, and, leading his horse, they rode away.

The miles grew long and the sun was hot. He was offered no water and he asked for none. The Indians ignored him. Once a young brave rode near and struck him viciously. Lane made no sound, gave no indication of pain. When they finally stopped, it was beside a huge anthill swarming with big red desert ants.

Roughly, they quickly untied him and jerked him from his horse. He dug in his heels and shouted at them in Spanish: "The Apaches are women! They tie me to the ants because they are afraid to fight me!"

An Indian struck him, and Ches glared at the man. If he must die, he would show them how it should be done. Yet he knew the unpredictable nature of the Indian, of his great respect for courage.

"Give me a knife, and I'll kill any of your warriors!"

They stared at him, and one powerfully built Apache angrily ordered them to get on with it. Cochise spoke, and the big warrior replied angrily.

Ches Lane nodded at the anthill. "Is this the death for a fighting man? I have fought your strong men and beaten them. I have left no trail for them to follow, and for months I have lived among you, and now only by accident have you captured me. Give me a knife," he added grimly, "and I will fight *him!*" He indicated the big, black-faced Apache.

The warrior's cruel mouth hardened, and he struck Ches across the face.

The white man tasted blood and fury. "Woman!" Ches said. "Coyote! You are afraid!" Ches turned on Cochise, as the Indians stood irresolute. "Free my hands and let me fight!" he demanded. "If I win, let me go free."

Cochise said something to the big Indian. Instantly, there was stillness. Then an Apache sprang forward and, with a slash of his knife, freed Lane's hands. Shaking loose the thongs, Ches Lane chafed his wrists to bring back the circulation. An Indian threw a knife at his feet. It was his own bowie knife.

Ches took off his riding boots. In sock feet, his knife gripped low in his hand, its cutting edge up, he looked at the big warrior.

"I promise you nothing," Cochise said in Spanish, "but an honorable death."

The big warrior came at him on cat feet. Warily, Ches circled. He had not only to defeat this Apache but to escape. He permitted himself a side glance toward his horse. It stood alone. No Indian held it.

The Apache closed swiftly, thrusting wickedly with the knife. Ches, who had learned knife-fighting in the bayou country of Louisiana, turned his hip sharply, and the blade slid past him. He struck swiftly, but the Apache's forward movement deflected the blade, and it failed to penetrate. However, as it swept up between the Indian's body and arm, it cut a deep gash in the warrior's left armpit.

The Indian sprang again, like a clawing cat, streaming blood. Ches moved aside, but a backhand sweep nicked him, and he felt the sharp bite of the blade. Turning, he paused on the balls of his feet.

He had had no water in hours. His lips were cracked. Yet he sweated now, and the salt of it stung his eyes. He stared into the malevolent black eyes of the Apache, then moved to meet him. The Indian lunged, and Ches sidestepped like a boxer and spun on the ball of his foot.

The sudden side step threw the Indian past him, but Ches failed to drive the knife into the Apache's kidney when his foot rolled on a stone. The point left a thin red line across the Indian's back. The Indian was quick. Before Ches could recover his balance, he grasped the white man's knife wrist. Desperately, Ches grabbed for the Indian's knife hand and got the wrist, and they stood there straining, chest to chest.

Seeing his chance, Ches suddenly let his knees buckle, then brought up his knee and fell back, throwing the Apache over his head to the sand. Instantly, he whirled and was on his feet, standing over the Apache. The warrior had lost his knife, and he lay there, staring up, his eyes black with hatred.

Coolly, Ches stepped back, picked up the Indian's knife, and tossed it to him contemptuously. There was a grunt from the watching Indians, and then his antagonist rushed. But loss of blood had weakened the warrior, and Ches stepped in swiftly, struck the blade aside, then thrust the point of his blade hard against the Indian's belly.

Black eyes glared into his without yielding. A thrust, and the man would be disemboweled, but Ches stepped back. "He is a strong man," Ches said in Spanish. "It is enough that I have won."

Deliberately, he walked to his horse and swung into the saddle. He looked around, and every rifle covered him.

So he had gained nothing. He had hoped that mercy might lead to mercy, that the Apache's respect for a fighting man would win his freedom. He had failed. Again they bound him to his horse, but they did not take his knife from him.

When they camped at last, he was given food and drink. He was bound again, and a blanket was thrown over him. At daylight they were again in the saddle. In Spanish he asked where they were taking him, but they gave no indication of hearing. When they stopped again, it was beside a pole corral, near a stone cabin.

When Jimmy spoke, Angie got quickly to her feet. She recognized Cochise with a start of relief, but she saw instantly that this was a war party. And then she saw the prisoner.

Their eyes met and she felt a distinct shock. He was a white man, a big, unshaven man who badly needed both a bath and a haircut, his clothes ragged and bloody. Cochise gestured at the prisoner.

"No take Apache man, you take white man. This man good for hunt, good for fight. He strong warrior. You take 'em."

Flushed and startled, Angie stared at the prisoner and caught a faint glint of humor in his dark eyes.

"Is this here the fate worse than death I hear tell of?" he inquired gently.

"Who are you?" she asked, and was immediately conscious that it was an extremely silly question.

The Apaches had drawn back and were watching curiously. She could do nothing for the present but accept the situation. Obviously they intended to do her a kindness, and it would not do to offend them. If they had not brought this man to her, he might have been killed.

"Name's Ches Lane, ma'am," he said. "Will you untie me? I'd feel a lot safer."

"Of course." Still flustered, she went to him and untied his hands. One Indian said something, and the others chuckled; then, with a whoop, they swung their horses and galloped off down the canyon.

Their departure left her suddenly helpless, the shadowy globe of her loneliness shattered by this utterly strange man standing before her, this big, bearded man brought to her out of the desert.

She smoothed her apron, suddenly pale as she realized what his delivery to her implied. What must he think of her? She turned away quickly. "There's hot water," she said hastily, to prevent his speaking. "Dinner is almost ready."

She walked quickly into the house and stopped before the stove, her mind a blank. She looked around her as if she had suddenly waked up in a strange place. She heard water being poured into the basin by the door, and heard him take Ed's razor. She had never moved the box. To have moved it would—

"Sight of work done here, ma'am."

She hesitated, then turned with determination and stepped into the doorway. "Yes, Ed—"

"You're Angie Lowe."

Surprised, she turned toward him, and recognized his own startled awareness of her. As he shaved, he told her about Ed, and what had happened that day in the saloon.

"He—Ed was like that. He never considered consequences until it was too late."

"Lucky for me he didn't."

He was younger looking with his beard gone. There was a certain quiet dignity in his face. She went back inside and began putting plates on the table. She was conscious that he had moved to the door and was watching her.

"You don't have to stay," she said. "You owe me nothing. Whatever Ed did, he did because he was that kind of person. You aren't responsible."

He did not answer, and when she turned again to the stove, she glanced swiftly at him. He was looking across the valley.

There was a studied deference about him when he moved to a place at the table. The children stared, wide-eyed and silent; it had been so long since a man sat at this table.

Angie could not remember when she had felt like this. She was awkwardly conscious of her hands, which never seemed to be in the right place or doing the right things. She scarcely tasted her food, nor did the children.

Ches Lane had no such inhibitions. For the first time, he realized how hungry he was. After the half-cooked meat of lonely, trailside fires, this was tender and flavored. Hot biscuits, desert honey . . . Suddenly he looked up, embarrassed at his appetite.

"You were really hungry," she said.

"Man can't fix much, out on the trail."

Later, after he'd got his bedroll from his saddle and unrolled it on the hay in the barn, he walked back to the house and sat on the lowest step. The sun was gone, and they watched the cliffs stretch their red shadows across the valley. A quail called plaintively, a mellow sound of twilight.

"You needn't worry about Cochise," she said. "He'll soon be crossing into Mexico."

"I wasn't thinking about Cochise."

That left her with nothing to say, and she listened again to the quail and watched a lone bright star in the sky.

"A man could get to like it here," he said quietly.

The Woman at Apache Wells

JOHN JAKES

TRACY RODE DOWN from the rimrock with the seed of the plan already in mind. It was four days since they had blown up the safe in the bank at Wagon Bow and ridden off with almost fifty thousand dollars in Pawker's brown leather satchel. They had split up, taking three different directions, with Jacknife, the most trustworthy of the lot, carrying the satchel. Now, after four days of riding and sleeping out, Tracy saw no reason why he should split the money with the other two men.

His horse moved slowly along the valley floor beneath the sheet of blue sky. Rags of clouds scudded before the wind, disappearing past the craggy tops of the mountains to the west. Beyond those mountains lay California. Fifty thousand dollars in California would go a long way toward setting a man up for the rest of his life.

Tracy was a big man, with heavy capable hands and peaceful blue eyes looking out at the world from under a shock of sandy hair. He was by nature a man of the earth, and if the war hadn't come along, culminating in the frantic breakup at Petersburg, he knew he would still be working the rich Georgia soil. But his farm, like many others, had been put to the torch by Sherman, and the old way of life had been wiped out. The restless postwar tide had caught him and pushed him westward to a meeting with Pawker and Jacknife, also ex-Confederates, and the robbery of the bank filled with Yankee money.

Tracy approached the huddle of rundown wooden buildings. The valley was deserted now that the stage had been rerouted, and the Apache Wells Station was slowly sagging into ruin. Tracy pushed his hat down over his eyes, shielding his face from the sun.

Jacknife stood in the door of the main building, hand close to his

---

holster. The old man's eyes were poor, and when he finally recognized Tracy, he let out a loud whoop and ran toward him. Tracy kicked his mount and clattered to a stop before the long ramshackle building. He climbed down, grinning. He didn't want Jacknife to become suspicious.

"By jingoes," Jacknife crowed, "it sure as hell is good to see you, boy. This's been four days of pure murder, with all that cash just waitin' for us." He scratched his incredibly tangled beard, unmindful of the dirt on his face or the stink on his clothes.

Tracy looked toward the open door. The interior of the building was in shadows. "Pawker here yet?" he asked.

"Nope. He's due in by sundown, though. Least, that's what he said."

"You got the money?" Tracy spoke sharply.

"Sure, boy, I got it." Jacknife laughed. "Don't get so worried. It's inside, safe as can be."

Tracy thought about shoving a gun into Jacknife's ribs and taking off with the bag right away. But he rejected the idea. He didn't have any grudge against the oldster. It was Pawker he disliked, with his boyish yellow beard and somehow nasty smile. He wanted the satisfaction of taking the money away from Pawker himself. He would wait.

Then Tracy noticed Jacknife's face was clouded with anxiety. He stared hard at the old man. "What's the trouble? You look like you got kicked in the teeth by a Yankee."

"Almost," Jacknife admitted. "We're right smack in the middle of a sitcheation which just ain't healthy. A woman rode in here this morning."

Tracy nearly fell over. "A woman! What the hell you trying to pull?"

"Nothin', Tracy. She said she's Pawker's woman and he told her to meet him here. You know what a killer he is with the ladies."

"Of all the damn fool things," Tracy growled. "With cash to split up and every lawman around here just itching to catch us, Pawker's got to bring a woman along. Where is she?"

"Right inside," Jacknife repeated, jerking a thumb at the doorway.

"I got to see this."

He strode through the door into the cool shadowy interior. The only light in the room came from a window in the west wall. The mountains and the broken panes made a double line of ragged teeth against the cloud-dotted sky.

She sat on top of an old wooden table, whittling a piece of wood. Her clothes were rough, denim pants and a work shirt. Her body, Tracy could see, was womanly all over, and her lips were full. The eyes that looked up at him were large and gray, filled with a strange light that seemed, at succeeding moments, girlishly innocent and fiercely hungry for excitement. Just Pawker's type, he decided. A fast word, and they came tagging along. The baby-faced Confederate angered him more than ever.

"I hear you joined the party," Tracy said, a bit nastily.

"That's right." She didn't flinch from his stare. The knife hovered over the whittled stick. "My name's Lola."

"Tracy's mine. That doesn't change the fact that I don't like a woman hanging around on a deal like this."

"Pawker told me to come," she said defiantly. From her accent he could tell she was a Yankee.

"Pawker tells a lot of them to come. I been riding with him for a couple of months. That's long enough to see how he operates. Only a few of them are sucker enough to fall."

Her face wore a puzzled expression for a minute, as if she were not quite certain she believed what she said next. "He told me we were going to California with the money he stole from the bank."

"That's right," Tracy said. "Did he tell you there were two more of us?"

"No."

Tracy laughed, seating himself on a bench. "I thought so." Inwardly he felt even more justified at taking the money for himself. Pawker was probably planning to do the same thing. He wouldn't be expecting Tracy to try it.

"If I were you, miss, I'd ride back to where I came from and forget about Pawker. I worked with him at Wagon Bow, but I don't like him. He's a thief and a killer."

Her eyes flared with contempt. She cut a slice from the stick. "You're a fine one to talk, Mister Tracy. You were there too. You just said so. I suppose you've never robbed anybody in your life before."

"No, I haven't."

"Or killed anybody?"

"No. I didn't do any shooting at Wagon Bow. Pawker killed the teller. Jacknife outside didn't use his gun either. Pawker likes to use his gun. You ought to know that. Anybody can tell what kind of a man he is after about ten minutes."

Lola threw down the knife and the stick and stormed to the window. "I don't see what call you've got to be so righteous. You took the money, just like Pawker."

"Pawker's done it before. I figured this was payment for my farm in Georgia. Your soldiers burned me out. I figured I could collect this way and get a new start in California."

She turned suddenly, staring. "You were in the war?"

"I was. But that's not important. The important thing is for you to get home to your people before Pawker gets here. Believe me, he isn't worth it."

"I haven't got any people," she said. Her eyes suddenly closed a bit. "And I don't have a nice clean town to go back to. They don't want me back there. I had a baby, about a month ago. It died when it was born. The baby's father never came home from the war—" She looked away for a moment. "Anyway—Pawker came into the restaurant where I was working and offered to take me West."

"Somebody in the town ought to be willing to help you."

Lola shook her head, staring at the blue morning sky. Jacknife's whistle sounded busily from the broken-down corral. "No," she said. "The baby's father and I were never married."

Tracy walked over to her and stood behind her, looking down at her hair. He suddenly felt very sorry for this girl, for the life lying behind her. He had never felt particularly attached to any woman, except perhaps Elaine, dead and burned now, a victim of Sherman's bummers back in Georgia. He could justify the Wagon Bow robbery to himself. Not completely, but enough. But he couldn't justify Pawker or Pawker's love of killing or the taking of the girl.

"Look, Lola," he said. "You don't know me very well, but I'm willing to make you an offer. If you help me get the money, I'll take you with me. It'd be better than going with Pawker."

She didn't answer him immediately. "How do I know you're not just like him?"

"You don't. You'll have to trust me."

She studied him a minute. Then she said, "All right."

She stood very close to Tracy, her face uplifted, her breasts pushing out against the cloth of her shirt. A kind of resigned expectancy lay on her face. Tracy took her shoulders in his hands, pulled her to him and kissed her cheek lightly. When she moved away, the expectancy had changed to amazement.

"You don't need to think that's any part of the bargain," he said.

She looked into his eyes. "Thanks."

Tracy walked back to the table and sat down on the edge. He couldn't understand her, or know her motives, and yet he felt a respect for her and for the clear, steady expression of her eyes. Something in them almost made him ashamed of his part in the Wagon Bow holdup.

Jacknife stuck his head in the door, his watery eyes excited. A big glob of tobacco distended one cheek. "Hey, Tracy. Pawker's coming in."

Tracy headed outside without looking at Lola. A big roan stallion with Pawker bobbing in the saddle was pounding toward the buildings over the valley floor from the north, sending a cloud of tan dust into the sky. Tracy climbed the rail fence at a spot where it wasn't collapsing and from there watched Pawker ride into the yard.

Pawker climbed down. He was a slender man, but his chest was large and muscled under the torn Union cavalry coat. He wore two pistols, butts forward, and cartridge belts across his shirtfront under the coat.

Large silver Spanish spurs jingled loudly when he moved. His flat-crowned black hat was tilted at a rakish angle over his boyish blond-whiskered face. Tracy had always disliked the effect Pawker tried to create, the effect of the careless guerrilla still fighting the war, the romantic desperado laughing and crinkling his childish blue eyes when his guns exploded. Right now, the careless guerrilla was drunk.

He swayed in the middle of the yard, blinking. He tilted his head back to look at the sun, then groaned. He peered around the yard. His hand moved aimlessly. "Hello, ol' Jacknife, hello, ol' Tracy. Damned four days, too damned long."

"You better sober up," Jacknife said, worried. "I want to split the money and light out of here."

"Nobody comes to Apache Wells any more," Pawker said. "Tracy, fetch the bottles out o' my saddlebags."

"I don't want a drink," Tracy said. Lola stood in the doorway now, watching, but Pawker did not see her. If he had, he would have seen the disillusionment taking root. Tracy smiled a little. Grabbing the money would be a pleasure.

"Listen, Pawker," Jacknife said, approaching him, "let's divvy the cash and forget the drink—"

Suddenly Pawker snarled and pushed the old man. Jacknife stumbled backward and fell in the dust. Pawker spat incoherent words and his right arm flashed across his body. The pistol came out and exploded loudly in the bright air. A whiff of smoke went swirling away across the old wooden roofs.

Jacknife screamed and clutched his hip. Tracy jumped off the fence and came on Pawker from behind, ripping the gun out of his hand and tossing it away. He spun Pawker around and hit him on the chin. The blond man skidded in the dust and scrabbled onto his knees, some of the drunkenness gone. Glaring, he slid his left hand across his body and down.

Tracy pointed his gun straight at Pawker's belly. "I'd like you to do that," he said. "Go ahead and draw."

Cunning edged across the other man's face. His hand moved half an inch further and he smiled. Then he giggled. "I'm going to throw my gun away, Tracy boy. I don't want trouble. Can I throw my gun away and show you I'm a peaceable man?"

Tracy took three fast steps forward and pulled the gun from its holster before Pawker could seize it. Then he turned his head and said, "Lola, find the satchel and get horses."

Pawker screamed the girl's name unbelievingly, turning on his belly in the dust to stare at her. He began to curse, shaking his fist at her, until Tracy planted a hand on his shoulder, pulled him to his feet and jammed him against the wall of the building with the gun pressing his ribs.

"Now listen," Tracy said. "I'm taking the satchel and I don't want a big muss."

"Stole my money, stole my woman," Pawker mumbled. "I'll get you, Tracy, I'll hunt you up and kill you slow. I'll make you pay, by God." His eyes rolled crazily, drunkenly.

Jacknife was trying to hobble to his feet. "Tracy," he wheezed, "Tracy, help me."

"I'm taking the money," Tracy said.

"That's all right, that's fine, I don't care," Jacknife breathed. "Put me on my horse and slap it good. I just want to get away from him. He's a crazy man."

Tracy shoved Pawker to the ground again and waved his gun at him. "You stay right there. I've got my eye on you." Pawker snarled something else but he didn't move. Tracy helped Jacknife onto his horse. The old man bent forward and lay across the animal's neck.

"So long, Tracy. Hit him good. I want to get away—"

"You need a doctor," Tracy said.

"I can head for some town," Jacknife breathed. "Come on, hit him!"

Tracy slapped the horse's flank and watched him go galloping out of the station yard and across the valley floor. Lola came around the corner of the building leading two horses. The satchel was tied over one of the saddlebags.

Tracy turned his head for an instant and when he turned back again, Pawker was scrabbling in the dust toward his gun which lay on the far side of the yard. Tracy fired a shot. It kicked up a spurt of dust a foot in front of Pawker's face. He jerked back, rolling over on his side and screaming, "I swear to God, Tracy, I'll come after you."

Lola was already in the saddle. The horses moved skittishly. Tracy swung up and said, "Let's get out of here." He dug in his heels and the horses bolted. They headed west across the floor of the valley.

They rode in silence. Tracy looked back once, to see Pawker staggering away from the building with his gun, firing at them over the widening distance. Until they made camp in the early evening at a small grove, with the mountains still looming to the west, Tracy said almost nothing.

Finally, when the meal with its few necessary remarks was over, he said, "Pawker will follow us. We'll have to keep moving."

She answered absently, "I guess you're right." A frown creased her forehead.

"What's the trouble?" He was beginning to sense the growth of a new feeling for this woman beside him. She was as silent and able as the hardened men with whom he had ridden in the last few years. Yet she was different, too, and not merely because she was female.

"I don't know how to tell you this right, Tracy." She spoke slowly. The firelight made faint red gold webs in her hair and the night air stirred it. "But—well—I think you're an honest man. I think you're decent and that's what I need." She stuck her finger out for emphasis. "Mind you, I don't mean that I care anything about you, but I think I could."

Tracy smiled. The statement was businesslike, and it pleased him. He knew that there was the possibility of a relationship that might be good for a man to have.

"I understand," he said. "I sort of feel the same. There's a lot of territory in California. A man could make a good start."

She nodded. "A good start, that's important. I made a mistake, I guess. So did you. But now there's a chance for both of us to make up for that. I'm not asking you if you want to. I'm just telling you the chance is there, and I'd like to see if what I think of you is right."

"I've been thinking the same," he said.

They sat in silence the rest of the evening, but it was a silence filled with a good sense of companionship that Tracy had seldom known. For the first time in several years, he felt things might work out right after all. Right according to the way it had been before the war, not since.

The next morning, they doubled back.

It was a five-day ride to Wagon Bow. The job was carried off at around four in the morning. Tracy rode through the darkened main street at a breakneck gallop and flung the satchel of money on the plank walk in front of the bank. By the time the sun rose he and Lola were miles from Wagon Bow. The only troubling factor was Pawker, somewhere behind them.

He caught up with them when they were high in the mountains, heavily bundled, driving their horses through the lowering twilight while the snow fell from a gray sky. Actually, they were the ones who caught up with Pawker. They saw him lying behind a boulder where he had been waiting. A rime of ice covered his rifle and his yellow boy's beard. His mouth was open. He was frozen to death.

Tracy felt a great relief. Pawker had evidently followed them, knowing the route they would probably take, and circling ahead to wait in ambush. It would have fitted him, rearing up from behind the boulder with his mouth open in a laugh and his avenging rifle spitting at them in the snow.

They stood for a time in the piercing cold, staring down at the body. Then Tracy looked at Lola through the dim veil of snow between them. He smiled, not broadly, because he wasn't a man to smile at death, but with a smile of peace. Neither one spoke.

Tracy made the first overt gesture. He put his thickly clad arm around her and held her for a minute, their cold raw cheeks touching. Then they returned to the horses.

Two days later, they rode down out of the mountains on the trail that led to California.

Law of the Hunted Ones

ELMORE LEONARD

PATMAN SAW IT first. The sudden flash of sun on metal; then, on the steepness of the hillside, it was a splinter of a gleam that hung unmoving amidst the confusion of jagged rock and brush. Just a dull gleam now that meant nothing, but the first metallic flash had been enough for Virgil Patman.

He exhaled slowly, dropping his eyes from the gleam up on the slanting wall, and let his gaze drift up ahead through the narrowness, the way it would naturally. But his fists remained tight around the reins. He muttered to himself, "You damn fool." Cover was behind, a hundred feet or more, and a rifle can do a lot of pecking in a hundred feet.

The boy doesn't see it, he thought. Else he would have been shooting by now. And then other words followed in his mind. Why do you think the boy's any dumber than you are?

He shifted his hip in the saddle and turned his head halfway around. Dave Fallis was a few paces behind him and to the side. He was looking at his hands on the flat dinner-plate saddle horn, deep in thought.

Patman drew tobacco and paper from his side coat pocket and held his mount in until the boy came abreast of him.

"Don't look up too quick and don't make a sudden move," Patman said. He passed the paper along the tip of his tongue, then shaped it expertly in his bony, freckly fingers. He wasn't looking at the boy, but he could sense his head come up fast. "What did I just tell you!"

He struck a match and held it to the brown paper cigarette. His eyes were on the match and he half mumbled with the cigarette in his mouth. "Dave, hold on to your nerve. There's a rifle pointing at us. Maybe two hundred feet ahead and almost to the top of the slope." He handed the makings across. "Build yourself one like it was Sunday afternoon on the front porch."

76

Their horses moved at a slow walk close to the left side that was smooth rock and almost straight up. Here, and as far as you could see ahead, the right side slanted steeply up, gravel, rock, and brush thrown violently together, to finally climb into dense pines overhead. Here and there the pines straggled down the slope. Patman watched the boy put the twisted cigarette between his lips and light it, the hand steady, up close to his face.

"When you get a chance," Patman said, "look about halfway up the slope, just this side of that hollow. You'll see a dab of yellow that's prickly pear, then go above to that rock jam and tell me what you see."

Fallis pulled his hat closer to his eyes and looked up-canyon before dragging his gaze to the slope. His face registered nothing, not even a squint with the hat brim resting on his eyebrows. A hard-boned face, tight through the cheeks and red-brown from the sun, but young and with a good mouth that looked as if it smiled most of the time, though it wasn't smiling now. His gaze lowered to the pass and he drew on the cigarette.

"Something shining up there, but I don't make out what it is," he said.

"It's a rifle, all right. We'll take for granted somebody's behind it."

"Indian?"

"Not if the piece is so clean it shines," Patman answered. "Just keep going, and watch me. We'll gamble that it's a white man—and gamble that he acts like one."

Fallis tried to keep his voice even. "What if he just shoots?" The question was hoarse with excitement. Maybe the boy's not as scared as I am, Patman thought. Young and too eager to be afraid. You get old and take too damn much time doing what kept you alive when you were young. Why keep thinking of him, he thought, you got a hide too, you know.

Patman answered, "If he shoots, we'll know where we stand and you can do the first thing that comes to your mind."

"Then I might let go at you," Fallis smiled, "for leading us into this jackpot."

Patman's narrow face looked stone-hard with its sad smile beneath the full mustache. "If you want to make jokes," he said, "go find someone else."

"What're we going to do, Virg?" Fallis was dead serious. It made his face look tough when he didn't smile, with the heavy cheekbones and the hard jawline beneath.

"We don't have a hell of a lot of choices," Patman said. "If we kick into a run or turn too fast, we're likely to get a bullet. You don't want to take a chance on that gent up there being the nervous type. And if we just start shooting, we haven't got anything to hide behind when he shoots back."

He heard the boy say, "We can get behind our horses."

He answered him, "I'd just as soon get shot as have to walk home. You got any objections to just going on like we don't know he's there?"

Fallis shook his head, swallowing. "Anything you say, Virg. Probably he's just out hunting turkeys . . ." He dropped behind the older man as they edged along the smooth rock of the canyon wall until there was ten feet between their horses.

They rode stiff-backed, from habit, yet with an easy looseness of head and arms that described an absence of tension. Part of it was natural, again habit, and part was each trying to convince the other that he wasn't afraid. Patman and Fallis were good for each other. They had learned it through campaigning.

Now, with the tightness in their bellies, they waited for the sound. The clop of their horses' hooves had a dull ring in the awful silence. They waited for another sound.

Both men were half expecting the heavy report of a rifle. They steeled themselves against the worst that could happen, because anything else would take care of itself. The sound of the loose rock glancing down the slope was startling, like a warning to jerk their heads to the side and up the slanting wall.

The man was standing in the spot where Patman had pointed, his rifle at aim, so that all they could see was the rifle below the hat. No face.

"Don't move a finger, or you're dead!" The voice was full and clear. The man lowered the rifle and called, "Sit still while I come down."

He turned and picked his way over the scattered rock, finally half sliding into the hollow that was behind his position. The hollow fell less steeply to the canyon floor with natural rock footholds and gnarled brush stumps to hold on to.

For a moment the man's head disappeared from view, then was there again just as suddenly. He hesitated, watching the two men below him and fifty feet back up the trail. Then he disappeared again into a deeper section of the descent.

Dave Fallis's hand darted to the holster at his hip.

"Hold onto yourself!" Patman's whisper was a growl in his heavy mustache. His eyes flicked to the hollow. "He's not alone! You think he'd go out of sight if he was by himself!"

The boy's hand slid back to the saddle horn while his eyes traveled over the heights above him. Only the hot breeze moved the brush clumps.

The man moved toward them on the trail ahead with short, bowlegged steps, his face lowered close to the upraised rifle. When he was a dozen steps from Patman's horse, his head came up and he shouted, "All right!"

to the heights behind them. Fallis heard Patman mumble, "I'll be damned," looking at the man with the rifle.

"Hey, Rondo!" Patman was grinning his sad smile down at the short, bowlegged man with the rifle. "What you got here, a toll you collect from anybody who goes by?" Patman laughed out, with a ring of relief to the laugh. "I saw you a ways back. Your toll box was shining in the sun." He went on laughing and put his hand in his side coat pocket.

The rifle came up full on his chest. "Keep your hand in sight!" The man's voice cut sharply.

Patman looked at him surprised. "What's the matter with you, Rondo? It's me. Virg Patman." His arm swung to his side. "This here's Dave Fallis. We rode together in the Third for the past five years."

Rondo's heavy-whiskered face stared back, the deep lines unmoving as if they had been cut into stone. The rifle was steady on Patman's chest.

"What the hell's the matter with you!" Patman repeated. "Remember me bringing you your bait for sixty days at Thomas?"

Rondo's beard separated when his mouth opened slightly. "You were on the outside, if I remember correctly."

Patman swore with a gruff howl. "You talk like I passed sentence! You damn fool, what do you think a Corporal of the Guard is—a judge?" His head turned to Fallis. "This bent-legged waddie shoots a reservation Indian, gets sixty days, then blames it on me. You remember him in the lock-up?"

"No. I guess—"

"That's right," Patman cut in. "That was before your time."

Rondo looked past the two men.

"That wasn't before my time." The voice came from behind the two men.

He was squatting on a hump that jutted out from the slope, just above their heads and a dozen or so feet behind them, and he looked as if he'd been sitting there all the time. When he looked at him, Fallis thought of a scavenger bird perched on the bloated roundness of a carcass.

It was his head and the thinness of his frame that gave that impression. His dark hair was cropped close to his skull, brushed forward low on his forehead and coming to a slight point above his eyebrows. The thin hair pointed down, as did the ends of a shadowy mustache that was just starting to grow, lengthening the line of his face, a face that was sallow-complexioned and squinting against the brightness of the afternoon.

He jumped easily from the hump, his arms outstretched and a pistol in each hand, though he wore only one holster on his hip.

Fallis watched him open-mouthed. He wore a faded undershirt and pants tucked into knee-high boots. A string of red cotton was knotted tight to his throat above the opening of the undershirt. And with it all, the yellowish death's-head of a face. Fallis watched because he couldn't take his eyes from the man. There was a compelling arrogance about his movements and the way he held his head that made Fallis stare at him. And even with the shabbiness of his dress, it stood out. It was there in the way he held his pistols. Fallis pictured a saber-slashing captain of cavalry. Then he saw a black-bearded buccaneer.

"I remember when Rondo was in the lock-up at Fort Thomas." His voice was crisp, but low, and he extra-spaced his words. "That was a good spell before you rode me to Yuma, wasn't it?"

Patman shook his head. The surprise had already left his face. He shook his head wearily as if it was all way above him. He said, "If you got any more men up there that I policed, get 'em down and let me hear it all at once." He shook his head again. "This is a real day of surprises. I can't say I ever expected to see you again, De Sana."

"Then what are you doing here?" The voice was cold-clear, but fell off at the end of the question as if he had already made up his mind why they were there.

Patman saw it right away.

It took Fallis a little longer because he had to fill in, but he understood now, looking at De Sana and then to Patman.

Patman's voice was a note higher. "You think we're looking for you?"

"I said," De Sana repeated, "then what are you doing here?"

"Hell, we're not tracking you! We were mustered out last week. We're pointing toward West Texas for a range job, or else sign for contract buffalo hunters."

De Sana stared, but didn't speak. His hands, with the revolving pistols, hung at his sides.

"What do I care if you broke out of the Territory prison?" Patman shouted it, then seemed to relax, to calm himself. "Listen," he said, "we're both mustered out. Dave here has got one hitch in, and I've got more years behind me than I like to remember. But we're out now and what the army does is its own damn business. And what you do is your business. I can forget you like that." He snapped his fingers. " 'Cause you don't mean a thing to me. And that dust-eatin' train ride from Wilcox to Yuma, I can forget that too, 'cause I didn't enjoy it any more than you did even if you thought then you weren't going to make the return trip. You're as bad as Rondo here. You think 'cause I was train guard it was my fault you got sent to Yuma. Listen, I treated you square. There were some troopers would have kicked your face in just on principle."

De Sana moistened his lower lip with his tongue, idly, thinking about the past and the future at the same time. A man has to believe in something, no matter what he is. He looked at the two men on the horses and felt the weight of the pistols in his hands. There was the easy way. He looked at them watching him uneasily, waiting for him to make a move.

"Going after a range job, huh?" he said almost inaudibly.

"That's right. Or else hunt buffalo. They say the railroad's paying top rate, too," Patman added.

"How do I know," De Sana said slowly, "you won't get to the next sheriff's office and start yelling wolf?"

Patman was silent as his fingers moved over his jaw. "I guess you'll have to take my word that I've got a bad memory," he said finally.

"What kind of memory has your friend got?" De Sana said, looking hard at Dave Fallis.

"You got the biggest pistols he ever saw," Patman answered.

Rondo mounted behind Patman and pointed the way up the narrow draw that climbed from the main trail about a quarter of a mile up. It branched from the pass, twisting as it climbed, but more decidedly bearing an angle back in the direction from which they had come. Rondo had laughed out at Patman's last words. The tension was off now. Since De Sana had accepted the two men, Rondo would too, and went even a step further, talking about hospitality and coffee and words like "this calls for a celebration," even though the words were lost on the other three men. The words had no meaning but they filled in and lessened the tension.

De Sana was still standing in the pass when they left, but when Fallis looked back he saw the outlaw making his way up the hollow.

When the draw reached the end of its climb they were at the top of the ridge, looking down directly to the place where they had held up. Here, the pines were thick, but farther off they scattered and thinned again as they began to stretch toward higher, rockier ground.

De Sana was standing among the trees waiting for them. He turned before they reached him and led the way through the pines. Fallis looked around curiously, feeling the uneasiness that had come over him since meeting De Sana. Then, as he looked ahead, the hut wasn't fifty feet away.

It was a low structure, flat-roofed and windowless, with rough, uneven logs chinked in with adobe mud. On one side was a lean-to where the cooking was done. A girl was hanging strips of meat from the low ceiling when they came out of the pines, and as they approached she turned with a hand on her hip, smoothing a stray wisp of hair with the other.

She watched them with open curiosity, as a small child stares at the mystery of a strange person. There was a delicateness of face and body that accentuated this, that made her look more childlike in her open sensitivity. De Sana glanced at her and she dropped her eyes and turned back to the jerked meat.

"Put the coffee on," De Sana called to her. She nodded her head without turning around. "Rondo, you take care of the mounts and get back to your nest."

Rondo opened his mouth to say something but thought better of it and tried to make his face look natural when he took the reins from the two men and led the horses across the small clearing to the corral, part of which could be seen through the pines a little way off. A three-sided lean-to squatted at one end of the small, fenced area.

"That's Rondo's." De Sana pointed to the shelter. Walking to the cabin, he called to the girl again. This time she did not shake her head. Fallis thought perhaps the shoulders tensed in the faded gray dress. Still, she didn't turn around or even answer him.

The inside of the cabin was the same as the outside, rough log chinked with adobe, and a packed dirt floor. A table and two chairs, striped with cracks and gray with age, stood in the middle of the small room. In a far corner was a straw mattress. On it, a blanket was twisted in a heap. Along the opposite wall was a section of log with a board nailed to it to serve as a bench, and next to this was the cupboard: three boxes stacked one on the other. It contained a tangle of clothing, cartridge boxes and five or six bottles of whiskey.

The two men watched De Sana shove his extra pistol into a holster that hung next to the cupboard. The other was on his hip. He took a half-filled bottle from the shelf and went to the table.

"Looks like I'm just in time." Rondo was standing in the doorway, grinning, with a canteen hanging from his hand. "Give me a little fill, *jefe,* to ease sitting on that eagle's nest."

De Sana's head came up and he moved around the table threateningly, his eyes pinned on the man in the doorway. "Get back to the pass!" His hand dropped to the pistol on his hip in a natural movement. "You watch! You get paid to watch! And if you miss anything going through that pass . . ." His voice trailed off, but for a moment it shook with excitement.

"Hell, Lew. Nobody's going to find us way up here," Rondo argued halfheartedly.

Patman looked at him surprised. "Cima Quaine's blood-dogs could track a man all the way to China."

"Aw, San Carlos's a hundred miles away. Ain't nobody going to track us that far, not even 'Pache Police."

De Sana said, "I'm not telling you again, Rondo." Rondo glanced at the hand on the pistol butt and moved out of the doorway.

But as he walked through the pines toward the canyon edge, he held the canteen up to his face and shook it a few times. He could hear the whiskey inside sloshing around, sounding as if it were still a good one-third full. Rondo smiled and his mind erased the scowling yellow face. Lew De Sana could go take a whistlin' dive at the moon for all he cared.

The girl's fingers were crooked through the handles of the three enamel cups, and she kept her eyes lowered to the table as she set the coffeepot down with her other hand, placing the cups next to it.

"Looks good," Patman said.

She said nothing, but her eyes lifted to him briefly, then darted to the opposite side of the table where Fallis stood and then lowered just as quickly. She had turned her head slightly, enough for Fallis to see the bruise on her cheekbone. A deep blue beneath her eye that spread into a yellowish cast in the soft hollow of her cheek. There was a lifelessness in the dark eyes and perhaps fear. Fallis kept staring at the girl, seeing the utter resignation that showed in her face and was there even in the way she moved her small body. Like a person who has given up and doesn't much care what happens next. He noticed the eyes when her glance wandered to him again, dark and tired, yet with a certain hungriness in their deepness. No, it wasn't fear.

De Sana picked up the first cup as she filled it and poured a heavy shot from the bottle into it. He set the bottle down and lifted the coffee cup to his mouth. His lips moved, as if tasting, and he said, "It's cold," looking at the girl in a way that didn't need the support of other words. He turned the cup upside down and poured the dark liquid on the floor.

Fallis thought, what a damn fool. Who's he trying to impress? He glanced at Patman, but the ex-corporal was looking at De Sana as if pouring the coffee on the floor was the most normal thing in the world.

As the girl picked up the big coffeepot, her hand shook with the weight and before her other hand could close on the spout, she dropped it back on the table.

"Here, I'll give you a hand," Fallis offered. "That's a big jug."

But just as he took it from the girl's hands, he heard De Sana say, "Leave that pot alone!"

He looked at De Sana in bewilderment. "What? I just want to help her out with the coffeepot."

"She can do her own chores." De Sana's voice was unhurried. "Just put it down."

Dave Fallis felt heat rise up over his face. When he was angry, he always wondered if it showed. And sometimes, as, for instance, now, he didn't care. His heart started going faster with the rise of the heat that tingled the hair on the back of his head and made the words come to his mouth. And he had to spit the words out hard because it would make him feel better.

"Who the hell are you talking to? Do I look like somebody you can give orders to?" Fallis stopped but kept on looking at the thin, sallow face, wishing he could think of something good to say while the anger was up.

Patman moved closer to the younger man. "Slow down, Dave," he said with a laugh that sounded forced. "A man's got a right to run things like he wants in his own house."

De Sana's eyes moved from one to the other, then back to the girl and said, "What are you waiting for?" He kept his eyes on her until she passed through the doorway. Then he said, "Mister, you better have a talk with your boy."

Fallis heard Patman say, "That's just his Irish, Lew. You know, young and gets hot easy." He stared at the old cavalryman—not really old, but twice his own age—and tried to see through the sad face with the drooping mustache because he knew that wasn't Virg Patman talking, calling him by his first name as if they were old friends. What was the matter with Virg? He felt the anger draining and in its place was bewilderment. It made him feel uneasy and kind of foolish standing there, with his big hands planted on the table, trying to stare down the skeletal-looking gunman who looked at him as if he were a kid and would be just wasting his time talking. It made him madder, but the things he wanted to say sounded too loudmouth in his mind. The words seemed blustering, hot air, compared to the cold, slow-spoken words of De Sana.

Now De Sana said, "I don't care what his nationality is. But I think you better tell him the facts of life."

Fallis felt the heat again, but Patman broke in with his laugh before he could say anything.

"Hell, Lew," Patman said. "Let's get back to what we come for. Nobody meant any harm."

De Sana fingered the dark shadow of his mustache thoughtfully, and finally said, hurriedly, "Yeah. All right." Then he added, "Now that you're here, you might as well stay the night and leave in the morning. If you have any stores with you, break them out. This isn't any street mission. And remember, first light you leave."

Later, during the meal, he spoke little, occasionally answering Patman in monosyllables. He never spoke directly to Fallis and only answered Patman when he had to. Finally he pushed from the table before he had finished. He rolled a cigarette, moving toward the door. "I'm going out to relieve Rondo," he said. "Don't wander off."

* * *

Fallis watched him walk across the clearing and when the figure disappeared into the pines he turned abruptly to Patman sitting next to him.

"What's the matter with you, Virg?"

Patman put his hand up. "Now just slow it down. You're too damn jumpy."

"Jumpy? Honest to God, Virg, you never sucked up to the first sergeant like you did to that little rooster. Back in the pass you read him out when he started jumping to conclusions. Now you're buttering up like you were scared to death."

"Wait a minute." Patman passed his fingers through his thinning hair, his elbow on the table. He looked very tired and his long face seemed to sag loosely in sadness. "If you're going to play brave, you got to pick the right time, else your bravery don't mean a damn thing. These hills are full of heroes, and nobody even knows where to plant the flowers over them. Then you come across a man fresh out of Yuma—out the hard way, too—" he added, "a man who probably shoots holes in his shadow every night and can't trust anybody because it might mean going back to an adobe cell block. He got sent there in the first place because he shot an Indian agent in a holdup. He didn't kill him, but don't think he couldn't have—and don't think he hasn't killed before."

Patman exhaled and drew tobacco from his pocket. "You run into a man like that, a man who counts his breaths like you count your blessings, and you pick a fight because you don't like the way he treats his woman."

"A man can't get his toes stepped on and just smile," Fallis said testily.

Patman blew smoke out wearily. "Maybe your hitch in the army was kind of a sheltered life. Brass bands and not having to think. Trailing a dust cloud that used to be Apaches isn't facing Lew De Sana across a three-foot table. I think you were lucky."

Fallis picked up his hat and walked toward the door. "We'll see," he answered.

"Wait a minute, Dave." Fallis turned in the doorway.

"Sometimes you got to pick the lesser of evils," the older man said. "Like choosing between a sore toe or lead in your belly. Remember, Dave, he's a man with a price on his head. He's spooky. And remember this. A little while ago he could have shot both of your eyes out while he was drinking his coffee."

Patience wasn't something Dave Fallis came by naturally. Standing idle ate at his nerves and made him move restlessly like a penned animal. The army hitch had grated on him this way. Petty routines and idleness. Idleness in the barracks and idleness even in the dust-smothering parade during the hours of drill. Routine that became so much a part of you it ceased being mentally directed.

The cavalry had a remedy for the restless feeling. Four-day patrols. Four-day patrols that sometimes stretched to twenty and by it brought the ailment back with the remedy. For a saddle is a poor place for boredom, and twelve hours in it will bring the boredom back quicker than anything else, especially when the land is flat and vacant, silent but for a monotonous clop, blazing in its silence and carrying only dust and a sweat smell that clung sourly to you in the daytime and chilled you at night. Dave Fallis complained because nothing happened—because there was never any action. He was told he didn't know how lucky he was. That he didn't know what he was talking about because he was just a kid. And nothing made him madder. Damn a man who's so ignorant he holds age against you!

Now he stood in the doorway and looked out across the clearing. He leaned against the door jamb, hooking his thumbs in his belt, and let his body go loose. The sun was there in front of him over the trees, casting a soft spread of light on the dark hillsides in the distance. Now it was a sun that you could look at without squinting or pulling down your hat brim. A sun that would be gone in less than an hour.

He saw the girl appear and move toward the lean-to at the side of the hut. She walked slowly, listlessly.

Fallis left the doorway and idled along the front of the hut after she had passed and entered the shelter. And when he ducked his head slightly and entered the low-roofed shed, the girl was busy scooping venison stew from the pot and dishing it onto one of the tin plates.

She turned quickly at the sound of his step and almost brushed him as she turned, stopping, her mouth slightly open, her face lower than his, but not a foot separating them.

He was grinning when she turned, but the smile left his face as she continued to stare up at him, her mouth still parted slightly and warm looking, complementing the delicately soft lines of nose and cheekbones. The bruise was not so noticeable now, in the shadows, but its presence gave her face a look of sadness, yet adding lustre to the deep brown eyes that stared without blinking.

His hands came up to grip her shoulders, pulling gently as he lowered his face to hers. She yielded against the slight pressure of his hands, drawing closer, and he saw her eyes close as her face tilted back, but as he closed his eyes he felt her shoulders jerk suddenly from his grip and in front of his face now was the smooth blackness of her hair hanging straight about her shoulders.

"Why did you do that?" Her voice was low, and with her back to him, barely audible.

Fallis said, "I haven't done anything yet," and tried to make his voice sound light. The girl made no answer, but remained still, with her shoulder close to him.

"I'm sorry," he said. "Are you married to him?"

Her head shook from side to side in two short motions, but no sound came from her. He turned her gently, his hands again on her shoulders, and as she turned she lowered her head so he could not see her face. But he crooked a finger beneath her chin and raised it slowly to his. His hand moved from her slender chin to gently touch the bruised cheekbone.

"Why don't you leave him?" He half whispered the words.

For a moment she remained silent and lowered her eyes from his face. Finally she said, "I would have no place to go." Her voice bore the hint of an accent.

"What's worse than living with him and getting beat like an animal?"

"He is good to me—most of the time. He is tired and nervous and doesn't know what he is doing. I remember him when he was younger and would visit my father. He smiled often and was good to us." Her words flowed faster now, as if she was anxious to speak, voluntarily lifting her face to look into his with a pleading in her dark eyes that seemed to say, "Please believe what I say and tell me that I am right."

"My father," she went on, "worked a small farm near Nogales which I remember as far back as I am able. He worked hard but he was not a very good farmer, and I always had the feeling that papa was sorry he had married and settled there. You see, my mother was Mexican," and she lowered her eyes as if in apology.

"One day this man rode up and asked if he may buy coffee. We had none, but he stayed and talked long with papa and they seemed to get along very well. After that he came often, maybe two, three times a month, and always he brought us presents and sometimes even money, which my papa took and I thought was very bad of him, even though I was only a little girl. Soon after that my mother died of sickness, and my papa took me to Tucson to live. And from that time he began going away for weeks at a time with this man and when he returned he would have money and he would be very drunk. When he would go, I prayed to the Mother of God at night because I knew what he was doing.

"Finally, he went away and did not return." Her voice carried a note of despair. "And my prayers changed to ones for the repose of his soul."

Fallis said, "I'm sorry," awkwardly, but the girl went on as if he had not spoken.

"A few months later the man returned and treated me differently." Her face colored slightly. "He treated me older. He was kind and told me he would come back soon and take me away from Tucson to a beautiful place I would love . . . But it was almost two years after this that the man called Rondo came to me at night and took me to the man. I had almost forgotten him. He was waiting outside of town with horses and made me go with them. I did not know him he had changed so—his face, and even his voice. We have been here for almost two weeks, and only a few days ago I learned where he had been for the two years."

Suddenly, she pressed her face into his chest and began to cry silently, convulsively.

Fallis's arms circled the thinness of her shoulders to press her hard against his chest. He mumbled, "Don't cry," into her hair and closed his eyes hard to think of something he could say. Feeling her body shaking against his own, he could see only a smiling, dark-haired little girl looking with awe at the carefree, generous American riding into the yard with a warbag full of presents. And then the little girl standing there was no longer smiling, her cheekbone was black and blue and she carried a half-gallon coffeepot in her hands. And the carefree American became a sallow death's-head that she called only "the man."

With her face buried against his chest, she was speaking. At first he could not make out her words, incoherent with the crying, then he realized that she was repeating, "I do not like him," over and over, "I do not like him." He thought, how can she use such simple words? He lifted her head, her eyes closed, and pressed his mouth against the lips that finally stopped saying, "I do not like him."

She pushed away from him lingeringly, her face flushed, and surprised the grin from his face when she said, "Now I must get wood for in the morning."

The grin returned as he looked down at her childlike face, now so serious. He lifted the hand-ax from the wood box, and they walked across the clearing very close together.

Virgil Patman stood in the doorway and watched them dissolve into the darkness of the pines.

Well, what are you going to do? Maybe a man's not better off minding his own business. The boy looks like he's doing pretty well not minding his. But damn, he thought, he's sure making it tough! He stared out at the cold, still light of early evening and heard the voice in his mind again. You've given him a lot of advice, but you've never really done anything for him. He's a good boy. Deserves a break. It's his own damn business how quick he falls for a girl. Why don't you try and give him a hand?

Patman exhaled wearily and turned back into the hut. He lifted De Sana's handgun from the holster on the wall and pushed it into the waist of his pants. From the cupboard he took the boxes of cartridges, loading one arm, and then picked up a Winchester leaning in the front corner that he had not noticed there before. He passed around the cooking lean-to to the back of the hut and entered the pines that pushed in close there. In a few minutes he was back inside the cabin, brushing sand from his hands. Not much, he thought, but maybe it'll help some. Before he sat down and poured himself a drink, he drew his pistol and placed it on the table near his hand.

Two Cents knew patience. It was as natural to him as breathing. He could not help smiling as he watched the white man, not a hundred feet away and just above him on the opposite slope, pull his head up high over the rim of the rocks in front of him, concentrating his attention off below where the trail broke into the pass. Rondo watched the pass, like De Sana had told him, and if his eyes wandered over the opposite canyon wall, it was only when he dragged them back to his own niche, and then it was only a fleeting glance at almost vertical smooth rock and brush.

Two Cents waited and watched, studying this white man who exposed himself so in hiding. Perhaps the man is a lure, he thought, to take us off guard. His lips straightened into a tight line, erasing the smile. He watched the man's head turn to the trees above him. Then the head turned back and he lifted the big canteen to his mouth. Two Cents had counted, and it was the sixth time the man had done so in less than a half hour. His thirst must be that of fire.

He felt a hand on his ankle and began to ease his body away from the rim that was here thick with tangled brush. He backed away cautiously so that the loose gravel would not even know he was there, and nodded his head once to Vea Oiga who crept past him to where he had lain.

A dozen or so yards back, where the ground sloped from the rim, he stood erect and looked back at Vea Oiga. Even at this short distance he could barely make out the crouched figure.

He lifted the shell belt over his head and then removed the faded blue jacket carefully, smoothing the bare sleeves before folding it next to Vea Oiga's on the ground. If he performed bravely, he thought, perhaps Cima Quaine will put a gold mark on the sleeves. He noticed Vea Oiga had folded his jacket so the three gold stripes were on top. Perhaps not three all at once, for it had taken Vea Oiga years to acquire them, but just one. How fine that would look! Surely Cima Quaine must recognize their ability in discovering this man in the pass.

Less than an hour before, they had followed the trail up to the point where it twisted into the pass, but there they stopped and back-trailed to a gradual rockfall that led up to the top of the canyon. They had tied up there and climbed on foot to the canyon rim that looked across to the other slope. They had done this naturally, without a second thought, because it was their business, and because if they were laying an ambush they would have picked this place where the pass narrowed and it was a hundred feet back to shelter. A few minutes after creeping to the rim, Rondo had appeared with a clatter of gravel, standing, exposing himself fully.

Vea Oiga had whispered to him what they would do after studying the white man for some time. Then he had dropped back to prepare himself. With Cima Quaine and the rest of the Coyotero Apache scouts less than an hour behind, they would just have time to get ready and go about the ticklish job of disposing of the lookout. Two Cents hoped that the chief scout would hurry up and be there to see him climb up to take the guard. He glanced at his cast-off cavalry jacket again and pictured the gold chevron on the sleeve; it was as bright and impressive as Vea Oiga's sergeant stripes.

Now he looked at the curled toes of his moccasins as he unfastened the ties below his knees and rolled the legging part of his pants high above his knees and secured them again. He tightened the string of his breechclout, then spit on his hands a half dozen times, rubbing the saliva over his arms and the upper part of his body until his dull brown coloring glistened with the wetness. When he had moistened every part of skin showing, he sank to the ground and rolled in the dust, rubbing his arms and face with the sand that clung to the wet skin.

He raised himself to his knees and knelt motionless like a rock or a stump, his body the color of everything around him, and now, just as still and unreal in his concentration.

Slowly his arms lifted to the dulling sky and his thoughts went to U-sen. He petitioned the god that he might perform bravely in what was to come, and if it were the will of U-sen that he was to die this day, would the god mind if it came about before the sun set? To be killed at night was to wander in eternal darkness, and nothing that he imagined could be worse, especially coming at the hands of a white man whom even the other white men despised.

When Two Cents had disappeared down through the rocks, Vea Oiga moved back from the rim until he was sure he could not be seen. Then he ran in a crouch, weaving through the mesquite and boulders, until he found another place along the rim that was dense with brush clumps. From here, Rondo's head and rifle barrel were still visible, but now he could also see, down to the right, the opening where the trail cut into the pass. He lay motionless, watching the white man until finally the low, wailing call lifted from down canyon. At that moment he watched Rondo more intently and saw the man's head lift suddenly to look in the direction from which the sound had come; but after only a few seconds the head dropped again, relaxed. Vea Oiga smiled. Now it was his turn.

The figure across the canyon was still for a longer time than usual, but finally the scout saw the head move slowly, looking behind and above to the pines. Vea Oiga rolled to his side and cupped his hands over his mouth. When he saw the canteen come up even with the man's face, he whistled into his cupped hands, the sound coming out in a moan and floating in the air as if coming from nowhere. He rolled again in time to see Two Cents dart from the trail opening across the pass to the opposite slope. He lay motionless at the base for a few minutes. Then, as he watched, the figure slowly began to inch his way up-canyon.

By the time the sergeant of scouts had made his way around to where trail met pass, Two Cents was far up the canyon. Vea Oiga clung tight to the rock wall and inched his face past the angle that would show him the pass. He saw the movement. A hump that was part of the ground seemed to edge along a few feet and then stop. And soon he watched this moving piece of earth glide directly under the white man's position and dissolve into the hollow that ran up the slanting wall just past the yellowness of the patch of prickly pear. And above the yellow bloom the rifle could no longer be seen. A splash of crimson spreading in the sky behind the pines was all that was left of the sun.

Vea Oiga turned quickly and ran back up-trail. He stopped on a rise and looked out over the open country, patched and cut with hills in the distance. His gaze crawled out slowly, sweeping on a small arc, and then stopped. There! Yes, he was sure. Maybe they were three miles away, but no more, which meant Cima Quaine would be there in fifteen to twenty minutes. Vea Oiga did not have time to wait for the scouting party. He ran back to the mouth of the pass and there, at the side of the trail, piled three stones one on the other. With his knife he scratched marks on the top stone and at the base of the bottom one, then hurried to the outcropping of rock from which he had watched the progress of his companion. And just as his gaze inched past the rock, he saw the movement behind and above the white man's position, as if part of the ground was sliding down on him.

Vea Oiga moved like a shadow at that moment across the openness of the pass. The shadow moved quickly up the face of the slope and soon was lost among rock and the darkness of the pines that straggled down the slope.

Crossing the clear patch of sand, Lew De Sana didn't like the feeling that had come over him. Not something new, just an intensifying of the nervousness that had spread through his body since the arrival of the two men. As if every part of his body was aware of something imminent, but would not tell his mind about it. As he thought about it, he realized that, no, it was not something that had been born with the arrival of the two men. It had been inside of him every day of the two years at Yuma, gaining strength the night Rondo aided him in his escape. And it had been a clawing part of his stomach the night north of Tucson when they had picked up the girl.

He didn't understand the feeling. That's what worried him. The nervousness would come and then go away, but when it returned, he would find that it had grown, and when it went away there was always a part of him that had vanished with it. A part of him that he used to rely on.

One thing, he was honest with himself in his introspection. And undoubtedly it was this honesty that made him see himself clearly enough to be frightened, but still with a certain haze that would not allow him to understand. He remembered his reputation. Cold nerve and a swivel-type gun holster that he knew how to use. In the days before Yuma, sometimes reputation had been enough. And, more often, he had hoped that it would be enough, for he wasn't fool enough to believe completely in his own reputation. But every once in a while he was called on to back up his reputation, and sometimes this had been hard.

Now he wasn't sure. Men can forget in two years. They can forget a great deal, and De Sana worried if he would have to prove himself all over again. It had come to him lately that if this were true, he would never survive, even though he knew he was still good with a gun and could face any situation if he had to. There was this tiredness inside of him now. It clashed with the nervous tension of a hunted man and left him confused and in a desperate sort of helplessness.

Moving through the pines, thoughts ran through his mind, one on top of the other so that none of them made sense. He closed his eyes tightly for a moment, passing his hand over his face and rubbing his forehead as if the gesture would make the racing in his mind stop. He felt the short hair hanging on his forehead, and as his hand lowered, the gauntness of his cheeks and the stubble of his new mustache. He saw the cell block at Yuma and swore in his breath.

His boots made a muffled, scraping sound moving over the sand and pine needles, and, as if becoming aware of the sound for the first time, he slowed his steps and picked his way more carefully through the trees.

The muscles in his legs tightened as he eased his steps on the loose ground. And then he stopped. He stopped dead and the pistol was out in front of him before he realized he had even pulled it. Instinctively his knees bent slightly as he crouched, straining his neck forward as he looked through the dimness of the pines, but if there was movement before, it was not there now.

Still, he waited a few minutes to make sure. He let the breath move through his lips in a long sigh and lowered the pistol to his side. He hated himself for his jumpiness. It was the strange tiredness again. He was tired of hiding and drawing when the wind moved the branches of trees. How much can a man take, he wondered. Maybe staying alive wasn't worth it when you had to live this way.

He was about to go ahead when he saw it again. The pistol came up and this time he was sure. Through the branches of the tree in front of him, he saw the movement, a shadow gliding from one clump to the next, perhaps fifty paces up ahead. Now, as he crouched low to the bole of the pine that shielded him, the lines in his face eased. At that moment he felt good because it wasn't jumpiness anymore, and there was another feeling within him that hadn't been there for a long time. He peered through the thick lower branches of the pine and saw the dim shape on the path now moving directly toward him.

He watched the figure stop every few feet, still shadowy in the gloom, then move ahead a little more before stopping to look right and left and even behind. De Sana felt the tightness again in his stomach, not being able to make out what the man was, and suddenly the panic was back. For a split second he imagined one of the shadows that had been haunting him had suddenly become a living thing; and then he made out the half-naked Apache and it was too late to imagine anymore.

He knew there would be a noise when he made his move, but that couldn't be helped. He waited until the Indian was a step past the tree, then he raised up. Coal-black hair flared suddenly from a shoulder, then a wide-eyed face even with his own and an open mouth that almost cried out before the pistol barrel smashed against the bridge of his nose and forehead.

De Sana cocked his head, straining against the silence, then slowly eased down next to the body of the Indian when no sound reached him. He thought: a body lying motionless always seemed to make it more quiet. Like the deeper silence that seemed to follow gunfire. Probably the silence was just in your head.

He laid his hand on the thin, grimy chest and jerked it back quickly when he felt no movement. Death wasn't something the outlaw was squeamish about, but it surprised him that the blow to the head had killed the Indian. He looked over the half-naked figure calmly and decided there was something there that bothered him. He bent closer in the gloom. No war paint. Not a line. He fumbled at the Indian's holster hurriedly and pulled out the well-kept Colt .44. No reservation-jumping buck owned a gun like that; and even less likely, a Sierra Madre broncho who'd more probably carry a rusted cap and ball at best. He wondered why it hadn't occurred to him right away. Apache police! And that meant Cima Quaine . . .

He stood up and listened again momentarily before moving ahead quickly through the pines.

He came to the canyon rim and edged along it cautiously, pressing close to the flinty rock, keeping to the deep shadows as much as he could, until he reached the hollow that sloped to the niche that Rondo had dug for himself.

He jumped quickly into the depression that fell away below him and held himself motionless in the darkness of the hollow for almost a minute before edging his gaze over the side and down to the niche a dozen yards below. He saw Rondo sprawled on his back with one booted leg propped on the rock parapet next to the rifle that pointed out over the pass.

There was no hesitating now. He climbed hurriedly, almost frantically, back to the pine grove and ran against the branches that stung his face and made him stumble in his haste. The silence was still there, but now it was heavier, pushing against him to make him run faster and stumble more often in the loose footing of the sand. He didn't care if he made noise. He heard his own forced breathing close and loud and imagined it echoing over the hillside, but now he didn't care because they knew he was here. He knew he was afraid. Things he couldn't see did that to him. He reached the clearing, finally, and darted across the clearing toward the hut.

Virgil Patman pushed the glass away from his hand when he heard the noise outside and wrapped his fingers around the bone handle of the pistol. The light slanting through the open doorway was weak, almost the last of the sun. He waited for the squat figure of Rondo to appear in this dim square of light, and started slightly when suddenly a thin shape appeared. And he sat bolt upright when next De Sana was in the room, clutching the door frame and breathing hard.

Patman watched him curiously and managed to keep the surprise out of his voice when he asked, "Where's Rondo? Thought you relieved him."

De Sana gasped out the word. "Quaine!" and wheeled to the front corner where the rifle had been. He took two steps and stopped dead. Patman watched the thin shoulders stiffen and raised the pistol with his hand still on the table until the barrel was leveled at the outlaw.

"So you led them here after all." His voice was low, almost a mumble, but the hate in the words cut against the stillness of the small room. He looked directly into Patman's face, as if not noticing the pistol leveled at him. "I must be getting old," he said in the same quiet tone.

"You're not going to get a hell of a lot older," Patman answered. "But I'll tell you this. We didn't bring Quaine and his Apaches here. You can believe that or not. I don't much care. Just all of a sudden I don't think you're doing anybody much good by being alive."

De Sana's mouth eased slightly as he smiled. "Why don't you let your boy do his own fighting?" And with the words he looked calmed again, as if he didn't care that a trap was tightening about him. Patman noticed it, because he had seen the panic on his face when he entered. Now he saw this calm returning and wondered if it was just a last-act bravado. It unnerved him a little to see a man so at ease with a gun turned on him and he lifted the pistol a foot off the table to make sure the outlaw had seen it.

"I'm not blind."

"Just making sure, Lew," Patman drawled.

De Sana seemed to relax even more now, and moved his hand to his back pocket, slowly, so the other man wouldn't get the wrong idea. He said, "Mind if I have a smoke?" while he dug the tobacco and paper from his pocket.

Patman shook his head once from side to side, and his eyes squinted at the outlaw, wondering what the hell he was playing for. He looked closely as the man poured tobacco into the creased paper and didn't see any of it shake loose to the floor. The fool's got iron running through him, he thought.

De Sana looked up as he shaped the cigarette. "You didn't answer my question," he said.

"About the boy? He can take care of himself," Patman answered.

"Why isn't he here, then?" De Sana said it in a low voice, but there was a sting to the words.

Patman said, "He's out courting your girlfriend," and smiled, watching the dumbfounded expression freeze on the gunman's face. "You might say I'm giving him a little fatherly hand here," and the smile broadened.

De Sana's thin body had stiffened. Now he breathed long and shrugged his shoulders. "So you're playing the father," he said. Standing half-sideways toward Patman, he pulled the unlit cigarette from his mouth and waved it at the man seated behind the table, "I got to reach for a match, Dad."

"Long as you can do it with your left hand," Patman said. Then added, "Son."

De Sana smiled thinly and drew a match from his side pocket.

Patman watched the arm swing down against the thigh and saw the sudden flame in the dimness as it came back up. And at that split second he knew he had made his mistake.

He saw the other movement, another something swinging up, but it was off away from the sudden flare of the match and in the fraction of the moment it took him to realize what it was, it was too late. There was the explosion, the stab of flame, and the shock against his arm. At the same time he went up from the table and felt the weight of the handgun slipping from his fingers, as another explosion mixed with the smoke of the first and he felt the sledgehammer blow against his side. He went over with the chair and felt the packed-dirt floor slam against his back.

His hands clutched at his side instinctively, feeling the wetness that was there already, then he winced in pain and dropped his right arm next to him on the floor. He closed his eyes hard, and when he opened them again he was looking at a pistol barrel, and above it De Sana's drawn face.

Unsmiling, the outlaw said, "I don't think you'da made a very good father." He turned quickly and sprinted out of the hut.

Patman closed his eyes again to see the swirling black that sucked at his brain. For a moment he felt a nausea in his stomach, then numbness seemed to creep over his body. A prickling numbness that was as soothing as the dark void that was spinning inside his head. I'm going to sleep, he thought. But before he did, he remembered hearing a shot come from outside, then another.

Cima Quaine walked over to him when he saw the boy look up quickly. Dave Fallis looked anxiously from Patman's motionless form up to the chief scout who now stood next to him where he knelt.

"I saw his eyes open and close twice!" he whispered excitedly.

The scout hunkered down beside him and wrinkled his buckskin face into a smile. It was an ageless face, cold in its dark, crooked lines and almost cruel, but the smile was plain in the eyes. He was bareheaded, and his dark hair glistened flat on his skull in the lantern light that flickered close behind him on the table.

"You'd have to tie rocks to him and drop him in a well to kill Virgil," he said. "And then you'd never be sure." He glanced at the boy to see the effect of his words and then back to Patman. The eyes were open now, and Patman was grinning at him.

"Don't be too sure," he said weakly. His eyes went to Fallis, who looked as if he wanted to say something, but was afraid to let it come out. He smiled back at the boy, watching the relief spread over his face, and saw him bite at his lower lip. "Did you get him?"

Fallis shook his head, but Quaine said, "Vea Oiga was crawling up to take the horses when De Sana ran into the corral and took one without even waiting to saddle. He shot at him, but didn't get him." He twisted his head and looked up at one of the Apaches standing behind him. "When we get home, you're going to spend your next two months' pay on practice shells."

Vea Oiga dropped his head and looked suddenly ashamed and ridiculous with the vermilion sergeant stripes painted on his naked arms. He shuffled through the doorway without looking up at the girl who stepped inside quickly to let him pass.

She stood near the cupboard, not knowing what to do with her hands, watching Dave Fallis. One of the half dozen Coyotero scouts in the room moved near her idly and she shrank closer to the wall, nervously picking at the frayed collar of her dress. She looked about the room wide-eyed for a moment, then stepped around the Apache hurriedly and out through the doorway. She moved toward the lean-to, but held up when she saw the three Apaches inside laughing and picking at the strips of venison that were hanging from the roof to dry.

After a while, Fallis got up, stretching the stiffness from his legs, and walked to the door. He stood there looking out, but seeing just the darkness.

Cima Quaine bent closer to Patman's drawn face. The ex-trooper's eyes were open, but his face was tight with pain. The hole in his side had started to bleed again. Patman knew it was only a matter of time, but he tried not to show the pain when the contract scout lowered close to him. He heard the scout say, "Your partner's kind of nervous," and for a moment it sounded far away.

Patman answered, "He's young," but knew that didn't explain anything to the other man.

"He's anxious to get on after the man," Quaine went on. "How you feel having an avenging angel?" Then added quickly, "Hell, in another day or two you'll be avenging yourself."

"It's not for me," Patman whispered, and hesitated. "It's for himself, and the girl."

Quaine was surprised, but kept his voice down. "The girl? He hasn't even looked at her since we got here."

"And he won't," Patman said. "Until he gets him." He saw the other man's frown and added, "It's a long story, all about pride and getting your toes stepped on." He grinned to himself at the faint sign of bewilderment on the scout's face. Nobody's going to ask a dying man to talk sense. Besides, it would take too long.

After a silence, Patman whispered, "Let him go, Cima."

"His yen to make war might be good as gold, but my boys ain't worth a damn after dark. We can pick up the man's sign in the morning and have him before sundown."

"You do what you want tomorrow. Just let him go tonight."

"He wouldn't gain anything," the scout whispered impatiently. "He's got the girl here now to live with long as he wants."

"He's got to live with himself, too." Patman's voice sounded weaker. "And he doesn't take free gifts. He's got a funny kind of pride. If he doesn't go after that man, he'll never look at that girl again."

Cima Quaine finished, "And if he does go after him, he may not get the chance. No, Virg. I better keep him here. He can come along tomorrow if he wants." He turned his head as if that was the end of the argument and looked past the Coyoteros to see the girl standing in the doorway.

She came in hesitantly, dazed about the eyes, as if a strain was sapping at her vitality to make her appear utterly spent. She said, "He's gone," in a voice that was not her own.

Cima Quaine's head swung back to Patman when he heard him say, "Looks like you don't have anything to say about it."

At the first light of dawn, Dave Fallis looked out over the meadow from the edge of timber and was unsure. There was moisture in the air lending a thickness to the gray dawn, but making the boundless stillness seem more empty. Mist will do that, for it isn't something in itself. It goes with lonesomeness and sometimes has a feeling of death. He reined his horse down the slight grade and crossed the gray wave of meadow, angling toward the dim outline of a draw that trailed up the ridge there. It cut deep into the tumbled rock, climbing slowly. After a while he found himself on a bench and stopped briefly to let his horse rest for a moment. The mist was below him now, clinging thickly to the meadow and following it as it narrowed through the valley ahead. He continued on along the bench that finally ended, forcing him to climb on into switchbacks that shelved the steepness of the ridge. And after two hours of following the ridge crown, he looked down to estimate himself a good eight miles ahead of the main trail that stayed with the meadow. He went down the opposite slope, not so steep here, but still following switchbacks, until he was in level country again and heading for the Escudillas in the distance.

The sun made him hurry. For every hour it climbed in the sky lessened his chances of catching the man before the Coyoteros did. He was going on luck. The Coyoteros would use method. But now he wondered if it was so much luck. Vea Oiga had told him what to do.

He had been leading the horse out of the corral and down through the timber when Vea Oiga grew out of the shadows next to him, also leading a horse. The Indian handed the reins to the boy and held back the mare he had been leading. "It is best you take gelding," he whispered. "The man took stallion. Leave the mare here so there is no chance she will call to her lover."

The Apache stood close to him confidently. "You have one chance, man," he said. "Go to Bebida Wells, straight, without following the trail. The man will go fast for a time, until he learns he is not being followed. But at dawn he will go quick again on the main trail for that way he thinks he will save time. But soon he will tire and will need water. Then he will go to Bebida Wells, for that is the only water within one day of here. When he reaches the well, he will find his horse spent and his legs weary from hanging without stirrups. And there he will rest until he can go on."

He had listened, fascinated, while the Indian read into the future and then heard how he should angle, following the draws and washes to save miles. For a moment he wondered about this Indian who knew him so well in barely more than an hour, how he had anticipated his intent, why he was helping. It had made no sense, but it was a course to follow, something he had not had before. The Apache had told him, "Shoot straight, man. Shoot before he sees you."

And with the boy passing from view into the darkness, Vea Oiga led the mare back to the corral, thinking of the boy and the dying man in the hut. Revenge was something he knew, but it never occurred to him that a woman could be involved. And if the boy failed, then he would get another chance to shoot straight. There was always plenty of time.

The sun was almost straight up, crowding the whole sky with its brassy white light, when he began climbing again. The Escudillas seemed no closer, but now the country had turned wild, and from a rise he could see the wildness tangling and growing in gigantic rock formations as it reached and climbed toward the sawtooth heights of the Escudillas.

He had been angling to come around above the wells, and now, in the heights again, he studied the ravines and draws below him and judged he had overshot by only a mile. On extended patrols out of Thomas they had often hit for Bebida before making the swing-back to the south. It was open country approaching the wells, so he had skirted wide to come in under cover of the wildness and slightly from behind.

A quarter of a mile on he found a narrow draw dense with pines strung out along the walls, the pines growing into each other and bending across to form a tangled arch over the draw. He angled down into its shade and picketed the gelding about halfway in. Then, lifting the Winchester, he passed out of the other end and began threading his way across the rocks.

A yard-wide defile opened up on a ledge that skirted close to the smoothness of boulders, making him edge sideways along the shadows of the towering rocks, until finally the ledge broadened and fell into a ravine that was dense with growth, dotted with pale yucca stalks against the dark green. He ran through the low vegetation in a crouch and stopped to rest at the end of the ravine where once more the ground turned to grotesque rock formations. Not a hundred yards off to the left, down through an opening in the rocks, he made out the still, sand-colored water of a well.

More cautiously now, he edged through the rocks, moving his boots carefully on the flinty ground. And after a dozen yards of this he crept into the narrowness of two boulders that hung close together, pointing the barrel of the Winchester through the aperture toward the pool of muddy water below.

He watched the vicinity of the pool with a grimness now added to his determination; he watched without reflecting on why he was there. He had thought of that all morning: seeing Virg die on the dirt floor . . . But the outlaw's words had always come up to blot that scene. "I think you better teach him the facts of life." Stepping on his toes while he was supposed to smile back. It embarrassed him because he wanted to be here because of Virg. First Virg and then the girl. He told himself he was doing this because Virg was his friend, and because the girl was helpless and couldn't defend herself and deserved a chance. That's what he told himself.

But that was all in the past, hazy pictures in his mind overshadowed by the business at hand. He knew what he was doing there, if he wasn't sure why. So that when the outlaw's thin shape came into view below him, he was not excited.

He did not see where De Sana had come from, but realized now that he must have been hiding somewhere off to the left. De Sana crouched low behind a scramble of rock and poked his carbine below toward the pool, looking around as if trying to determine if this was the best position overlooking the well. His head turned, and he looked directly at the aperture behind him, where the two boulders met, studying it for a long moment before turning back to look down his carbine barrel at the pool. Dave Fallis levered the barrel of the Winchester down a fraction and the front sight was dead center on De Sana's back.

He wondered why De Sana had taken a carbine from the corral lean-to and not a saddle. Then he thought of Vea Oiga who had fired at him as he fled. And this brought Vea Oiga's words to memory. "Shoot before he sees you."

Past the length of the oiled gun barrel, he saw the Y formed by the suspenders and the faded underwear top, darkened with perspiration. The short-haired skull, thin and hatless. And at the other end, booted long legs, and toes that kicked idly at the gravel.

For a moment he felt sorry for De Sana. Not because the barrel in front of him was trained on his back. He watched the man gaze out over a vastness that would never grow smaller. Straining his eyes for a relentless something that would sooner or later hound him to the ground. And he was all alone. He watched him kick his toes for something to do and wipe the sweat from his forehead with the back of his hand. De Sana perspired like everyone else. That's why he felt sorry for him. He saw a man, like a thousand others he had seen, and he wondered how you killed a man.

The Indian had told him, "Shoot before he sees you." Well, that was just like an Indian.

He moved around from behind the rocks and stood there in plain view with the rifle still pointed below. He felt naked all of a sudden, but brought the rifle up a little and called, "Throw your gun down and turn around!"

And the next second he was firing. He threw the lever and fired again— then a third time. He sat down and ran his hand over the wetness on his forehead, looking at the man who was now sprawled on his back with the carbine across his chest.

He buried the gunman well away from the pool and scattered rocks around so that when he was finished you wouldn't know that a grave was there. He took the outlaw's horse and his guns. That would be enough proof. On the way back he kept thinking of Virg and the girl. He hoped that Virg would still be alive, but knew that was too much to ask. Virg and he had had their good times and that was that. That's how you had to look at things.

He thought of the girl and wondered if she'd think he was rushing things if he asked her to go with him to the Panhandle, after a legal ceremony . . .

And all the way back, not once did he think of Lew De Sana.

Snowblind

EVAN HUNTER

HE RODE THE big roan stiffly, the collar of his heavy mackinaw pulled high on his neck. His battered Stetson was tilted over his forehead, crammed down against his ears. Still, the snow seeped in, trailing icy fingers across the back of his neck.

His fingers inside the right-hand mitten were stiff and cold, and he held the reins lightly, his left hand jammed into his pocket. Carefully, he guided the horse over the snow-covered trail, talking gently to him. He held a hand up in front of his eyes, palm outward to ward off the stinging snow, peered into the whirling whiteness ahead of him.

The roan lifted its head, ears back. Quickly, he dropped his hand to the horse's neck, patted him soothingly.

He felt the penetrating cold attacking his naked hand, withdrew it quickly and stuffed it into the pocket again, clenching it into a tight fist, trying to wrench whatever warmth he could from the inside of the pocket.

"Damnfool kid," he mumbled. "Picks a night like this."

The roan plodded on over the slippery, graded surface, unsure of its footing. Gary kept staring ahead into the whiteness, looking for the cabin, waiting for it to appear big and brown against the smoke gray sky.

His brows and lashes were interlaced with white now, and a fine sifting of snow caked in the ridges alongside his eyes, lodged in the seams swinging down from his nose flaps. His mouth was pressed into a tight, weary line. He kept thinking of the cabin, and a fire. And a cup of coffee, and a smoke.

It was the smoke that had started it all, he supposed. He shook his head sadly, bewildered by the thought that a simple thing like a cigarette could send a kid kiting away from home. Hell, Bobby was too young to be smoking, and he'd deserved the wallop he'd gotten.

He thought about it again now, his head pressed against the sharp

102

wind. He'd been unsaddling Spark, a frisky sorrel if ever there was one, when he saw the wisp of smoke curling up from behind the barn. At first, he thought it was a fire. He swung the saddle up over the rail and took off at a trot, out of breath when he rounded the barn's corner.

Bobby had been sitting there, his legs crossed, gun belt slung low on his faded jeans, calm as could be. And puffing on a cigarette.

"Well, hello," Gary'd said in surprise.

Bobby jumped to his feet and ground the cigarette out under his heel. "Hello, Dad," he said soberly. Gary remembered wondering why the boy's face had expressed no guilt, no remorse.

His eyes stared down at the shredded tobacco near the boy's boot. "Having a party?" he asked.

"Why, no."

"Figured you might be. See you're wearing your guns, and smoking and all. Figured you as having a little party for yourself."

"I was headin' into town, Dad. Feller has to wear guns in town, you know that."

Gary stroked his jaw. "That right?"

"Ain't safe otherwise."

Gary's mouth tightened then, and his eyes grew hard. "Feller has to smoke in town, too, I suppose."

"Well, Dad . . ."

"Take off them guns!"

Bobby's eyes widened, startling blue against his tanned features. He ran lean fingers through his sun-bleached hair and said, "But I'm goin' to town. I just told . . ."

"You ain't goin' nowheres. Take off them guns."

"Dad . . ."

"No damn kid of mine's goin' to tote guns before he's cut his eyeteeth! And smoking! Who in holy hell do you think you are? Behaving like a gun slick and smoking fit to . . ."

Bobby's voice was firm. "I'm seventeen. I don't have to take this kind of . . ."

Gary's hand lashed out suddenly, open, catching the boy on the side of his cheek. He pulled his hand back rapidly, sorry he'd struck his son, but unwilling to acknowledge his error. Bobby's own hand moved to his cheek, touched the bruise that was forming under the skin.

"Now get inside and take them guns off," Gary said.

Bobby didn't answer. He turned his back on his father and walked toward the house.

The snow started at about five, and when Gary called his son for supper at six, the boy's room was empty. The peg from which his guns usually hung, the guns Gary'd said he could wear when he was twenty-one, was bare. With a slight twinge of panic, Gary had run down to the barn to find the boy's brown mare gone.

Quickly, he'd saddled the roan and started tracking him. The tracks were fresh in the new snow, and before long Gary realized the boy was heading for the old cabin in the hills back of the spread.

He cursed now as the roan slipped again. Damned if he wasn't going to give that boy the beating of his life. Seventeen years old! Anxious to start smoking and frisking around, anxious to wrap his finger around a trigger. It would have been different if Meg . . .

He caught himself abruptly, the old pain stabbing deep inside him again, the pain that thoughts of her always brought. He bit his lip against the cold and against the memory, clamped his jaws tight as if capping the unwanted emotions that threatened to overflow his consciousness again.

This was a rough land, a land unfriendly to women. For the thousandth time he told himself he should never have brought her here. He'd made a big mistake with Meg, perhaps the biggest mistake of his life. He'd surrendered her to a wild, relentless land, and he was left now with nothing but a memory and a tombstone. And Bobby. He would not make the same mistake with Bobby.

How long ago had it been? he asked himself. *How long?*

Was Bobby really seventeen, had it really been that long?

"All right, mister," the voice said.

He lifted his hand, tried to shield his eyes. The snow whirled before them, danced crazily in the knifing wind. Through the snow, he made out the shadowy bulk of three men sitting their horses. His hand automatically dropped to the rifle hanging in the leather scabbard on his saddle.

"I wouldn't, mister," the same voice said.

He squinted into the snow, still unable to make out the faces of the three riders. "What's this all about, fellers?" he asked, trying to keep his voice calm. Through the snow, he could see that two of the riders were holding drawn guns.

"What's it all about, he wants to know," one of the men said.

There was a flurry of movement and the rider in the middle spurred his horse forward, reining in beside Gary's roan.

"Suppose you tell *us* what it's all about, mister."

Gary's eyes dropped inadvertently to the holster strapped outside his mackinaw, the gun butt pointing up toward his pocket.

"Don't know what you mean, fellers."

"He don't know what we mean, Sam."

The rider close to Gary snickered. "What you doin' on this trail?" His breath left white pockmarks on the air. Gary stared hard at his face, at the bristle covering his chin, at the shaggy black brows and hard eyes. He didn't recognize the man.

"I'm lookin' for a stray," Gary said, thinking again of Bobby somewhere on the trail ahead.

"In this weather?" Sam scoffed. "Who you kiddin', mister?"

Another of the riders pulled close to the pair, staring hard at Gary. "He's poster-happy, I think," he said.

"Shut up, Moss," Sam commanded.

The third rider sat his horse in the distance, his hands in his pockets, his head tucked low inside his upturned collar. "Moss is right, Sam. The old geezer's seen our pictures and . . ."

"I said shut up!" Sam repeated.

"Hell, ain't nobody chases strays in a storm," the third rider protested.

Sam lifted the rifle from Gary's scabbard, then took the .44 from the holster at his hip. Gary looked down at the empty holster, raised his eyes again.

"Ain't no need for this," he said. "I'm lookin' for a stray. Wandered off before the storm started, and I'm anxious to get him back 'fore he freezes board-stiff."

"Sure," Sam said, "you're lookin' for a stray. Maybe you're lookin' for *three* strays, huh?"

"I don't know what you're talking about," Gary said. "You feel like throwing your weight around, all right. You're three and I'm one, and I ain't goin' to argue. But I still don't know what you're talking about."

"We gonna freeze out here while this bird gives us lawyer talk?" Moss asked.

The third rider said, "You know of a cabin up here, mister?"

"What?" Gary asked.

"You deaf or some . . ."

"Rufe gets impatient," Sam interrupted. "Specially when he's cold. We heard there was a cabin up here somewheres. You know where?"

"No," Gary said quickly.

"He's poster-happy," Moss insisted. "What the hell're we wastin' time talking for?" He pulled back the hammer of his pistol, and the click sounded loud and deadly beneath the murmur of the wind.

Gary combed his memory, trying to visualize the "wanted" posters he'd seen. It wasn't often that he went to town, and he didn't pay much attention to such things when he did ride in. He silently cursed his memory, realizing at the same time that it didn't matter one way or the other. He didn't know why these men were wanted, or just what they were running from. But he sure as hell knew they *were* wanted. The important thing was to keep them away from Bobby, away from the cabin up ahead.

"Seems I do remember a cabin," he said.

"Yeah? Where is it?"

Gary pointed down the trail, away from the cabin. "That way, I think."

"We can't afford thinkin'," Rufe said. "And we can't afford headin' back toward town either, mister."

"That ain't the way to town," Gary said softly.

"We just come from there," Sam said. He yanked his reins, pulling his horse around. "I think we'll go up this way, mister. Stay behind him, Moss."

Rufe, up the trail a ways, turned his horse and started pushing against the snow, Sam close behind him. Gary kept the roan headed into the wind, and behind him he could hear the labored breathing of Moss's horse.

"We'll have to hole up for tonight," Rufe said over his shoulder.

"Yeah, if we can find that damn cabin," Sam agreed.

"We'll find it. The old geezer ain't a very good liar."

They rode into the wind, their heads bent low. Gary's eyes stayed on the trail, searching for signs beneath the tracks of the lead horse. Bobby had sure as hell been heading for the cabin. Suppose he was there already? The boy was wearing his guns, and would probably be fool enough to try shooting it out with these killers. Maybe they weren't killers, either. Maybe they were just three strangers who weren't taking any chances. Then why had the one called Moss kept harping on posters, and why had Rufe mentioned pictures of the trio? *Stop kidding yourself,* Gary thought. *They'd as soon shoot you as look at you.*

"Well, now ain't that funny!" Rufe shouted back. "Looks like the cabin was up this way after all, mister."

Gary raised his eyes, squinted at the squat log formation ahead on the trail. The ground levelled off a bit, and they walked the horses forward, pulling up just outside the front door. Sam dismounted and looped his reins over the rail outside. Gary felt the sharp thrust of a gun in his back.

"Come on," Moss said.

Gary swung off his saddle, patting the roan on its rump. "These animals will freeze out here," he said.

"You can bring out some blankets," Sam said. Together, he and Rufe kicked open the door of the cabin, their guns level. Gary's heart gave a lurch as he waited for sound from within.

" 'Pears to be empty," Rufe said.

"Ummm. Come on, Moss. Bring the old man in."

They stomped into the cabin, closing the door against the biting wind outside. Sam struck a match, fumbled around in the darkness for a lantern. There was the sound of a scraping chair, the sudden thud of bone against wood.

"Goddamnit!" Sam bellowed.

Gary waited in the darkness, the hard bore of Moss's pistol in his back. The wick of the lantern flared brightly, faded as Sam lowered it.

"Right nice," Rufe commented.

"Better get a fire going," Sam said.

Rufe crossed the room to the stone fireplace, heaped twigs and papers into the grate, methodically placed the heavier pieces of wood over these. He struck a match, held it to the paper, watched the flames curl upward as the twigs caught.

"There," he said. He shrugged out of his leather jacket. "This ought to be real comfy."

"There's some blankets on the bunk," Sam said. "Take 'em out and cover the horses, mister."

Gary walked to the bunk, filled his arms with the blankets, and started toward the door. Just inside the door, he stopped, waiting.

Moss shrugged out of his mackinaw. "Go on," he told Gary. "We'll watch you from here. Too damn cold out there."

Gary opened the door, ducked his head against the wind, and ran toward the horses. He dropped the blankets, gave one quick look at the door, and then swung up onto the roan's saddle.

"You want a hole in your back?" Sam's voice came from the window.

Gary didn't answer. He kept sitting the horse, staring down at the blankets he'd dropped in the snow.

"Now cover them horses and get back in here," Sam said. "And no more funny business."

Gary dropped from the saddle wearily. Gently, he covered all the horses, feeling the animals shiver against the slashing wind and snow. He was grateful that Bobby hadn't been in the cabin, but he was beginning to wonder now if the boy hadn't been lost in this storm. The thought was a disturbing one. He finished with the horses and headed back for the cabin. Moss pulled open the door for him, slamming it shut behind him as soon as he'd entered.

"Get out of those clothes," Sam said, "and sit over there by the table. One more fool stunt like that last one, and you're a dead man."

Gary walked over to the table, folding his mackinaw over the back of a chair. Rufe was sitting in a chair opposite him, his feet on the table, the chair thrust back at a wild angle.

Gary sat down, his eyes dropping to Rufe's hanging gun.

"Wonder how long this'll last," Sam said from the window.

"Who cares?" Moss said. He was poking around in the cupboard. " 'Nough food here to last a couple of weeks."

"Still, we should be moving on."

"You know," Rufe drawled, "maybe we shoulda split up."

"What the hell brought that on?" Sam asked impatiently.

"Just thinkin'. They'll be lookin' for three men. They won't be expectin' single riders."

"That's what the old man's for," Sam said, smiling.

"I don't follow."

"They won't be expectin' *four* riders, either. The old man's coming with us when we leave."

"The hell I am," Gary said loudly.

"The hell you *are,*" Sam repeated.

Gary looked at the gun in Sam's hand. He made a slight movement forward, as if he would rise from his chair, and then he slumped back again. They were treating him like a kid, like a simple, addlebrained . . . He caught his thoughts abruptly. He suddenly knew how Bobby must have felt when he'd slapped him this afternoon.

Sam walked away from the window, stood warming the seat of his pants at the fireplace.

"Four riders," he said. "A respectable old man and his three sons." He looked at Gary and chuckled noisily.

He was still chuckling when the front door was kicked open. Gary turned his head swiftly, his eyes widening at sight of the white-encrusted figure in the doorway. The figure held two guns, and they gleamed menacingly in the firelight.

Sam clawed at his pistol, and a shot erupted in the stillness of the cabin. The gun came free, and Sam brought it up as the second shot slammed into his chest. He clutched at the stone mantel, swung around, his legs suddenly swiveling from under him. He dropped down near the fire, his hand falling into it in a cascade of sparks.

The men in the room seemed to freeze. Moss with his back to the cupboard, Rufe with his feet propped up on the table, the figure standing in the doorframe with smoking guns.

Gary looked at the figure, trying to understand that this was Bobby, that this was his son standing there, his son who had just shot a man.

And suddenly, action returned to the men in the room. Moss pushed himself away from the cupboard in a double-handed draw. At the same instant, Rufe began to swing his legs off the table.

Gary kicked out, sending the chair flying out from under Rufe. From the doorway, Bobby's guns exploded again and Moss staggered back against the glass-paned cupboard, his shoulders shattering the doors. Bobby kept shooting, and Moss collapsed in a shower of glass shards. Rufe sprawled to the floor, tried to untangle himself from the chair as Gary reached down and yanked the gun from his holster, backing away from the table quickly. Rufe crouched on the floor for an instant, then viciously threw the chair aside and reached for his remaining gun. Gary blinked as he saw flame lance out from the gun in his fist. The bullet took

Rufe between the eyes, and he clung to life for an instant longer before he fell to the floor, his gun unfired.

Bobby came into the cabin, hatless, his hair a patchwork of snow.

"I figured you were trailin' me," he said. "I swung around the cabin, trying to lose you."

"Lucky you did," Gary said softly. He stood staring at his son. For a moment, their eyes met, and Bobby turned away.

"I ain't goin' back with you, Dad," he said. "A . . . a man's got to do things his own way. A man can't have . . ."

"Suppose we talk about it later, Bob," Gary said.

He saw his son's eyes widen. He'd never called him anything but Bobby until this moment.

Gary smiled. "Suppose we talk about it later," he repeated. "After we've had a cup of coffee." And then, though it was extremely difficult, he added, "And a smoke together."

The Corpse Rides at Dawn

JOHN D. MACDONALD

1

Vengeance Trail

DAVE AUSTIN RODE into the hot dusty little town of Oracle on the tall trail-weary black. He had hated the smallness and the sameness and the dullness of it when he had left four years before, his jaw sore and swollen from where his brother's fist had connected. He hated the town even more after the absence.

The hooves of the black kicked up little puffs of white dust as he rode by the store, the livery stable, Ike Andres's saddlery, the closed office of the deputy sheriff, the frame and adobe Oracle House, the Easy Do Saloon.

Two wagons were hitched in front of the Oracle House, and some hot saddle stock stood and fretted at the flies in front of the Easy Do and the Gay Gold farther down the street.

He pulled up the black, and the packhorse, stupefied by the heat, walked into the black and dodged stiffly as the black kicked at it. He pulled around and went to the stable, swinging down from the black and peering into the dark hay-smell of the place. An old man in broken boots slept on a pile of hay.

Dave unsaddled and slapped the black into a stall; he grunted as he slid the bedroll off the packhorse. It thudded onto the board floor. The old man woke up, blinked at him blearily and went back to sleep.

Dave walked over and kicked him lightly in the ribs. "Get up and take care of my stock."

The old man sat up. "I see you was doing everything yourself and—" The old man stopped abruptly. "Dave Austin, ain't you?"

"Yes."

The old man bounced up with surprising agility. "What you going to do about your brother Pete?" Dave looked at him steadily, didn't answer. "All right, forget I asked you. I know what I'd do."

"And what would you do?"

"I'd get to hell back on my horse and get out of here. Hawson'll send his boys onto you one by one until one of 'em guns you down."

"And what about Hawson?"

"He don't carry no gun no more. Best thing you can do is get on out of Oracle. Hawson has brought in maybe seven bad ones in the last two years. One of 'em got Pete. You haven't got a chance."

Dave Austin looked at the old man for a long moment, shouldered the heavy bedroll, yanked his carbine out from under the *rosadero,* and headed out into the sunlight. It was only a hundred feet to the wide porch of the Oracle House, but he was sweating heavily before he reached it.

An old man dozing on the wide porch took a long look at Dave, swallowed heavily, and the front legs of his chair thumped down onto the boards. As Dave walked in the door, the old man on the porch spat across the railing with great deliberation and little accuracy.

Martha Deen, the fat, pleasant, sloppy wife of Sid Deen who owned the Oracle House, came from the back of the place when Dave thumped on the desk.

She walked heavily to the desk, stopped suddenly and then walked toward him more slowly. "Hello, Dave."

"Hello, Martha."

"The town's been sort of waiting on you, Dave."

"I heard five days ago. I was about a hundred and forty mile down the line."

"You shouldn't have come back, Dave."

"I want a room, not advice, Martha. So far you're the second one I've talked to. And you both tell me to get out of town."

"You shouldn't be silly for Pete's sake, Dave. He was a mean, stubborn man, and forty people told him he shouldn't have set up his spread right in the way of Hawson."

"How about that room?"

She sighed. "Second floor. The one facing the stairs. Door's unlocked. Where do you want your stuff sent?"

"Sent?"

"After one of Hawson's boys kills you."

"You keep it, Martha. I was going to ride on through and stay out to Pete's place, but I figured this'd be handier."

She laughed. It was a flat, mirthless sound. "You wouldn't of liked it out there, Dave. Pete had lots of notes outstanding to Ryan over to the store. Maybe half again the value of the place after this hot spell. Stock

dying all over. Hawson just upped and bought up the notes and fore-
closed the place and sold it to himself. Using it as a line camp right now I
hear. Intends to, anyway."

Dave shouldered the bedroll, trudged up the stairs and pushed the
door to his room open. He dropped the bedroll on the floor, stripped,
poured water into the basin and sponged the trail dust off his body. He
squatted by the roll, opened it up and took out fresh clothes.

He was lean and hard and too thin for his height. A white puckered
scar cut across the ridges of muscle on his back. His features were so
regular as to have been characterless were it not for a deep hardness in
his eyes, a rigidity about the set of his mouth. He dressed, strapped the
gun belt around his thin waist, sat on the edge of the bed and wiped trail
dirt from the butt of his single-action peacemaker. The walnut grip fitted
comfortably into his palm.

He sat for a long time and pondered what the old man in the stable had
said. He thought of what Martha had said. Finally he unstrapped the gun
belt, tossed it into the open bedroll and threw a corner of the tarp over it.

Ike Andres came to the door of the saddlery, took Dave's right hand in
both of his and drew him inside. Ike, in spite of his smallness, had been a
foreman for Dave's father during the early days. A bronc he had been
breaking had crushed him against the snubbing post in the middle of the
round corral. He had mended, but he would never swing up onto a pony
again. He was a gray little man with wide soft eyes and a bitter, twisted
mouth.

"Dave, boy!" he said gently. "Dave!"

Dave permitted himself the first smile since entering Oracle. "Hello,
you old horse thief!"

They went into the back room where Ike slept. Ike sat on the bed and
Dave leaned against the wall and smiled down at him. They were both
uncomfortable.

"How did it happen, Ike?" Dave asked.

"The dryness, boy. Hawson's holes dried, and he moved in on Pete.
Pete and his two hands shot about thirty head, but Hawson's men pulled
down the fence Pete had put up around his best hole and the Hawson
beef trampled the hole to a mud wallow. The next day somebody found
Pete over near Spike Ridge. Shot in the back of the neck. The horse had
bucked him into the rocks. He wasn't pretty. I had him buried over on the
hill next to your folks."

"I owe you whatever it cost."

"You don't owe me a damn thing!" Ike said angrily. "Your old man set me up in this place when I couldn't ride no more. So don't you try to talk slop to me."

"Where's Pete's stuff?"

"Over there in the corner. Clothes. And that box there is full of things I took out of the house. Some silver that belonged to your ma. The old man's books. Family Bible. Pete's roan is over to Louis Besa's place. I had it took over there before Hawson could grab it along with the spread. The horse and stuff belong to you."

Dave looked at the rough wooden box that held his patrimony and his inheritance. He rolled a smoke and found that he was pinching it so tight between thumb and finger that it wouldn't draw. He dropped it to the floor.

He thought of the bitter, back-breaking labor that had been the lot of his father and mother until they had gotten far enough ahead to hire ranch hands. He remembered the day during the long drought when his father, bone weary from trying to save weak stock, had been caught in the dry wash by a ten-foot flood wall coming down from the mountains. His mother had died a month later.

The foreman who had replaced Ike had been no good. The ranch had been sold to pay the debts. He and Pete had been too young to work it. Hawson, his saddlebags heavy with gold from the Black Hills, had bought in. Pete and Dave had gone to stay with Ike, and one day Pete had hit the adobe wall with his hard young fist and said, "I'm going to get it all back. Every square foot of it. Every blade of grass!"

They had worked for day wages, and in the end Pete had insisted on claiming at the base of the hills just beyond the west boundary of Hawson's spread. They had argued about the location. At twenty, Dave had ridden out of Oracle, his jaw sore, his mind full of the harsh quarrel with Pete.

Dave looked at the box and said hoarsely, "That's about the same amount of stuff we had when the four of us first come out here. Haven't got far, have we?"

"What you been doing?" Ike asked quickly.

"Everything. Trapped and broke mustangs. Trail boss. Winter line camp. Deputy in a silver town."

"Can you shoot?"

"As well as most. Not as good as some that live off it."

"Hawson stayed right quiet until he started to make money. Then he began to elbow little spreads out of his way. Unexpected fires during the night. Brawls picked by his men. He's got maybe thirty regular cowhands now. He pays 'em good.

"But he's also got maybe seven men he's brought in. A rough string. He don't give those boys no cow work. Some of them ride with him wherever he goes. Hawson wants to be king of this country. Right now you might say he's crown prince. Where's your gun?"

"I hear Hawson don't carry one. I hear that if I carried one, his boys'd nudge me into a fight."

Ike looked thoughtful. "What are you fixing to do?"

"Damn if I know. Pete was shot in the back of the neck. I'd like to get Hawson the same way."

"You don't stand a chance, boy. Not a chance."

"Tell me more about Jud Hawson."

Ike scratched his lean jaw. His eyes were somber. "Not much to tell. His hair's gone white, and he's took to wearing it long. He's got kind of a wild look in his eye, and he talks to folks about seeing visions of people coming to him and telling him that he is the king wheel of this part of the country. Heard tell that out at his spread he makes the folks bow from the waist when they want to talk to him."

Dave was silent for long moments. He rolled another smoke, dragged deeply on it. His mouth was like a deep gash in saddle leather.

Ike said softly, "Going to miss Pete a lot, Dave. He was a stubborn fool, but he did what he thought right. Kind of vain about hisself, too. Wore that big old white-colored hat and had Ryan over to the store stock those yella shirts from Mexico.

"Maybe you better ride back out and forget this mess, Dave," Ike said. "In order to get to Hawson you'll have to gun your way through the seven rannies he's got, and by the time you've knocked off a couple he'd have more hired. Besides, it's a good bet that every damn one of them is faster than you."

Dave smiled tightly. "Look at this, Ike. See? Nothing in my hands." He yanked his right arm up, the elbow sharply bent so that his fist came close to his ear. The arm flashed down, and a lean knife with a slim blade and a rawhide handle buried itself in the doorframe with a chunking sound.

Ike said softly, "I'll be damned! How'd you do that?"

"Broke a leg in Mexico. While it was mending a *paisano* taught me. See how the right cuff on this shirt is loose? I got this piece of rubber around my arm. The knife goes under it with the hilt toward my wrist. It stays there until I snap my arm back. Then it slips out, and I grab the blade as it goes by.

"I've won over two hundred dollars with that little knife. Stand side by side with a gunfighter and somebody gives the word and I put the knife into a tree twelve feet away before he can get a slug into it."

Ike frowned. "Knife work is dirty."

"And shooting a man in the back of the neck is good clean fun!" Dave said hoarsely.

"I'm sorry, boy," Ike said. "I forget the kind of competition you got."

Dave walked across the room, kicked the wooden box gently, frowned down at it. "You say Hawson is maybe a little crazy?"

"He could be. Maybe is."

"You got Pete's clothes here?"

"That's right. Why?"

"Wait a minute. I'm doing some thinking." Dave frowned for a few minutes. "Is that roan fast?"

"One of the best."

Dave squatted on the floor close to Ike's bed and talked for ten minutes in a low tone. Ike looked at him incredulously for a long time, and then a slow grin crept across his face. "Dave boy, it just might. It just might. And there's not another damn thing you can do except wait with a rifle and try to bushwack him."

2

Buzzard Bait

DAVE AUSTIN SHOULDERED his way through the swinging doors into the Gay Gold, Saturday night. Two games of pócar robado were going on at the round tables in the rear of the place. Fat Wesser, huge and red-faced with eyes like chilled skim milk, stood behind the bar. Two men stood at the end of the bar, and Dave realized immediately that they matched Ike's description of Hawson's men.

One was a kid too young to shave, with thin pale hands and dark eyes that were luminous and beautiful. They had the look of candles around a bier, of sunlight on silver coffin handles, of the raw metal of a filed sear. He had a quiet confidence far beyond his years. He stood with his back to the bar, his elbows hooked over it. Thin white fingers dangled above the grip of the .44 in the shallow holster against his right thigh. His name, at the moment, was Randy Adams.

The second one was much older, a squat sandy man in his early forties with thick shoulders, no neck, freckled hands and small sleepy eyes. His underlip was severed by a vertical scar which bisected his square chin. Dave guessed that he would be Quinn. Dave glanced quickly around the saloon and decided that, of the seven Ike had carefully described, these were the only two in town. He had already stopped in at the Easy Do.

In a needlessly loud voice, Fat Wesser said, "Hello there, Dave Austin!"

Quinn lost his sleepy look, and the luminous eyes of Adams turned sharply toward Dave, flicked down to the empty holster and registered disappointment.

Before Dave had a chance to order a drink, Quinn hitched up his belt, swaggered over to him and said, "What's your business in town, Austin?"

Dave heard the silence that filled the saloon. There was no slap of cards, rattle of chips, from the tables in the rear.

"Who the hell is he?" Dave said to Wesser.

Quinn grabbed Dave's shoulder, yanked him around. "I'm talking to you, friend. Jud Hawson likes to know everybody's business. What's yours?"

Dave felt the quick red tide of anger and was glad he had left the Colt behind. He kept all expression off his face and said, "You look like the sort of scum that would work for Hawson."

Quinn went so pale that the freckles on his thick face stood out. He said over his shoulder, "Loan this punk your gun."

"I never use them, friend."

Quinn sneered at him. "What do you keep in that empty holster—knitting?"

"Suppose you haul that ugly nose of yours to your end of the bar and keep it out of my business."

Quinn was amazingly fast. Dave was braced for the punch and had hoped to duck it entirely. He slipped most of the blow, but enough of the force of it caught him high on the cheekbone to drive him back several steps. He shook his head clear as Quinn charged in.

Quinn's sledgehammer blow went around the back of Dave's neck. Dave pivoted and put all his lean strength into a short right hook into Quinn's middle. The diaphragm muscles that he hit were as hard as woven leather, but Quinn grunted and stepped back. Dave smashed Quinn's mouth with an overhand left and was in turn driven back, almost falling, by a thudding blow under the heart.

Blood ran down Quinn's chin. He shook his head and followed up his advantage. Dave was driven back by the grunting fury of Quinn's heavy blows. A hard fist caught Dave high on the temple, and, as he fell to one side, Quinn straightened him up with a blow to the jaw.

Dave was faced by two figures. Both of them were Quinn. They drifted apart and then together, refusing to merge into one opponent. Dave hit Quinn in the face with a feeble right and then went down as Quinn's fist hit him between the eyes.

He caught a flash of movement and turned his head sharply, putting his arm across his face. Quinn's heel dug deep into his arm with such force that he thought at first that the bone was shattered.

As the dimness faded away, Dave saw that Fat Wesser was holding a gun on Quinn, saying, "I won't have you killing him with your boots in here, Quinn."

"Get up, Austin!" Quinn roared.

Dave lifted his shoulders from the floor and gasped, "My legs! I can't move my legs!" He groaned and sank back to the floor.

There was a heavy buzz of conversation, and Dave caught the words, "His back . . . Must have hurt his back when he fell . . . Maybe he's just yellow . . ."

"Get Ike Andres," Dave said, groaning again. . . .

Bart Case, who called himself a doctor, sat by the bed in Ike's back room and heated the end of a long needle in a match flame. He said, "Son, this sort of thing is a little over my head. I got to know if you got any feeling in them legs. Now I'm going to jab you in a couple of places with this here needle, and if you feel anything, you holler."

Ike stood close to the head of the bed. The light flickered on his gray face, his twisted mouth. "Sure, Bart," Dave said.

Bart, with odd deftness, jabbed Dave four times. Right and left thigh. Right and left calf. Dave said, "Come on, Bart. Stick me with it. What are you waiting for?"

Bart sighed. "I already stuck you, son. You sure enough got dead legs on you. I don't know enough to tell you what the answer is. Maybe after a few days the feeling will come back slow. I hope so. Maybe never. Hard to tell."

Dave bit his lip and said, "I'll be okay." His voice was flat and dead.

Bart left. Ike said gently, "He'll go right on back to the Gay Gold and tell 'em." Ike walked over and slipped the bolt on the door, drew the thick curtains across the one window.

Dave swung his feet over the side of the bed, stood up and stretched. He felt his jaw. "That Quinn had rocks in his hands."

"I was afraid that needle business would give you away."

"Got tossed into a hill of red ants once. Felt just about like that. Did you see Louis?"

"Sure, As far as Louis is concerned, the roan fought his way out and ran off into the hills. I got him up in that little box canyon a half mile beyond Pete's place. The place that Pete used to own."

Jud Hawson walked out onto his *placita,* yawned and stretched. In a few moments the Mexican woman would bring his breakfast out. He was a big man, thick-shouldered and tall, with a brown face too young for his long white hair. His eyes were a cold clear blue and his profile was taken from a Roman coin.

During the past three years he had trained himself to move slowly, speak slowly. He carried himself with enormous dignity. Each morning of his life he stood in his dooryard and looked at the distant blue of the mountains and thought of the day when his holdings would reach the edge of those mountains.

There was no limit, no ceiling, for a man with vision, with the guts to make that vision come true. The rest of them were stupid and lazy. They clung to their land and hoped for the best. He, Jud Hawson, would gobble up their little spreads and turn the range into bright yellow gold. The gold would buy more range, and what he couldn't buy he'd take.

They were stupid to resist him. The sheriff had bucked him, so he had bought the sheriff. If he couldn't have been purchased, he would have died. Ryan at the store resisted him for a time. He bought Ryan. Men could be either purchased or beaten or killed. They had small hearts and small visions. They lived with their stupid noses in the dust.

Hawson lived with the great men of the past who came to him during his long dreams at night and spoke softly to him. "You grow bigger, Hawson. Someday it will be impossible to ride across your land in a week's time. After you have all the land, there are other things. You will have many men then. You must raise and equip an army. The rest of them are weak. Only you, Hawson. Only you. Only you."

He stretched again and noticed that the golden sun of the dawn shone on a soft layer of mist that clung to the hollows, spread thinly across the flats. It was good land. The best.

He heard a faint shout, an unidentifiable sound that came from a great distance. He peered into the sun and saw a horse and rider. The horse cut through the mist in a slow lope, looking as if its hooves didn't touch the ground. He heard the distant thud of hooves.

He squinted into the sun, wondering who it was. Suddenly he was very still. The rider wore a yellow shirt that blazed in the sunlight. The big hat was dead white. There was something familiar about the way the man sat the horse. The horse itself . . .

Hawson gasped. The rider was soon lost in the mist.

Randy Adams stood with his hat in his hand in front of the table where his employer was having breakfast.

"Hell yes, he was dead!" Adams said flatly. "His horse tossed him into the rocks, and I went over and took a good look. The bullet went in the back of his neck and busted his chin all to hell on the way out the front. Besides, he landed on his head in them rocks."

"You say Louis Besa got his horse? Go see if Besa still has it. Send Quinn up here to see me."

When Quinn arrived, Hawson snapped, "Take off your hat and stand straight!"

Quinn looked sullen, but he removed his hat and straightened his shoulders. Hawson questioned him in detail about the episode with Dave Austin. When he had all the information, Hawson gave Quinn his instructions.

Both men were back within three hours. Hawson saw them together in the main room of the ranch house.

Adams said, "I saw Besa. He told me the roan got away from him and run off onto the open range. I backed him up against the gate to his corral and smashed his nose with the barrel of my gun. He got down on his knees and begged and blubbered and said that he'd told me the truth. He was too damn scared to lie. Why did you send me to see him?"

"Shut up! And how did you come out, Quinn?"

"Andres didn't want to let me in, but finally he agreed. I went in and told Austin I was sorry about his legs, and he cursed me for about five minutes. I let him rave. He looked sick as hell. I got over by the bed; and when Andres went out into the front of the shop, I leaned down and grabbed Austin by the throat.

"I watched his legs. He fought like hell with his arms. Knocked this here tooth loose. But he didn't move his legs at all. Finally he thumped on the wall with his fist and Andres came in and I had to leave go of him. He ain't faking, Mr. Hawson. His face was black as your boots, and still he didn't move those legs none."

Hawson stood up suddenly and paced over to the big fireplace. He looked down at the gray ashes of the previous winter and said, "I might as well tell the two of you what this is all about. But don't tell any of the others. This morning I saw Pete Austin ride across my range. Just to the east of the house."

Quinn gasped. Adams said, "Must have been somebody looks like Pete looked."

"It was Austin's roan. I know the gait on that animal. He wore one of those special yellow shirts and that white hat with the extra-high crown. He sat his horse like Pete Austin."

Hawson's back was turned to the two of them. Adams looked at Quinn and smiled crookedly, touching his finger to his temple. Quinn shrugged.

"Sun was pretty bright this morning," Quinn said.

Hawson turned and glared at him. "Damn it, man! I know what I saw! I saw Pete Austin ride by out there, and I want it stopped. You understand? Stopped!"

"Sure, sure," Adams said gently.

"Don't use that tone of voice on me, Adams!" Hawson yelled.

Hawson sat at breakfast again with Quinn and Adams standing in front of his table. He lifted a forkful of food with a trembling hand. His face was gray under the tan, and there was a new deepness to the lines bracketing his mouth.

He said gently, "I want to thank you gentlemen for following my orders so explicitly. This morning Pete Austin rode by here again. I trust that both you gentlemen were enjoying your sleep at the time?"

Hawson, for the first time in nearly two years, was wearing a gun belt. Adams glanced at it and then looked at Quinn. There was quiet scorn in Adams's eyes.

Hawson continued in a louder voice, "When I give orders, I want them followed. Tomorrow morning you two will be out there on the flats before dawn. You'll both have rifles. You'll be on foot. You'll wait for Pete Austin, and when he rides by you'll fire. Understand?"

Quinn looked down at the flagstones. He said sullenly, "Pete Austin is dead. I'll be damned if I'll lay on my belly out there on the flats just because you start seeing things."

The table upset as Hawson came up out of his chair. He swung his long arm, and his open palm cracked against Quinn's face. "You'll do as you're told!"

Quinn snarled and started to turn away. His hard palm slapped against the holster at his thigh and came up fast, levering the gun to bear on Hawson. The sound of the shot was flat and hard in the open air. Quinn took one step forward and fell onto his face. His gun slid, spinning, toward Hawson's feet.

Hawson's mouth worked. He turned toward Adams, who was shoving his gun back into the holster. "Thanks, Adams."

"Don't thank me. You handle the payroll. That ought to be worth two hundred. I sort of liked Quinn. Better make it two-fifty."

A Mexican woman came to the door to the *placita,* took a look at Quinn, threw her apron up over her head and ran back into the house.

"The hands are out. She won't say anything," Hawson said quietly. "Get Quinn's stuff out of the bunkhouse. Bury it with him. Keep any money you find on him. Get Miguel to dig the grave. That'll be worth three hundred to me."

Adams grinned broadly. "I'll do all that, but I won't chase no ghosts for you, Hawson."

"You'll call me Mr. Hawson!"

"I won't chase ghosts, *Mister* Hawson."

In midafternoon Randy Adams rode out to the east of the ranch house. He swung down from his horse and walked until he came on the tracks. He squatted on his heels, rolled a smoke and looked at the tracks for a long time. There was a half-smile on his lips, but his eyes were puzzled. At last he went back and got Miguel. Miguel was very good at tracking. Just before dusk Miguel, panting with exertion, stood aside proudly while

Adams rode into the little box canyon. The roan nickered. Adams grinned broadly and told Miguel to run along back to the ranch.

The door closed behind Bart Case. Dave sat up in bed and smiled ruefully at Ike Andres. "If that old fella don't stop coming around with that needle of his, I'm going to hire out for a pincushion."

"Needles feel better than bullets, Dave. I don't like the way you're pushing this thing. You can't show up at the same time again. Damn it, old Hawson'll be waiting with a rifle even if he doesn't get any of his boys to work on you."

Dave frowned. "I spoil the effect if I don't show up at the right time, Ike." He laughed. "I think I got the old boy going. His face looked as white as Pete's hat this morning. Just one more morning ride and then we try the hole ace."

"I don't like it," Ike said sourly. "Go along with me this far. Don't try it in the morning. Catch him just at dusk, and ride close enough so that he can catch a flash of the shirt. Then light on out of there."

Dave thought for long moments. "Okay. Maybe you're right. Maybe if he doesn't know what time to expect the ghost it'll rattle him worse. Did you bring back the thing from Louis's place?"

"It's out in the wagon bed. I'll get it."

Andres hobbled out and brought it in. Dave looked it over. Two pieces of strap iron bolted together in the form of a T. Bolt holes were drilled in the base of the T. It was about thirty inches high, and the crosspiece was about twenty inches long.

Ike said, "I didn't bother to bring the saddle in. We braced the horn the way you said and drilled through it."

Dave fingered the sharp curve in the base of the T. "You figure this curves enough?"

"Seems to when you get it set up. If it don't, we can wedge it between a couple of rocks and bend it just a little bit more."

"Tonight, Ike, after the town's abed, you better take the wagon and take all the stuff out to where the roan is. I'll go on out way before dawn as usual, and I'll stay in the canyon all day and hit Hawson's place at dusk. You better roll up some blankets and stick them in this here bed and tell folks I'm sleeping."

Jud Hawson sat in his big chair in the dark and looked out the window across the sighing plains, looked at the speckled infinity of stars. He sighed heavily. He thought of the dawn rider, and the palms of his hands grew clammy. He shivered. Lately the great men of the past hadn't come to him in his dreams. He had dreamed of the face of Pete Austin. There was a smile on Austin's lips. He had whispered, "You, too, Hawson. You, too. *You, too.*"

In his room Hawson lighted the lamp, took his favorite rifle from the gun cabinet. He spent over an hour cleaning and polishing it. At last he held it in his hands and snicked the bolt shut. It made a slick, heartening click.

He sat with the chill steel against his hands and thought of Pete Austin. He saw himself kneeling on the small terrace at dawn, the quick shots whipping the air, the butt thudding against his shoulder. He looked through the sights and fired shot after shot into the yellow shirt. He saw holes appear in the fabric. The rider laughed and kept riding.

Hawson looked toward the black square of his window and shuddered. He blew out the lamp and undressed in the dark. He stretched out, stiff and weary, and stared up at the dark ceiling. The muscles of his neck and back ached. He thought of the way Quinn's gun had spun at his feet. He thought of Adams's eyes.

3

Dead Man's Blood

IKE ANDRES SADDLED up the swaybacked gray with practiced fingers, climbed with difficulty up into the seat and slapped the gray's rump with the reins, clucked to it softly. The wagon started with a jolt. The horse clumped down the narrow alley, and he turned right on the main street. No light showed in all of Oracle. Andres guessed that it was about two o'clock. A pale moon rode near the horizon.

He swayed on the wagon seat and thought of Dave, whom he had left sleeping. Dave was a good boy. A little hard and bitter for his age. Couldn't hardly blame the boy. A tough deal all the way around. A no-limit game with death for the low hole card.

The slow rumble of the wagon made him sleepy. He swayed from side to side, peering through the night, clucking to the gray once in a while. It was a sad thing not to be able to ride after so many years in the saddle. He remembered the times he had rode the point on the big herds of longhorns, all the way from Texas to the Kansas yards.

It had been a fine life. He thought, as he had thought many times before, that the horse that had crippled him should have crushed his life out against the brutal hardness of the snubbing post. Then he wouldn't be condemned to live out his years as half a man.

He turned off the main road, braced himself as the wagon lurched down the steep side of a small washout, clung to the seat as the gray scrambled up the far side, the stones rolling under its hooves.

At last he came to the turnoff to the canyon. The last quarter mile was across the open prairie. The dry grasses rustled against the wheels. He reined in at the entrance to the canyon and sat for a time savoring the beauty of the night before climbing stiffly down. He had decided that a tangle of chokeberry bushes near the canyon entrance would be the best place to hide the things he had brought.

He tethered the gray, pulled down the tailgate and grabbed the T of scrap iron. He had it half out of the wagon when he heard the sound close behind him. He froze.

He heard a quiet sigh. "You made me wait a long time, Andres. Maybe you can tell me about the ghost."

Ike recognized the silky voice of Adams. He knew that Adams's eyes were as adjusted to the faint moonlight as his own. He stood motionless, still clutching the heavy T of scrap iron.

Suddenly, with a wild yell, he whirled, hurling the heavy device at the dim figure behind him. There was the sound of an impact, a hoarse exclamation, and the figure melted down against the ground.

Ike tried to move quickly, tried to force his broken body to carry him forward to where he could get his gnarled hands on the throat of Adams. He took two steps and the world exploded into fire, the heavens cracked open with a noise of thunder. He was on his back with something bubbling in his chest. The dry grass brushed his cheek. The stars swirled madly above. He couldn't take a deep breath . . .

Dave jumped up quickly and hurried to the window. There was a hint of gray in the east. He had slept too long.

Ike should have been back long ago. He stepped quietly out the back door. The wagon wasn't back. Something had happened to Ike.

He dressed in haste, pulling on a dark shirt over the bright yellow one that he put on first. He had to make up time. The town would soon be stirring. He yanked his boots on, buckled on his belt and jammed the white hat on his head.

The door to the livery stable was unlatched. It creaked as he opened it. He stood still, heard the snores of the old man. The boards creaked as he walked back to the stalls. The old man snored on. He stepped into the stall, quieted the welcoming whinny with a hand over the tall black's muzzle.

He saddled up, led the horse out of the stall. He swung up, hinted with the hooks, and the black pounded across the boards. Dave ducked low as the black ran out the wide front door. Behind him he heard the yell of the old man. He lifted the black into a dead run.

He pulled in the black at the canyon and advanced cautiously. He was up to the wagon before he saw Ike's body.

He jumped up, his fingers tight on the gun grip, the muzzle swinging in slow horizontal arcs. Six feet beyond Ike the T of scrap iron bent the grass over. One end of the crossbar was stained dark. Near it was a dark spot in the grass.

At the crash of the shot, he dropped flat. The muzzle flash had come from a spot twenty feet away. He fired twice in the direction of the flash. The sky grew lighter. Flat on his belly, he wormed his way forward. At last he saw a dim shape in the grass. He aimed carefully, saw it jerk as the bullet hit.

Seconds later he rolled it over. Adams!

He touched the flesh of the man's hand. It was like ice. Adams had been dead for some time. Adams had his gun in his right hand. Burning grass glowed near the muzzle. Dave suddenly understood. Some reflex had caused it. Some tremor in the dead, stiffening body.

Adams's chin was smashed, and his throat was torn where the heavy scrap iron had hit it. A trail of blood led back through the grass. The picture was clear. Ike had hurled the iron at Adams, tearing his throat. Adams had killed Ike and then bled to death as he tried to crawl back to his horse, his gun on cock.

Dave glanced at the east. The rim of the sun would soon show. There was no point in waiting until dusk. The death of Ike spoiled the entire plan. Everything was ruined. By the time he could construct the dummy of the sacking that Ike had hauled in the wagon, it would be broad day. Back in the town they would go into the back room and find him gone. Word would reach Hawson before noon. They would no longer think of ghosts. They would have guns ready for him.

He stood up, holstered his gun and looked down for several minutes at the dead face of Adams. He snapped his fingers suddenly. His mouth twisting with disgust, he squatted, unbuttoned Adams's sodden shirt and ripped it off.

He got rope out of the wagon, laid the T of scrap iron on Adams's chest, and tied it there with knots that bit into the cold flesh. It took a long time to work Adams's limp arms into the sleeves of the yellow shirt. Dave got the roan, hobbled it and bound sacking over its eyes. It stood quivering.

He picked up Adams's body, hoisted it into the saddle. The roan smelled death and tried to shy away. The saddle horn had been reinforced and two holes bored through it which matched the holes in the base of the T. He fed the bolts he had taken tightly through the holes.

Adams sat upright in the saddle, his legs dangling limply. Dave tied his feet into the stirrups, tied his wrists loosely together in front of him, and fed the reins into the limp hands. He stepped back.

Since the first gray of dawn, Jud Hawson had stood on the flagstones of the *placita,* looking toward the east. During the night he had been tempted to go down to the bunkhouse, wake up the other five in his rough string and station them out in the flats to the east of the house. But he remembered how Quinn had reacted. And Adams.

The sun crept up until the great golden ball was above the horizon. Overhead the gray changed slowly to morning blue. Hawson felt a deep relief. The time was past. Pete Austin would not come again.

Hawson slowly relaxed. He sat down heavily in the chair behind his small breakfast table. He put the rifle on the flagstones at his feet.

He heard the distant thud of hoof, jingle of rowel hook, and suddenly he was standing, trembling.

His eyes widened and his breath stopped as he saw that the roan was headed directly for the *placita.* It came shouldering out of the mist, and on it was a silent man in a white hat, a yellow shirt.

He lifted the rifle, centered it.

Hawson smiled tightly and squeezed down on the trigger. He cursed. A miss! He forced steadiness into his arms, fired again. The rider came on. The big white hat was pulled down low over his eyes, shadowing his face.

Hawson knew that he hadn't missed.

The roan was much closer. He saw the shattered chin, the blood on the shirt. The voice of Quinn sounded in his ears . . . *and busted his chin all to hell on the way out the front.*

Hawson saw the dark holes appear in the yellow shirt. The roan was wide-eyed, foaming. Hawson knew that he was screaming, felt the muscles of his jaw crack as his mouth opened. He continued to yank on the trigger after the rifle was empty. He had no more breath for screaming. He threw the rifle full at the man fifteen feet away, and, as the horse thundered up to him, he dropped onto his face, covering his head.

The horse veered off across the flats, the hooves thudding ever more softly until at last Hawson could hear nothing but the excited servants around him.

He wanted the darkness. He didn't want eyes with which he could see a man in a yellow shirt riding a horse—a man long dead. A man whose head bobbed grotesquely.

He jumped up so quickly that those standing around him moved back in confusion. He saw the flat swarthy face of Miguel. He said softly, "Take your knife and take out my eyes, Miguel."

Miguel backed off, palms out in horror.

They looked at his face, heard his soft and wheedling voice, saw the clawing motions of his hands. They turned and fled.

When they were gone, Dave Austin slid off the black and came up the slope.

Hawson heard his step and turned. His face lighted up. In a voice like the voice of a child finding a delicious surprise, he said, "You have come to kill me!"

Dave stood for a moment and listened to the begging, the babbling. Dave holstered his gun and walked away.

It took him the best part of a half hour to ride slowly back to the canyon. By midmorning he had captured the badly spooked roan. Back at the mouth of the canyon he took the spade from the wagon and buried Adams, the T of iron and the doctored saddle. He replaced the turf and swept it clean of traces. He lifted Ike gently into the bed of the wagon, tied the black and the roan to the tailgate, and drove slowly back into Oracle.

He felt oddly light-headed. Once, as the wagon jolted along, he licked dry lips and said, "Ike, you understand, don't you? He'll be dead by nightfall."

But Dave found out later that he was wrong. Hawson didn't kill himself until a half hour before dawn the next day.

The Time
of the Wolves

MARCIA MULLER

"IT WAS IN the time of the wolves that my grandmother came to Kansas." The old woman sat primly on the sofa in her apartment in the senior citizens' complex. Although her faded blue eyes were focused on the window, the historian who sat opposite her sensed Mrs. Clark was not seeing the shopping malls and used-car lots that had spilled over into what once was open prairie. As she'd begun speaking, her gaze had turned inward—and into the past.

The historian—who was compiling an oral account of the Kansas pioneers—adjusted the volume button on her tape recorder and looked expectantly at Mrs. Clark. But the descendant of those pioneers was in no hurry; she waited a moment before resuming her story.

"The time of the wolves—that's the way I thought of it as a child, and I speak of it that way to this very day. It's fitting; those were perilous times, in the 1870s. Vicious packs of wolves and coyotes roamed; fires would sweep the prairie without warning; there were disastrous floods; and, of course, blizzards. But my grandmother was a true pioneer woman: She knew no fear. One time in the winter of 1872 . . ."

Alma Heusser stood in the doorway of the sod house, looking north over the prairie. It was gone four in the afternoon now, and storm clouds were building on the horizon. The chill in the air penetrated even her heavy buffalo-skin robe; a hush had fallen, as if all the creatures on the barren plain were holding their breath, waiting for the advent of the snow.

Alma's hand tightened on the rough door frame. Fear coiled in her stomach. Every time John was forced to make the long trek into town she stood like this, awaiting his return. Every moment until his horse appeared in the distance she imagined that some terrible event had taken him from her. And on this night, with the blizzard threatening . . .

127

The shadows deepened, purpled by the impending storm. Alma shivered and hugged herself beneath the enveloping robe. The land stretched before her: flat, treeless, its sameness mesmerizing. If she looked at it long enough, her eyes would begin to play tricks on her—tricks that held the power to drive her mad.

She'd heard of a woman who had been driven mad by the prairie: a timid, gentle woman who had traveled some miles east with her husband to gather wood. When they had finally stopped their wagon at a grove, the woman had gotten down and run to a tree—the first tree she had touched in three years. It was said they had had to pry her loose, because she refused to stop hugging it.

The sound of a horse's hooves came from the distance. Behind Alma, ten-year-old Margaret asked, "Is that him? Is it Papa?"

Alma strained to see through the rapidly gathering dusk. "No," she said, her voice flat with disappointment. "No, it's only Mr. Carstairs."

The Carstairs, William and Sarah, lived on a claim several miles east of there. It was not unusual for William to stop when passing on his way from town. But John had been in town today, too; why had they not ridden back together?

The coil of fear wound tighter as she went to greet him.

"No, I won't dismount," William Carstairs said in response to her invitation to come inside and warm himself. "Sarah doesn't know I am here, so I must be home swiftly. I've come to ask a favor."

"Certainly. What is it?"

"I'm off to the East in the morning. My mother is ill and hasn't much longer; she's asked for me. Sarah is anxious about being alone. As you know, she's been homesick these past two years. Will you look after her?"

"Of course." Alma said the words with a readiness she did not feel. She did not like Sarah Carstairs. There was something mean-spirited about the young woman, a suspicious air in the way she dealt with others that bordered on the hostile. But looking after neighbors was an inviolate obligation here on the prairie, essential to survival.

"Of course we'll look after her," she said more warmly, afraid her reluctance had somehow sounded in her voice. "You need not worry."

After William Carstairs had ridden off, Alma remained in the doorway of the sod house until the horizon had receded into darkness. She would wait for John as long as was necessary, hoping that her hunger for the sight of him had the power to bring him home again.

"Neighbors were the greatest treasure my grandparents had," Mrs. Clark explained. "The pioneer people were a warmhearted lot, open and giving, closer than many of today's families. And the women in particular were a great source of strength and comfort to one another. My grandmother's friendship with Sarah Carstairs, for example . . ."

* * *

"I suppose I must pay a visit to Sarah," Alma said. It was two days later. The snowstorm had never arrived, but even though it had retreated into Nebraska, another seemed to be on the way. If she didn't go to the Carstairs' claim today, she might not be able to look in on Sarah for some time to come.

John grunted noncommittally and went on trimming the wick of the oil lamp. Alma knew he didn't care for Sarah, either, but he was a taciturn man, slow to voice criticism. And he also understood the necessity of standing by one's neighbors.

"I promised William. He was so worried about her." Alma waited, hoping her husband would forbid her to go because of the impending storm. No such dictum was forthcoming, however: John Heusser was not one to distrust his wife's judgment; he would abide by whatever she decided.

So, driven by a promise she wished she had not been obligated to make, Alma set off on horseback within the hour.

The Carstairs' claim was a poor one, although to Alma's way of thinking it need not be. In the hands of John Heusser it would have been bountiful with wheat and corn, but William Carstairs was an unskilled farmer. His crops had parched even during the past two summers of plentiful rain; his animals fell ill and died of unidentifiable ailments; the house and outbuildings grew ever more ramshackle through his neglect. If Alma were a fanciful woman—and she preferred to believe she was not —she would have said there was a curse on the land. Its appearance on this grim February day did little to dispel the illusion.

In the foreground stood the house, its roof beam sagging, its chimney askew. The barn and other outbuildings behind it looked no better. The horse in the enclosure was bony and spavined; the few chickens seemed too dispirited to scratch at the hard-packed earth. Alma tied her sorrel to the fence and walked toward the house, her reluctance to be there asserting itself until it was nearly a foreboding. There was no sign of welcome from within, none of the flurry of excitement that the arrival of a visitor on the isolated homesteads always occasioned. She called out, knocked at the door. And waited.

After a moment the door opened slowly and Sarah Carstairs looked out. Her dark hair hung loose about her shoulders; she wore a muslin dress dyed the rich brown of walnut bark. Her eyes were deeply circled— haunted, Alma thought.

Quickly she shook off the notion and smiled. "We've heard that Mr. Carstairs had to journey East," she said. "I thought you might enjoy some company."

The younger woman nodded. Then she opened the door wider and motioned Alma inside.

The room was much like Alma's main room at home, with narrow, tall windows, a rough board floor, and an iron stove for both cooking and heating. The curtains at the windows were plain burlap grain sacks, not at all like Alma's neatly stitched muslin ones, with their appliqués of flowers. The furnishings—a pair of rockers, pine cabinet, sideboard, and table —had been new when the Carstairs arrived from the East two years before, but their surfaces were coated with the grime that accumulated from cooking.

Sarah shut the door and turned to face Alma, still not speaking. To cover her confusion Alma thrust out the corn bread she had brought. The younger woman took it, nodding thanks. After a slight hesitation she set it on the table and motioned somewhat gracelessly at one of the rockers. "Please," she said.

Alma undid the fastenings of her heavy cloak and sat down, puzzled by the strange reception. Sarah went to the stove and added a log, in spite of the room already being quite warm.

"He sent you to spy on me, didn't he?"

The words caught Alma by complete surprise. She stared at Sarah's narrow back, unable to make a reply.

Sarah turned, her sharp features pinched by what might have been anger. "That is why you're here, is it not?" she asked.

"Mr. Carstairs did ask us to look out for you in his absence, yes."

"How like him," Sarah said bitterly.

Alma could think of nothing to say to that.

Sarah offered her coffee. As she prepared it, Alma studied the young woman. In spite of the heat in the room and her proximity to the stove, she rubbed her hands together; her shawl slipped off her thin shoulders, and she quickly pulled it back. When the coffee was ready—a bitter, nearly unpalatable brew—she sat cradling the cup in her hands, as if to draw even more warmth from it.

After her earlier strangeness Sarah seemed determined to talk about the commonplace: the storm that was surely due, the difficulty of obtaining proper cloth, her hope that William would not forget the bolt of calico she had requested he bring. She asked Alma about making soap: Had she ever done so? Would she allow her to help the next time so she might learn? As they spoke, she began to wipe beads of moisture from her brow. The room remained very warm; Alma removed her cloak and draped it over the back of the rocker.

Outside, the wind was rising, and the light that came through the narrow windows was tinged with gray. Alma became impatient to be off for home before the storm arrived, but she also became concerned with leaving Sarah alone. The young woman's conversation was rapidly growing erratic and rambling; she broke off in the middle of sentences to laugh irrelevantly. Her brow continued moist, and she threw off her shawl, fanning herself. Alma, who like all frontier women had had considerable experience at doctoring the sick, realized Sarah had been taken by a fever.

Her first thought was to take Sarah to her own home, where she might look after her properly, but one glance out the window discouraged her. The storm was nearing quickly now; the wind gusted, tearing at the dried cornstalks in William Carstairs's uncleared fields, and the sky was streaked with black and purple. A ride of several miles in such weather would be the death of Sarah; do Alma no good, either. She was here for the duration, with only a sick woman to help her make the place secure.

She glanced at Sarah, but the other woman seemed unaware of what was going on outside. Alma said, "You're feeling poorly, aren't you?"

Sarah shook her head vehemently. A strand of dark brown hair fell across her forehead and clung there damply. Alma sensed she was not a woman who would give in easily to illness, would fight any suggestion that she take to her bed until she was near collapse. She thought over the remedies she had administered to others in such a condition, wondered whether Sarah's supplies included the necessary sassafras tea or quinine.

Sarah was rambling again—about the prairie, its loneliness and desolation. ". . . listen to that wind! It's with us every moment. I hate the wind and the cold, I hate the nights when the wolves prowl . . ."

A stealthy touch of cold moved along Alma's spine. She, too, feared the wolves and coyotes. John told her it came from having Germanic blood. Their older relatives had often spoken in hushed tones of the wolf packs in the Black Forest. Many of their native fairy tales and legends concerned the cruel cunning of the animals, but John was always quick to point out that these were only stories. "Wolves will not attack a human unless they sense sickness or weakness," he often asserted. "You need only take caution."

But all of the settlers, John included, took great precautions against the roaming wolf packs; no one went out onto the prairie unarmed. And the stories of merciless and unprovoked attacks could not all be unfounded . . .

"I hear the wolves at night," Sarah said. "They scratch on the door and the sod. They're hungry. Oh, yes, they're hungry . . ."

Alma suddenly got to her feet, unable to sit for the tautness in her limbs. She felt Sarah's eyes on her as she went to the sideboard and lit the oil lamp. When she turned to Sarah again, the young woman had tilted her head against the high back of the rocker and was viewing her through slitted lids. There was a glitter in the dark crescents that remained visible that struck Alma as somehow malicious.

"Are you afraid of the wolves, Alma?" she asked slyly.

"Anyone with good sense is."

"And you in particular?"

"Of course I'd be afraid if I met one face-to-face!"

"Only if you were face-to-face with it? Then you won't be afraid staying here with me when they scratch at the door. I tell you, I hear them every night. Their claws go *snick, snick* on the boards . . ."

The words were baiting. Alma felt her dislike for Sarah Carstairs gather strength. She said calmly, "Then you've noticed the storm is fast approaching."

Sarah extended a limp arm toward the window. "Look at the snow."

Alma glanced over there, saw the first flakes drifting past the wavery pane of glass. The sense of foreboding she'd felt upon her arrival intensified, sending little prickles over the surface of her skin.

Firmly she reined in her fear and met Sarah's eyes with a steady gaze. "You're right; I must stay here. I'll be as little trouble to you as possible."

"Why should you be trouble? I'll be glad of the company." Her tone mocked the meaning of the words. "We can talk. It's a long time since I've had anyone to talk to. We'll talk of my William."

Alma glanced at the window again, anxious to put her horse into the barn, out of the snow. She thought of the revolver she carried in her saddlebag as defense against the dangers of the prairie; she would feel safer if she brought it inside with her.

"We'll talk of my William," Sarah repeated. "You'd like that, wouldn't you, Alma?"

"Of course. But first I must tend to my horse."

"Yes, of course you'd like talking of William. You like talking *to* him. All those times when he stops at your place on his way home to me. On his way home, when your John isn't there. Oh, yes, Alma, I know about those visits." Sarah's eyes were wide now, the malicious light shining brightly.

Alma caught her breath. She opened her mouth to contradict the words, then shut it. It was the fever talking, she told herself, exaggerating the fears and delusions that life on the frontier could sometimes foster. There was no sense trying to reason with Sarah. What mattered now was to put the horse up and fetch her weapon. She said briskly, "We'll discuss this when I've returned," donned her cloak, and stepped out into the storm.

The snow was sheeting along on a northwesterly gale. The flakes were small and hard; they stung her face like hailstones. The wind made it difficult to walk; she leaned into it, moving slowly toward the hazy outline of her sorrel. He stood by the rail, his feet moving skittishly. Alma grasped his halter, clung to it a moment before she began leading him toward the ramshackle barn. The chickens had long ago fled to their coop. Sarah's bony bay was nowhere in sight.

The doors to the barn stood open, the interior in darkness. Alma led the sorrel inside and waited until her eyes accustomed themselves to the gloom. When they had, she spied a lantern hanging next to the door, matches and flint nearby. She fumbled with them, got the lantern lit, and looked around.

Sarah's bay stood in one of the stalls, apparently accustomed to looking out for itself. The stall was dirty, and the entire barn held an air of neglect. She set the lantern down, unsaddled the sorrel, and fed and watered both horses. As she turned to leave, she saw the dull gleam of an ax lying on top of a pile of wood. Without considering why she was doing so, she picked it up and carried it, along with her gun, outside. The barn doors were warped and difficult to secure, but with some effort she managed.

Back in the house, she found Sarah's rocker empty. She set down the ax and the gun, calling out in alarm. A moan came from beyond the rough burlap that curtained off the next room. Alma went over and pushed aside the cloth.

Sarah lay on a brass bed, her hair fanned out on the pillows. She had crawled under the tumbled quilts and blankets. Alma approached and put a hand to her forehead; it was hot, but Sarah was shivering.

Sarah moaned again. Her eyes opened and focused unsteadily on Alma. "Cold," she said. "So cold . . ."

"You've taken a fever." Alma spoke briskly, a manner she'd found effective with sick people. "Did you remove your shoes before getting into bed?"

Sarah nodded.

"Good. It's best you keep your clothes on, though; this storm is going to be a bad one; you'll need them for warmth."

Sarah rolled onto her side and drew herself into a ball, shivering violently. She mumbled something, but her words were muffled.

Alma leaned closer. "What did you say?"

"The wolves . . . they'll come tonight, scratching—"

"No wolves are going to come here in this storm. Anyway, I've a gun and the ax from your woodpile. No harm will come to us. Try to rest now, perhaps sleep. When you wake, I'll bring some tea that will help break the fever."

Alma went toward the door, then turned to look back at the sick woman. Sarah was still curled on her side, but she had moved her head and was watching her. Her eyes were slitted once more, and the light from the lamp in the next room gleamed off them—hard and cold as the icicles that must be forming on the eaves.

Alma was seized by an unreasoning chill. She moved through the door, out into the lamplight, toward the stove's warmth. As she busied herself with finding things in the cabinet, she felt a violent tug of home.

Ridiculous to fret, she told herself. John and Margaret would be fine. They would worry about her, of course, but would know she had arrived here well in advance of the storm. And they would also credit her with the good sense not to start back home on such a night.

She rummaged through the shelves and drawers, found the herbs and tea and some roots that would make a healing brew. Outside, there was a momentary quieting of the wind; in the bedroom Sarah also lay quiet. Alma put on the kettle and sat down to wait for it to boil.

It was then that she heard the first wolf howls, not far away on the prairie.

"The bravery of the pioneer women has never been equaled," Mrs. Clark told the historian. "And there was a solidarity, a sisterhood among them that you don't see anymore. That sisterhood was what sustained my grandmother and Sarah Carstairs as they battled the wolves . . ."

For hours the wolves howled in the distance. Sarah awoke, throwing off the covers, complaining of the heat. Alma dosed her repeatedly with the herbal brew and waited for the fever to break. Sarah tossed about on the bed, raving about wolves and the wind and William. She seemed to have some fevered notion that her husband had deserted her, and nothing Alma would say would calm her. Finally she wore herself out and slipped into a troubled sleep.

Alma prepared herself some tea and pulled one of the rockers close to the stove. She was bone-tired, and the cold was bitter now, invading the little house through every crack and pore in the sod. Briefly she thought she should bring Sarah into the main room, prepare a pallet on the floor nearer the heat source, but she decided it would do the woman more harm than good to be moved. As she sat warming herself and sipping the tea, she gradually became aware of an eerie hush and realized the wind had ceased.

Quickly she set down her cup and went to the window. The snow had stopped, too. Like its sister storm of two days before, this one had retreated north, leaving behind a barren white landscape. The moon had appeared, near to full, and its stark light glistened off the snow.

And against the snow moved the black silhouettes of the wolves.

They came from the north, rangy and shaggy, more like ragged shadows than flesh-and-blood creatures. Their howling was silenced now, and their gait held purpose. Alma counted five of them, all of a good size yet bony. Hungry.

She stepped back from the window and leaned against the wall beside it. Her breathing was shallow, and she felt strangely light-headed. For a moment she stood, one hand pressed to her midriff, bringing her sense under control. Then she moved across the room, to where William Carstairs's Winchester rifle hung on the wall. When she had it in her hands, she stood looking irresolutely at it.

Of course Alma knew how to fire a rifle; all frontier women did. But she was only a fair shot with it, a far better shot with her revolver. She could use the rifle to fire at the wolves at a distance, but the best she could hope for was to frighten them. Better to wait and see what transpired.

She set the rifle down and turned back to the window. The wolves were still some distance away. And what if they did come to the house, scratch at the door as Sarah had claimed? The house was well built; there was little harm the wolves could do it.

Alma went to the door to the bedroom. Sarah still slept, the covers pushed down from her shoulders. Alma went in and pulled them up again. Then she returned to the main room and the rocker.

The first scratchings came only minutes later. *Snick, snick* on the boards, just as Sarah had said.

Alma gripped the arms of the rocker with icy fingers. The revolver lay in her lap.

The scratching went on. Snuffling noises, too. In the bedroom Sarah cried out in protest. Alma got up and looked in on her. The sick woman was writhing on the bed. "They're out there! I know they are!"

Alma went to her. "Hush, they won't hurt us." She tried to rearrange Sarah's covers, but she only thrashed harder.

"They'll break the door, they'll find a way in, they'll—"

Alma pressed her hand over Sarah's mouth. "Stop it! You'll only do yourself harm."

Surprisingly, Sarah calmed. Alma wiped sweat from her brow and waited. The young woman continued to lie quietly.

When Alma went back to the window, she saw that the wolves had retreated. They stood together, several yards away, as if discussing how to breach the house.

Within minutes they returned. Their scratchings became bolder now; their claws ripped and tore at the sod. Heavy bodies thudded against the door, making the boards tremble.

In the bedroom Sarah cried out. This time Alma ignored her.

The onslaught became more intense. Alma checked the load on William Carstairs's rifle, then looked at her pistol. Five rounds left. Five rounds, five wolves . . .

The wolves were in a frenzy now—incited, perhaps, by the odor of sickness within the house. Alma remembered John's words: "They will not attack a human unless they sense sickness or weakness." There was plenty of both here.

One of the wolves leapt at the window. The thick glass creaked but did not shatter. There were more thumps at the door; its boards groaned.

Alma took her pistol in both hands, held it ready, moved toward the door.

In the bedroom Sarah cried out for William. Once again Alma ignored her.

The coil of fear that was so often in the pit of Alma's stomach wound taut. Strangely, it gave her strength. She trained the revolver's muzzle on the door, ready should it give.

The attack came from a different quarter: The window shattered, glass smashing on the floor. A gray head appeared, tried to wriggle through the narrow casement. Alma smelled its foul odor, saw its fangs. She fired once . . . twice.

The wolf dropped out of sight.

The assault on the door ceased. Cautiously Alma moved forward. When she looked out the window, she saw the wolf lying dead on the ground—and the others renewing their attack on the door.

Alma scrambled back as another shaggy gray head appeared in the window frame. She fired. The wolf dropped back, snarling.

It lunged once more. Her finger squeezed the trigger. The wolf fell.

One round left. Alma turned, meaning to fetch the rifle. But Sarah stood behind her.

The sick woman wavered on her feet. Her face was coated with sweat, her hair tangled. In her hands she held the ax that Alma had brought from the woodpile.

In the instant before Sarah raised it above her head, Alma saw her eyes. They were made wild by something more than fever: The woman was totally mad.

Disbelief made Alma slow. It was only as the blade began its descent that she was able to move aside.

The blade came down, whacked into the boards where she had stood.

Her sudden motion nearly put her on the floor. She stumbled, fought to steady herself.

From behind her came a scrambling sound. She whirled, saw a wolf wriggling halfway through the window casement.

Sarah was struggling to lift the ax.

Alma pivoted and put her last bullet into the wolf's head.

Sarah had raised the ax. Alma dropped the revolver and rushed at her. She slammed into the young woman's shoulder, sent her spinning toward the stove. The ax crashed to the floor.

As she fell against the hot metal Sarah screamed—a sound more terrifying than the howls of the wolves.

"My grandmother was made of stronger cloth than Sarah Carstairs," Mrs. Clark said. "The wolf attack did irreparable damage to poor Sarah's mind. She was never the same again."

Alma was never sure what had driven the two remaining wolves off—whether it was the death of the others or the terrible keening of the sick and injured woman in the sod house. She was never clear on how she managed to do what needed to be done for Sarah, nor how she got through the remainder of that terrible night. But in the morning when John arrived—so afraid for her safety that he had left Margaret at home and braved the drifted snow alone—Sarah was bandaged and put to bed. The fever had broken, and they were able to transport her to their own home after securing the battered house against the elements.

If John sensed that something more terrible than a wolf attack had transpired during those dark hours, he never spoke of it. Certainly he knew Sarah was in grave trouble, though, because she never said a word throughout her entire convalescence, save to give her thanks when William returned—summoned by them from the East—and took her home. Within the month the Carstairs had deserted their claim and left Kansas, to return to their native state of Vermont. There, Alma hoped, the young woman would somehow find peace.

As for herself, fear still curled in the pit of her stomach as she waited for John on those nights when he was away. But no longer was she shamed by the feeling. The fear, she knew now, was a friend—something that had stood her in good stead once, would be there should she again need it. And now, when she crossed the prairie, she did so with courage, for she and the lifesaving fear were one.

Her story done, Mrs. Clark smiled at the historian. "As I've said, my dear," she concluded, "the women of the Kansas frontier were uncommon in their valor. They faced dangers we can barely imagine today. And they were fearless, one and all."

Her eyes moved away to the window, and to the housing tracts and shoddy commercial enterprises beyond it. "I can't help wondering how women like Alma Heusser would feel about the way the prairie looks today," she added. "I should think they would hate it, and yet . . ."

The historian had been about to shut off her tape recorder, but now she paused for a final comment. "And yet?" she prompted.

"And yet I think that somehow my grandmother would have understood that our world isn't as bad as it appears on the surface. Alma Heusser has always struck me as a woman who knew that things aren't always as they seem."

Gamblin' Man

DWIGHT V. SWAIN

STIFF-LIPPED AND grim, Mr. Devereaux fingered the double eagle and wondered bleakly if all hulking, loudmouthed men were scoundrels; or was it merely that Fate chose only uncommon blackguards to send his way? Even worse, why did he not discover their connivings before they'd stripped him down to twenty dollars? He had one double eagle left. His last.

Across the table the man called Alonzo Park scooped up the cards, squared the deck, and riffled it in an expert shuffle. In the process he also managed an incredibly deft bit of palming that ended with six cards missing, just as in previous games.

Almost without thinking, Mr. Devereaux left off fingering the gold piece and instead caressed his sleeve-rigged double derringer.

This table around which they played was jammed in a corner at one end of the El Dorado's bar. It was out of the way, yet close to the source of supply of the red-eye of which Park, who owned the place, seemed so fond. It was a good twenty feet to the door, twenty feet past cold-eyed, gun-slung loungers who wandered about the saloon.

Park's voice cut in, a reverberant, bull-throated bellow. The man's meaty features glistened red as his own raw forty-rod whiskey.

"Lafe! Drinks all around!"

In silent, studied apathy, Mr. Devereaux allowed the cross-eyed barkeep to refill his glass and continued his appraisal.

A sheepherder sat to his left, no gun showing. Beyond him, a rat-visaged nondescript from the livery stable, toting a rusted .45. Then Park, ostensibly unarmed; probably he favored a hideout gun. And finally, to Mr. Devereaux's right, completing the circuit, a brawny, freckle-faced young fellow, Charlie Adams, who swayed drunkenly in his chair and held solemn, incongruous converse with a long-skirted, china-headed doll over a foot tall which he kept propped on the table before him.

Mr. Devereaux's hand turned out a mediocre pair, augmented by another—equally mediocre—on the draw.

Again he weighed that last remaining gold piece and studied Park. Finally he shoved the double eagle forward.

The sheepherder and the nondescript threw in their cards. Charlie Adams hesitated, ogling Mr. Devereaux owlishly from behind the doll, then followed suit. For a moment Park, too, hung back. But only for a moment.

"Raise you, Devereaux! I'll call your bluff!"

Mr. Devereaux could feel his own blood quicken, the hackles rise along his neck. Imperceptibly, he hunched his left shoulder forward, just enough for the black frock coat to clear his armpit-holstered Colt. The sleeve-rigged derringer held an old friend's reassurance.

"And raise you back, Park," he said softly. He reached into the pot, removed his double eagle as if to replace it with something larger.

A harsh, raw note crept into Alonzo Park's bull voice. He thrust his chin belligerently forward. "Put in your money, Devereaux. Put up or shut up."

Mr. Devereaux allowed himself the luxury of a thin, wry smile. He breathed deep—and savored the fact that this very breath might be his last. He pushed the thought back down and brought out the Colt in one swift, sure gesture.

He let his voice ring, then.

"Misdeal, Park. I'm betting my gun against your stack that there are less than fifty-two cards on this table—and that we'll find the others in a holdout on your side!"

Silence. Echoing eternities of silence, spreading out across the room. The sheepherder and the nondescript sat stiff and shriveled. Adams stared stupidly, jaw hanging, the big doll clasped to his chest.

Gun poised, feet flat against the floor, Mr. Devereaux waited. He watched the muscles in Park's bull neck knot, the hairy hands contract. "God help you, you dirty son!" Park rasped thickly. "I'll have your hide for this!"

"No doubt," Mr. Devereaux agreed. He gestured with his Colt to the livery groom. "Look under the table-edge for a holdout."

The man flicked one nervous glance at the gun, then bent to obey. He came up with two aces and three assorted spades.

Mr. Devereaux let his thin smile broaden. "I win." He rose, started to reach for Alonzo Park's stack. And he realized, even in that moment, the magnitude of his error.

The cross-eyed bartender whipped up a sawed-off shotgun with a bore that loomed big as twin water buckets. It seemed to Mr. Devereaux in that moment that he could hear the faint, sweet song of angel voices.

A gun's roar cut them short.

Sheer reflex sent Mr. Devereaux floorward, wrapped in vast disbelief at finding himself alive. He glimpsed the scattergun, flying off across the room. He stared at the cross-eyed bartender, while that worthy swore and clutched at a bleeding hand.

Big Adams, drunk no longer, came to his feet. He still gripped the doll, but now the china head was gone. The muzzle of a .45 protruded from its shredded, smoldering neck. Left-handed, he reached a nickeled star from his pocket and pinned it on. His freckled, good-natured face had gone suddenly cold, his voice hard and level.

"You're under arrest, Park. The town council held a private confab last night. They decided Crooked Lance needed a marshal an' gave me the job. The first chore on the list was to clean up the El Dorado."

The day dragged drowsily, even for Crooked Lance town. September's shimmering, brazen sun hung at two o'clock, the straggled clumps of cholla and Spanish bayonet a-ripple in its heat. The choked, close scent of sun on stone, and dust and dirt and baking 'dobe, rose faint yet all-pervasive. Even the thrumming flies droned lethargy, and the tail of breeze from distant, cloud-capped mountains alone kept the sparse shade tolerable.

Peace came to Mr. Devereaux. He loved such sleepy days as this, days for dreams and smiles and reveries. Relaxed and tranquil, he contemplated the padlocked El Dorado from his chair on the hotel porch. He wondered, in turn, how Alonzo Park liked his cell in the feedstore that served Crooked Lance as a makeshift jail.

The man was a fool, Mr. Devereaux decided soberly. Else why would he stay here, insisting on trial, instead of thankfully accepting Adams's offer to let him ride out of town unfettered, on his own agreement never to return? What possible defense could he offer? Did he actually believe he could salvage his fortunes?

The thought brought Mr. Devereaux's own financial state to mind. Adams was holding last night's poker pots as evidence till after the trial this afternoon. It left Mr. Devereaux with only the one twenty-dollar gold piece. He contemplated the coin wryly. He flipped it. His last double eagle, still.

The scuff of feet and the acrid breath of rising dust cut short his reveries. He looked around to see Crooked Lance's new marshal and a chubby, fresh-scrubbed cherub in pigtails and starched gingham round the corner hand in hand, the cherub wobbling ludicrously as she vainly tried to make her short legs match the lawman's long strides.

Adams nodded greetings, dropped into a chair beside Mr. Devereaux on the porch. He grinned boyishly.

"This here's my gal Alice, Devereaux. You better be nice to her, too. That was her doll I was totin' last night."

The cherub giggled and hid her face in her father's lap.

"You said you'd get me another dolly, Daddy. You promised." A tremor of excitement ran through her and she raised her head, eyes shining. "I know just the kind I want, Daddy. Missus Lauck's got one in her window. Blue eyes that close, and real gold hair."

Adams grinned again. He dandled her, gleeful and squealing, on one knee.

"Don't push me too fast, honey. Wait'll I draw at least one pay." Then, to Mr. Devereaux: "Guess we better mosey on over to the schoolhouse for court. Trial's set for two-thirty. Soon's it's over I can give you back your money."

Mr. Devereaux nodded, rose. Flat-crowned Stetson in hand, he stared off across the desert miles. An indefinable weariness washed over him, as if some queer, invisible shadow had crept across the turquoise sky. He caught himself wondering how it would feel to bounce a pigtailed daughter on one's knee . . .

It being Crooked Lance's first trial, the town council had voted in the mayor as judge. He sat behind the teacher's desk in the little adobe schoolhouse now, a thin, stooped, balding man, gavel in hand, gnawing his lips. He served as a barber, ordinarily, and these new responsibilities rode heavily upon him.

Mr. Devereaux chuckled benignly and let his gaze travel on. The little room was a babble of voices, the bare wood benches already filled. Whole families were out: fathers, mothers, children. Others, too—and over these he did not chuckle. Silent, too-casual men with guns lounging along the back wall. Last night they'd been lounging the same way at the El Dorado.

Adams brought in the prisoner.

Park had recovered his poise. Jaw outthrust, red face bright with what might pass for righteous indignation, he strode aggressively to his place. When, for the fraction of a second, his gaze met Mr. Devereaux's, his eyes were venomous, mocking, strangely mirthful.

Mr. Devereaux frowned despite himself. Almost without thinking, he touched his derringer's butt.

His Honor rapped for order, peered hesitantly down at the prisoner. "You want someone to help you, Park? You got a right, you know."

Park glowered. "I don't need help for what I've got to say."

Adams took the stand, told how he'd sat in on the game at Park's own table, feigning drunkenness. He'd picked that particular game, he explained, because he wanted to find out whether the El Dorado's owner, personally, was doing the cheating the council had ordered him to investigate. Further, he'd figured that table as most likely for action, Mr. Devereaux being a man who "looked like he knew his way around a deck of cards without no Injun guide, an' hard to buffalo, too!"

Park's only comment was a contempt-laden snort.

As before, Mr. Devereaux frowned. Instinctively, he shrugged the black frock coat smooth about his shoulders. The Colt's weight stood out sharp in his consciousness. Then the judge was calling him forward to take the stand.

In an instant Alonzo Park was on his feet. "Your Honor!" he bellowed.

His Honor started, cringed. Finally he made a feeble pass at pounding with his gavel. "Now, Park—"

"Don't 'Now Park' me!" the prisoner roared, his face the hue of a too-ripe plum. "Now's the time I speak my piece." He glowered and his eyes swept the room. Yet somehow, to Mr. Devereaux, there seemed to be a certain theatrical note about it all, as if the man were carefully building up a part.

Park went on. "You've called me a crooked tinhorn on the say of that jackass Charlie Adams, and I've kept quiet. But I'm damned if I'll let you ring in this gun-wolf, too!"

The judge chewed his lips, looked uneasily from Park to Adams to Mr. Devereaux and back again. "What you got agin' him, Lon?" he queried uneasily.

Mr. Devereaux saw the triumph in Park's eyes, then—the murderous glee the front of indignation veiled. He stared in dismay as the man whipped out a flimsy, too-familiar pamphlet.

"This is the 'wanted' list of the Adjutant General of Texas!" Park bellowed. "You've brought me up for crooked gambling, but your chief witness is a card shark and a killer, on the dodge from a murderous charge!"

Mr. Devereaux could feel the tension leap within the room. His own breath came too fast. As from afar he heard the El Dorado's owner shout on, work himself into a frenzy.

"Your haywire marshal gave me a chance to run out if I wanted to, but I stayed. I guess that shows whether I'm guilty or not! This tinhorn planted that holdout under the table. He figured to chase me out of town so he could take over the El Dorado—"

Somewhere at the back of the room a man yelled, "Park's right! Turn him loose! That Devereaux's the one should be in jail!"

The schoolroom exploded to a screaming madhouse. A tribute, Mr. Devereaux thought dourly as he maneuvered himself against the nearest wall, to Alonzo Park and his carefully stationed loungers.

The judge brought down his gavel with a bang. It was the first time since the beginning of the trial that he had showed such force and vigor.

"Case dismissed!"

"What about Devereaux?" somebody yelled.

As if in answer, Charlie Adams shoved forward, gun out. His good-natured face had gone worried and grim.

"I got no choice, Devereaux. You're under arrest!"

A cloud had swept down during that stormy schoolhouse session, Mr. Devereaux discovered. Already it impinged on the sun's bright sphere, a scudding wall of night stretched off to the distant mountains. The wind had quickened, too; freshened. Now it came whipping through Crooked Lance in gusts and buffets, sucking up little geysers of sand that swirled and rustled like dry leaves.

"Let's go, Devereaux," Adams said. His voice was flat.

Carefully, Mr. Devereaux adjusted his flat-crowned Stetson, shrugged smooth the black frock coat. It was a useless gesture, really, now that the heavy Colt was gone. Its absence gave him a queer, off-balance feeling. The sleeve-rigged derringer alone remained to comfort. That, and the gold piece. One double eagle. He laughed without mirth and flipped it in a glittering arc. Together, Devereaux and Adams moved out into the street.

The storm came faster now, blotting out light, racing hungrily on across the desert. The wind increased with it, drove tiny stones into Mr. Devereaux's face. Dust choked him. Sand gritted between his teeth.

Voiceless, he strode on. The thing was inevitable, he supposed, a peril that went with notoriety. Periodically he was bound to be recognized. The only marvel was that any lobo vindictive as Park had been content to leave an enemy to the law.

They passed the shuttered, padlocked El Dorado. The Silver Lady, too. Grant's Drygoods. Lettie Lauck's millinery.

Lettie Lauck. Mr. Devereaux pondered the name, remembered Alice and her doll. Alice, the fresh-scrubbed cherub in her pigtails and starched gingham. He wondered, a bit wistful, if he would ever see her again.

"Turn here," Adams said.

The feedstore that served as jail had an inner storage room—zinc-lined against rats—for a cell. The marshal prodded Mr. Devereaux toward it.

Mr. Devereaux sighed. It was coming now. It had to come. He touched the derringer's butt.

Marshal Adams swung open the storeroom's heavy door. "In there."

Mr. Devereaux studied him, caressed the derringer. "You believe it, then, Charlie?" He made his voice very gentle.

"Believe what?"

"The things Alonzo Park said."

Adams laughed. It had a harsh, unhappy sound. "What does it matter? Your name was in that book. You're on the owlhoot."

"A packed jury might call things murder that you wouldn't, Charlie."

He could see the sweat come to Adams's broad forehead. Then the jaw tightened.

"Sorry, Devereaux. That's twixt you an' the Adjutant Gen'ral of Texas. Folks here just hired me to hold up the law, not judge it."

Again Mr. Devereaux sighed. Nodded. The loose-holstered years went into his draw. "I'm sorry, too, Marshal. I can't take that chance." Cat-footed, he backed towards the open outer door.

Behind him, a gun roared.

Mr. Devereaux leaped sidewise—swiveling; firing. He glimpsed only a blur of motion as the gunman jumped away. That, and Adams pitching to the floor.

The minutes that followed never came quite clear to Mr. Devereaux. He acted by instinct, rather than logic, reloading the derringer as he ran. No need to ask himself what would happen if Crooked Lance's shouting citizenry should find him here by the fallen marshal, gun in hand.

But the townsmen were out already, a dozen or more of them, headed across the street towards him at a dead run even as he broke cover. Mr. Devereaux turned hastily, to the tune of oaths and bullets. He ducked between two buildings, to come out seconds later in an alley.

The jail-and-feedstore combination was of frame construction set on low, stone corner posts close to the ground. Mr. Devereaux dropped, rolled into the shallow space beneath the building.

There followed an eternity of dust and rocks and cobwebs, lasting well over an hour. When his pursuers finally gave up and silence once more reigned, he wriggled forth and stumbled stiffly to his feet.

The storm had brought with it an early dusk. Wind whipped the black frock coat tight about his legs as he tried to dust away the worst of the debris from beneath the building. Aching, irritable—and infinitely cautious—he gave it up, headed for the livery barn on down the alley.

The nondescript groom sprawled asleep in the haymow. Ever wary, Mr. Devereaux prodded him awake.

Grumbling, bleary-eyed, the man rose, peered at Mr. Devereaux through the stable's gloom. His lantern jaw dropped. "You!"

Mr. Devereaux favored him with one curt nod, brought up the derringer. "At your service. And now, if you'll saddle my black stallion . . ."

The nondescript swayed, still staring. His words came out a half-coherent mumble. "I thought you was over there at Park's."

"Park's?"

"Sure. The El Dorado. One o' Park's boys got scared about you bein' holed up there. He come round huntin' Adams."

Mr. Devereaux compressed his lips to a thin, straight line.

"Adams is dead."

"Dead?" The groom eyed him queerly. "Who says he's dead? He come in here lookin' for you not half a hour ago. Doc Brand patched up that hole in his shoulder."

"He . . . wasn't killed?"

"Uh-uh. Not even crippled bad."

One o' Park's boys come huntin' . . .

Mr. Devereaux stood very still. Discovered, with a strange abstraction, that he was hanging on the beats of his own heart. Of a sudden his mouth grew dry.

The nondescript was speaking again now, eyeing the derringer as he rubbed his lantern jaw. "You carry that thing in a sleeve-rig, don't you? Adams was tellin' 'bout it while Doc Brand fixed him up."

"Indeed?" Mr. Devereaux stiffened. "In that case, perhaps you'll favor me with the loan of your Colt." He stepped close, reached the rusting gun from its holster.

"Yeah, sure." The nondescript shifted uneasily, licked his lips. "I'll get your horse up, too."

As in a dream, Mr. Devereaux followed, patted the nickering stallion's sleek jet neck. "This is a time for travel, boy," he heard himself say. "We'll give this groom our double eagle for his gun and be on our way."

'One o' Park's boys come huntin' . . .'

One of Park's men had come hunting, to tell an honest marshal where a wanted man was hiding. Only it wasn't true. He, the hunted, hadn't been there.

In his mind's eye he pictured Alonzo Park with his bull neck and meaty, flushed face. Yes, Park would use a fugitive's name to bait a trap for an honest marshal.

"Did Park's man find Adams?" he asked, and in spite of all his efforts he could not make it sound quite casual.

"Uh-uh. He'd already left."

For a long, wordless moment Mr. Devereaux stood there. Slowly drew in a deep, full breath. His lips felt stiff, unreal.

The groom shuffled his feet. "If you'll just lemme get there . . ."

Ever so faintly, Mr. Devereaux smiled. Again he patted the stallion's neck. He replaced the gold piece in his pocket.

"That won't be necessary now. I've had a change of plans." And then, after a second: "If the marshal asks for me again, you can tell him I'm at the El Dorado."

Alonzo Park sprawled in the selfsame chair he'd occupied the night before, back to the bar, red-eye whiskey at his elbow.

"You scared me, Devereaux. I was beginning to be afraid you wouldn't come."

Mr. Devereaux raised his brows, allowed his curiosity to show. "You expected me, then?"

"Expected you? Of course I expected you." Park laughed. "You've got a rep for being a sentimental fool, Devereaux. They tell stories about it all the way to Montana. Last night Adams backed your play, so I knew you'd come when you heard he'd bought himself some trouble."

"And so?"

"So now we wait till Adams shows up to pinch you. Both of you'll turn up dead. Then I'll tell it that you forced me to hide you out at gunpoint. You killed Adams, and I killed you. The town will give me a vote of thanks." Again he leered. "Nice, eh?"

Wordless, Mr. Devereaux shrugged. It had seemed such a good idea, this check on Park. Interception by the cross-eyed, shotgun-toting barkeep was another story. They'd nailed him cold, overlooked nothing save the derringer in their search. They'd have found it, too, except that he'd transferred it to a new hideout within his flat-crowned Stetson after the stable groom's comment on the sleeve-rig.

So, now he stood here before Alonzo Park in the echoing, dimlit El Dorado. The scattergunner still covered him from behind the bar—grim, incongruous against the background of mirrors and pyramided bottles. Two other Park gunmen crouched by the street-front windows at the far end of the room, eyes glued to cracks in the shutters.

One of the men by the windows sang out, low, tense. "It's Adams! Here he comes!"

Park grinned wolfishly. "Well, Devereaux?"

A chill rippled through Mr. Devereaux in spite of his control. He had to fight to keep his tremor from his face. "I bow to superior talent, sir!" He took off the Stetson, mopped his brow. His sweating fingers closed round the derringer's butt. His knuckles showed white.

"He'll be here in ten seconds, Lon!" the gunman said.

Mr. Devereaux turned a trifle, stared straight into the bartender's crossed eyes. The shotgun's barrels loomed like cannon. Desperately, he tried to give his voice the right inflection.

"These maneuverings raise a thirst. Make mine Mill's Bluegrass, please."

For the fraction of a second the bartender's gaze wavered toward the bottles stacked behind him.

Mr. Devereaux brought the derringer up past the Stetson's brim, fired once. A black spot the size of a dime appeared just above the man's left cheekbone.

Chill, rock-steady now, Mr. Devereaux swiveled.

Park snarled, clawed a pistol from beneath his coat.

Mr. Devereaux fired the other barrel. He watched two of Park's bared teeth disappear, the man himself totter over backwards.

Behind him, the street end of the room reverberated gunfire. He swung. Park's gunmen were already down, Charlie Adams coming forward stiff-legged, a smoking .45 in his hand. The marshal bent, twisted the pistol away from the dead Park.

"A .31. That's what Doc Brand said shot me," Adams said.

Other men were crowding through the door now, bug-eyed, excited men with loud voices. Mr. Devereaux ignored them, held his own tone steady. He even managed to inject a faint, ironic note. "You were looking for me, Marshal?"

The other's freckled face froze. "I still am. You're wanted back in Texas."

"And duty's duty?" Mr. Devereaux sighed. Of a sudden he felt very old, very weary. "So be it, Marshal. A man must play it as he sees it." Then: "Dry work, Marshal. If you don't mind, I'll have a drink."

Very carefully, he rounded the end of the bar, stared down at the fallen, cross-eyed barkeep.

"Dead." He bent, as if to move the man away. Then, instead, he snatched up the scattergun and straightened fast. "Buckshot means burying, gentlemen. Do I have any takers?"

No one moved. Then Adams let out his breath, scowled.

"Damn you, Devereaux!"

Somehow, to Mr. Devereaux, it sounded like a benediction.

Wordless, he backed through the El Dorado's open doorway, whipped loose the reins of a big, snake-eyed bay at the rail, and led the beast out of view beside the building. He fired the scattergun into the air as he booted the bay across the rump, hard.

The horse let out a snort second cousin to a Comanche war whoop and took off with a thunder of hoofs. Mr. Devereaux ducked back into the shadows and stood stock-still.

The rush of feet in the El Dorado came like an echo to the big bay's thunder. Shouting, cursing, the marshal and his men boiled out the door, forked saddles and raced off in wild pursuit.

Mr. Devereaux waited till they were out of sight. He'd pick up the black stallion at the livery barn according to plan and head off south. There'd be plenty of time. Yes, plenty of time . . .

Again Lettie Lauck's shop caught his eye. It was lighted. He could see a tall young woman moving about inside.

The doll was still there, a big one, even bigger than the one Charlie Adams had carried. The eyes were wide and blue, the hair shimmering gold, the gown of silk. It was a beautiful doll.

The price tag was there, too: twenty dollars.

Almost without thinking, Mr. Devereaux reached into his pocket, fingered the double eagle. His last double eagle, still.

With a start, it came to him that the sky had cleared. The stars were out and the wind no longer blew. For an instant he almost thought he could hear Charlie Adams's shouts as he spurred his riders on. He smiled . . .

Still smiling, he stepped inside the shop. He doffed the flat-crowned Stetson politely as the tall young woman came forward.

"The doll in the window, please," said Mr. Devereaux.

Vigilante

H. A. DeROSSO

BILL LEAHY BROUGHT the word. "The Committee's meeting tonight, John."

John Weidler set down his newspaper and removed his spectacles. "Childress?" he asked.

"Yes."

Weidler carefully placed his spectacles in their case and cast a slight smile at his wife. He was glad that the two children were outside. He could hear their calls and laughter as they played in the backyard. John Weidler placed a hand momentarily on Martha's shoulder, then followed Leahy outside.

The evening air carried a crisp coolness and Weidler buttoned his jacket. They were silent as they walked along, the rasp of their shoe leather on the hard-packed ground the only sound.

Finally Weidler said, "It's come to a head this time."

Leahy nodded. He was a big man with a wide face and a violent redness to his features. For all his weight his step was light and soft—the tread of a stalking cat.

"He has asked for it," said Leahy heavily. "Matt Childress raised hell last night. Shot up half a dozen places, broke the windows of the Mercantile. When the marshal tried to arrest him this morning, Matt tore up the writ and threw it in the marshal's face. Matt sure did go and ask for it."

They walked along in the quickly gathering twilight. Virginia City was unnaturally quiet—such a quiet that it had never known. A far call from the Virginia City of a year ago—the Virginia City of Henry Plummer and the Innocents.

Weidler kept envisioning the old Virginia City that had been a tent city with its gambling houses and saloons and its roughly clothed, roistering miners and thieving, murdering Innocents. Full of wild, primitive laughter and full of sudden death.

150

A year had wrought a lot of changes in Virginia City. The tents were gone, replaced by frame buildings, though the saloons and gambling houses remained. It was a changed Virginia City with its muted laughter and vibrant life. A place where a man could settle down and raise a family. And the Vigilantes had made it so.

"What's the word from Nevada?" Weidler asked.

"Hang him," Leahy said bluntly.

"That will be going kind of far," murmured Weidler, a sudden coldness gripping him. He was a short, stocky man in his early thirties and there was the appearance of great strength in his arms and shoulders. He had a rather plain face with a blunt jaw and there was the hint of the bulldog in his features and in his bearing. He looked like a cold man.

"It's up to the Committee," said Leahy.

"This is going to be hard, Bill. Matt was one of us. He's not a bad sort when he's sober. Drunk, he's a wild man. We've warned him time and again, but it hasn't done any good."

"He's been bragging that the Vigilantes are through."

"We'll see about that."

"Matt has friends. They'll put up a fuss. You can bet on Tom Kincaid putting up for Matt."

"Yes, Tom will do that. The hell of it is—Tom is our friend, too."

"So is Matt Childress."

They came to Day & Miller's store, where the Vigilante meeting was to be held. Miners crowded in front of the store and they all had rifles but they were a quiet, somber lot. Weidler and Leahy nodded to a few of them and entered the store.

Two kerosene lamps had been lit and their shadowy, wavering light left heavy patches of black shadow in the corners and on the far walls. About twenty men were waiting. They were all morose and quiet, carrying about them a nervous silence as though wanting everything over with as soon as possible.

One of the men spoke, "I just saw Childress. Warned him to leave town. He laughed and said the Vigilantes are played out. That they won't dare hang a man for shooting up the town."

Every man's glance was on Weidler. He'd been one of the early organizers of the Vigilantes and he'd placed the noose around George Ives's neck when that first member of the Innocents had been executed. The men were very silent now, only the scraping of their boots when they shifted their weight marring the stillness. Weidler knew they were awaiting his words.

They would put much weight to what he'd say, Weidler realized. They had always looked to him for leadership and he had never failed them. But this time things were different. Matt Childress was a friend, not a thieving, murdering outlaw. His only fault lay in his inability to hold liquor.

Weidler felt the cold sweat stand out on the back of his neck. This was not going to be easy.

"There's not much to say," Weidler said tonelessly. "You all know Matt Childress's record. He's not at all bad when sober. He has no criminal record. But this is not the first time that he has shot up the town, destroyed property and endangered the lives of citizens.

"And it is not the first time he has laughed at and ignored the law. He is a bad example. If he keeps on getting away with it, there will be others to follow his ways. He can't be reformed."

He paused awhile, searching his mind for more to say. He could go on and list Matt Childress's good points. In all fairness Matt had that much coming, but the time for loyalty and sentiment was past, Weidler told himself. He had to think of what Childress meant to Virginia City, not what he meant to John Weidler.

At length he went on. "Matt Childress is your friend—and my friend. But that should not prejudice our decision. Nevada has sent word that Matt Childress should hang and that is the voice of six hundred miners. Now that decision is up to us—the Executive Committee. We all want Virginia City and Montana Territory to be a law-abiding place where honest men can live in peace and security.

"You will vote 'Aye' or 'Nay'."

It was Bill Leahy who broke the silence, saying, "Aye." One by one the others echoed Leahy's vote and the matter was done. Leahy walked behind the counter and took down a rope.

They acted quickly, anxious to get a distasteful thing done and out of the way. John Weidler led them out of Day & Miller's store. The group of armed miners were still there. Silent. Waiting. Some of them had lighted torches.

Weidler read their unspoken query and he bobbed his head in a wordless answer. They fell in behind the Committee.

Matt Childress was in Fielding's saloon, standing at the bar with Tom Kincaid at his side. Childress's face went white and he seemed to shrink a little when he spied Weidler, but only for a moment. Childress squared his shoulders and there was a tight smile on his pale lips as he waited for the Vigilantes to speak.

Kincaid had tensed, his face taking on the color of his red hair. Heat came to his eyes. They were friends, these men. They'd ridden through storm and cold to bring summary justice to the cutthroat Innocents.

They'd worked side by side—John Weidler, Matt Childress, Bill Leahy, Tom Kincaid.

"We've come for you, Matt," said Weidler.

"This is a hell of a joke to play on a man, John." Childress's voice trembled a little.

"It's no joke, Matt."

Tom Kincaid pushed forward, facing Weidler. "Are you really going through with it, John?"

"Yes."

Kincaid's face worked and it seemed as though he was going to unloose a torrent of words. But no sounds came, although his eyes distended and a sneer curled his lips. His eyes were flat and ice-cold.

Childress's thick face was very white now. "You can't mean hanging," he said, forcing a quavering laugh. "I know I'm in the wrong and I'm damned sorry. I swear before God it won't happen again. I got something coming. Banishment, maybe—but not hanging!"

Slowly, wishing that it could be otherwise, John Weidler shook his head. He was thankful that he was a reticent man who could hide his emotions behind a cold exterior, or he could never have endured watching the life going out from Matt Childress's eyes and the way he leaned against the bar as though he could not stand alone.

"You'll give me a little time then?" Childress asked dully. "A little time to put my affairs in order and to write a few letters? And to see my wife?"

"You have an hour," said Weidler.

"But an hour isn't enough! She can't make it here in that time."

"One hour," said John Weidler, turning away.

They had taken Matt Childress to one of the back rooms of Fielding's saloon where the doomed man had been supplied with pen and paper. Weidler was outside in the cold darkness, leaning against the front of the saloon. There was a cold cigar in Weidler's mouth but he kept drawing on it as if unaware that it had died.

Presently Wayne Dunning came up. He was a young man who clerked in Day & Miller's store. "They've sent a rider for Elizabeth Childress. As soon as the meeting was over and the verdict known, the rider took out for Childress's place. His wife will sure raise hell if she gets here before the execution."

"A woman's tears have a way of moving a man," said Weidler, frowning. "Tears once saved Hayes Lyons and Buck Stinson and Ned Ray from the noose and left them free to murder and rob for almost a year. But she won't get here in time."

"She'll probably use Big Bay. That horse is the fastest thing around here."

"She won't make it. What bothers me is Tom Kincaid. I thought he'd take it much harder than he has. I wonder why he hasn't?"

The hour passed and Childress's guards came out of Fielding's saloon with the doomed man walking in their midst. In the torchlight Childress's face was pasty gray and his step was a trifle unsteady.

He looked at John Weidler out of wide, haunted eyes but Weidler would not meet the man's stare. Weidler led the crowd of men to the corral in back of Day & Miller's store.

The corral gate was swung open and a rope was tossed over the cross-bar. A Vigilante came out of the back of the store, carrying an empty packing box which he placed underneath the dangling noose. Bill Leahy and Wayne Dunning lifted Childress up on the box.

Childress's pale face glistened with sweat and his voice was raspingly harsh. "You can't mean this! You're all just playing a joke on me. You can't really mean to hang me for what I did last night! For getting drunk and having some fun? I'm not complaining. I deserve something for always getting out of hand and causing Virginia City a lot of trouble but I don't deserve hanging.

"I ain't ever killed but one man in all my life and he asked for it. I ain't ever robbed anyone. I've always been an honest man. Banish me. Cut off my ear or my arm but don't hang me!"

Bill Leahy had climbed up on the packing box beside Childress and Leahy fitted the noose about the doomed man's neck, and then signaled that the other end of the rope be tied to a corral post.

John Weidler stood by watching, the dead cigar still between his lips. For a while he could not believe that all this was real. But the torchlight and the milling men and Matt Childress's gray face were authentic enough and Weidler suddenly wished that all this were a dream that he might brush aside and forget upon awakening.

He hardly heard Wayne Dunning who kept whispering, "We haven't much time. She'll be here soon. We haven't much time."

There was a commotion within the crowd and Tom Kincaid came bulling his way through the armed miners. His face was very red and his eyes flashed. He bulled up close to Weidler, so close that the Vigilante leader had to fall back a step.

"Call it off, John!" Kincaid ordered.

Weidler shook his head.

"So you're really going through with it," Kincaid roared. "And I held back. Thinking that you were just trying to put the fear of death in Matt.

Let him know the feel of a rope around his neck and that would calm him. That's what I thought you were up to, so I held back. I didn't think you were kill-crazy."

Weidler chewed his cold cigar. "Take it easy, Tom. Take it easy."

"You'll hang Matt only over my dead body," yelled Kincaid, swinging a wild fist at Weidler. The Vigilante had been expecting the blow and he swayed his head aside and out of Kincaid's reach.

Bill Leahy came in fast and before Kincaid could try another blow Leahy had his pistol against the back of Kincaid's neck.

"Hold on, Tom," Leahy snapped.

Kincaid dropped his arms and his fists unclenched. He never took his stare off Weidler's face. When Kincaid spoke his lips curled back from his teeth as though the very words were unclean.

"You filthy, kill-crazy murderer! I always felt you had a bad streak in you, John, but I never would own up to it because I called you friend. I felt we needed a cold man like you to put an end to Henry Plummer and the Innocents. I never thought the killing craze would worm into you until you'd hang anyone just to satisfy your filthy craving.

"We need the Vigilantes. I was one of them, and I am not ashamed of what I did. But tonight you're tearing down all the good we ever built. You're blackening the name of the Vigilantes in a way that can never be forgotten. When histories of the Vigilantes are written you'll be marked down as a kill-crazy murderer, and all those associated with you will have to carry the same black brand."

Weidler took it all in silence. He stood there stolidly, the dead cigar clamped between his teeth, meeting Tom Kincaid's hot stare. Weidler's pulse was pounding and he could feel the throb of the vein at his temple.

He knew a coldness that filled him completely, the identical coldness he'd always felt at moments like these. Kincaid's words fell as from an alien world.

"One word from you and Matt could be saved," Kincaid went on. "Had you stood up for Matt, put in a good word for him, the Committee would never have voted as it did.

"It's an evil and dark day for Montana Territory when you've taken to hanging men for minor offenses. But Matt Childress will be the first and the last. I can't save him. I know that. But I'll see to it that you'll never hang another. Mind that, John."

Weidler turned his head and his stare away from Kincaid. Matt Childress was mumbling brokenly, incoherently on the packing box. Weidler felt a weakness creeping over his will. The time had come and he had to make his choice—between Matt Childress and a Virginia City that would be quiet and still and peaceful, where a man could live and be proud of his town.

And suddenly he realized that if he hesitated much longer, he could not go through with it.

So he took the cigar from his mouth and said clearly, coldly, "Men, do your duty!"

Afterward, when Childress's lifeless body was swaying in the night wind, there came the thunderous clopping of a horse's hoofs and a rider burst into the smoky torchlight. It was a woman, and she flung herself out of the saddle before the horse had halted. She stopped short when she spied the dangling body.

Weidler was up against the corral fence with Bill Leahy and Wayne Dunning on either side of him. They all watched Elizabeth Childress. She was a tall woman with a violently beautiful face. They knew little about her except that she lived with Matt Childress and he called her his wife. She stared at Childress's body a long while, but no tears or cries came. She spoke at last, her voice choking with grief.

"Oh, the shame of it," she cried as she knelt beneath the dead man and clasped her arms around his stiffening legs. "That Matt Childress should be hanged like a common felon. Where were his friends? Why did they let this happen to him who was a better man than all of them?

"Better that someone had taken a gun and shot my Matt down. If I had been here, I'd have done that—rather than suffer him to hang!"

She seemed to notice Weidler for the first time. The woman rose slowly to her feet and she walked haltingly, stooped forward a little as if to see better. And as she came close, Weidler saw the tightness of her features and the way the cords stood out on her neck.

He expected her to speak, to burst out in an orgy of denunciations, but she only stared at him, her lips working silently. Then she went back to Childress.

Weidler spat the shredded cigar from his teeth and walked away.

He found that Martha had put the children to bed and that she had a pot of boiling coffee on the stove for him. She didn't say anything but he could feel from her silent presence that she yearned for some comforting words to say to him.

He poured the coffee with fingers that were stiffly untrembling and, looking up, he caught her eyes and smiled a little.

"You'd better go to bed," he told her. "I'm staying up a while longer."

She left the room and he was instantly sorry she had gone. It felt so empty now—empty as he was himself. All he knew was a hollow feeling within him and a vast restlessness. He went to the kitchen door and threw it open, standing full in the soft sweep of the night wind.

He stood looking off at the sky but not seeing the stars or the moon or the scattered clouds flowing along with the wind. All he saw was Matt Childress's swaying body and the loathing and hatred in Tom Kincaid's eyes.

He was standing there in the chillness of the night when Bill Leahy came again.

"What is it, Bill?"

"Tom Kincaid is after you."

"He'll get over it."

Leahy placed a big hand against the doorjamb. His breathing had calmed. "He's taken on a load of drinks. He's in a bad mind, John. He's coming over here to have it out with you."

"He's drunk. He doesn't know what he's doing."

"But he's doing it just the same."

"Why has he got it in for me?" Weidler asked savagely.

"He blames you for Matt. Says if you'd put in a good word for Matt, he'd never been hanged. There's no telling Tom otherwise. I've tried for half an hour but Tom won't listen."

"Then I'll have to try," said Weidler.

"He's got a gun, John."

Weidler shrugged. Bill Leahy came in close and slipped something into Weidler's pocket. He reached down and felt the cold metal of a revolver.

They had turned out into the street when they spied the man coming toward them. He walked with a rolling step much like a sailor's but Weidler knew that the roll of the walk was due to too many drinks.

Kincaid had stopped, his legs planted wide. His head was thrust forward and he raised a hand and pushed his hat back from his forehead. Recognition came to him for he laughed and said:

"Well, well, if it ain't Bloody John!"

"Hello, Tom," said Weidler easily. "I'm on my way to Fielding's for a drink. Will you join me?"

"Drink, hell!" exploded Kincaid wrathfully. Then he laughed again. "I won't join you in a drink but you sure will join Matt in hell!"

He had been holding his right hand at his belt and he suddenly flung up his arm. Weidler saw moonlight flash on the polished metal of Kincaid's pistol.

"Hold it, you damn fool!" Weidler cried, rushing forward. Kincaid laughed and his cold eyes looked down the sights of his gun but his bullet was wide.

Before he could fire again, Weidler was on him.

Kincaid was bringing his weapon up again but Weidler grasped the gun, holding it away from him. Kincaid lunged, grunting, and he drove the hard toe of his boot into Weidler's shin. Weidler released his hold and as he wavered on the point of unbalance, Kincaid shoved out his leg, sending Weidler sprawling.

He rolled over quickly to find himself staring in the bore of Kincaid's weapon.

Weidler hardly realized his actions. Perhaps it was the instinct of self-preservation that prompted him to act so automatically. For the gun in his hand roared, and as Kincaid staggered, it roared again.

Kincaid made a half-turn and it looked as if he wanted to walk away when he said quite clearly, "Oh my God!" and fell.

They came running, the watching men, and they gathered around the fallen Tom Kincaid. Weidler's friends were about him, but he was heedless to their queries about his welfare. Two words stuck to his mind as he walked away. Two words hurled at him by someone looking down at dead Tom Kincaid.

"Bloody killer!"

A strange, cold loneliness settled down over Weidler. He knew that he'd never forget the double tragedy of this night. The memory of it would ever haunt him, but, looking about him, he saw that Virginia City was quiet now, a natural quiet, and that was consolation enough.

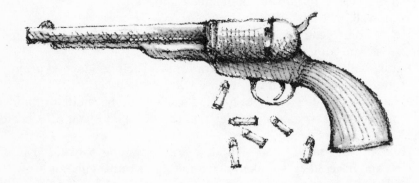

Markers

BILL PRONZINI

JACK BOHANNON AND I had been best friends for close to a year, ever since he'd hired on at the Two Bar Cross, but if it hadn't been for a summer squall that came up while the two of us were riding fence, I'd never have found out about who and what he was. Or about the markers.

We'd been out two weeks, working the range southeast of Eagle Mountain. The fences down along there were in middling fair shape, considering the winter we'd had; Bohannon and I sported calluses from the wire cutters and stretchers, but truth to tell, we hadn't been exactly overworking ourselves. Just kind of moving along at an easy pace. The weather had been fine—cool crisp mornings, warm afternoons, sky scrubbed clean of clouds on most days—and it made you feel good just to be there in all that sweet-smelling open space.

As it happened, we were about two miles east of the Eagle Mountain line shack when the squall came up. Came up fast, too, along about three o'clock in the afternoon, the way a summer storm does sometimes in Wyoming Territory. We'd been planning to spend a night at the line shack anyway, to replenish our supplies, so as soon as the sky turned cloudy dark we lit a shuck straight for it. The rain started before we were halfway there, and by the time we raised the shack, the downpour was such that you couldn't see a dozen rods in front of you. We were both soaked in spite of our slickers; rain like that has a way of slanting in under any slicker that was ever made.

The shack was just a one-room sod building with walls coated in ashes-and-clay and a whipsawed wood floor. All that was in it was a pair of bunks, a table and two chairs, a larder, and a big stone fireplace. First things we did when we came inside, after sheltering the horses for the night in the lean-to out back, were to build a fire on the hearth and raid the larder. Then, while we dried off, we brewed up some coffee and cooked a pot of beans and salt pork. It was full dark by then and that storm was kicking up a hell of a fuss; you could see lightning blazes outside the single window, and hear thunder grumbling in the distance and the wind moaning in the chimney flue.

When we finished supper Bohannon pulled a chair over in front of the fire, and I sat on one of the bunks, and we took out the makings. Neither of us said much at first. We didn't have to talk to enjoy each other's company; we'd spent a fair lot of time together in the past year—working the ranch, fishing and hunting, a little mild carousing in Saddle River— and we had an easy kind of friendship. Bohannon had never spoken much about himself, his background, his people, but that was all right by me. Way I figured it, every man was entitled to as much privacy as he wanted.

But that storm made us both restless; it was the kind of night a man sooner or later feels like talking. And puts him in a mood to share confidences, too. Inside a half hour we were swapping stories, mostly about places we'd been and things we'd done and seen.

That was how we came to the subject of markers—grave markers, first off—with me the one who brought it up. I was telling about the time I'd spent a year prospecting for gold in the California Mother Lode, before I came back home to Wyoming Territory and turned to ranch work, and I recollected the grave I'd happened on one afternoon in a rocky meadow south of Sonora. A mound of rocks, it was, with a wooden marker anchored at the north end. And on the marker was an epitaph scratched out with a knife.

"I don't know who done it," I said, "or how come that grave was out where it was, but that marker sure did make me curious. Still does. What it said was, 'Last resting place of I. R. Lyon. Lived and died according to his name.' "

I'd told that story a time or two before and it had always brought a chuckle, if not a horse laugh. But Bohannon didn't chuckle. Didn't say anything, either. He just sat looking into the fire, not moving, a quirly drifting smoke from one corner of his mouth. He appeared to be studying on something inside his head.

I said, "Well, *I* thought it was a mighty unusual marker, anyhow."

Bohannon still didn't say anything. Another ten seconds or so passed before he stirred—took a last drag off his quirly and tossed it into the fire.

"I saw an unusual marker myself once," he said then, quiet. His voice sounded different than I'd ever heard it.

"Where was that?"

"Nevada. Graveyard in Virginia City, about five years ago."

"What'd it say?"

"Said 'Here lies Adam Bricker. Died of hunger in Virginia City, August 1882.' "

"Hell. How could a man die of hunger in a town?"

"That's what I wanted to know. So I asked around to find out."

"Did you?"

"I did," Bohannon said. "According to the local law, Adam Bricker'd been killed in a fight over a woman. Stabbed by the woman's husband, man named Greenbaugh. Supposed to've been self-defense."

"If Bricker was stabbed, how could he have died of hunger?"

"Greenbaugh put that marker on Bricker's grave. His idea of humor, I reckon. Hunger Bricker died of wasn't hunger for food, it was hunger for the woman. Or so Greenbaugh claimed."

"Wasn't it the truth?"

"Folks I talked to didn't think so," Bohannon said. "Story was, Bricker admired Greenbaugh's wife and courted her some; she and Greenbaugh weren't living together and there was talk of a divorce. Nobody thought he trifled with her, though. That wasn't Bricker's way. Folks said the real reason Greenbaugh killed him was because of money Bricker owed him. Bricker's claim was that he'd been cheated out of it, so he refused to pay when Greenbaugh called in his marker. They had an argument, there was pushing and shoving, and when Bricker drew a gun and tried to shoot him, Greenbaugh used his knife. That was his story, at least. Only witness just happened to be a friend of his."

"Who was this Greenbaugh?"

"Gambler," Bohannon said. "Fancy man. Word was he'd cheated other men at cards, and debauched a woman or two—that was why his wife left him—but nobody ever accused him to his face except Adam Bricker. Town left him pretty much alone."

"Sounds like a prize son of a bitch," I said.

"He was."

"Men like that never get what's coming to them, seems like."

"This one did."

"You mean somebody cashed in his chips for him?"

"That's right," Bohannon said. "Me."

I leaned forward a little. He was looking into the fire, with his head cocked to one side, like he was listening for another rumble of thunder. It seemed too quiet in there, of a sudden, so I cleared my throat and smacked a hand against my thigh.

I said, "How'd it happen? He cheat you at cards?"

"He didn't have the chance."

"Then how . . . ?"

Bohannon was silent again. One of the burning logs slid off the grate and made a sharp cracking sound; the noise seemed to jerk him into talking again. He said, "There was a vacant lot a few doors down from the saloon where he spent most of his time. I waited in there one night, late, and when he came along, on his way to his room at one of the hotels, I stepped out and put my gun up to his head. And I shot him."

"My God," I said. "You mean you *murdered* him?"

"You could call it that."

"But damn it, man, why?"

"He owed me a debt. So I called in his marker."

"What debt?"

"Adam Bricker's life."

"I don't see—"

"I didn't tell you how I happened to be in Virginia City. Or how I happened to visit the graveyard. The reason was Adam Bricker. Word reached me that he was dead, but not how it happened, and I went there to find out."

"Why? What was Bricker to you?"

"My brother," he said. "My real name is Jack Bricker."

I got up off the bunk and went to the table and turned the lamp up a little. Then I got out my sack of Bull Durham, commenced to build another smoke. Bohannon didn't look at me; he was still staring into the fire.

When I had my quirly lit I said, "What'd you do after you shot Greenbaugh?"

"Got on my horse and rode out of there."

"You figure the law knows you did it?"

"Maybe. But the law doesn't worry me much."

"Then how come you changed your name? How come you traveled all the way up here from Nevada?"

"Greenbaugh had a brother, too," he said. "Just like Adam had me. He was living in Virginia City at the time and he knows I shot Greenbaugh. I've heard more than once that he's looking for me—been looking ever since it happened."

"So he can shoot you like you shot his brother?"

"That's right. I owe him a debt, Harv, same as Greenbaugh owed me one. One of these days he's going to find me, and when he does he'll call in his marker, same as I did mine."

"Maybe he won't find you," I said. "Maybe he's stopped looking by this time."

"He hasn't stopped looking. He'll never stop looking. He's a hardcase like his brother was."

"That don't mean he'll ever cross your trail—"

"No. But he will. It's just a matter of time."

"What makes you so all-fired sure?"

"A feeling I got," he said. "Had it ever since I heard he was after me."

"Guilt," I said, quiet.

"Maybe. I'm not a killer, not truly, and I've had some bad nights over Greenbaugh. But it's more than that. It's something I know is going to happen, like knowing the rain will stop tonight or tomorrow and we'll have clear weather again. Maybe because there are too many markers involved, if you take my meaning—the grave kind and the debt kind. One of these days I'll be dead because I owe a marker."

Neither of us had anything more to say that night. Bohannon—I couldn't seem to think of him as Bricker—got up from in front of the fire and climbed into his bunk, and when I finished my smoke I did the same. What he'd told me kept rattling around inside my head. It was some while before I finally got to sleep.

I woke up right after dawn, like I always do—and there was Bohannon, with his saddlebags packed and his bedroll under one arm, halfway to the door. Beyond him, through the window, I could see pale gray light and enough of the sky to make out broken clouds; the storm had passed.

"What the hell, Bohannon?"

"Time for me to move on," he said.

"Just like that? Without notice to anybody?"

"I reckon it's best that way," he said. "A year in one place is long enough—maybe too long. I was fixing to leave anyway, after you and me finished riding fence. That's why I went ahead and told you about my brother and Greenbaugh and the markers. Wouldn't have if I'd been thinking on staying."

I swung my feet off the bunk and reached for my Levi's. "It don't make any difference to me," I said. "Knowing what you done, I mean."

"Sure it does, Harv. Hell, why lie to each other about it?"

"All right. But where'll you go?"

He shrugged. "Don't know. Somewhere. Best if you don't know, best if I don't myself."

"Listen, Bohannon—"

"Nothing to listen to." He came over and put out his hand, and I took it, and there was the kind of feeling inside me I'd had as a button when a friend died of the whooping cough. "Been good knowing you, Harv," he said. "I hope you don't come across a marker someday with my name on it." And he was gone before I finished buttoning up my pants.

From the window I watched him saddle his horse. I didn't go outside to say a final word to him—there wasn't anything more to say; he'd been right about that—and he didn't look back when he rode out. I never saw him again.

But that's not the whole story, not by any means.

Two years went by without me hearing anything at all about Bohannon. Then Curly Polk, who'd worked with the two of us on the Two Bar Cross and then gone down to Texas for a while, drifted back our way for the spring roundup, and he brought word that Bohannon was dead. Shot six weeks earlier, in the Pecos River town of Santa Rosa, New Mexico.

But it hadn't been anybody named Greenbaugh who pulled the trigger on him. It had been a local cowpuncher, liquored up, spoiling for trouble; and it had happened over a spilled drink that Bohannon had refused to pay for. The only reason Curly found out about it was that he happened to pass through Santa Rosa on the very day they hung the puncher for his crime.

It shook me some when Curly told about it. Not because Bohannon was dead—too much time had passed for that—but because of the circumstances of his death. He'd believed, and believed hard, that someday he'd pay for killing Greenbaugh; that there were too many markers in his life and someday he'd die on account of one he owed. Well, he'd been wrong. And yet the strange thing, the pure crazy thing, was that he'd also been right.

The name of the puncher who'd shot him was Sam Marker.

In the Silence

PEGGY S. CURRY

DAYLIGHT WAS THERE at his eyes before it seemed he'd been asleep. Then he saw the big foot by the tarp-covered bedroll, and the foot moved to prod him again. "Are you sleepin' all day?" demanded Angus Duncan.

Jimmy McDonald sat up and blinked at the big red-haired man who towered above him. Then he reached into the breast pocket of his heavy wool shirt and his chapped fingers brought out the silver brooch with its glinting purple jewel. He'd worn the brooch on his kilt when he left the hills of Scotland to come to Wyoming and learn the sheep business.

"Ah, that miserable glass and cheap silver," Angus Duncan muttered. "What kind of a never-grow-up are you when you must carry a trinket in your pocket?"

Jimmy couldn't answer. There was no way to put into words what he felt about the brooch. It meant home, the home he'd left to be under the guidance of this distant cousin of his father, the home he hadn't seen for two years. *Aye, that was a green and wonderful land across the ocean,* Jimmy thought, trying to stretch himself awake. *Not mean country like this with its late, cold spring and its mountain always there, frowning down on you.*

Jimmy shivered. Already he feared the mountain that towered above the campground almost as much as he feared Angus Duncan. Terrifying tales were told of those who lived too long alone on the mountains. "In the silence," the herders called it, and sometimes, they said, a man too long in the silence was daft for the rest of his lifetime.

"Get up and stir the sheep," Angus Duncan said now. "Lambs should be at their breakfast before we start them up the mountain. Then we'll not have the ewes hiding from us among the rocks and brush to feed their young."

Jimmy bent to pull on his boots. Finally he stood, tall for his fourteen years, and looked up at Angus Duncan. "And what's my wages for sitting the summer alone on the mountain with your sheep?"

Angus Duncan's frosty blue eyes looked down on him from under the heavy red eyebrows and the stern mouth moved at the corners in what might have been a smile. "Not content with grub and decent blankets anymore, eh? Well, I'll tell you—" Angus Duncan paused and looked at the mountain, its pines still black against the first morning light.

"Your summer's wages," Angus Duncan said at last, "will be the long-tailed lambs."

A terrible empty ache began in Jimmy's stomach. "But—they can die. The coyotes can kill them, and the wild range horses run over them, trampling them. I—I could work the whole summer and have nothing left to show for it."

Angus Duncan grunted. "Well said for a lad that's slow to grow up. You've spoken the truth, and the truth can be a hard thing to face. If you save the lambs, you'll beat the best herder's wages. If you lose them, you've yourself to reckon with."

So Angus Duncan was laying out a hard lot for him, a mean job, and Jimmy recalled saying as much when he'd asked Angus Duncan to let him stay another month on the prairie with the other herders in their comfortable canvas-roofed wagons. "Let me stay with them," Jimmy had said. "Let me move to high country when they do."

Angus Duncan had laughed in his face. "Does a boy learn sheep business by sitting with old men under shelter? Why, when I was ten years old, I trailed to the Big Horn Mountains . . ."

Now, in the cold of this June morning, Jimmy went to where the sheep were bedded on the gentle slope that marked the beginning of the mountain. As he moved among them, they stirred like old gray stones coming suddenly to life and got up and stretched and nudged their sleeping lambs. These were the dock-tailed lambs, tails cut on the level prairie and with their legs already strong for the mountain trip.

He looked carefully for the swollen ewes, their bellies like gray barrels; the late lambs would run to sixty or seventy. *Aye,* he thought, *if I could keep only half I'd be a man of wealth.* But his lambs would be the late catches, born far from the familiar ground of the drop herd, prey to coyotes, early snowstorms that hit the mountain, and the salt-hungry horses that ran wild on the open range. Far from the world his lambs would be, brought to life near the sky, with no one to help him keep them from harm.

Jimmy's shoulders sagged as he moved toward the small fire with its smoke and fragrance of coffee. Angus Duncan silently handed him a tin plate, and they ate without speaking to each other, then loaded the packhorses and put saddles on the riding horses. On the packhorses were Jimmy's supplies for the summer—a tent, a small teepee, sacks of salt for the sheep, food and bedding.

It took five hours to get the sheep on the mountain, moving them slowly along the narrow paths between trees and rocks. But the dogs worked well. Jimmy and Angus walked, leading the horses, and it was hot before they nooned up in the high country. They rested while the sheep were quiet and in the afternoon moved them across the broad back of the mountain to where the snowdrifts still lay with their adjoining pools of water. Here the sheep would drink while there was water, and later use the springs that sometimes went dry by the end of summer.

"You'll set up your main tent here," Angus Duncan said, "and come back for food and to water the sheep. At night set up your teepee by the bed ground. I'll be back in a couple of weeks to move you on a bit. And one day, if you keep your wits about you, I'll let you be a camp mover instead of a herder."

He'll make me no camp mover, when my long-tailed lambs are dead, Jimmy thought bitterly. *I'll be at the herding till I'm an old man if all the wages I get are long-tailed lambs.* And in anger he said loudly, "Why do you come up here so soon—snow still on and nights like the middle of winter and not a soul to keep me company? I see no other sheep outfits up here."

"The early sheep get the best grass and plenty of water," Angus Duncan said. "You'll have company by July—and the finest lambs." Then Angus nodded to himself and rode away, leading the packhorses.

The silence of the mountain seemed to grow out of the grass and trees until it came to stand all around Jimmy. His heart beat loudly and sweat broke out on his body. He called to the sheepdogs, his voice sounding strange and hollow, then went into the tent where the small stove, left from last year's early camp, had been set up. He put his bacon in a white sack and hung it high in a tree, for the flies wouldn't go high in the wind or the thin air. He stacked his canned goods in the corner and put other groceries in a box with a strong catch to keep it shut. Here he had his flour, salt, sugar, baking powder, soda, and sourdough mix.

The silence kept coming into the tent while he worked. And suddenly he felt an overwhelming desire for candy. But Angus Duncan wasn't one to feed his herders anything sweet. Plain food, Angus Duncan always said, kept a man lean and strong and did no harm to his teeth.

Forget about teeth, Jimmy thought, finding a can of condensed milk and punching holes in it with his pocketknife. Then he got a tin cup and filled it with snow from a drift near the tent. He poured canned milk over the snow and covered this with sugar. He ate greedily. *Maybe the silence won't bother so much with a full belly.*

Jimmy set up a small teepee near where the sheep were gathering to bed down for the night. "Don't bull the sheep about their bed ground," Angus had cautioned. "They know better than you where they'll sleep best." He set his .22 rifle in the corner of the teepee. It was a single-shot and Angus

Duncan had said, "Enough gun for you, and see you don't ventilate a leg or foot with it. Nobody'll be around to bandage your bleeding."

No, Jimmy thought, feeling cold, *there is nobody around.*

Two of the late lambs were born just before twilight and no sooner had the mothers licked their faces clean and the yellow saddles of membrane started to dry on their backs than the coyotes began howling.

Jimmy hurried to build fires around the bed ground, heaping up broken tree limbs and sagebrush, swinging the ax until his arms ached. When darkness came, he lighted the fires that circled the sheep. The thin, eerie *yip-yapping* of the coyotes rang out from time to time. Jimmy got his gun and walked around the bed ground. Once he saw coyotes at the edge of the firelight, their eyes glowing red, and he rushed toward them, the gun ready. They slipped away into the darkness.

He slept little that night, curled half in and half out of the teepee, the rifle close beside him. And it wasn't until the sheep nooned up that he felt free to lie down among the sagebrush and sleep deeply, the sun pouring over him.

He wakened to the thunder of horses' hooves and sat up blinking. He knew before he saw them come racing out of the trees into the open plateau that these were the wild range horses. Some had broken away from corrals and jumped fences and had run for years on open ranges. Now they wandered onto the mountain and were crazy in their need for salt, for there no salt sage grew.

While he screamed and groped for rocks to throw, they thundered past him, scattering the sheep. When they had gone, one of his new long-tailed lambs lay trampled and bloody and dead. He put out more salt for the sheep and vowed to shoot the range horses if they came back.

That night Jimmy again built fires to keep away the coyotes and from time to time paced around the bed ground. Five late lambs came during the night. The wind blew in from the north, spitting rain, but this he didn't fear as much as the coyotes or the range horses. There was shelter for the new lambs under the big sagebrush, and Angus Duncan had told him that sheared ewes died from cold more easily than lambs. From the moment of breath, the lamb was at home in the chill, Angus said, but the sheared ewe was without the cover she'd grown used to and couldn't stand much cold.

When the sheep nooned again, Jimmy was in need of sleep, but now the great silence of the mountain plagued him more than weariness. He got on his saddle horse and rode quickly to the rim of the mountain where he could look down on the prairie and see the white-roofed sheepwagons of other herders.

It was almost like talking to another person to see the wagons. He reached in his shirt pocket and took out the silver brooch he'd worn on his kilt in that long-ago time when he'd left Scotland. He turned the brooch in his hand, as though the faraway herders could see it shining. The silence roared in his ears.

At last he rode back to the big tent near the melting snowdrift. He unsaddled the horse and put hobbles on him. Then he noticed the big footprints where the ground was moist near the water hole. *He was not alone in the silence.*

Jimmy ran to the tent, shouting, "Hey there!" But his voice seemed to bounce back at him from the canvas walls and he saw that the tent was empty. Disappointment filled him. It was surely a strange thing that a man would not stay and talk with him. In such a big, lonely country men didn't pass up the opportunity to talk to one another.

The silence of the mountain came pouring into the tent. He closed the tent flap as though to shut it out, but gigantic and real, the silence was there, all around him. *I must take hold of myself,* he thought. *I must look after the sheep.* And after a while the big silence ebbed out of the tent, much the way a tide draws back from the shore.

That night the coyotes were bad, circling the fringe of the lighted fires and making the sheep restless. Doggedly, Jimmy kept the fires going and walked around and around the ring of bedded sheep. Once he stopped and stared, for he was sure he had caught a glimpse of a man at the edge of the firelight. Then, it seemed, the man faded away. Queer little prickles ran up the back of Jimmy's neck. *Am I going daft?* he wondered.

At the end of ten days Jimmy was thin and hard, and his eyes, red from wind and sun, burned fiercely in his taut young face. Loneliness was in him, filling him like a bitter food he couldn't digest. Periodically the silence dropped over him in a smothering cloud and within it he'd stand, trembling and sweating. Once it was so terrifying he dropped to his knees and clutched the sagebrush to assure himself of his own reality.

There were now fourteen of the small long-tailed lambs. The bold, brassy blue sky mocked him, and out of it came the big eagles, plummeting down toward the new lambs. Sometimes he ran, shouting, to frighten them away. Sometimes he shot at them. Once, on the far side of the herd from where he stood, an eagle got a lamb, soared high with it, and dropped it. Returned and soared again and dropped it. By the time the eagle came in for the third catch, Jimmy was close enough to shoot at it. The eagle went away, but when Jimmy got to the lamb, the life had gone.

In these days that became more dream than reality, he ceased to hate Angus Duncan. He knew if Angus Duncan were to ride out of the aspen trees, now coming green in a quick mist, he'd run to the big man as though he were a lad again and running to his father.

On a late afternoon, when the wind was down and the shadows were long from the rocks and trees, a man came suddenly and stood by the big tent, a man with a gun in a bloody hand. There was something terrible and frightening about him; it breathed out of his dirty clothes, the blood on his hand, the mad light in his eyes.

He said clearly to Jimmy: "I've come to take the long-tailed lambs. The coyotes will get them anyhow."

Blinding anger came up in Jimmy. He tried to collect his wits, hold in check his rising terror. Then slowly he reached in his shirt pocket and brought out the silver brooch with the shiny purple stone that was the color of heather in bloom. He let the treasure lie in the palm of his hand where the sunlight struck it from the west.

"You'll kill me to get my lambs," Jimmy said quietly, turning the brooch to catch more sunlight so that it gleamed brighter than before.

"What's that in your fist?" the stranger asked.

"Silver and precious stone," Jimmy replied. "Worth more than all the band of sheep." He looked into the stranger's eyes and saw them glitter.

"If you steal this," Jimmy went on, "a curse will be on you. This can't be killed for or stolen. But it can be bargained for."

Now that he was making a story, he ceased to be afraid. It was like listening to his mother talk when the sea was rough and the fishing boats were in danger. Always his mother had told the children stories until the sea seemed a friend, and faith would come to them that their father would get home.

"I heard of a man who stole one of these jewels," Jimmy said, "killing a man to get it. Blindness struck him." And he turned the silver brooch until the sun glinted on the glass, making a light that fell full in the stranger's eyes.

"But," Jimmy went on, "it can be bargained for, and no harm done. I'll bargain with you—this for you, if you leave my long-tailed lambs." And he moved closer so the wild eyes could look more closely at the stone.

"I can take it—and the lambs." The stranger spat on the ground.

"Aye." Jimmy nodded. "That is so. And you'll have to kill me, for I'll fight. It's for you to choose whether there's a curse on you or not."

The stranger didn't speak.

Jimmy's hand tightened on the brooch. "I'll never be the same without it," he said, more to himself than to the stranger. "It is giving something inside me away."

Then the evil-smelling man moved close and held out the hand with the bloody fingers. "I'll take it—and leave your sheep."

When the brooch fell from his hand to the hand of the stranger, tears began to run down Jimmy's cheeks and the strength left his legs. He fell down to the ground and lay as one dead. When he awoke, it was dark, and he was cold and hungry. He jumped up, thinking only of the sheep, and ran to build fires and walk the bed ground. The dogs greeted him and licked his hands.

Two days later when Angus Duncan came riding up from the flat country, he looked sharply at Jimmy and said, "Have you forgotten to eat, boy? What's happened to you?" And the big man got off his horse and put his hand gently on Jimmy's shoulder.

Jimmy talked slowly and carefully, telling his story of the stranger. Afterward he waited for Angus Duncan to laugh at him or tease him. But Angus neither laughed nor spoke. He walked over to the dwindling water hole near the snowdrift that now was almost gone and looked at the ground. "There is no track of a man here," he said, "but, of course, the sheep have been in to drink and trampled the earth."

He came back to Jimmy and said, "I brought you some sweets. Strange, how a man hungers for them on the mountain." And he took a sack of candy and put it in Jimmy's hand.

Once Jimmy would have stood there and stuffed the candy in his mouth and eaten until the sack was empty. But now he only held the sack and said casually, "I may have some tonight after my supper. Thank you."

"In the silence," Angus Duncan said, "a man learns to be strong. And the silence is not only on the mountain, Jimmy. Somewhere—before he dies—every man must meet it and struggle with it on his own terms. In the silence we must face only ourselves." Again Angus Duncan's hand touched the boy's shoulder. "I see now you have done that."

Jimmy's hand moved to his empty shirt pocket. *I could have lost the brooch, there at the edge of the mountain when I was looking to the prairie and the wagons of other herders,* he thought. *Still—*

"Well," he said, "you'll want to take a look at the sheep over there. I've lost only two lambs—one to the wild horses and another to the eagles."

He walked with Angus Duncan toward the sheep. The light of later afternoon had given new shapes to everything, making even the grass look thicker and stronger. The silence was still there. But Jimmy smiled to himself, letting it move beside him as an old and familiar friend.

Wolf Night

BILL CRIDER
for Rodney Allbright

CARLOTTA LONGORIA WAS the first one to die that month. Down at the dance hall, they called her the Spanish Angel, and she danced in a full red dress with black trim, swinging it just high enough at the right times to give the boys a flash of ankle, and, if they were lucky, of her calves. There were those who claimed to have seen more, but no one really believed them. She had long black hair that she pulled tight, making a smooth and shiny covering for her head, with a white part right down the middle, and she always tucked a rose behind her right ear.

She was the prettiest woman most men in San Benito had ever seen.

She wasn't pretty when they found her that morning. Her throat had been ripped out by something with very sharp teeth, and that something had torn her up even worse than some of the others. The red dress was ripped to shreds, and the blood that stained it was dark and almost black in the morning light. Her face was virtually untouched, but the harsh sun made it look coarse and lined in a way that it never had in the dim light of the dance hall. No, she wasn't very pretty at all that morning.

"We got to do something about this, Sheriff," Tal Harper said. "This is the sixth one. The sixth!"

Sheriff Butch Whitney looked down at the mangled body with a sick churning in his belly. Harper was absolutely correct in his count. Carlotta was the sixth woman to die in San Benito in the last three months. There was a maniac on the loose, or something worse.

He was afraid it was something worse.

"It's a goddamned wolf, is what it is," Tom Strake said. Strake was Whitney's deputy. "Look at those marks. Couldn't nothin' but a wolf leave teeth marks like that, and no man would tear a woman up that way and just leave her layin' there. Good Lord!"

"Yeah," Harper said. "It's a wolf, all right. Ain't that what Willie Jackson told us it was?"

172

Sheriff Whitney belched, tasted something sour in his mouth. "Sure, he told us that. He told us he got off five shots at it, too, with his .44, and hit it at least four times. And we never found a speck of blood from it or any sign that he hit it. He's been known to have a couple. Or more than a couple. He was drunk as a lord. There aren't any wolves in these parts. Least not right in town."

They were standing in an alley not two blocks from the dance hall. Carlotta had no doubt been headed home after her last performance, unescorted as usual. She might have been a dance-hall girl, but it wasn't her practice to have anything to do with the men who came to watch her. If you got too familiar with them, they didn't want to see you anymore, or at least they didn't want to see you dance. They would have other things on their minds.

"If I told her once, I told her a hundred times," Harper said. He was the owner of the Golden Slippers, the dance hall where Carlotta had worked. "I told her, 'Carlotta, never leave here and walk home by yourself. Look what happened to Teeny.'" Teeny had been another of Harper's dancers. She had lost her throat about a month before.

"Hell, look what happened to all those other women," Strake said. "All of 'em. Torn all to goddamned pieces. You gotta do something, Sheriff."

Whitney knew that he had to do something. He just didn't know what it was that he could do. Personally, though, he believed what Willie Jackson had said. He believed that Jackson had shot that wolf. He would never tell Strake and Harper that, but he had seen Jackson's face and he never saw a man so sober.

"That son of a bitch was big, too, Sheriff," Jackson had said. "Bigger than a man, almost. I hope to God I never see a thing like that again in my life."

And to make sure that he never did, Jackson had moved away from San Benito the next day.

"I've noticed something else," Strake said. "I think we can tell when that booger's gonna do his killin'."

"How's that?" Harper said.

"It's a full moon," Strake said. "You think about it. Ever' woman that's been killed has been killed durin' a full moon."

"I'll be damned," Harper said. "I believe you're right. You hear that, Sheriff?"

Whitney heard, all right, and his stomach gave a sick lurch. He had already figured out that much for himself.

He turned away from the body. "You boys call Doc Robb," he said, not looking at them. "I got to talk to somebody."

"Who?" Harper said. "Who you got to talk to?"

"The schoolteacher," Whitney said, striding away from them, not looking back.

"What the hell?" Strake said.

Harper just shrugged, and they went to find the town doctor, who was also the undertaker. Carlotta didn't need a doctor, but she could use a good undertaker about then.

Adolph Stutz had come to the little town of San Benito at the beginning of the fall, only a few months before, and set up a school. He spoke English with a thick accent, but he was the only teacher in town, and a lot of families sent their children to him to learn reading and ciphering. When he answered the door for Whitney, his speech was already a little slurred, and he hadn't shaved that day. It was a Saturday, and there would be no school. Stutz was often drunk on the weekends, and occasionally during the week. Most folks considered that a small price to pay to have a teacher in town. If he didn't have some bad habits, he'd be in some bigger place, making a lot more money than the citizens of San Benito could afford to pay him.

"I need to talk to you, Dolph," Whitney said.

"C'm in, zir," Stutz said. He staggered a little as he stood back from the door to allow Whitney to enter.

Whitney entered the sour-smelling room. He had been there before, having come by to talk to the teacher when the man first came to town. The parents liked to know a little about the person who was going to teach their children. Whitney liked to talk, and so did Stutz, so they had gotten along all right. Stutz had not given much information about his background, but he had admitted his weakness for the bottle. He had also seemed to know a lot about such things as Shakespeare and Robert Browning. He had a shelf almost full of books. Suitably impressed, Whitney had reported his findings to the parents, who had contracted with Stutz for the instruction of their children. Since that time, Whitney had visited Stutz on several other occasions.

Stutz shoved a pile of dirty clothes off a horsehair-stuffed sofa and invited Whitney to sit down. Whitney lowered himself to the sofa, and Stutz walked over to a mahogany chair beside a small table. On the table there were a bottle of cheap whiskey and a shot glass.

Stutz sat and poured himself a glass from the bottle. "As you can zee, Zheriff, I do not drink heavily. Only two ounzes at a time!" He laughed heartily and knocked back the liquor. He did not offer any to Whitney.

"Zo," he said, wiping the back of his left hand across his mouth, "what it is that I can do for you this day?"

"I want you to tell me again about that stuff you told me before."

The windows of the room were heavily curtained, but some light came through them. Stutz held his glass up to that light and seemed to study it. "What 'stuff' do you mean?"

"You know. About that whatchamacallit—that *loop-garoo* or whatever it was."

Stutz set down his glass, folded his hands across his stomach. "Ah," he said.

"Look," Whitney said, beginning to get a little angry, "another woman's been killed. Just like the others. If you know anything about it, you better let it out."

Stutz smiled faintly in the dim light. "Do you want to hear what I know, or what I zuspect?" he asked.

"Just tell me," Whitney said wearily.

"Shape-changers," Stutz said. "In the old country, we know of them quite well. There are men, and women, too, who can alter their shapes and become animals. Bats. Bears." He paused. "Wolves."

Whitney shook his head. "I just don't see it," he said. "I just don't."

There was a clink of glass on glass as Stutz poured himself another drink. "'There are more things in heaven and earth,'" he said, tilting back his head and pouring the whiskey down. "Your red Indians know of such men. They have many stories. I have heard zome of them."

"But to do something like that," Whitney said.

"A man who becomes an animal is no longer a man," Stutz said. "Once the change begins, he is fully animal."

"But he can't be killed."

"That is what some believe. He can be killed, however. It is not easy, but he can be killed." He leaned forward in his chair, his palms resting on his knees. "He may even *want* to be killed."

Whitney found that hard to believe. "Nobody wants to die," he said.

"You are thinking like a normal man," Stutz told him. "We are discussing a man who is an animal, a man for whom to kiss is to bite and rend, a man for whom hot blood is the drink of the gods, a man—"

"All right," Whitney said.

Stutz leaned back, smiling.

"How can I kill him?" Whitney said.

Stutz told him.

"Jesus Christ," Harper said. "What are we talkin' about here? We got to get an outlaw to help us, is that what you're sayin'?"

"An outcast, maybe. Not an outlaw," Whitney said.

"That's what you say. You really think he'll do the trick?"

"How would I know?" Whitney said. His stomach was getting worse.

The whole thing was making him sick. The dead women, the visit with Stutz, the thought of having to go ask somebody to kill a *loop-garoo* for him. There was one thing for damned sure, though. He wasn't going to tell anybody about that *loop-garoo* business. That was going to be his own little secret.

"What do you know, then?" Strake asked him. "You seem to have a pretty damn good idea of what you want to do."

"I've heard this guy is a good wolf hunter, that's all. If it is a wolf doin' what you think it's doin', then this is the man to get. If it's not, then he may be able to help us, anyway."

"So who's goin' to talk to this fella?" Harper wanted to know.

"I'll go," Whitney said.

He located the man's camp outside of town late that afternoon.

"Hello, Sheriff," the man said when Whitney rode up. He had a strong voice and spoke extremely well, like an educated man. "Would you like a cup of coffee?"

The man apparently had had a small fire going, and a black coffeepot sat on some glowing coals.

"No thanks," the sheriff said. "I didn't come out here for any coffee."

"Well, then. Why did you come?"

Whitney told him.

"And you think I can help?"

"From what I've heard," Whitney said, "you may be the only one who can."

"Then I'll be glad to try. I believe strongly in law and order."

"Good," Whitney said. "I was hoping you'd say that."

The full moon rose pale that night, so pale that it looked almost like a faint, round cloud in the blackness of the sky. The stars had a hard, bright twinkle in the clear, still, cool air.

The dance hall was a happy place, but only because none of the customers had any idea of what was to happen later, and because most of them had already forgotten what had happened to Carlotta. Or if they hadn't forgotten, they had at least managed to put it out of their minds for the time being.

The girls were a different matter. *They* knew very well what had happened, and they knew that Teeny had died the same way the previous month. But they also knew that the killer wasn't picking on girls from the dance hall. After all, he'd killed the preacher's wife and three other women, too.

Still, the girls were scared, as were all the women of the town. It was hard to find a one of them who would even think about going outside her house after dark. Only a woman like Carlotta, a woman who had often told everyone that she wasn't afraid of the devil himself, would stroll outside in San Benito after the first shades of twilight began to draw on.

Scaredest of all was the one they called Francellen. She was the one Harper had talked to earlier.

"You have to do this for us," he said. "If you don't, there won't be anything left of the town within a year. Before long, folks will start moving away, like Willie Jackson, and there won't be any need for a dance hall. There won't be any job for a girl like you."

"I can move, too," Francellen said. She was a big blonde, and big in all the right places, with the full breasts and hips that men liked to look at in the tight dresses she wore to dance in. "This ain't the only place I can get a job. I bet I could go up to San Antone and make twice what I'm makin' here."

Harper thought she might be right, but he couldn't go with her. Oh, he could go, but he would take years to get established, if he ever did, and he didn't have enough money set by to take the risk. He had to stay right where he was, where he had a good business going and where he knew that he could continue to make money.

So he told Francellen he would double her salary if she'd do what he asked.

She thought about it awhile and then agreed. It was a risk, that was true, but to double her salary and not even have to move? Where could she ever get a deal like that? Besides, there was a cowboy or two who was beginning to look at her like they might like to make her an honest woman, and that was something that she might let some good-looking waddy talk her into once she had a considerable stack of gold eagles put away safely in the bank, say in another year or two. Sooner, maybe, if she really got her salary doubled.

Now it was getting on toward two o'clock on Sunday morning, and Francellen was getting worried. There were only a couple of drinkers left in the place, and most of the girls had left earlier, all of them accompanied by one, two, or even three men. Some of them stayed in places where the men would be welcome to spend the night with the girls, even all three men. That was fine with Francellen. She didn't have the same philosophy that Carlotta had. Some of the girls lived right on the premises. in the rooms on the second floor, rooms they sometimes used for other purposes. That was fine with Francellen, too.

Tonight, just tonight, she wished that she lived in one of those rooms, or that she had made plans to be accompanied home by several men. But that hadn't been part of Harper's strategy. No, he wanted her to walk to her room in the Widow Bradley's house all alone. He had even asked her to stick to the dark side of the street.

And she had said yes.

"Perfectly safe," he said. "You'll be perfectly safe. We'll be watching out for you."

"Who's 'we'?" she said.

"Never mind that. Trust me."

Trust him. Trust a dance-hall man. Well, she had said yes, and what was done was done.

She walked out through the big room, saying good night to the bartender and to the bouncer, who was trying to pry the last of the drunks off a bar stool and toss him outside.

She passed out the door and onto the board sidewalk, her shoes making a hollow sound on the boards as she walked.

She came to the alley. There was blackness pooled in it, blackness that the pale moon had no way of reaching. Her steps faltered, but she went on.

She passed the mouth of the alley. Nothing happened. No one sprang out of the dark to grab her and tear her.

She stepped up onto the next walk, a nervous laugh breaking from her. There was nothing to worry about. That was what she had really thought when Harper talked to her. Why would anyone bother her? Nothing would happen, and she would get double her salary for simply walking home alone. What could be easier?

She passed the next alley with hardly a thought, and her right foot was up on the walk when the thing attacked.

She smelled it before it hit her, the rank animal smell of it, the reek of its hot breath, the musky scent of its lust.

Then it was upon her.

She screamed as its hot, rough tongue washed over her face, its lips slavering down the front of her dress.

She felt—she saw!—the teeth, the teeth so white, so sharp in the pale light of the moon.

She screamed again, but the scream was muffled by the thing's hand, or its paw, it must have been a paw, so hairy, so hairy that she could taste the hair.

The teeth sank into her neck, and she fainted.

She never heard the shots.

The men waiting in the alleyway across the street were taken by surprise. They had seen nothing, no movement, no hint of a presence, nothing. The thing that attacked the dance-hall girl was like a piece of the darkness breaking off and falling on her. For a second, for only a second, they were too stunned to move.

"For God's sake!" Whitney said. "Shoot!"

The stranger, who couldn't quite believe what he was seeing, drew his pistol with what seemed to Whitney to be dreamlike slowness, and began firing.

The shots were spaced so closely that they were actually like one long, rumbling roar, but Whitney later thought that he could recall each individual shot and that he could have counted to ten between each one.

When the roll of sound died away, there was a haze of smoke in the street, and the men ran forward through it.

In the opposite alley lay the woman, Francellen, her throat bloody.

Across her lay a great, hairy beast. Blood was pumping from his wounds.

Whitney, panting, his face contorted with fury and fear, reached them first. He kicked the body of the beast aside, rolling it over on its back. Then he knelt down by the woman, reaching for her pulse.

"Is she . . . ?" Harper said.

"I think she's alive," Whitney said. "I think we made it in time. Somebody go get the Doc."

Harper turned to go, then turned back at Strake's cry.

"Jesus God!" Strake said. "Look at that thing!"

They looked. The beast was changing, its form altering.

It was beginning to look almost human.

It was beginning to look a lot like Adolph Stutz.

"Jesus God," Strake said again, much quieter this time.

"We couldn't have done it ourselves," Whitney said. "He's the one who told me how to do it."

"He told you to get—" Harper looked around. The stranger was gone. "Who the hell *was* that masked man, anyway?"

The thing that looked very much like the schoolteacher coughed. "I don't know," he managed to say. "But he left me these zilver bullets." He began to laugh. "Thank him for me. Please."

He coughed blood into the dirt of the alley, but he was smiling when he died.

Liberty

AL SARRANTONIO

THERE'S A STORY they tell in Baker's Flats that tells you everything you need to know about the town. It seems there was a Swede named Bergeson who moved in without permission from the town elders. He came from out East, and he was a little naive because he assumed that since this was the United States, and that he was now a United States citizen, that he could go anywhere and do whatever he liked. Seems he believed all that business they fed him in Europe about this being the land of True Freedom and Golden Opportunity, and like any other poor fool who isn't getting what he wants where he is, he packed up and got on a ship that sailed through the cold waters and came to America.

This was 1885, the year those Frenchmen were putting up that Statue of Liberty in New York Harbor. I know because I was helping them do it, working for five cents a day and drinking four cents of it at McSorley's. I like to think that this Swede, Bergeson, got a good look at that statue as he sailed into the United States. I like to think that he got a good look at it half finished, because that's just about where Liberty stands in this country.

Anyway, to make a long story shorter, because I've got other things to tell, they found this Swede staked out on his land in the sun, naked, blue eyes wide with surprise more than fright, because he was a big man and wouldn't have gone down without a fight. They found his legal deed to the land he owned stuffed in his mouth, and a circle of bullet holes outlining his chest where his heart had beat. There were seven holes, just as there are seven elders of the town of Baker's Flats, and the story they tell is that these town elders went and killed the Swede Bergeson and made a solemn oath doing it, a pact if you will, that they would take it to their deaths and conspire against anyone who conspired against them.

That's the story they tell, and I know the story because I came out West with the Swede, running from the law and the half-finished liberty that statue represented, looking for my own freedom, and eventually, unlike the poor Swede, finding it, which constitutes the rest of my story.

As I said, the Swede was a naive man, but he was a good man at heart, and when he told me the story of the land he'd purchased out West, the farm waiting for him in a town called Baker's Flats, a place so new and untamed that there wasn't a sheriff; was, in fact, no real law for three hundred miles to any compass point; only seven town elders who constituted the law and meted out justice; well, when he told me these things in McSorley's Bar, in New York, the night I met him, and I watched his blue eyes imagining the clear, hot plains, and the freedom they promised, we made a pact over the ale I bought him (because there is nothing in the world better than McSorley's Ale for pact making) that I would go out West with him, and that we would fulfill our dreams together. He would have his farm, and his wide-open spaces, and his America, and I would have—well, a chance at real liberty.

We laid out by freight that very night. The Swede insisted on taking a coach train and showed me his money, which would pay for two passages, but I told him no, and told him as much as I could of my reason for it, and he was wise enough (though so naive in other things) to see my point.

Our car was a cold one, but the Swede was used to the cold, even to the point of giving me his coat when he saw the distress I was in, his big, open face splitting into a smile as he said in his thick accent, "Take it. If two men can share a dream, they can also share a coat."

The night passed slowly. We kept the car door slid open partway, because the Swede wanted to see the moon, which had risen white and stark over the east.

"The East," he said, "is where stars rise, and the moon too."

"But the West," I answered, "is where we're going, and where your face should be." So I threw open the door on the other side of the car, and we looked out there together.

We talked about a lot of things that night, about our hopes and dreams for a better life, and he showed me the Colt and the Winchester he'd bought "for the Wild West," as he called it, and somewhere, just as the sun was pushing the sky from purple to blue, he said the thing I had been hoping to hear, the thing that made me trust him as I'd hoped I could: "You don't have to tell me what you're running from. I don't believe you did it." And with that he lay down and turned his back on me and slept, and I sat looking out to the west, knowing my chance at liberty was safe.

We traveled a week by rails, till Reading, Pennsylvania, by boxcar, and then by first-class coach. The Swede insisted, showing me the roll of money he had saved and convincing me what I already knew: that the telegraphs weren't likely to have my picture up on the wall out here yet, and so, this far from New York, I was no longer a wanted man. I balked a little at him spending his money on me, but only a little, because to tell the truth, I was getting sick of the bum's life and craved a little cleanliness and a good cigar, and the Swede provided all this and good food to boot. And so on through St. Louis and then out to the territories, where the land got flatter but where, the Swede said, he could smell his new farm calling to him. I remember that day because it was the day he first showed me the picture he had of his wife and young daughter, and they were as blond as he was. The girl would be strong when she got older, and they would both join him when he was settled. I half wished, seeing the picture of that pretty blond girl, that she were here already.

It was another half week before we reached Baker's Flats, by short railway and then by stage and flatbed wagon, and when we got in there and the Swede made claim to his land, it was not a week later that the trouble started and the Swede was dead.

The day after the funeral, being as there was no law for three hundred miles, I began to hunt the town elders of Baker's Flats, one by one. It was not a quiet thing, and it got louder as it went along, and I have to say that in many ways I enjoyed it. I can tell you now I wasn't a stranger to killing when it was necessary, and hadn't been in New York. I kept the picture of the Swede in my mind as I went about it, and I kept the picture of his pretty daughter and wife in my pocket, and I thought about my own freedom, which made the killing easier.

The first was a man named Bradson, who owned the General Store. He had given the Swede and I a hard time right at our arrival in town and had made a remark that had told me all I needed to know about him. We'd walked into his store for some chewing tobacco, and maybe a cigar, since the Swede knew I liked them so much, and when the little bell over the door had tinkled, he looked our way, and a look filled his eyes when he saw us that I immediately didn't like, and he turned the bald back of his head to us and muttered, not so low that I didn't hear, "Foreigner," and went into his back room.

We waited fifteen minutes for him, the Swede with patience and me with growing anger, but he didn't come out. I had decided by that time that I wanted a cigar very badly, and was about to march into the back room after Bradson, but the Swede took my arm and quietly said, "Let's be going." I looked up into his broad face, and I knew at that moment that he had heard Bradson's remark, too, but had chosen to ignore it. This told me that he was sharper than I'd thought, but I was still mad, and finally he took my arm and said again, gently, "Let's go."

I went then, but I came back after the Swede's death, and I found

Bradson where I'd hoped I would, in the back room of his store. It was after dark and the store was closed, but the lamp was lit on his little desk and he sat doing accounts. He didn't hear me slip open the front door and come in, and he didn't hear anything again after I cocked the butt of my Colt across the back of his ear and laid him out on the floor. I put a bullet in his heart, at the top, where the top of a circle might be, the start of a circle, just the way the Swede had been killed. There was a cigar humidor on a shelf behind the counter in the front of the store, and I filled my pocket with coronas before I left.

It was a dark night and stayed quiet after my shot into Bradson, and it stayed quiet after two more single shots, each continuing to advance a circle around two more hearts, rang out. There was the liveryman, Polk, who put up some fight and was strong but not strong enough, and the telegraph man, Cooper, who had a beard and was said to abuse his wife. He was in his office, too, with a bottle of whiskey instead of his wife for company, and I left him sprawled next to his telegraph, a bullet in the right of his heart, his spilled bottle inches from his cooling hand.

I hit the hills for a while after that, because I knew they'd be after me the next day. And I was right. I went high up, where it was cold and even colder at night, but I had the Swede's coat to warm me, just as it had that first night in the freight car, and I made camp where they couldn't see a small fire and where I could hear the echo of their horse's movements a mile off. I waited two days and gave them enough time to get close, and then I fell in behind them and waited for them to splinter off, as I knew they would when they found the false clues I'd left for them that told them I'd gone one of two ways.

They split off just as I'd wanted them to. The two toughest stayed together, and the two weakest, who I wanted to take together, rode off down what they thought to be the least likely trail, which was where I waited for them. I had the Swede's rifle, and I waited in the V between two rocks, and I almost felt bad when I picked them off because they rode right into me and never looked up. I took them out with two quick shots because the other two were the dangerous ones, and they weren't all that far away and were sure to hear the gunshots.

The two I took out were Maynard and Phillips, the bar owner and the fat banker, and I know I shot Maynard below the heart where I wanted, but I wasn't so sure that my shot into Phillips continued the circle up toward the eight-o'clock position, because he didn't go down right away and almost made me shoot again. But his horse was only carrying the dead body, and when momentum failed and Phillips fell, I took the time to check the body and found I had indeed hit him right on the eight.

I had a bit of a rough time of it for the next twelve hours. It turned out that Jeppson and Baker, the two remaining, were closer than I'd thought.

Baker even got a shot off at me as I rode off, and he was a good shot and took part of my right earlobe off, which only added to my resolve.

They hunted me well, and for a while I thought they had me, but then they made a few blunders and I was able to play fox again. I left my trail in a stream, then falsified it on the other side, circling back to the water and running back past their position to fall in behind them. I was not stupid enough to try to pick them off then, but contented myself with letting them lose me, and I went back to the Swede's farm.

His body was long gone, buried out behind the farmhouse in the beginnings of his tilled field, but there was a bed to sleep in and a stable to hide my horse and some food in the larder to drive the hunger for real food from my belly. I even smoked a cigar after my meal, remembering the Swede, and took out the picture of his wife and daughter and looked at it for a while before I went to sleep for a couple of hours.

I was up before sunrise. I had breakfast, and then I went out and fed the horse so he wouldn't get hungry, and then I walked into town. It was Sunday. The moon was a thick crescent, waxing, much the same as it had been that night on the train when the Swede and I had looked to the west.

The cock was crowing when I reached Jeppson's church. It was small and empty, and I let myself into the back room where Jeppson bunked and waited. He had a nice collection of guns, and a bowie knife, and I admired the couple of Comanche scalps he had hanging on hooks over his shaving mirror. Services started at eleven, so I expected him around ten. I was disturbed once, about eight o'clock, but it proved to be a dog scratching at the door. I found a scrap bone for him and he went away.

There was a Bible on the desk, which I began to read, and I was so absorbed in my reading that I didn't hear the Reverend Jeppson enter his church a little while later and open the door to his office. He froze, and so did I, but he was more startled than I was, and that gave me enough time to get my gun up and drill him in the heart. His Colt was halfway out of his holster, and it fell to the floor as he dropped. He said, "Oh, God," which I thought appropriate. I walked over to him and was pleased to see I had hit him just where I'd wanted, around the eleven-o'clock mark.

I figured that if Jeppson was home, then so was Baker. He had the biggest house in town, because he was the biggest man, and naturally leader of the town elders, and the best shot. I had my healing earlobe to attest to that.

I figured rightly. I found him at breakfast with his family, ranged round their big oak table as if nothing had happened. His wife, a pretty little thing with dark red hair, was dishing out potatoes and eggs to three boys and a little girl, and there was Baker at the head of the table, dressed in his churchgoing best. I saw all this through the picture window. I could have broken the window, but I thought it would be better to go in the front door and make sure of my shot.

Again he proved to be the sharpest of the seven. He must have seen me move away from the window, because he was waiting for me behind the stairway banister when I pushed the door open. He winged me in the left shoulder, but I did the same to him, and then he panicked and ran for the stairs. I heard his wife and children screaming in the dining room as I mounted the steps after him.

We went through the upstairs of the house, and I got him to empty his revolver. I found him cowering in the room of his little girl, squeezed down in the corner next to her crib. He had his six-shooter on his lap, with the empty chambers out so I could see it. A scatter of unloaded bullets spilled from his shaking hand. "Please, don't do this to my family," he begged, but I took careful aim at his flushed face and then lowered the gun to his chest and put the last bullet into his heart at the twelve-o'clock spot, completing the circle I'd started with Bradson.

I was tired then. I told Baker's wife to leave with her children and get the rest of the town together for a meeting at three o'clock. Then I bolted the doors and slept in Baker's big, comfortable bed. The Colt was loaded under my pillow, but I didn't think I'd need it, and I was right.

At three o'clock I got up and shaved and took one of Baker's fine cigars from his study and lit it and walked out into the street to have my say.

They were all waiting for me out there. I showed them the Swede's Colt, and his Winchester, and I told them how I had killed the Swede and the seven town elders. I told them about the story they would tell in Baker's Flats about how all this had happened, and I told them what would happen to any of them if they got it wrong. They were farmers and women and children, and they all knew what I meant. They knew there wasn't any other law for three hundred miles.

Just to be sure they understood me, I told them about the man I had murdered in New York, throwing him from the scaffolding of the Statue of Liberty when he laughed when I told him that no man can be free under the thumb of any other man or government, that a man can only achieve true liberty by controlling all other men around him.

I knew they understood me, because they went home when I told them to. I stood on the porch of my new house and watched them go, and then I took out the picture of the Swede's beautiful wife and daughter and thought I'd write, in the Swede's name, to tell them to hurry out here, that there was a fine life waiting for them.

For the first time in my life I felt true liberty.

In Baker's Flats, they tell my story still.

Hacendado

JAMES M. REASONER

Cobb reached the border about noon. He reined in his horse on the slight rise overlooking the Rio Grande and thought about the problem facing him. The Ranger badge pinned to his shirt didn't mean a damn thing across the river. All it was good for was a target.

But he had been chasing Frank Shearman for nearly a week. He didn't much feel like letting the outlaw go now, just because Shearman had crossed the river.

Cobb heeled his horse into motion again. He rode down the slope and sent the animal splashing through the shallow, slow-moving stream.

Here along the river, Mexico was just as flat and dusty as Texas was. Gray and blue peaks rose in the distance, though, a rugged-looking range with deep shadows along its base. Shearman's tracks headed straight for the mountains.

Cobb was a big man, barrel-chested, with a week's growth of dark stubble on his face. He gnawed on some jerky and a stale biscuit as he followed the trail. The sun was hot, riding high in the sky overhead. The glare stabbed at Cobb's eyes.

He almost didn't see the men who rode out of a dry wash and started shooting at him.

Cobb swallowed the last bite of biscuit and grabbed for his gun. A bullet sang close by his ear as he palmed out the Colt and lined it on one of the two men charging toward him on horseback. Cobb triggered off a couple of shots, saw the vaquero rock back in his saddle and then pitch to the side. The other man kept coming, blasting away.

Cobb's horse was spooked by the gunfire. It tried to rear, but Cobb's strong arm on the reins hauled it back down. He aimed carefully, trying to ignore the whine of lead around him, and fired a third time.

The attacker was close now, only twenty yards away. Cobb heard his cry

186

of pain as the bullet caught him in the shoulder. The gun in the man's hand flew out of his fingers. He sagged but managed to stay in the saddle.

Cobb holstered his pistol and slid the Winchester out of the saddle boot. Levering a round into the chamber, he lined the rifle on the man and called out, "Just hold it, fella! Sit still!"

The man's horse had slowed to a halt. Cobb walked his mount forward slowly, keeping the man covered. As he studied the man, Cobb saw that he wore the big battered sombrero and rough range clothes of a working vaquero, just like his sprawled companion. Neither man was particularly good with a gun. They had loosed plenty of rounds in his direction without hitting anything but air.

Reining in a few feet away, Cobb said to the man, "You speak English?"

"Sí."

"Why the hell'd you start shootin' at me like that? It was right unfriendly."

The man glowered at him as he clutched his bloody shoulder. He was swaying slightly in the saddle, and his face was pale under its dark tan. "You are on the range of Don Luis Melendez, señor. Our orders are to shoot all who trespass on Don Luis's land."

"Damned unfriendly, all right." Cobb snorted.

The man's eyes rolled up in his head, and he fell from his horse, landing heavily on the ground. Dust billowed up around his crumpled form.

Cobb spat and said, "Hell." Cautiously he dismounted and rolled the man over with a booted foot. The vaquero was still breathing, but he was out cold. Cobb left him there and strode over to the second man. This one was still alive, too. The side of his shirt was bright red where the Ranger's bullet had torn through his body, but the wound was fairly shallow.

Cobb straightened from checking on the man and shook his head. Regardless of the fact that they had tried to kill him, he couldn't just leave them out here to die. He thought both of them might pull through if he could get them back to the hacienda of that Melendez fella they rode for.

The Mexicans' horses were nearby, watching him nervously. Cobb started trying to round them up. Damned if he was going to carry the wounded men on his back.

Cobb wondered how much of a lead Frank Shearman was going to have before this day was over.

Cobb had no idea where the ranch was located, so once he had the two unconscious men tied onto their horses, he kept following Shearman's tracks. Might as well, he thought. He couldn't ask the vaqueros for directions.

The land became more rolling as he approached the foothills. There was more vegetation here. Pastures of lush grass told him this was good cattle country.

In the middle of the afternoon Cobb rode up a ridge and topped it to see a cluster of adobe buildings in the small valley below. There was a large structure in the center with whitewashed walls and a red tile roof. The outbuildings were plainer, more functional. Even at this distance Cobb could see the ornate wrought-iron gate that led onto the house's patio.

He had a feeling he had found the hacienda of Don Luis Melendez.

Someone on the place must have seen him coming, because several men hurried into a corral and threw saddles on horses. Cobb started down the slope, leading the horses bearing the two wounded men. He drew his rifle as the men from the ranch mounted up and rode hurriedly to meet him.

Cobb pulled his mount to a stop and lifted the Winchester as the men approached. Raising his voice, he called, "Howdy! Got a couple of hurt men here!"

The riders were vaqueros like the ones who had attacked him. They came to a stop a few yards away, and the looks they gave Cobb were icy and hostile. One man was dressed a little better than the others, and he edged his horse forward a step or two. Cobb pegged him as the foreman of the ranch crew.

The man had a weathered face and a drooping mustache. He gestured at the wounded men and said, "What happened to them, señor?"

"They came ridin' out of a wash and tried to shoot me," Cobb answered bluntly. "Figured I'd better stop 'em as best I could."

He saw hands edging toward the butts of pistols. The Winchester's magazine was full. They'd probably take him down, but some of them were going with him.

The foreman made a curt gesture and rattled off a command in harsh Spanish. Cobb understood enough of it to know that he was telling the other men not to shoot.

"We will take them to the house," the foreman said. "Don Luis will wish to speak with you."

Cobb nodded. "That's fine with me."

He moved his horse aside and let a couple of the vaqueros come forward to take charge of the wounded men. His grip on the Winchester remained firm. The foreman said solemnly, "It is not polite to ride up to another man's house with a weapon drawn, señor."

Cobb nodded toward the wounded men. "One of them told me their orders were to shoot strangers on sight. That ain't too polite, neither."

"You have my word of honor that no one will molest you, señor."

Cobb considered, then slowly slipped the rifle back in the boot. It was still close to hand, and so was his Colt.

He rode toward the hacienda, the foreman falling in beside him. The other men rode behind them. Cobb felt his back crawling, but he wasn't sure it was from being followed by angry Mexicans.

There was something strange about the hacienda itself.

As Cobb studied it, he saw that it looked like any other good-sized ranch headquarters on this side of the border. But one of the peaks behind it was casting a shadow over the house. The rest of the buildings were all still in the sun.

A trick of the light and the time of day, Cobb decided.

As the group of riders approached the wrought-iron gate, it swung open and a tall man strode out. He wore fine whipcord pants, a loose linen shirt, and tall black boots. The beard he sported was dark and neatly trimmed.

The hair on his head was white.

It was a striking combination, Cobb thought. The man was in his forties, still handsome and vital. But the gaze he turned toward the newcomer was quick and nervous. As Cobb and the foreman came to a stop in front of him, he asked sharply, "Who are you? What do you want with us?"

"Name's Cobb," the Ranger answered. "I'm a lawman trackin' an outlaw."

"You are a Texan." Don Luis sounded bitter.

The foreman spoke up. "He shot Pedro and Estaban, Don Luis."

"They started shootin' at me first," Cobb pointed out. "I was just defendin' myself."

"You had no right to be on my land," Melendez said. "You have no right to be on this side of the river."

Cobb nodded slowly. "Reckon you may be right. But I didn't come to cause you trouble, mister. I'm sorry about your men. If you want me off your land, I'll be glad to get on about my business."

Don Luis raised a hand and passed it over his face. His fingers shook slightly, Cobb noticed. The hacendado took a deep, ragged breath and said, "I apologize, Señor Cobb. You are right, of course. I should not have ordered my men to keep strangers away." He raised his head and met Cobb's level gaze. "Please, señor, accept my hospitality. I would like for you to remain here tonight."

Cobb shook his head. "I've got to be ridin'." He glanced around. The wounded men had been taken to the back of the house, no doubt to be carried in through a rear entrance. But the foreman and several of the vaqueros were still sitting on their horses behind him.

"I insist, señor," Don Luis said smoothly. "If you do not accept, I shall know that you are offended by my offer. I would not like that."

The foreman barked an order, and guns came out this time. Cobb heard the ominous sound of hammers being eared back. He looked back at Melendez. The man was smiling, but his eyes were as cold and hard as the mountain peaks in the distance.

"Looks like you got a guest, Don Luis," Cobb said curtly.

"Two," the hacendado replied. The smile remained on his face as he went on, "Another gringo rode in earlier today. Somehow he had avoided my men. His name, he said, is Shearman."

Frank Shearman almost dropped his glass of wine as Don Luis Melendez strode into the big living room of the hacienda, followed by Cobb. The outlaw's eyes fastened on the silver star on silver circle pinned to Cobb's shirt. His hand moved toward his gun.

Melendez shook his head. "No gunplay, gentlemen," he said sharply. The foreman and a couple of vaqueros crowded into the room behind Cobb. "This is my home."

Shearman forced himself to relax with a visible effort and sank back against the cushions of the big chair in which he sat. After a moment a smile curved his thin lips. "Of course, Don Luis," he said. "I apologize for the rashness of my actions. Who's your new guest?"

"This is Señor Cobb," Don Luis replied. "I believe he comes from Texas, like you, Señor Shearman."

"Howdy, Frank," Cobb said, letting a grin play over his wide mouth.

"We know each other?" Shearman asked.

"Nope. But I've seen your picture on plenty of reward dodgers. I got to San Angelo a couple of days after you held up the bank there."

Melendez looked shrewdly at Cobb. "I see that your reason for crossing the border is Señor Shearman here."

"That's right. And if you'll allow me, Don Luis, I'll take him off your hands."

The hacendado shook his head. "As I told you, Señor Shearman is also my guest. I could not permit such a breach of hospitality as to permit you to arrest him."

Shearman's grin became cocky as he took in the situation. "That's right, Cobb," he said mockingly. "Where's your manners?"

"Left 'em back there with that deputy you gunned down in San Angelo," Cobb growled, the smile dropping off his face. Turning to

Melendez, he said, "This man's a wanted outlaw, Don Luis. I'd appreciate your cooperation."

Don Luis shook his head. "I will hear no more about this matter, gentlemen. There will be no talk of business until after we have dined."

Movement in the corner of the room caught Cobb's eye. He looked over to see a small man gliding out of a doorway. The man was slender, past middle age, with a thin mustache and a few strands of hair plastered over his bald head. At first glance he was unimpressive in his servant's clothes, but something in the way he stared at Cobb made the Ranger frown. The man was so thin that his head resembled a skull as he bowed in Don Luis's direction.

"You wish a meal prepared for your guests, Don Luis?" he asked in a rasping voice.

"Yes, please, Jorge. And a glass of wine for Señor Cobb."

The servant poured the wine from a jug and brought it to Cobb. His fingers touched Cobb's as he handed over the glass, and the Texan was struck by how cold the man's hand was. He still didn't like the smile on the man's face, either.

Cobb kept an eye on Shearman as he sipped the wine. The outlaw might decide to take a chance on offending Don Luis if he thought he could get away with gunning down Cobb. Don Luis seemed to be staying between the two men, though—whether accidentally or by design, Cobb couldn't say.

As he glanced around the room Cobb saw that it was well appointed. There was a thick rug under his feet, and an equally elaborate tapestry hung on one wall. The furniture was low and heavy, built to last.

The sound of footsteps made Cobb turn his head. Two women came into the room through an arched doorway. Cobb's fingers tightened on the glass he held. He had already decided to play along with Don Luis, bide his time, and wait for a chance to grab Shearman. The presence of women was just an added obstacle to his plans. He didn't want any female getting in the way of a stray bullet.

He had to admit that these two dressed up a room, though. They were both slender, of medium height, and their lovely features showed a strong resemblance to each other. Mother and daughter, Cobb decided, the younger one in the full bloom of her youth, the older still a damned handsome woman. Melendez smiled broadly as they entered.

"Ah, gentlemen, allow me to introduce the two most precious jewels in my possession. My wife Pilar and my daughter Inez."

Cobb just nodded to them and said, "Ma'am," letting the single word do for both of them. Shearman, on the other hand, stood up quickly, a broad smile on his face.

"Ladies," he said, reaching out to take Doña Pilar's hand. He bent over and kissed it, murmuring, "I'm charmed to meet you, madam, and your lovely daughter as well."

Cobb's mouth twitched. There was nobody smoother with the ladies than a damned outlaw.

He frowned as he looked closer at them. Both of the women were pale, their features drawn. It was probably a hard life for a female, out here in this isolated hacienda, but despite their attractiveness, Pilar and Inez looked like they were under some sort of strain.

Don Luis introduced Cobb and Shearman to his wife and daughter. Inez briefly said hello to Shearman, then moved over in front of Cobb. "Good evening, Señor Cobb," she said softly.

Cobb felt like a big awkward bear standing next to this pretty slip of a girl. He muttered something, and then Don Luis moved in and rescued him. "I'm sure Jorge has dinner ready," he said. "Shall we go into the dining room?"

It seemed to Cobb like there hadn't been much time to fix a meal, but the little majordomo called Jorge had probably already had dinner under way. It was late afternoon now, and as they went into the dining room Cobb could see the purple light of dusk through the big windows.

The long hardwood table shone, and it was piled high with food. Cobb hadn't seen such a spread since the last time he had gone to church. There had been dinner on the grounds after the preaching. The food there had been plentiful and good, but it wasn't served on such finery as was displayed here.

Don Luis took his place at the head of the table, with Pilar to his right and Inez to his left. Shearman managed to sit next to Pilar. Inez indicated with her dark eyes that Cobb should take the seat next to her.

Cobb settled into the high-backed chair, feeling like an old longhorn bull in a fancy parlor. He was more at home eating cold beans on the trail than sitting down to a meal like this. But there seemed to be nothing else he could do. That foreman and several of the vaqueros were just outside. Any ruckus would bring them running.

Jorge hovered near the table as the Melendez family and their two guests ate. The servant's hands were clasped in front of him, and the smile never left his face.

Cobb didn't like him, not a damn bit. Something about Jorge reminded him of diamondback rattlers he had seen lazing in the sun.

The sky outside darkened rapidly during the meal. Cobb had to admit that the food was good. Tender *cabrito,* warm tortillas, a crisp salad, plenty of beans, and more than enough wine. Every time his glass was empty, Jorge scurried forward to fill it. It was a good thing he was used to drinking good old Texas whiskey, Cobb thought. The wine didn't pack much of a wallop compared to the who-hit-John he usually drank.

Shearman kept up a running conversation with Doña Pilar, and Cobb could see that the woman was taken with him. For his part, he ate in silence, despite Inez's efforts to draw him into conversation. He didn't want to be rude; he just wanted to be out of here and on the way back to Texas with a bank robber and killer as his prisoner.

When the meal was finished, Don Luis leaned back in his chair and smiled at his guests. He had been drinking heavily throughout dinner, and he seemed more at ease now. The wine had helped soothe whatever was gnawing at him. He said, "Now, gentlemen, that you have enjoyed my hospitality, I will beg your indulgence while you listen to a story."

"Don't know that I've got time for a story, Don Luis," Cobb rumbled. "You said we'd talk business when dinner was over. I got a prior claim on this smooth-talkin' feller over there." He nodded toward Shearman.

"Come on, Cobb," the handsome outlaw said. "Let's not ruin a lovely evening."

Doña Pilar spoke up. "I do not understand," she said. "There is some . . . trouble between you and this man, Señor Shearman?"

"He wants to take me back to Texas and see me hung," Shearman replied. "He's a Ranger."

Cobb put his palms on the table. "That's right. And I intend to do it."

"Señor Cobb!" Melendez said sharply. "I will not allow this. As I said, I insist you listen to my story."

Cobb took a deep breath. If Don Luis yelled, plenty of help would come boiling in here. "All right," he said. He'd wait a little while longer.

Melendez took out a thin black cigar and lit it, not offering one to his guests. He said, "Gentlemen, I have quite a successful rancho here. I have worked hard, and I have seen my efforts bear much fruit. And the most succulent fruits of my life are Pilar and Inez." He smiled at them, then went on. "So you can see why I was devastated when they died last spring."

The room was warm, but Cobb felt cold knives stab into his nerves. What the hell was Don Luis talking about? A glance across the table told him that Shearman was just as shocked and confused.

Melendez went on after a second's pause. "If it had not been for Jorge, I do not know what I would have done. I could not have survived without my two lovely flowers. So I summoned Jorge."

Cobb looked at the servant and saw the superior smirk on his face. Suddenly he wasn't sure who was the master and who was the servant in this house.

"Jorge is a *bruja*. A . . . witch, I suppose you would say. He restored my wife and daughter to life and agreed to stay here with us, to keep them alive and vital. All he required in return was a small amount of tribute—and an occasional sacrifice."

Shearman was pale. He licked his lips and said, "Sacrifice?"

Melendez nodded. "That is why I have ordered my men to drive off any strangers who venture onto my land. I will not inflict my misfortune on innocent travelers. Whenever Jorge requires a sacrifice, I pay one of the peasant families who live on my land to provide it. I pay handsomely, gentlemen." He waved a hand. "However, there are times when providence dictates otherwise. Such as now."

Shearman pushed his chair back and stood up. "I don't know what the devil you're talking about, Melendez, but I don't like it. I'm riding on."

Cobb laughed abruptly. He had listened to Don Luis's yarn, and he knew what the hacendado wanted. "Forget it, Shearman," he said harshly. "These folks are figurin' to let that fella kill us both." He jerked a thumb at the still smiling Jorge.

"But . . . but that's crazy!" Shearman protested.

Don Luis shook his head. "Only one of you will be turned over to Jorge. The two of you will fight, and the loser will remain. The victor will be allowed to leave this rancho in peace."

Cobb didn't believe him for a second. If he and Shearman went along with this nonsense, both of them would wind up dead. He was sure of that.

"Shearman," he said softly, "we got to get out of here together, Shearman. It's our only chance."

The outlaw looked around, eyes wild. His hand darted toward the gun on his hip.

Cobb surged up out of his chair. The women screamed as he grabbed the table and lifted it. The muscles in his back and shoulders bulged as he heaved, upsetting the table with a huge crash. He whirled, grabbing for his gun.

Don Luis shouted in Spanish. The door of the dining room burst open, and the foreman and his men came running in with their guns up and ready. Shearman twisted toward them, an incoherent yell on his lips as he started triggering his pistol.

He jerked backward as bullets slammed into him. The vaqueros cut him down mercilessly.

Sacrifices could always be found.

Cobb didn't bother firing at the vaqueros. He lunged away from the wrecked table, one long arm lashing out toward Jorge. The little man tried to leap away, but Cobb was moving with a speed born of desperation. He caught Jorge's collar and yanked him off his feet.

Cobb jammed the barrel of his Colt against the man's head and yelled, "Hold it!"

Don Luis screamed a command, and the foreman and his men stopped firing. The hacendado's face was haggard as he pleaded, "No, Señor

Cobb! If you harm Jorge, Pilar and Inez will die again! He is all that is keeping them here with me."

Cobb clamped an arm around Jorge's neck and growled, "That true, little man?"

Jorge stopped his feeble struggles. He gasped for breath and then hissed, "You will die, gringo! I have powers—"

Cobb pressed down harder with the barrel of his Colt. "I'm a superstitious man, mister," he said heavily. "I believe if somebody blows your brains out, you die. And I don't believe anybody can bring dead folks back to life." His lips drew back from his teeth in a grin. "You want to try your powers against ol' Colonel Sam's here?"

For a long moment following Cobb's challenge, no one in the room moved or spoke. The Ranger gave an instant's glance toward Shearman's sprawled body and grimaced. He wouldn't be taking the outlaw back to Texas to hang. Justice had been served in a different way.

Finally Jorge said, snarling, "I will destroy you—"

"Do it," Cobb shot back. His finger tightened on the trigger of the pistol. "Do it damn quick, mister, 'cause I'm about to ventilate that bald head of yours."

Jorge sagged in his grasp then, a sob welling up from him.

"Tell 'em the truth," Cobb ordered, sensing the man's defeat. "Those ladies didn't really die, did they?"

Jorge shook his head. "I . . . I know about the healing herbs. Doña Pilar and her daughter were very, very sick, but they were not dead. I . . . I did what I could for them."

"And when they got better, you decided to cash in. You had Don Luis under your thumb, and you didn't want to let him out. You came up with this sacrifice business to keep everybody scared of you." Cobb tightened his grip on the man's neck again. "And maybe you enjoyed it some, too."

Jorge nodded as best he could.

Cobb shoved him away and looked at Don Luis. An awful realization had dawned on the hacendado's face. He understood now what his own fear had made him do, how he had given in to a human monster's demands. The word would spread through the peasants, the source of Jorge's sacrifices.

And there would be retribution, Cobb was sure of that.

"I'm ridin' out," he said, "and I'm takin' Shearman's body with me."

Jorge had sunk to his knees and was crying. The women were weeping, too.

"No one will stop you, Señor Cobb," Melendez said softly. "Please. Go."

Cobb slung Shearman's body over his shoulder and went.

He rode hard, not looking back as he left the hacienda behind him. He figured he would see the flames and hear the screams—

And there was always trouble enough for a Ranger, back on the Texas side of the border.

Death Ground

ED GORMAN
To Sara Ann Freed
my good and gentle phone friend

1

YOU COULD TELL it was a well-kept house. On the way up the stairs with the straw-haired girl in the gingham dress and the high-button shoes one size too big, Leo Guild had to step aside to let an Indian woman toting a bucket of soapy water pass by him. She carried a mop and had a forehead shiny with sweat, and she sure looked as if she knew how to keep things clean. If the girls took equal care of themselves, Guild tonight would have himself a pleasant if slightly lonely birthday. He was fifty-four today.

The girl said, half an hour later, "I bet you're mad."

Guild said nothing.

"I bet you wish you woulda picked one of the other girls, don't ya?"

Guild still said nothing.

"I can't help it. Sometimes I just can't do it. Sometimes I get to thinkin' about all the things the preacher used to say, and then I just can't do it. I just can't." She paused. "It's nothin' personal. I mean, you don't offend me or nothin'."

"Gosh, thanks."

"You just got a kind face. I figgered you'd understand. Some men do and—"

"—and some men don't."

The girl got flustered and looked scared.

In the small room with the too-soft bed and the melancholy shadows of kerosene light, Guild laughed somewhat sadly. "I guess it's just the way my luck's been running."

"Bad luck, huh?"

"Tracked a man six hundred miles through the snow and damn near lost a finger to frostbite, and the day before I caught up with him and the two-thousand-dollar reward I would have gotten, he dropped dead of a heart attack."

"Gol."

"Then I signed on as a stagecoach guard and before I reached the first stage stop, the company went bankrupt."

"Cripes."

He looked her over in the lamp glow. She hadn't taken her clothes off. She looked like a farm girl dressed up for a Saturday night with a farm boy. His body wanted her, but his soul didn't because her soul didn't want him. He never liked it in the houses, but he was fifty-four and in many ways he had lived too much and in many ways he had lived too little, and even though he couldn't talk about too much or too little with anybody, he could hold somebody in the darkness, and the mere fact of holding them would be enough to get him through this night of fifty-four years.

But the girl, too skinny and plain to ever be particularly profitable for a house like this, did not want to hold him, so now he took the rye from the bedstand and the cigarette he'd rolled earlier in the day and he had his own little celebration.

"You mad?"

"Nope." He smoked his cigarette.

"You gonna tell Patty?"

"Nope." He drank his rye.

"You gonna hit me?"

"Nope." He stared into the deep shadows of the room and listened to the cold October night rattle the window. Then he thought of the little girl. Sometimes it happened like that. Suddenly she was there in his mind, and so was what he'd done.

"You look sad, mister."

"Old is all."

"Fifty-four ain't old."

"Some fifty-fours ain't old. Mine is."

He was already up and straightening his clothes, the black suit coat and white boiled shirt and gray serge trousers and black Texas boots. He eased the black Stetson onto his gray hair. Finally he tugged the holster holding his .44 around his waist and into proper place.

She glanced up at him with her quick kid face. "You sure you ain't gonna tell Patty?"

He leaned over and kissed her on the forehead. "I'm not going to tell Patty."

He left the money on the battered bureau, and then he ducked his six feet under the door frame and went on downstairs.

Several men sat anxiously in the parlor, waiting. They might have been at a train depot waiting for some big black engine to take them someplace fantastic. They looked that excited.

Patty, the woman who ran the place, came up and said, "She good?"

"Real good."

She poked him in the ribs and grinned. She had food in her teeth. "All my girls are good."

He went to the door, and on the way out she said to his back, "All of them."

He was ten steps down the sidewalk, dead leaves scraping the boards of the walk, the silver alien moon full and ominous in the cloudless sky, when he saw a short man in a three-piece suit carrying a Winchester hurrying toward him.

The man, breathlessly, said, "You Guild?"

Guild nodded.

"I'm Deputy Forbes."

"Glad to meet you."

"Sheriff wants to see you."

"He say why?"

"He said why, but he also said I wasn't supposed to say why."

Guild, expansive on the rye, said, "He say why you weren't supposed to say why?"

"Your cheeks cold?"

"No, but my nose is."

"Good," Deputy Forbes said. "Then let's go back to the office and we can discuss this in a nice warm place." Then he raised his young, pudgy face to the fancy house whose light faltered in the prairie shadows behind. "She's got some good girls in there, that Patty does."

"Yes," Guild said, "that's what I heard."

2

DECKER WAS TYPICAL of the kind of law you saw in the Territory these days. The old kind, the gunfighters who'd roamed town to town taking a piece of prostitution and gambling and liquor, were gone. Just this summer four of them had been hanged in Yankton. The territorial governor had called it "a symbol of our new dedication to law and order." Such statements always made Guild smile. If it was your neck in the noose, it was a lot more than symbolic.

Decker stood maybe five-eight and weighed maybe one-forty. He had a handsome but unremarkable face and wore eyeglasses. His brown hair was thinning and he wore a three-piece brown suit on the right lapel of which rested the smallest three-pointed star Guild had ever seen. He looked like a banker who might get tough with you after a few beers.

His office continued the impression that he was a businessman. Behind a wide mahogany desk was a glass-paneled bookcase with enough law tomes to make a young lawyer envious. On the desk itself was a tintype of Decker, a pretty plump woman, and two pretty plump little girls. To the right of the desk was a long glass case filled with rifles and shotguns. The floor had a gray hooked rug. On a small service table to the left of the desk was a nickel-plated coffeepot from which Decker poured Guild a cup without asking.

Guild thanked him for it and sat down.

"Across the alley is the back door of the undertaker's," Decker said.

"I see."

"We put two men in there about an hour ago."

Guild sipped his coffee. He knew what was coming.

"One of them was Merle Rig. He a good friend of yours?" Decker said.

"Actually, he was sort of an enemy."

Decker put down his tin cup and seemed to give Guild a reassessment, as if Guild had been hiding something only now revealed.

"Kind of funny you would be a bodyguard for a man you consider an enemy."

"He paid me."

"Still."

"Winter's coming and I'm fifty-four and I don't have much money. He paid me two hundred dollars."

"Why was he your enemy?"

Guild shrugged. "Ten years ago we were doing some bounty hunting together. The day we were to collect, he knocked me out and went in and got the reward for himself."

"But you agreed to be his bodyguard anyway?"

"I was passing through town here and he heard about it and he came to me and said that somebody was after him. He said he'd been sick the last week or so and couldn't defend himself and would I watch him."

"Ever wonder why he didn't come to me for protection?"

"Didn't have to wonder. I assumed he was in trouble the law could only make worse."

"You live in a nice world, Mr. Guild."

"It's the only one that'll have me," Guild said, thinking about the little girl again and how people reacted once they knew who he was and what he'd done.

"A month ago he robbed the local bank here of fifteen thousand dollars," Decker said. "He and a mountain man named Kriker."

"The hell."

"I'm sure it was Kriker who came into town and killed him and the kid." He paused, following Guild's eyes to the certificate on the wall. These days in the Territory, lawmen went to one of the territorial capitals where they taught courses in being a lawman. Decker said, "The kid has a mother here. You shouldn't have gotten him involved."

"I'm sorry I did, but he wanted to. He said he wanted to be a deputy but you wouldn't let him."

"He was too raw. He had a head full of fancy notions that wouldn't do this office or himself a damn bit of good."

"He wasn't a bad bodyguard. He stayed sober and he was punctual and he was reasonably good with a Remington. That's why he was there to-night. Spelling me."

"He was back shot."

Guild sighed. "You talk to his mother?"

"That's a privilege I'm going to give you, Mr. Guild. Technically, you were his employer. Seems to me it would only be fitting."

Guild finished his coffee and set the tin cup carefully on the fine shiny wood of the desk. Decker pushed a round leather coaster over to him. Decker was exactly the sort of man who would use coasters.

Decker said, "Tomorrow two of my deputies are going after Kriker. You have any interest in joining them?"

"Thought I'd just be moving on."

"They're young and they could use help."

"You could always go."

"I could if I didn't have to testify in a very important case tomorrow morning in the next county."

"I see."

"It's time we got Kriker. You know him?"

"No."

"Has his own little encampment up in the sand hills. Suspected him of a lot of things over the years but was never able to prove anything. There's a thousand-dollar reward for the money and the men who robbed the bank."

"What makes you think you can prove anything now?"

"Day of the robbery the dead man and Kriker were seen together in a local saloon. Plus I've got a strong suspicion that we'll find the money somewhere in Kriker's encampment."

"Why would Kriker kill him?"

"He was weakening, your friend. Or enemy. Or whatever the hell he was. He sent me a note."

"A note?"

"Yes."

"When did you get it?"

"Just this afternoon."

"Funny he didn't mention anything to me about a note."

Decker made a face that said a lot funnier things had happened.

"You mind if I see the note?" Guild said.

Decker opened a drawer and took out a long white envelope and opened the flap. From inside the envelope he took a piece of gray paper that had been folded several times. He handed it across the desk to Guild. The paper was cheap and smudgy. In a broad shaky hand were written the words: *I'd like to talk to you about me and Kriker's part in the First Citizen Bank robbery.* It was signed *Merle Rig.*

Guild frowned.

"Something wrong, Mr. Guild?"

"Far as I knew, Merle Rig couldn't either read or write."

"Maybe he had somebody write it for him."

"Maybe."

Decker took the note back and put it in the envelope and put the envelope in the drawer and then put his social face on again, the one he wore in the tintype with the plump Decker brood.

Decker said, "I need you to go across the alley with me. All right, Mr. Guild?"

There were two of them and they were naked. They lay on tables in a back room noisy with the banging of creaky shutters caught in a Halloween wind. Blood soaked the sheets that covered them.

He looked at the kid first and nodded, and then he looked at Merle Rig and nodded. Rig had nickels covering his eyes. Pennies stained green.

The undertaker, a stout man with the flushed cheeks and bloodstained apron of a good German butcher, started to draw the sheet back over Merle Rig's face, but Guild stopped him.

Guild wanted to stare at the face a moment longer. He wasn't sure why. They hadn't been so different, not in the final tally of things, Rig and Guild. Rig made one kind of mistake and Guild another, and that was about all. He stood there and thought how he should have told Rig that he didn't give a particular damn about Rig knocking him out and taking the reward all for himself. People were just people and sometimes they did terrible things. Everybody did.

The Halloween wind came. The guttering kerosene lamps in the death room fluttered and cast long cavelike shadows.

Decker said, "I don't know about you, Mr. Guild, but it's real easy to get tired of staring at dead people. How about letting him draw the sheet back up?"

Guild looked up at the undertaker, who was wiping his bloody hands off on his apron.

Guild nodded and the undertaker drew the sheet back over Merle Rig.

Decker put a piece of paper in Guild's hand. "Here's where the kid's mother lives."

"You don't think this is your job?"

Decker said, "I wasn't stupid enough to hire him."

3

THE WOMAN LIVED in a boardinghouse that smelled of laundry soap and cabbage and pipe tobacco. She lived in a wide room built off the east end of the two-story frame house. He went up two steps and started to knock and then he looked through the glass and past the curtain to where the lamplight was like butter and where she sat in cheap calico and a shawl, darning a pair of gray work socks. She was old not so much in years, but worn-out old. When he did knock finally and she looked up finally, he saw that in fact she was no older than forty and that buried in the rawboned face were beautiful blue eyes.

She got up and came to the door and said, "Help you, mister?"

"You'd be Kenny's mother."

She knew right away something was wrong. She crossed herself. "My God."

Guild said, "I'd like to come in."

"You're that man who hired him, ain't you?" ·

"Please," he said, taking off his hat and nodding to the interior.

There was a daybed covered now with a quilt and throw pillows so it would resemble a couch. Against the opposite wall was a bed. The furniture consisted of a rocking chair and a kitchen table and a cupboard and a stove. The air smelled of cinnamon. Guild thought of his own mother and his boyhood on a farm when even in the best of times you got twenty-five cents for wheat and two cents a pound for dressed pork.

She put a hand on his wrist and said, "He's dead, ain't he?"

"Yes."

"My God."

"I'm sorry, ma'am."

"You there?"

"When it happened?" Guild asked.

"Yup."

"No. No, I wasn't there."

"Where was you?"

He thought of the fancy house and the farm girl who hadn't wanted to.

"I had business. Tonight's my birthday." He thought maybe the last re-mark would buy him a little sympathy. Then he was ashamed of himself. Her son was dead. She should be the one seeking sympathy, not him.

She backed into the room. She had the dazed look that often accompa-nies news of death. In Guild's experience people tended to do one of two things: just kind of float and fade the way she was, or get angry. She floated over to the daybed and sat down, so light the springs didn't squeak at all, and folded her old-woman hands one across the other in her lap and then looked up at him with her young-woman eyes.

She began sobbing then, and he just stood there and listened to her. She swore and she prayed and then she did them both again.

Finally he went over through the cinnamon-smelling air in the butter-gold light of the little room and sat on the bed. This time the springs did squeak and he put his big arm around her and sort of tucked her inside him, and then, as he knew she would, she just cried all the more.

They sat there for a very long time like this beneath the cheap print of a very sad Jesus. Knowing what Jesus knew, Guild had good reason to be sad.

"He nearly died soon as they took him from my womb." She looked over at him. "His lungs, the doc said. Never did have good lungs."

Guild nodded.

This was half an hour later.

She had insisted on fixing them tea. It was cinnamon tea. The wind rattled the windows.

She said, "You hear him cough?"

"Yes."

"Never did have good lungs."

She was crazed, repeating herself. The least he could do was sit there and listen and drink her cinnamon tea.

"He wanted to be a sheriff."

"That's what he told me."

"Wouldn't have made a good one, though. Too skittish."

"Oh."

"Our whole family's skittish."

Guild didn't know what to say. He felt unable to move, unable to speak. He just sat there. There were three of them in the room. Her and Guild and the dead son, Kenny.

"His pa was skittish, too. Died in the mines, his pa did."

"I'm sorry."

"Kenny was all I had." She started crying again. "He never should have started hanging around that Bruckner."

"Bruckner?"

"One of the sheriff's deputies. He was always doin' little favors for Bruckner and his brother James, and they was always fillin' his head with the idea that he was gonna be a deputy someday." She looked at him and her grief made him glance away, ashamed. "You filled his head, too."

"He came to me, ma'am."

"But you should've known better."

He sighed. "Now that I think about it, yes, I think I should have."

"They offered him twenty-seven cents an hour to work over to the wagonworks, and he turned it down just so's he could be a bodyguard to that Rig fella. Rig wasn't no good."

Guild was surprised by the familiarity in her voice. "You knew Rig?"

"Sure. He come here several times."

"Rig came here? When?"

"About a month and a half ago."

When Guild hired him, Kenny Tolliver had been careful to pretend that he didn't know Rig at all. Guild said, "So they knew each other pretty well?"

"Kenny, he came home drunk several nights and said he'd been with them."

"Them?"

"Sure. Rig and Bruckner and James."

"The deputies and Rig knew each other?"

"Sure." She looked at him more carefully now.

"Something wrong?"

"Don't know yet, I guess."

She said, "You work six months at the wagonworks, they give you a raise."

"It sounds like a decent job."

"I know a fellow making thirty-nine cents an hour there. Been there fourteen years."

"I'm sorry, Mrs. Tolliver." Then: "He ever mention a man named Kriker?"

"Kriker? No, not that I recollect."

He stood up. He made a very elaborate thing out of putting his hat on and fixing it just so on his head. She sat once more in the buttery light with her old body and young eyes and watched him.

"You never should have hired him," she said.

She was crying once more.

"No," he said. "No, Mrs. Tolliver, I shouldn't have."

4

HE GOT UP at 4:00 A.M. Even then, he had to hurry. There was a lot to do.

He went down the rooming house hallway to the pump and filled his pitcher and then went back to the commode basin and washed himself very well. It might be days before he got a chance to clean himself this well again. He even washed behind his ears the way his older sister had always told him to. She was dead now from consumption, and so the memory was bittersweet.

In his saddlebags he'd been carrying a brand-new red union suit from Sears he hadn't gotten around to wearing. He put the long johns on this morning and then his regular clothes and then he gathered up everything, including the rifle he intended to trade and his .44 and his sheepskin.

Dawn was a pinkish streak behind the peaks and turrets of the town's fancier houses. The wagon tracks in the streets were frozen solid. Guild's breath was a pure white plume. His nose was cold and he was glad he'd used the hemorrhoid salve a doc had given him. Chill temperatures and saddle leather got tough on you.

The first stop was a Catholic church. A plump priest was saying an early mass for immigrant women and a few male workers. The church was crude, wood instead of the marble you saw in the big Territory towns, but the stations of the cross had been rendered in Indian art, probably Sioux, and were interesting to look at. The smell of incense was very sweet and he enjoyed hearing the small choir chant in Latin. Even though he had no idea what the words meant, they carried dignity and reassurance.

He sat in the last pew, in the shadows, and he did not kneel when the rest of them knelt, and he did not rise for communion when the rest of them rose. He kept staring at the stations of the cross. In them Christ had slightly Indian features.

Then mass ended and he got up and walked up the center aisle to the altar and called out for the priest, who was skinny and bald and had a wart on his cheek. The two Indian altar boys watched Guild curiously. To the priest, Guild said, "I would like you to hear my confession, Father." The priest nodded and waved the two altar boys away.

The priest looked around and said, "The church is empty. We can do it right here."

"That would be fine."

"You look troubled."

"I am troubled."

The priest in his silk vestments pointed to a corner over by the votive candles. There were two chairs there. The priest said, "Why don't we sit down?"

"I've never made a confession sitting down."

The priest smiled. "Tradition isn't everything."

So they went over and sat down and Guild said, "Forgive me, Father, for I have sinned. It has been three months since my last confession."

"All right, my son. What weighs on you?"

"A little girl," Guild said. Ordinarily he followed the usual form for making a confession, starting with the lesser sins first and leading up to the more important ones. But he decided that since they had already broken formality by sitting down, he might as well break formality by talking only about one thing. "I killed a little girl."

The priest had to pretend not to be shocked, but of course he was shocked. You could not hear about killing little girls and not be shocked.

"You did this on purpose?"

"No."

The priest looked enormously relieved. "Then why do you confess it?"

So Guild told him, as Guild always did whenever the dreams of the little girl got particularly bad again, as they had been lately. Guild was not even a Catholic. It was simply that confession, unlike whiskey, seemed to help the dreams. At least temporarily.

The second stop was at the livery stable. The liveryman had furry white muttonchops and wore a Prince Albert suit and a homburg. He obviously wanted to be seen as a prosperous merchant. The right hand he put forth for Guild to shake sparkled with diamonds. He had a Negro to do the real work, cleaning up the manure, grooming the animals, gentling them out back in a rope corral.

What lay ahead required a better animal than the grulla he'd come into town on.

The liveryman showed him several animals. When Guild saw the shave-tailed Appaloosa, he thought about the time he'd served a three-day sentence for assault and battery. He'd seen a drunken wrangler showing off for friends by trying to break a particularly troublesome stallion. Finally the wrangler got so humiliated that he took out a knife and slashed the stallion's throat. Guild had gone over and kicked in three of the man's ribs and broken his nose. He had one of those tempers.

He looked at the Appaloosa and said, "How much?"

"Too cold to dicker," the liveryman said, patting his hands together.

They made a deal.

By now the town of false fronts and two-story brick buildings was well
awake. The sky was low and gray and wintry. The trees were naked and
the grass was brown and you could smell serious snow coming. In the
distance the mountains showed snow on their caps. Below this were the
sand hills where the man named Kriker resided. Guild ate three eggs and
sausage and slice browns in a restaurant filled with angry talk about the
Territory's latest political crisis—the notion that the Territory could force
your child to go to school for five years, whether you needed that child as
a farmhand or not. At least in this restaurant, the idea was not a popular
one.

The woman at the general store was fifty but very attractive in a gingham dress and spectacles with gold rims. She put Guild in mind of women
who made good cherry pies and knew when, as lovers, to be ferocious and
when, the night suddenly oppressive with a man's memories, to be gentle.

But there were other things to be done than spark a lady, and Guild
wasn't all that comfortable in the sparking department anyway.

She showed him ten weapons and he held them all and sighted them
and held them some more. Finally he asked her how much she'd give him
in trade for the Remington and so they concluded their deal.

He walked out of there with a double 10-gauge.

Now he was ready. He had thought about how Rig had been killed, and
he had thought about how young Kenny Tolliver had been killed, and he
had thought about how they'd both known the deputies, and he had
thought about how the bank had been held up, and he had thought about
the man named Kriker.

None of it seemed to make sense, of course, but then when you
thought about it, it all made a great deal of sense.

He figured he owed Rig a death. Maybe he even owed the Tolliver kid a
death, and so he hefted his new-bought double 10-gauge.

5

THE FIRST DEPUTY, Thomas Bruckner, turned out to be a tall man in a
beaver coat and a fedora and a brilliant blue glass eye, the other one
being all right. He also had a gold tooth and an almost constant grin short
on mirth and long on malice. When Guild walked into Sheriff Decker's
office, Thomas Bruckner looked at his partner, his brother James Bruckner, and winked.

. Guild recognized the wink.

He had seen it many times over the past four years, ever since the trial.

It meant that the man winking and the other man grinning in response knew all about Guild.

Or thought they did, anyway.

James was an awkward man in a greasy duster and several layers of clothes beneath. His knuckles had been busted so many times they sat on his hands like ornaments. But that wasn't what you really noticed about James Bruckner. No, what you really noticed was how the left side of his face had an unnatural, leathery look, the result of burns that must have occurred in childhood. The stretched texture of the skin looked as if the scars did not quite want to cover the man's face.

Sheriff Decker and the kid deputy Forbes were behind Decker's desk, going over papers.

Guild said, "I'm going with these two for Kriker."

The grins faded fast and Decker's head came up.

"Morning, Mr. Guild." He had changed suits. He wore a western-cut number this morning, but it was tweed and it was immaculate and he still looked more merchant than lawman. He looked neither distressed nor surprised, though certainly the Bruckners did. "What changed your mind?"

Guild decided to make things simple. No reason to share his suspicions. He said, "You said there was a thousand-dollar reward for return of the money."

"Indeed."

"Well, that's why I'm going."

The room smelled of coffee and cigar smoke. Outside in the hall ragged prisoners were being pushed out the door on the way to court appearances at the county courthouse down the street. One of them glanced in at the men in the office and gathered a great wad of white spit and sent it flying into the room.

Thomas Bruckner lifted his Sharps and pointed it at the man. "Give me a double eagle if I can hit him in the balls?"

James laughed.

A deputy pushed the prisoner out of the way.

Then the Bruckners turned back to Decker.

Thomas Bruckner said, "Won't ride with him, Sheriff."

This time Decker did look surprised. "Why not? Said you wouldn't mind an extra man."

"You know what you found out over the telegraph," Thomas said, " 'bout the little girl and all."

"He was acquitted," Decker said.

"Still and all," Thomas said.

Guild said, "Makes no never-mind to me, Sheriff. If they want an extra man, I'll go along with them. If not, I'll find this Kriker on my own."

Thomas grinned his hateful grin. "Bounty man. Lots of confidence. You ever been in the sand hills in this weather, bounty man?"

"So happens I have."

Thomas said, "You ever stalked a man so crazy even the goddamn Indians are scared of him?"

Guild nodded to Decker. "I'll be going now, Sheriff. Just thought you'd like to know my intentions."

The Bruckners glanced at each other and then Thomas said to Guild, "Thought you were goin' with us."

"Thought you didn't ride with a man like me."

Another glance. Guild could guess what they were thinking: He would be easier to control if he were with them.

"You're all right," Thomas said. "Just kind of testin' your mettle a little."

Guild said, "I wouldn't do that real often if I were you."

Thomas laughed. "You got a lot of pride for a bounty man. Especially for a bounty man who killed a little girl."

James said, touching his burned skin, "Ease off on him, Thomas. Ease off on him."

For a moment Guild and James stared at each other. They had something in common—James, his burned face; Guild, the dead girl. It made them outcasts; it made them prey.

Thomas glared at his brother and then yanked on his sleeve. "Come on, we'll go get ready so we can meet the bounty man here in half an hour."

He tilted his hat to the sheriff and then jerked his brother through the door. Obviously he didn't like the idea of his brother telling him to "ease off" anybody.

When the Bruckners went to get ready, Guild said to Decker, "Strange company for a man like you."

"Meaning?"

"Meaning I doubt they went up to Yankton and took one of those courses on law."

Deputy Forbes smiled his kid smile. Obviously he had gone to Yankton.

Decker pushed a tin cup of coffee Guild's way, stuck a pipe in his mouth, and said, "Territory's changing, but it hasn't changed completely yet. We've got telegraph and a few telephones and transcontinental railroads, but we still have need of men like the Bruckners."

"You trust them?"

Decker's smile, so friendly, was quick. "About as much as I trust you, Mr. Guild. About as much as I trust you."

6

KRIKER PUSHED BACK the burlap curtain and came into the small room inside the soddie that was veined with buffalo grass thick as a man's arm and that generally stayed cool in summer and warm in winter. At noon on the overcast day, the shadows were deep and the moisture-swollen walls cold to touch.

The girl lay on a cot beneath a pile of buffalo hides lively with ticks and other vermin. The girl was eight or nine; Kriker had never been sure. Even from here he could see that she was not better. She was worse.

Kneeling next to her was a raw, angular old woman dressed in a man-like getup of different kinds of hide that she'd cured herself and wore year round. Even by standards of this settlement, the old woman smelled, and even the men who worked the kill told jokes about her.

She raised her gray head to Kriker. She was angry. "You got to give it time to work."

Kriker was a chunky man but not fat. He shaved no oftener than every few weeks and wore a buckskin jacket and a buckskin hat. He carried two .44s stuck into a wide belt and a knife with which he'd cut out the innards of squirrels for dinner. Of course he cut other things with it, too. He said he was in his fortieth summer but no one, especially Kriker, could be sure of this.

He was known throughout the Territory as a man who had robbed banks, trains, and wealthy homes, and who had shot, stabbed, and drowned any number of people who he felt were in need of such fates. He was known in the settlement as the man who'd bitten off the Mountie's nose, this being up near the territorial border where a young and over-zealous Mountie had tried to arrest Kriker for something he hadn't done. Kriker calmly presented his side of the case, but still the Mountie wanted to take him in. Kriker threw the man to the ground and there ensued a terrible wrestling match, the Mountie having won his post wrestling title many times, and finally Kriker resorting to something he'd heard mountain men talk about but had never seen done. He clamped his teeth on to the Mountie's nose and bit down hard as he could. It was no easy task to tear off a man's nose. But that afternoon Harry Kriker did exactly that. After three minutes or so, all that was left of the Mountie's nose was a red, running hole. Kriker returned to the encampment. Three other encampment men had been with him. They never tired telling the story, and encampment people never tired of hearing it.

But that sort of frivolity was long past Kriker now as he stood staring down at the frail blond girl with the sweaty face and death-shut eyes.

Kriker moved closer to the girl. Looked at her carefully.

He reached down and put his hand beneath the buffalo robes and took her wrist, frail as a flower stem, and felt for a pulse. Faintly, he felt one.

"You do what you said you was goin' to?" he said to the granny woman.

The woman was nervous now. At one time Kriker had had a wife and son, the story went, and they took sick from milk that had not been put far enough down the well for keeping. A doc was brought from the closest town. Kriker's wife and son died anyway. That night the doc was found on the stage trail back to town. His eyes had been dug out with just the sort of knife you'd cut up squirrels with. A sheriff had come out and there had been an investigation and all of the local newspapers had run angry editorials about Harry Kriker and all the things he had been suspected of over the years, but as usual Kriker and the encampment went on. The doc was buried with a mask over his eyes.

Obviously the granny woman thought of the doc now as she rose, her old knees cracking, and said, "I give her the rattlesnake."

"The heart?"

"The heart."

"And nothin' more?"

"And nothin' more."

"Then why the hell's she still sick? You said it would work."

Her worn brown eyes grew evasive. "I said it might take a day or two."

All his life Kriker had trusted granny women. He had been raised in the hills, and in the hills you did not trust docs because when you did your wife and your son died. But granny women knew things docs didn't know at all. How to get rid of birthmarks by rubbing the marks for three days against the hand of a newly dead corpse; how to get rid of whooping cough by putting the cougher's neck through a horse collar three times; and how to cure bed-wetting—this as a last resort if beating the child didn't work—by feeding the child the hind legs of a rat fried just so.

Granny women knew all about these things.

Yet this granny woman, Sadra, had been working with the girl now three days and the girl was only getting worse.

Sadra said, "It ain't like she's your kin."

Kriker raised angry eyes to her. Nobody in the settlement understood. Three years ago he'd held up a stage and the men he'd been with had been too full of fear to go gentle. Driver and passengers had all been killed—except for the girl. They'd wanted to kill her, too, but Kriker had said, no, he would take her back to the encampment. The girl had become his life. When in town he bought her dresses. When in the timber he cut her up rattlesnakes and gave her their rattles as toys. He fed her, he sang to her mountain songs in his sure strong voice, and he cradled her when she became afraid of the lightning and thunder of summer storms.

Yet never once in the three years had the girl said a word. He saw in the blue of her eyes that her life had stopped somehow when she'd seen her parents shot to death on the stage road that day, and that no pretty dress or gentle mountain song could ease those blue eyes.

And so he simply revered her.

He slept on a hide cot next to hers, and he brought her her meals, and on a day he designated as a birthday he brought her something new and shiny from town.

But she never thanked him, of course. She just sat huddled in the corner of the soddie and watched him, though mostly she seemed to be looking at something no one but she could see.

He told her of the flowers and how they smelled and how you could hold them like infants; and he told her of the mountain streams and how pure and cold the water was; and he told her of how animals could be more loyal and trustworthy friends than human beings ever could, and that was why there was no pleasure in killing animals but sometimes there was pleasure in killing human beings.

He told her all of these things many times—this big hairy shaggy man that judges all over the Territory were just waiting to hang—told her in the soft voice he used to use with his wife and son . . . and she didn't hear.

Or didn't seem to, anyway.

And now she lay ill and he feared the worst and his voice grew threatening with the granny woman.

He stood up. "I got to go see priest." He nodded to the bed. "You take care of this girl, hear? I want her up on her feet before tomorrow."

He leaned down and kissed the girl on the forehead.

"You hear me, granny woman?"

The threat was clear.

The granny woman nodded and he left.

If you stood on one of the smaller sand hills and looked into the valley below, you saw it, the settlement of sixteen soddies, with a cleared common square for meetings and children. To the east, near the stream, was where the slaughtering was done, usually by the men. The cows were knocked out and then stabbed through the breast and then bled, this blood becoming blood meal for fertilizer. Then each carcass was cut in half, right down the spine, then into quarters. Tanners in town bought the hides, with hooves and horns going to the glue factory. Even the offal was used, for tankage. This was men's work, of course.

The women did not want to do this kind of work, but it was about the only kind of work they did not do. They did candlemaking, knitting, weaving, soapmaking, spinning, herding, milking, wood carrying, planting, and harvesting (there was a woman named Beulah who could drive a team of ten oxen). The married women bore children and the young girls stockpiled clothes and skills as part of their trousseaus. A woman who could do heavy fieldwork, for example, was looked on just as fondly as a beauty.

This then was the settlement, and it had been his settlement for ten years now, ever since Kriker had first come here on the run from a shootout in Montana. He had cleared the trees and made his peace with those Indians who had yet to drift to the drab reservations constructed by the Yankees. He had also invited the rabble who made up the settlement, "rabble" because the first generation here was much like Kriker himself: thieves and counterfeiters and arsonists and killers. They had come to escape prison or the treachery of streets in Chicago or St. Loo or Toronto.

They had come because Kriker had told them that they could establish a settlement and raise everything they needed to feed and clothe themselves, and it had been a wonderful ringing dream delivered in Kriker's pulpitlike oratory. So they had come, in rags and tatters, men of rage and melancholy, women without virtue or loyalty, and even though at first many of them had deserted, returning to the familiar filth of the cities, enough of them stayed that the settlement prospered and those who stayed were transformed from rubble into human beings with purpose and dignity. The first corn came up and blackbirds had to be chased off; wild strawberries were picked in June and grain yellow as gold was toted in smoky September; and the women, the tireless ceaseless women, found that butter and eggs fetched good prices for a mere day's buckboard ride into town.

The settlement was born and grew and prospered, and the first generation bore a second generation. Now, as he thought of all this, the priest had only one regret—that, ironically, the man responsible for all this had not himself changed.

Kriker.

His rage had been too deep somehow, his ways too instinctive and reckless, for even the accomplishment of the settlement to calm him.

And so, only a month ago, they had struck a bargain, the priest and Kriker.

Kriker would be involved in one more robbery and then he would take his part of the proceeds and take the little girl and he would leave the settlement. Forever.

The people here were tired of being afraid of Kriker, and tired of being afraid that he would someday be responsible for the destruction of the settlement he had helped build.

Father Healy stood now as Kriker came up the small sand hill toward him. The day was raw. Kriker huddled into his sheepskin. He carried his carbine, as always.

Behind Kriker everything was gray. The grass and foliage were barren with winter. Smoke from chimneys curled from the roof of each cabin. The cows huddled together in the lean-to next to a long line of scrub oaks forming a windbreak.

Kriker said, "She ain't no better."

The priest could see tears in Kriker's eyes.

The priest sighed. "I'm sorry, Kriker."

"The granny woman even give her the rattlesnake heart."

The priest felt Kriker studying him. He knew that his disbelief in the granny woman's ways angered Kriker. "The girl needs a doctor."

Kriker hefted his carbine. "You ain't bringin' no doc out here, you understand?"

Carefully, for this was the first time the priest had said anything about the subject to anyone in the settlement: "There's a possibility we've got a problem on our hands."

"What kind of problem?"

"Other people are getting sick, too."

Kriker stared at him. "Like Maundy?"

"Just like Maundy."

"Maybe it's somethin' we et. Meat maybe."

"Meat doesn't make people sick this way." The priest pulled himself to full height, about five-eight. Inside his dusty black cassock, he was a chunky man with white hair and blue eyes. Inexplicably, there was a knife scar just below his left ear. Nobody in the settlement could ever remember seeing a priest with a knife scar before. But the priest stayed and nobody asked questions. Given the background of the settlement itself, questions were kept to a minimum.

"We need a doctor," the priest said.

Kriker shook his head, waved his rifle at the encampment below. "By mornin' the granny woman will have Maundy fixed up and then we can travel. Two men are stoppin' by in the mornin' and then Maundy and I will be gone."

"Two men?" There was recrimination in the priest's voice. "I thought we had an agreement. We abide by the law here now, Kriker. That's why Sheriff Decker leaves us alone."

Kriker grinned. "Sheriff Decker. If he only knew."

"What sort of men are these?"

"Just the sort of men you'd expect me to be with, Father. Just that sort exactly."

"We can't afford trouble." The priest added, "You were part of it, weren't you?"

"Part of what?"

"You know what. That bank robbery in town."

"I needed a stake. For me and Maundy. We're headed west."

"You should find that girl a good family and leave her be."

Kriker's anger was quick and startling, and in it the priest could see the mountain-man ferocity that had made Kriker so frightening both in fact and in legend. He grabbed the priest by the shoulder and said, "I lost my real child and now all I've got is Maundy. A man ain't nothin' without his offspring. Nothin'. You understand me?"

He let the priest go.

The gray clouds, promising snow in the west, lay like fog on the tops of the pines in the mountains surrounding them. The wind was cold enough to make the priest's cheeks red.

"Them men are gonna be here, and then we're gonna split the money, and then they're gonna go one direction and me and Maundy's goin' another," Kriker said, "and then the settlement's all yours. You do anything you like with it."

This was Kriker's way of making peace after he had lost his temper. He never apologized. He merely made his voice gentler.

"You understand, Father?"

"I understand."

"You say some prayers for Maundy, too, you hear?"

"I will, Kriker. I will."

Kriker nodded and then returned to the settlement below, leaving the priest to think of the symptoms he'd encountered in the settlement the past few days, and of the word he hadn't heard since a single terrible spring a decade or so ago in St. Louis when 4,500 people had died of the same disease.

The word held unimaginable power for being such a simple few syllables.

Cholera.

7

It was land of ugly beauty, scoria buttes rising into rounded hills of red volcanic rock, hard ground littered with buffalo skulls bleached white by sun and now made even whiter by the snow that blew in the harsh north-easterly wind. Then there was the endless tireless prairie, untold miles of it, brown grass, the rusted ribs of deserted Conestoga wagons, and then an area of alkali desert and sagebrush spiny cactus, dead as a man's worst fear of what lay beyond death. Two emaciated magpies fed here on the fetid meat of a gangrened deer, and thin little creeks were already frozen in the gray twenty-degree afternoon weather that continued lashing the three riders with sticky blasts of wet snow.

They rarely spoke, James riding a grulla several lengths away, Thomas Bruckner and Guild back a ways, staying within a pace of each other. Obviously neither man wanted the other behind him with a gun.

They stopped once to ride down into a gulley where they ate salt pork, beans, and bread, and drank water by kicking in a membrane of ice and scooping up creek water. Wind was trapped in here and it had a frightening majesty, chafing their faces, whistling off the volcanic rock that dinosaurs had once prowled. Still, they talked very little. Guild said, "How you planning to do this?"

"We're gonna go in at night and surprise him," Thomas Bruckner said. "Why?"

"Because I don't see any reason to shoot him."

"He killed two men, didn't he?"

Guild said, "Did he?"

"That supposed to mean something?"

Guild said nothing. He went back to his mount and adjusted the bedding he carried, and the oilskin coat in case things got very bad, and a small waterproof bag for personal things, among which was a picture of the little girl. He wasn't sure why he carried it. Once a priest had advised him to tear it up, but when Guild had tried he couldn't. It rode with him everywhere.

According to Guild's Ingram it was 3:18 when they started riding again.

They found the Indian just before nightfall.

At first they weren't sure what it was. The prairie, flat, without detail, played more tricks than a desert. A man could look a quarter mile off and see something, and then before he reached it it would change apparent shape half a dozen times.

But they saw birds, crows, and magpies mostly, and they didn't have to wonder much here in the now-drifting snow what it was. It might be a mule or a plump rabbit, but whatever it was it was most certainly flesh of some kind or the birds would not be here on the grasses. Light faded now, and everything on the ground was becoming white, and Guild's cheeks were red and numb and so he pulled a red bandanna robber-style across his face.

At least there was no smell, he thought, when they reached what proved to be the Indian.

He'd been an old man, gray-haired, toothless. The birds had eaten out his eyes and a part of his mouth and some of his belly.

Guild hefted his double 10-gauge with one gloved hand and shot at the birds to scare them off. There was no sense killing them. They were birds and they did what birds did and you could not judge them otherwise.

Thomas Bruckner raised his rifle and began firing, too.

It took Guild a moment, there in the dusk, to realize what Bruckner was shooting at.

Not the birds but the dead man.

He put four bullets in the dead Indian's forehead and then he laughed, "Sumbitch." He looked back to his burn-faced brother. "Indian sumbitch."

The Indian lay there in his garish rags, the kind white men gave red men on reservations. No telling what he'd been doing out here or what had killed him. Could have been anything from a heart attack to simply stumbling and cracking his skull.

"No call for that, Thomas," James Bruckner said. There was weariness and a certain resentment in his voice. "He's already dead."

Thomas Bruckner put one more bullet into the dead man. "Yeah," he said. "But he ain't dead enough." He looked at Guild.

They rode on to the settlement.

As they rode, James Bruckner kept thinking of how his brother had shot the dead man back there. He had started twitching, James had, the way he always twitched when his brother did something like this.

The way he had started twitching when, as small boys, Thomas had doused his little brother in kerosene and then thrown a match.

"Not near as bad as it could have been," the circuit doc had said, complimenting the missus on applying wet tea leaves to the boy. "Not as bad as it could have been. He didn't die."

But there were different ways to die, of course. You died when people laughed at you and pointed. You died when you knew you would never hold any but a house-bought woman.

There were a lot of different ways to die.

The sounds of his brother's rifle still echoed in his brain, as did his own screams from years ago when his brother had poured kerosene on him.

He tilted the brim of his hat lower.

The snow was getting bitter.

And he was still twitching, one involuntary spasm after another, a sight ugly in his own eyes as the leathery patch of burned skin covering half his cheek.

8

BY GUILD'S INGRAM it was 8:07 P.M. when they reached the top of the barren hill below which sprawled the valley where the settlement, in summer, yielded its bounty.

The moon was round and silver and alien. The tired horses crunched the icy earth and snorted wearily. Blowing snow was an off-white sheet covering everything, even the deep jet shadows cast by the jagged volcanic rock. Wind came like unearthly song down the mountains and across the silver shine of creek and the grassy cradle of cultivated land where only a month ago wheat yellow as gold had been scythed. But now there was just the wind and the rock and the three men sitting on their horses, staring at the settlement below.

Guild, leaning forward in his saddle, jerked the double 10-gauge from its scabbard. This was the surprise he'd been waiting to visit on the Bruckners ever since last night and the deaths of Rig and young Kenny Tolliver.

He put the double 10-gauge right to the burned part of James Bruckner's face and said, "I'll kill you right here if you don't both throw down your guns."

"What the hell you doin', Guild?" Thomas Bruckner said.

Into the wind, Guild said, "The way I read all this, you killed Rig and Tolliver so you could get your share of the bank money."

"What bank money?" Thomas Bruckner said.

"He knows, Thomas, he knows." Guild jabbed James Bruckner's face with the 10-gauge right where the burned area was. James Bruckner sounded ready to cry.

"You were all in it together. You and this Kriker and Rig and Tolliver," Guild said. "No easier trick than to have the law provide the lookout while the robbers empty out the bank."

"You'd really shoot him, Guild?" Thomas Bruckner said.

Guild pulled back the hammer. "You want to try me?"

"So what're you proposin'?"

"First your weapons get thrown and then I want you to get down."

"I don't think he's foolin', Thomas," James Bruckner said. His face was lost in the shadows beneath his hat rim, but you could hear his tears.

"You sumbitch," Thomas Bruckner said. "I knew you was trash. I knew it."

He threw down his rifle.

Guild said, "Now the guns and the knife."

"You sumbitch."

Then came the handguns and the knife.

Guild prodded James Bruckner with the double 10-gauge. "Now you
do the same."

"You're goin' to get it, James," Thomas Bruckner said, obviously needing to threaten somebody, and with Guild holding the gun there was no
point in threatening him. "Just the way I used to give it to you in the barn
when Pa was out in the fields. Just that way, James."

James threw down his weapons. They made a chinking sound against
the volcanic rock.

Guild took the rope from his saddle and swung it over to James. "Now
get down real easy and go over and tie your brother to that pine down the
hill there."

James Bruckner said, "He'll kill me if I do, mister."

"I'll kill you if you don't."

"Oh, Jesus, mister, you're puttin' me in a real pickle."

Guild prodded him with the gun again. "You walk down that hill and
tie him up or I'll shoot you right here."

"He's just talkin', James. You don't listen to him."

"He shot a little girl, Thomas. Nobody who shoots a little girl is just
talkin'."

Apparently Thomas now saw the inevitable. "This all over, James,
you're gonna get it real good. Real, real good."

"Ain't my fault, Thomas. Ain't my fault."

Guild was tired of the talk. He walked the Appaloosa over to where
Thomas Bruckner had dismounted. Guild slugged the man once, hard in
the mouth.

"Jesus Christ, Jesus Christ!" Thomas Bruckner cried into the wind. He
was holding a handful of thick blood. His own.

So his brother took him downhill and lashed him to the pine that grew on
a slant on the snowy slope.

Guild dropped off the Appaloosa to check James Bruckner's handi-
work. The man had done a good job.

Guild took a rope from Thomas Bruckner's grulla and then tied up
James on the other side of the same tree.

"You sumbitch," Thomas Bruckner said. "You sumbitch."

Guild rode into the settlement fifteen minutes later, coming down a
grassy hill sleek with snow. Cinders from log fires cracked against the

black night sky. The air was pleasantly smoky. Through pieces of burlap in windows you could see the reddish glow of fires and hear the soft crying of infants.

Guild, his double 10-gauge cradled in his right arm, dismounted.

In the center cabin, a door opened and a man in long black garb stood there. A priest.

He came forward into the gloom, his breath frosty, his left hand wrapped around a tin coffee cup.

"Good evening, sir," the priest said in a formal way.

"Good evening, Father."

"You wish a place to sleep tonight?"

"No," Guild said. "I'm looking for a certain man."

"Who would that be?"

"A man named Kriker."

"Kriker. I see."

"He's here, then?"

"No. I'm afraid he's gone."

"I didn't know priests told lies."

The priest paused, looked around. "You're with the sheriff?"

"No."

The priest stared at him a long moment. A collie dog came up. He was covered with snow. He was panting. He looked like he was enjoying himself.

"You're a bounty man."

"Yes," Guild said.

"That is a shameful occupation."

"Where's Kriker?"

"He's not as bad as you may have heard."

"Some men were killed. He may have had something to do with it."

The priest frowned.

Guild lifted the double 10-gauge. "I want to speak with him, Father. Now."

Even from here, even from behind, Guild could hear the safety clicking off the rifle.

"You want to talk, bounty man? You got your chance."

Given the size and the wildness of the man who appeared in the center of the circle of cabins, Guild knew he was finally seeing Harry Kriker.

But apparently Kriker changed his mind, because just as Guild began to speak, Kriker brought his fist down hard on the back of Guild's head.

Guild was unconscious instantly, the collie dog mewling as Guild's face slammed to the ground and was partially buried in deep snow.

9

THOMAS WILLIAM BRUCKNER had been raised, along with six brothers and
seven sisters, in a large soddie in the southernmost tip of the Territory,
down where days were generally longer by forty-five minutes and temperatures generally warmer by ten degrees. He was the second brother in
line and at once the wiliest. Even his older brother, Earle, had had the
good sense to fear him. After age six, when Thomas had locked Earle in
the barn with a boar widely known to have eaten at least ten piglets right
down to the bone—and Thomas had sat on the roof watching Earle trying
to get out of the barn as the boar continually charged at him—Earle had
not only stayed out of Thomas's way but had deferred to him in any
matter in which Thomas demanded deference.

About his sisters, he did not think much at all, good or bad, except to
note that three of them had very large breasts and three of them had
virtually no breasts at all, and the ones with breasts he occasionally tried
to spy on when they took baths in the tin tub on nights before wagon rides
to church. Of the six Bruckner brothers, only two had any interest in
getting off the farm, the others being perfectly content (as were Pa and
Ma) to stay here and farm land that yielded twenty-five cents a bushel for
wheat (and half the time you had to take your share in trade). The high-
light of the whole year, it seemed, was the agricultural society meeting,
where you got to see such exciting things as a squash that weighed 148
pounds and "really took the rag off the bush" (as Pa always liked to say)
and where prizes were awarded in categories as diverse as Three-year-old
Steers and Oxen and Best Buggy and Best Pleasure Carriage and Best
Double and Single Plow. For the women there was Best Shawl and Best
Woolen Sheets and Best Roll Stair Carpeting and Best Woolen Knit
Socks. None of this was the least tolerable for a boy who read, with
difficulty (having gone only through the fourth grade), exciting newspaper
accounts of what life on the frontier was like back in the raw and early
fifties.

It was, surprisingly, his second youngest brother, James, who joined
him in long and fantastic talks out in the woods, where they put prairie
grass in corncob pipes and smoked till their throats were raw and
dreamed aloud of what life in frontier towns would be like. Surprisingly
for two reasons. One, James was the slightest in size and ambition. Pa
always said, "He's more comfortable doin' the woman's work," and so, in
fact, he'd been. And surprisingly for a second reason, too—because even
though Thomas had only been playing the day he'd thrown kerosene on
James and then tossed a wooden match at the soaked ground around

James just to scare him, he was amazed, given the ugliness of James's face, that James would have much to do with him.

But somehow James let Thomas become his boss, Thomas sensing that James did not know how to become as manly as his other brothers, and also sensing that James expected Thomas to teach him. So Thomas taught him to wrestle and shoot game and use a slingshot and make sly little jokes with the Indians who they'd see in the tiny four-buggy village where Pa sent them for certain store-bought provisions from time to time.

Then one April night, the air sweet with spring and prairie grasses already long and the moon bright as madness itself, Thomas, who was then sixteen, and James, who was then twelve, left the farm with such belongings as they could rightfully claim (though technically the hunting rifle belonged to the oldest brother, Earle) and set out to find that type of excitement peculiar to the Territory in those days.

What they found was exactly the opposite, of course. In town after town they worked in restaurants washing dishes or in livery stables with coloreds hauling manure or on farm crews for ten cents a day cutting grain with a cradle and binding it with a band of straw (a feat nobody today knew how to accomplish). Many times as they lay on hard cold ground, the stars chill and distant as their old dreams, James, now fourteen, would cry from loneliness and confusion or some pain a towny had put on him that day for the ugliness of his burned face; and even Thomas, remote and angry as he usually was, felt like crying, too, for what they'd found in the frontier towns were boys like themselves, long on dreams and short on money, comprising a kind of underclass of little more stature than Indians or runaway slaves, sleeping in lofts and alleys and tarp-covered wagons, and always waiting to be run in by bored or mendacious police officers.

Then Thomas William Bruckner shot and killed his first man and everything changed abruptly and much for the better.

It happened up near the Montana border, and actually it happened by mistake. The Bruckner brothers were in a tavern where men fought as much for pleasure as passion and where every sort of illegal deed—from theft to murder—could be planned and a man found to carry out the plan. Thomas William Bruckner was now twenty. He had lost, in the past year, three teeth in four fistfights, a cache of fifty-seven dollars he'd managed to save from farm work, and his virginity. This had happened in a fancy house, and of course he'd gotten the clap and it had all ended in about fifteen excited seconds anyway. She'd looked relieved. An easy fifty cents for fifteen seconds.

Anyway. The tavern.

A man, quite large and quite drunk, had accosted another man, making delirious accusations about the other's advances toward his wife.

The larger man, even though he did not need any help in defeating the smaller one, began to take out a pistol, his certain intent to kill the smaller man.

It was at this moment that Thomas William Bruckner, standing down the bar, tried to get out of the way of the gunfire, and in so doing instinctively drew his own Peacemaker. And then he tripped. The floor was crude pine and the tenpenny nails had not been nailed flat and the toe of his boot had caught the nub of a nail and—

—and his Peacemaker fired and he shot exactly in the heart the large man who had been about to shoot exactly in the heart the smaller man and—

—and it turned out that the smaller man was a good friend of the man who virtually ran the town—or anyway ran those things in the town that mattered, which was to say the women and the liquor and the labor force.

And so it was that the Bruckner brothers learned what the frontier was all about. Not heroic or legendary gun battles. Not the beauty of the sprawling Territory. Not the sense of holding your own destiny in your own hands. Control: that's what the frontier was really all about.

So the Bruckners went to work for the man who controlled the town, and then they moved on to another, larger town where another, more powerful man decided what went on and what didn't go on, and they worked for him, doing jobs large and small, including occasional killings.

Thomas became particularly good at running a shakedown business— offering protection from the law to people who ran whorehouses and saloons, and that was easy enough to do because the first person you always paid off in any town was the lawman.

This was all ten years earlier. There had been a marriage that ended— or so Thomas said—when the woman had fallen down the stairs the night before. (James knew better than to talk about what he'd seen.) There had been some arson in Chicago in which forty Chinese had died and a man named Fitzsimmons got the block he'd been after at the price he'd been wanting to pay. The brothers had hated Chicago, having, like most Territory people, an equal aversion to slavery and to black people. Finally there had been innumerable jobs for innumerable lawmen in innumerable small towns where whores were sold on the hoof and almost any kind of violence could be disguised as accidental.

James himself had killed only once. Thomas had gutshot a saloon owner who'd refused to pay protection. As the man was gagging and puking his last, Thomas, quite calmly, had handed James the rifle and said, "You need the experience, brother. Now you go on and do it, hear me?" James shook his head and backed away and refused to do it. And he would have kept on refusing, only the man was in such misery—this is what he told Thomas later—that he reckoned he was doing him a favor, so he took the rifle and cocked it and shot the man twice in the face, exploding his brain, and then he was just one more dead animal and there was no more pain for him.

These were the Bruckner brothers, the two lashed now to the pine tree on the downslope in the hammered-silver moonlight and the white whipping snow.

"I'm gonna put that gun as far up his ass as it'll go," Thomas Bruckner said, making obvious reference to Guild. "Then I'm just gonna keep loadin' and reloadin' till my arm gets tired."

The wind took his voice and made it vanish down the piny slope of volcanic rock.

10

HE WAS IN a cabin in a straight-backed chair, and Kriker stood over him with a gun. The cabin smelled of cooked meat and illness. In a corner on the cot, in shadows cast by a kerosene lamp, lay a little girl beneath several layers of buffalo hides. You could see by the way she sweated and by the flat white of her skin and by the fever blisters on her tiny gentle mouth that she was very very ill.

Kriker slapped Guild once clean and hard across the side of the face. Guild started to get up out of the chair—anger over being slapped hurting his pride—but then through the door the priest came and he looked at both of them and said, "Kriker. You said there would be no violence."

Kriker set his Sharps down and said, "I want to know why he's here."

"You know why. He's a bounty man." The priest nodded to Guild, and said to Kriker, "You should take that as a sign. You should take your money and leave. With winter coming they won't find you in Canada."

"I won't leave without her."

"She can't travel," the priest said.

Guild sensed how softly the priest spoke when the subject of the girl came up. Obviously he was afraid of infuriating Kriker.

"Where's the granny woman?" Kriker demanded.

"The granny woman can't help."

"She knows the secrets."

"There are no secrets, Kriker. Except for a medical doctor."

"No!" Kriker said, leaning toward the priest.

As Guild watched them talk, he noticed that the priest was missing the final two fingers on his right hand. When he gestured with the hand, the movement gave the man an odd vulnerability. But beyond that, something else troubled Guild. He knew there was some significance to the missing fingers but he did not know what. Something he was failing to remember . . .

Guild said, "I've got the Bruckner brothers tied to a tree."

Kriker turned back to him. "The Bruckner brothers?"

Guild nodded. "I'd like to get up, Kriker. I've got a bad headache from where you hit me. I'd like to get up and have some coffee and walk around."

"I want you to tell me about the Bruckner brothers. What the hell are you doing with them?"

Guild looked to the priest, who said, "Let him have some coffee and walk around. You have the gun, Kriker. He's unarmed."

Kriker glared at Guild, but then he nodded approval.

The priest got Guild some coffee and poured it into a chipped china cup that he handled with some reverence—people this poor in the Territory valued beyond reason chipped castoffs from the rich that they bought in secondhand stores where they stood in line with handfuls of pennies to buy bitter bits of real civilization. While the priest was busy with Guild, Kriker went over and knelt by the girl.

She moaned and Guild saw Kriker jerk back as if he'd been shot. In that simple movement Guild sensed how much the mountain man loved the little girl.

Kriker took a pitcher of water from the nightstand and filled a glass and then raised the girl's head and gave her a drink.

Guild saw tears shine in Kriker's eyes.

Guild looked back at the priest. "She been throwing up?"

"Yes."

"Drinking a lot of water?"

The priest nodded.

"Bad intestinal cramps?"

"Yes, Mr. Guild. Why?"

Guild's face grew tight in the soft lamplight. He did not want to say the word. He did not want to see the pain on Kriker's face.

In a whisper, Guild said, "You know what's going on here, Father."

"Yes."

"But he doesn't, apparently."

"No."

Kriker was talking to the girl.

Guild said, "You need to get a doctor out here right away."

"I know."

Kriker got up, came over. "She seems to be doing better."

He wanted them to agree.

The priest said, "Maybe that's so, Kriker."

"We'll bundle her up. I can take her with me tonight."

Guild said, "She can't travel, Kriker."

"What the hell you talking about?"

"She's got cholera."

There was no other way around it now. He had to look away from Kriker.

Kriker said to the priest, "What the hell's he talking about?"

"He's right, Kriker. She's got cholera and so do several other people in the settlement. We're having a meeting in half an hour." The priest paused. "That's why we need you to clear out. Because we've got to bring in a doctor, and when he sees the cholera, he'll bring in the law. They'll want to make sure this doesn't spread any farther than it has to."

"I won't leave without her."

The priest touched Kriker's arm. The huge man in the dirty buckskins and the wild hair looked lost suddenly—as if his eyes could not focus, his tongue and lips unable to form words.

The priest said, "They're going to vote."

"Who is?"

"The people of the settlement."

"On what?"

"On you."

"Me?"

"Whether to force you out."

"I founded this place. I felled the trees and cleared the fields. There wouldn't be any settlement if it wasn't for me."

"But now you can destroy it, Kriker, and you can't see that. The law is looking for you because they think you killed two men in town and that means they'll destroy this settlement to get you."

Kriker swung around to Guild. "Is this why you come out here, bounty man?"

Guild said, "Yes."

"They're offering a reward because I'm supposed to have killed two men."

"Yes."

"What men?"

"Rig and Tolliver."

"Rig and Tolliver? I didn't kill them."

"I know you didn't. But the Bruckner brothers have convinced the sheriff you did, and they came out here to take you in."

"They'd shoot me."

"Sure they would, Kriker. First chance."

"I didn't kill them men."

"I know."

Kriker said, "Shit," and slammed his right fist into the palm of his left hand. He glanced at the girl. "I've got to get her out of here."

"Why don't you go back with me?" Guild said.

"What?"

"Talk to Decker. I'll make sure the Bruckners don't get to you, and you can tell your side of things."

"I helped stick up the bank. Me and Rig planned it. Tolliver and the deputies was part of it."

"Tell that to Decker."

"They'll still arrest me for robbery."

Guild said, "It's easier than running, Kriker. You're not young anymore and running isn't easy. It isn't easy at all."

Kriker, still seeming dazed by the events of the past half hour, said, "They need to get to me."

"Who?"

"The Bruckners."

"Why?"

"Because I got the bank money hid."

"Why don't you turn it over to me?"

For the first time, Kriker laughed. "You're some hopped-up sonabitch, aren't you? You goddamn bounty men. A little girl is layin' here sick and two deputies are comin' to kill me and all you can think about is the reward."

"Winter's coming," Guild said. "I'm no younger than you and I need money." He shrugged. "It's my job." He nodded to the priest. "Besides, the priest is right. If you don't want to deal with Decker, then you should leave clean. Pack up and head out fast. By the time the Bruckners and Decker catch up with you, you'll be long gone."

"How come you don't want to take me in?"

"I want the robbery money. I return that, I've got my reward. Plus I think I can convince Decker that you didn't have anything to do with killing Rig or the Tolliver kid. I owe the kid and his mother that much."

Kriker glanced at the sleeping girl. She was moaning again, her face white except for the cheeks where the fever was deep red fire.

Kriker said, seeming to forget everything they'd been talking about, "She needs some more water."

He went over to her and poured another glass and then knelt down.

He touched her head, kissing her, and this time there could be no mistaking the sounds he made.

Kriker was sobbing.

* * *

He was old enough to remember when a white Canadian named Theophile Brughier had married the daughter of the Dakota Sioux Chief War Eagle and thereby brought a measure of peace, however temporary, to the area.

He was old enough to remember when Indian women did the gardening with antler rakes and hoes made from bison shoulders.

He was old enough to remember when Indian men were not farmers at all but were hunters. It was the white man and his reservations who had turned hunter into farmer, and failed farmer at that, for now Indians not only his age but Indians small as infants waited in line at army posts for scraps of food and the quick pitying smile of the blue-coated supply sergeant.

He was old enough to remember when he could have erections he did not even want and old enough to remember what this part of the Territory had been like before the buffalo were killed and before the blue sky was crosshatched with telephone and electrical poles and before the river bore the taint of ore from the factory waters upstream.

His name was Pa-wa-shi-ka and he was coming to see his friend, the priest at the settlement. The seventy-nine-year-old Indian had begun coughing up blood again, and last time the priest had told him to come at once if this happened again.

So even tonight in this cold without mercy, he had left his soddie downstream and come up onto the area of rock, his dun slipping on the soft snow, up over the hill, and down to the settlement below.

At first he imagined the sickness that came with the coughing blood was playing tricks on his ears. That and the whipping wind.

Hunched down inside the robes, he imagined he could hear sounds. Desperate sounds. Human sounds.

He stuck his face outside the robe draped over his head.

In the cutting snow, it was almost impossible to see. Even given the curious silver illumination of the full moon.

He did not see the men at first. He did not even see the tree.

He merely continued on up the rocky hill, his dun now no faster than an aged burro.

Then for a moment—as if a fabric had been torn and his gaze allowed to see inside—he saw the two men lashed to the scrubby pine tree on the deep slope of the hill.

At first he did not slow the course of his dun at all. The two men were white, and he had learned long ago never to become involved in a white man's affairs unless you had absolutely no choice. White men were crazed, and even those who seemed friendly were capable of turning on you suddenly, the way animals suddenly and for no reason turn on humans.

He went on.

But they continued yelling, their voices slapping at him on the downdraft of the snow wind, and so finally he reined the dun to a stop and turned around and peeked out of his robe again at the two men.

"We won't make it through the night, Grandpa!" one of them shouted. "Please help us out."

Pa-wa-shi-ka turned his horse to the right, toward the tree. He had a coughing fit then and simply let the horse walk over by the tree.

"Who tied you up?" the Indian asked from his horse.

The two men writhed against their lashes. The one without the burned face said, "Robbers. We're deputies and they captured us. You help us out, Grandpa, and we'll see that you get part of the reward."

The old man shook his head. "It is not good to help white people. They turn on you."

"Please," said the one with the burned face. "We won't last the night. It'll get in our lungs and we'll die of pneumonia."

"Look at my goddamn jacket, old man," the other white man said, shouting above the wind. It was as if they were in a tunnel and the tunnel was roaring with wind.

And then the Indian saw it. The shine of silver—the white man's badge of authority.

"You are law?"

"Law. Yes. Jesus." The man without the burns sounded frantic.

"I will be in trouble if I don't help you, then," the old man decided.

"Very bad trouble," the man without the burns said.

Pa-wa-shi-ka began choking with a coughing spasm again.

Finally he got down from his dun and went over to the two lashed men and cut them free.

The man without the burn did not wait long. He grabbed the Indian's knife away from him and then said, "I want your rifle there, Grandpa."

"My rifle?"

"And your horse."

"Horse? But why?"

But the white man said nothing. He simply walked over to the horse, helped the other white man up, and left Pa-wa-shi-ka standing there to think of the days when he had been a hunter and when nobody would ever have been able to take his knife that way, let alone steal his rifle and horse.

But then he fell to coughing and the blood was thick and hot now, spilling down the front of his cotton shirt.

He went over and picked up the hide robe they had flung from the dun as they'd set off up the hill.

The Indian wrapped himself in the robe and started off walking.

The way he was coughing, he wondered if he would have strength enough to reach the settlement.

11

THE BIRD WAS a barn swallow trapped by the granny woman fifteen minutes ago and brought here to the cabin where the sick girl lay.

The priest had gone several cabins away, where the meeting between the settlement people was taking place.

Kriker with his rifle and Guild with his sense of helplessness stayed here. Sometimes he watched the little girl and then recalled the little girl he'd shot. Life was fragile enough, but for children it was doubly so. He thought of small hands reaching out with no grasp strong enough to save them.

Kriker, now sitting by the girl in a chair angled so that he could watch Guild with no problem, said to the granny woman, "You better hurry up. She's hotter than she was an hour ago."

"I got no guarantees, Kriker."

"You said you could handle it all right."

"I said I could handle it all right if the demons wasn't in her." She shrugged aged shoulders. "If the demons is in her, ain't much I can do."

"A doc could help," Guild said. "She needs a doc."

"You shut up, bounty man. I'm sick of you already." Kriker glared up at the granny woman. The kerosene lamp still cast strong shadows and the wind slammed like a fist against the burlap of cabin windows.

The girl started up in bed abruptly and began vomiting. Guild went over to her and without a word held her frail little shoulders as the puking jerked her about. Kriker held a pan under her mouth.

When she was done and Kriker had laid her back down again, he looked at Guild and said, as if surprised by Guild's tenderness, "Thanks."

"She's a nice little girl."

"She's a beautiful, lonely little girl. She never complains." Then he dropped his gaze to her again and shook his head and whispered "Son of a bitch" at whatever gods he held responsible for this.

The brown barn swallow was little more than a chick, and so the area of its breast was small and the location of its heart difficult to find. "I'm gonna need one of you to hold this bird for me," the granny woman said.

Kriker said, "I'll do it."

He got up and went over to the table where the granny woman worked.

He clamped big hands on the tiny bird that gazed up at him with terrified alien eyes.

The granny woman stabbed the bird in the breast area. Some kind of mucus ran out of the bird's mouth. The eyes grew very large and then a thin membranous haze covered its gaze and then it was dead.

The granny woman worked efficiently now. She cut out the innards and searched with hard white hands through the soft red innards until she came to the heart, which was smaller than a pea. She had been boiling milk in a pan on a small fire in the corner. She took the hot milk and poured some in a tin coffee cup and then dropped the tiny heart into the burned crust of milk floating on top.

Guild shook his head. It was too late on the frontier for anybody reasonable to still practice granny medicine, and yet tens of thousands of people still did. Day in and day out their patients died after drinking tea made of water and the cleaved-off tail of a black cat or eating a handful of fish worms or tying the nail of a coffin to a foot to take care of rheumatism.

The little girl was dying and they were feeding her the heart of a barn swallow. He hated them for their mountain-born stupidity and yet he was moved by their grief and their earnestness.

"You hold her head and I'll pour it down her," the granny woman said.

"This better work," Kriker said.

"It will, Kriker," the granny woman said.

But she glanced anxiously at Guild, and he saw that she looked afraid because she knew what Kriker would do to her if the girl died.

The granny woman stuck a stick in the tin cup. "We want to get the blood good and stirred," she said.

"Good and stirred," said Kriker. He sounded dazed again.

They went over and gave the girl the heart of the barn swallow.

Guild looked back at the bird's carcass on the table. The blood didn't bother him so much as the eyes. They were open and staring, and he went over and closed them.

The little girl puked up the milk less than three minutes after they gave it to her.

He was not really a priest, of course, and those in the settlement knew it. He had come here eight years ago, the law back in Chicago interested in his part in the murder of a cardsharp (John Healy was himself a cardsharp), but he found both himself and the settlement in need of a priest and so he became one.

At first they did not honor him. They would scoff and curse and deride him. But a woman, whose baby strangled at bloody birth, was comforted by the fake priest, as was her husband, and so Healy made two converts among the forty or so settlement people. Then a woman asked Healy to baptize her infant and then a man asked him to give his consumptive wife last rites. And then, Healy having long worn the black cassock and white collar now, children began calling him "Father." There came a flood and Healy offered succor as well as prayers spoken in a tongue touched with brogue, manly and fine, here in the forest where they'd fled. And at planting season he stood as Jesus had stood, arms wide and praying to the blue sky for bountiful harvest and the balm of friendship. By then even the adults had come to call him Father Healy, and now there was no question that he was a priest. The settlement, wanting its own form of civilization, wanting its children to learn the secrets of print on paper and the ways of men who did not beat their wives and work their children as slaves—the settlement had forgotten utterly about a man named Healy who'd been a Chicago cardsharp. They knew only a Healy who was a priest, and a good one.

Father Healy himself had only one problem with his role. He knew the social necessity of the settlement having a priest, yet he did not believe in a God. He tried. He held the most delicate flowers and splashed in his hands the purest of water and watched unblinking the steep and unfaltering arc of the hawk against the blue summer sky. He saw all the evidence of a God, and yet in his heart he could not believe in one.

He blamed this on his boyhood near the Union Stockyards in Chicago, where his father came home day after numbed day bloody as a stillborn babe, the entrails of dead animals clinging to him like the white larvae of maggots to spoiled meat. What a place the Union Stockyards had been. Two million dollars to construct. Three hundred fifty-five acres alone of cattle pens. And the animals themselves. Twenty-five thousand cattle. Eighty thousand hogs. Twenty-five thousand sheep. All this carrying the stench and sound of hell itself, for it was estimated that ten thousand animals a day died there, that on some killing floors the blood was so deep it splashed the knees in waves.

This was how the young Healy came to think of life and death. The men who owned the yards got you and they killed at their whim. And then, as with the sad-eyed cows and the plump pink pigs and the sweet frightened lambs—then there was just the darkness. Just the darkness.

He had been forced to be a priest because he saw early on that he had none of the skills the other settlement men could claim. He was too clumsy for farm work and too unskilled for building. But he spoke in his fine voice and he knew how to read, and his gambling days had left him with a gift for reassuring others (nobody needing more reassurance than a man you were cheating), and so it was that Healy followed in the footsteps of Jesus and tried to believe in Jesus but did not—even on the most overpowering of star-flung spring nights—much as he so desperately prayed to.

But it was important for him to be a priest because there was no other thing he could be for this settlement, and it was important for the settlement to have him be its priest because even the strongest of men were frightened of the things that lay just beyond daylight. So his words soothed them the way a baby is soothed in the lap and arm, even though the words are often meaningless to the parent uttering them, just soft imbecilic songs of reassurance on the long night's air.

During all this time, Kriker had been the unquestioned master of the settlement and great deference had been paid to him.

But now, years of his robberies, years of the settlement's dreading an invasion by the law, had come to an end because now the settlement was faced with something that not even Kriker's rage could manage—the prospect of cholera.

Crowded into the largest cabin now—the cabin usually used for meetings—were twenty men and women dressed in shabby winter clothes, shirt piled on shirt, torn gloves pulled over raw knuckles. Yet in all there was a sense of purpose and pride that their stay at the settlement here had given them. They had been thieves and worse, and now they knew the satisfaction of real work. They had been plunderers, and now they knew the joy of having families and protecting that most precious gift of all, children.

And now they stood facing Kriker. Father Healy was between him and the others, while Kriker leaned against one corner of the cabin, smoking a cob pipe, his face drained of its usual animation because only five minutes before he had seen that the girl's condition continued to deteriorate.

A man named Silas, a man big as Kriker himself in bib overalls and a red wool sweater, said, "We owe you our lives, Kriker. We're not meanin' to be ungrateful."

Kriker said, "I can't leave now. The girl's too sick to travel."

A woman said, without anger, "Kriker, we need a doc. The granny woman can't help us. And when the doc comes the law'll come, too, because they think you murdered those people in town. You know there been some people in town just waitin' to burn this place down. We don't want to give them no excuses, Kriker."

Kriker came away from the wall and glared at them—the young, the old, the lame among them, and the strong. They'd been his people, his flock, as it were, all these years, and now they regarded him as a stranger.

"It's our settlement, Kriker," said another man. He was bald and wore a rough denim jacket and rough denim jeans. "You kept to the old ways—

the ways we fled. But we learned the land, Kriker, and now those are our ways. We don't rob no more, and we don't have no law on us."

Kriker's grief turned to anger as he leaned on his Sharps. "You think I couldn't kill you, Jonathan?"

"You could kill me, Kriker." The man waved his hand to the others. They had guns of various kinds, too. "But you couldn't kill them."

Father Healy said, "We need to remember two things here. Without Kriker there would be no settlement. Each of us owes him more than we can say. Isn't that right?"

He addressed the group of them. Heads hung now, both with shame and with an obvious sense that perhaps the priest was going to try and persuade them not only to let Kriker stay, but to put off sending somebody for a doc in town.

"Isn't that right?" Father Healy repeated.

He was chastising them, the way a parent scolds children.

"Right," somebody at the back of the group said.

Then most of the people took it up, there in the cabin with the potbellied stove and the walls lined with jars of strawberry preserves and corn and string beans. There were quilts here, too, warm and beautiful ones, and a fiddle in the corner that sang sweetly on nights of festivity—and what Healy did with his words and hard glances was remind the people of who in the first place was responsible for all this.

Kriker.

Then the priest surprised everybody by turning to Kriker and saying, "But as grateful as we are, Kriker, I have to put the good of everybody ahead of your own good."

Kriker seemed to sense what was coming.

The priest said, "You must leave tonight."

"Without the girl?"

"She can't travel, Kriker."

"You're supposed to be my friends."

"There are other children here, Kriker, and the threat of cholera. That comes before anything."

Kriker started to heft his gun.

Guild, who had been rolling a cigarette in the corner and just watching the proceedings, said, "The way cholera moves, you should send somebody right now."

"Tonight?" a man asked.

Guild nodded. "With the best horse you've got." Guild stood up and started edging toward Kriker because he could see what was about to happen. Kriker was getting ready to raise his Sharps.

Guild moved then, grabbing a chair and smashing it across the back of Kriker's head just as the man raised the Sharps.

Several people screamed, and for the next few moments there was great confusion as Guild threw himself down on the still-conscious Kriker. Guild needed to get a punch off clean and hard enough to knock the man out completely.

The man named Jonathan saved him the trouble by coming over and kicking Kriker in the side of the head.

Kriker's head slammed against the floor. He was unconscious. Guild got his handcuffs from his gun belt and cuffed Kriker and then dragged him over to the wall.

When he got up he saw the man named Jonathan standing there staring down at Kriker. "I didn't want to do that." He sounded on the verge of tears. "We owe him everything."

"You didn't have any choice," Guild said. To the priest he said, "Now let's get a rider. We need a doc and we need Sheriff Decker and a few deputies out here. One of you a good rider?"

He looked at the group and they pushed forth a young woman in braids and freckles. She was maybe sixteen. "She's the best," the priest said. He smiled affectionately. "She likes horses better than people."

"Yeah, all except for Jim Courtner over to the other village," a voice from the rear said. "She likes him best."

The young woman blushed.

"You think you can reach town in this storm?" Guild asked.

She nodded.

"All right," Guild said, "here's what you need to tell Decker, and here's what you need to tell the doc."

12

THOMAS BRUCKNER CROUCHED next to a pine just on the edge of the settlement.

His brother James, walking on his haunches, came up from behind. James said, "Maybe he won't give a damn about her anymore."

"You heard the way he'd talk about her to Rig and Tolliver."

The moonlight sparkled through the blowing snow. Thomas Bruckner's eyebrows were white with the freezing stuff.

James said, "It wouldn't be right."

Which was what Thomas had been waiting to hear—the thing that was really bothering his brother. Ever since Thomas had suggested taking the girl and using her as a way of getting the bank money from Kriker, James had been acting the way he usually did when he didn't want to do something but was afraid to say so.

A spindle-legged doe appeared in the moonlit clearing. Then, sensing the two men, it took off faster than seemed possible west of the cabins.

Thomas said, "You want to make me mad?"

"You know better'n that, Thomas."

"Then you do what I say."

"She's a little girl."

Thomas wiped snow from his face, then sighed. "You remember that time in Kansas City?"

"What time?"

"The time with the red-haired woman who said you were ugly."

James waited a very long time before speaking as he crouched there next to his brother. "Yes," he said. "Yes, I remember."

"You remember what I did for you?"

Nothing.

"You remember, James?"

"Yes, I remember."

"Well, you think it's right that I'd do something like that for you, and here I ask you a simple little favor and you won't do nothin' for me at all?"

Nothing.

"You think that's right, James?"

"No, I guess not."

"I wish you'd say that louder so's I'd know you mean it."

"No, I guess it isn't right."

"I cut up her face real good for you, didn't I?"

"I didn't want you to do that, Thomas."

"But I did it."

"I didn't even want you to do it."

"But I love you, James. You're my brother and I love you and that's why I was obliged to do it."

"If you loved me, maybe you wouldn't have thrown that kerosene on me in the first place."

"I thought we had that agreement."

Nothing.

"I thought we had that agreement."

"I'm sorry."

"I thought we had that agreement that said I feel so bad about throwin' that kerosene on you that I never want to hear about it again."

"I'm sorry."

"But about once every couple weeks you go and break that agreement. You ever notice how you do that, James?"

"I'm sorry, Thomas."

"Now I cut up that whore for you and it seems to me that the least thing you could do for me is go in there and get that little girl and bring her back out here while I stand guard. Doesn't that seem like the least little thing you could do for me?"

"I guess so."

"You don't sound sure."

"Sometimes I'm not sure, Thomas. Sometimes I'm not sure about anything."

The wind came again, and the freezing snow, silver dust devils of it now. Thomas said, "There's a line shack about a mile from here. We'll take her there and we'll all be nice and warm. Then we'll tell Kriker we've got her and then we'll get the money and then you and me can head for California."

"You shouldn't have cut her."

"Hell," Thomas Bruckner said. "Hell if I shouldn't have." Then, into the smell of fire and human warmth downwind on the shadowy night, he said, "You go get her, James. You go get her right now."

Once he reached the camp, James Bruckner felt a familiar fear—that of desertion. As a boy he'd been lost in a rainstorm and he'd felt that he would never find his way home again. He felt surrounded by hostile entities he could not see. But then his brother Thomas had come looking for him and had guided him home.

Now James felt surrounded by hostile entities again. Only these he could see—or at least glimpse: the people of the settlement. People whose eyes would settle on the burned part of his face and narrow in disgust. People who would snicker and point behind his back. People who could never see what he was—but only what he appeared to be. Ever since being doused with the kerosene, he had imagined that people wanted to get their hands on him, to tear him apart the way a lynch mob had torn apart a black man in Keokuk one day when he and Thomas had been riding through, literally rending the man with their fingers and fists.

If the people of this settlement caught him stealing the girl, then the same fate would be his.

For the next ten minutes, he went cabin to cabin. In three cabins mothers sat with broods of children, humming, knitting, rocking infants. In one cabin an older man sat reading a yellow paperbound book by a kerosene lamp.

In the fourth and largest of all the cabins, he heard the meeting taking place and heard what the settlement people were saying about Kriker, and what Kriker said about the little girl.

From this, James Bruckner learned what he should be looking for—a young girl who was sick from something, though he could not quite decide what from the conversation.

So he set about checking out other cabins, and finally he came to the one where an old woman sat in a rocking chair next to a cot where a fevered-looking young girl lay asleep.

The old woman held in her right hand, by its tiny feet, a dead bird which she was switching back and forth over the face of the sleeping girl.

A granny woman, James Bruckner realized.

He leaned back from the burlap window and pressed himself against the rough bark of the cabin wall as he heard feet crunching through the ice and snow.

His heart hammered as he thought of the black man in Keokuk and what the mob had done to him, what it wanted to do to anybody who was different from itself.

The crunching feet drew closer.

Cherry pipe smoke trailed on the night air.

The moon was so round and clear, even through the haze of snow, it looked unreal.

He pressed himself against the wall so hard the back of his head hurt from the pressure.

Please just go on by. Please just go on by.

Which is what they did, finally, two men, one of whom said, "I never seen Kriker like that. The way he looked back there."

"He looked old."

"It's the girl. It's like she's his own."

"She's never spoken since the day he took her. Never a word."

"He shouldn't have taken her. He should have left her."

"Never a word."

Then they were gone and James Allan Bruckner knew that he needed to move quickly now.

He yanked his Navy Colt from his holster—the leather sodden with snow—and walked carefully around to the front door of the cabin.

He moved almost without sound, having become, during his years since leaving home, very good at jobs that required stealth. Or at least that's what Thomas always told him when he insisted it was James Allan who should go into this place or that while Thomas stood some distance away "watching out."

He eased in the door, and before the granny woman quite had time to look up, he had the Colt aimed straight at her face and the hammer cocked.

"I don't want to hurt you, granny woman."

She had frozen now, holding the dead bird still above the sleeping girl's face.

"I just want the girl."

"Oh, no," the granny woman said. "This is Kriker's girl."

"I need to take her, granny woman. I need to take her and I want to do it without hurtin' you. Do you understand me?"

"She's Kriker's girl," the granny woman said again.

But for the moment, James Bruckner wasn't listening. He had been so long out in the bitter cold—first lashed to the tree and then hiding out on the edge of the settlement—that now all he could do was stare at the warm and comfortable cabin. There was food in the pantry—bread and rice and beans—and there was a potbelly stove and a tin tub for soaking in steamy hot water and a beautiful painting of the Lord and—

And the granny woman was staring at his face.

He sensed it and his head snapped around and then his eyes confirmed it.

Obviously fascinated and repelled at the same time, the granny woman rested her eyes on his patch of burned skin.

Most people couldn't.

"What happened to your face?"

"Why would you care?" He sounded mean now.

" 'Cause I might know a treatment for it."

"There ain't no treatment for it."

"You sure?"

"I'm sure. Knew this granny woman in Wisconsin. She said there was a treatment for it and she spent several days tryin' but it came to nothin'." Then softly, "Nothin'."

"She try a robin's egg?"

"Yep."

"She try tyin' a mackerel to your head?"

"Yep."

"She try a—"

"She tried everything. Everything."

The granny woman, small but not at all frail, sat back in her rocking chair thoughtfully. "What you goin' to do with her?"

"Can't see how that's your business."

"You're shiverin'."

"I'm cold."

"You're shiverin' 'cause you're scared, too. You don't really want to take this little girl."

"Got to."

"Why?"

"Like I said, can't see how that's any of your business."

"She's got the cholera."

Without moving his Colt from the granny woman's face, he eased his gaze to the girl. She almost looked dead, so still and pale. Only the sweat on her face spoke of fevered life.

"I got to take her, granny woman."

"She'll die if you move her."

"I got to take that chance."

"You know what Kriker'll do to you?"

"Help me git her bundled up, granny woman."

"It's gonna be terrible, what Kriker's gonna do."

"Help me git her bundled up," he said.

She helped him. She tugged a heavy woolen coat on the girl and then boots and then mittens and then a heavy woolen scarf around her head.

The first time James Bruckner touched her, he felt how hot the girl was. He couldn't see how anybody could be that hot and still be alive. He thought of cholera and the stories he'd heard about it and of a marshal he'd known who'd been fine at nine one morning and then dropped straight down dead at four that afternoon.

Cholera.

He hefted the girl under his arm like a bundle and said, "I'm gonna have to put you out, granny woman."

"Hit me?"

"Yep."

"You don't sound like you want to do that."

"Ain't a matter of want. Matter of need."

Which is when he struck her. He had learned over the years how to hit somebody just to put them out briefly and how to hit somebody to hurt them. She would not be out more than ten or fifteen minutes the way he'd just done her, and then all she'd have at worst would be a headache. He had only made a mistake once, in a Northeastern Territory town where Thomas had briefly been sheriff, when he'd hit a Mexican prisoner. The man had had epilepsy and had gone into convulsions right there at James Allan's feet. And he had died at James Allan's feet, too, and not for months could James Allan forget it, the way the man had spewed silver froth from his mouth, the crazed animal eyes, and the entire twitching body.

James Allan Bruckner hefted the girl under his arm and ran out into the night.

13

GUILD GOT KRIKER set up in a chair, still handcuffed, of course, and then got himself set up in a chair and then had a cigar while he waited for the big man to come to.

By now the others had left the central cabin. Guild sat there listening to the fire pop inside the potbellied stove and to the way the snow sounded like salt granules sprayed against the west side of the cabin.

When Kriker made a noise, Guild said, "I need you to tell me where the money is."

Kriker made no intelligible response. He moved his head from side to side as if he were in a great deal of pain, and then he said, "The girl."

"The granny woman's with her."

He was coming awake now, Kriker was. "She all right?"

"She needs a doc, Kriker. The priest is right."

"He ain't a priest."

"What?"

"He ain't a priest."

"He wears a cassock and a collar."

"He still ain't no priest."

"What is he, then?"

"Cardplayer from Chicago."

"I'll be damned," Guild said, and knew instantly who the man was. The missing fingers became a wanted poster and the wanted poster became a man. A cardsharp wanted for second-degree murder in the death of another cardsharp. Guild had one of those memories. He didn't recall everything about the poster—couldn't, for example, recall the amount of the reward—but he remembered the words "cardsharp" and "missing fingers."

But now that wasn't so important as the robbery money. To get that reward, all Guild needed to do was ride back to Sheriff Decker. To claim the priest he'd have to go all the way back to Chicago.

He said, "You're being selfish, Kriker."

"What's that supposed to mean?"

"The girl. She needs a doc and you need to let her go."

"She's my daughter."

"She's your daughter the way Healy is a priest."

"Her folks got killed and I took care of her."

"She needs a doc."

"A doc killed my wife and son."

Guild sighed. "They told me what happened, and it doesn't sound like it was the doc. It sounds like it was the disease."

"What disease?"

"Same one as this one. Cholera."

"She's got a touch of the bug is all."

"You know better."

"Hell."

"Hell, too," Guild said, "and you know it." He paused. "Where's the money?"

Kriker grinned. "We're talkin' about a little girl's life here and all you give a damn about is the money."

Guild grinned back. "I like your piety, Kriker."

"What's 'piety'?"

"You've been killing people and robbing people all over the Territory for twenty years and I try to collect a reward on you and you get all pissed up and self-righteous."

"I never killed nobody innocent."

"Somebody killed the girl's folks."

"Wasn't me." He sighed. "Anyway, later on I killed the man what done it."

"I've got half of what I wanted."

"What's that supposed to mean?"

"It means I've got the Bruckner brothers tied up. Now I get the money and I'll have all I wanted. I'll take the money and the brothers back to Sheriff Decker and get the reward and ride out of here."

"What about me? You don't want to take me in?"

"We're going to make a trade."

"A trade?"

"You're going to tell me where the money is, and then you're going to get on your horse and get out of here."

"What about Maundy?"

"The girl's staying so a doc can help her."

Tears came into the mountain man's eyes again, and Guild could see that his fear and hatred of docs was just as powerful in the voodoo sense as the granny woman's medicines. "The doc'll kill her! The doc'll kill her!"

But Guild was past it now with the man. He felt sorry for him and was moved by his love for the little girl, but the little girl needed a doc and Guild needed the reward money and needed to turn over the Bruckners, who'd killed Rig and young Tolliver. The one part of hunting bounty he'd never liked was that not everybody made it easy for you. Sometimes Guild saw that he was very little different from the man he was stalking, and sometimes that made things difficult indeed. But you got past it and the professional part of yourself took over and while it was not an admirable part of yourself perhaps but it was a necessary part.

Kriker had put his head down and was starting to sob, and Guild said, "I'll stay here with the doc personally, Kriker. I'll be with him all the time. I'll make sure that he doesn't do anything to the girl. You understand that?"

Kriker raised his head. His eyes and nose were running and his beard was filled with mucus. "I don't want her to die, Guild. I don't want her to die."

He sounded unimaginably young and terrified, and now all Guild himself could do was put his own head down.

When he raised it, he said, "Where'd you put the money, Kriker?" He said it very softly, so softly the popping of the potbellied stove nearly covered his words.

"There's a cave on a ridge to the north of here. There's a crooked oak in front of it. The money's in there. I don't give a damn about the money no more. I just want Maundy to be all right." He stared at Guild. "You promise you won't let that doc hurt her?"

"I promise."

" 'Cause I'd find you."

"I know."

"And I'd kill you."

"I wouldn't blame you."

" 'Cause I love her."

Guild stood up and that's when somebody burst through the cabin door and said, "Somebody took the girl and knocked out the granny woman!"

Kriker made a noise Guild could equate only with a huge animal that had been badly wounded.

Guild picked up his double 10-gauge and said, "Son of a bitch. Son of a bitch."

Then they all went to Kriker's cabin.

14

"You got what you wanted, didn't you?" Kriker shouted at the priest half an hour later.

The two men stood only inches apart in the center of the cabin where the girl had lain.

The granny woman, favoring her head with a knobby hand, sat in a corner shaking her head as if she could still not believe what had taken place.

Inside the stove, wind from the chimney chased the flames in a whoosh of fire.

Three settlement men stood and watched as Kriker, still cuffed, paced back and forth in the cabin after screaming at the priest.

"You got what you wanted, you miserable son of a bitch! I wouldn't be surprised if you had something to do with it!"

The granny woman glanced up and said, softly and sorrowfully, "He didn't have nothin' to do with it, Kriker. Nothin' at all."

Kriker waved his cuffed fists in frustration and fury.

The snow was getting heavy and wetter. Guild went down the long slope of the hill, digging in his heels. By now the moon was so snowed over there was nothing but shadow and snowdrifts on the land. The only sound was the wind and, faintly, his own boots, the creak of leather and crunch of ice.

They were gone from the tree, the Bruckner brothers, just as he'd expected.

Uselessly, he bent down and picked up the rope that had bound them. He hefted it in his hands as if it had the power to impart some knowledge he vitally needed.

But he was stalling and he knew it. He just didn't want to have to see Kriker's face again. The girl gone, Kriker had become the sort of animal the human mind cannot comfortably deal with, one so lost in grief he is capable of any act at all.

Guild threw the rope down and started back up the slope, the wind knocking him to the left and then to the right, not permitting him straight passage.

He was about halfway up the hill, black sky behind the rocks and pines on the rim, when he heard a moan he first dismissed as the wind.

But the moan came again and he knew better, and now he went left on purpose, over across a sheer shine of ice coating to a jagged boulder. The closer he got, the clearer two thick black sticks became.

Then he realized that the thick black sticks were human legs.

The old Indian had crawled behind the boulder for protection from the wind. It hadn't done him much good. He had ten or twenty breaths in him and no more.

Guild raised the man's head and said, "Where's your horse?"

The Indian, parchment brown, parchment wrinkled, smelled of urine and sweat despite the cold. He said, "Lawman."

The Bruckners, of course. "Burned face?"

The Indian nodded.

Guild said, "I'm taking you to the settlement."

The Indian started to cry.

Guild threw the old man over his shoulder and started once more down the hill. The old man had the effect of anchoring Guild. The strain was greater, but the wind no longer blew Guild around.

He could feel him dying. You could tell by the coughing. The old

Indian's lungs pressed against Guild's back and he could feel death come that way. In little spasms. Then there weren't any spasms at all.

Guild didn't put him down, though. He carried him the rest of the way to Kriker's cabin and then set him on the floor and everybody there looked at the dead brown man and shook their heads, and one said, "Bruckners?"

And all Guild could do was nod and stare over at Kriker, who had his face buried in the pillow where the girl's head had lain.

Guild was watching Kriker roll his face back and forth on the pillow when one of the settlement men started gagging just before he started vomiting.

Guild said to Healy the priest, "It's starting. The cholera."

Healy the priest said something he probably shouldn't have. He said, "Shit."

Guild said, "Now we've got to wait for two things."

"What's that?" Healy said.

"Word from the Bruckners on how they want to make the trade for the girl."

"And?"

Guild nodded to the two men helping the sick man out of the door. "And the cholera to start. You know how it goes. Half this settlement could be dead by tomorrow night."

This time the priest responded more appropriately. He said, "My God."

15

ONCE THERE HAD been a city named Yankton, and it had been a fine city with electric lights that glowed in the darkness and fine shiny carriages pulled by fine shiny horses and a park where a calliope could be heard on summer nights and a band shell where a hundred musicians played music so beautiful that even the stars seemed to brighten.

Once there had been a two-story house with the kind of exterior decoration called gingerbread (which the girl always giggled at hearing, thinking of gingerbread as something little girls such as herself ate as special treats). Once there had also been a sunny room where a gray cat named Naomi stretched in the sunlight and where a plump pink doll named Estelle watched everything that went on in the room with her blue button eyes. Maundy was the only one in the world who knew that Estelle could talk; she had decided it would be best for all concerned to keep Estelle's abilities a secret.

Once there had been a tall, handsome father given to three-piece suits and working late at his law office, and once there had been a short, pretty mother given to holding Maundy on her knee and reading to her stories by a man named Sir Walter Scott and a woman named Louisa May Alcott. Maundy liked especially Louisa May.

Then one summer there had been a stage trip (Father having said, "There's no direct train route there," and then cursing as always the territorial government for its inadequacies) to see Cousin Daniel on his farm.

And that's when it happened—the frightened shout of the stagecoach driver, the pounding of hooves coming from the surrounding woods, and then the quick sharp ear-hurting sound of gunfire, and the tart gray smell of it, too.

The robbers had made Father, Mother, and herself step down from the stage and raise their hands the way people had to in the melodramas her parents liked to attend, and then for no reason two of the robbers simply started shooting and—

—and she could remember nothing else about that period of her life.

Occasionally she would try to reconstruct the rest of what had happened that day, but something in her mind would not let the images form.

The gunfire . . . and Father screaming and Mother leaning down to him and screaming herself and . . .

Then there was the man named Kriker. He had a beard like a bear's and a belly like a bison's, and he wore hide for clothes instead of cotton or flannel, and when he spoke he talked the way the poor people of Yankton did, with "ain'ts" and "ain't a gonnas" and all those other things that Miss Meister always said made her "positively cringe."

Kriker was one of the four robbers, but he hadn't done any of the shooting. In fact, he shouted for the shooting to stop, but by then it had been too late.

Kriker took her back to the settlement then and began the long process of trying to get her to talk. That was the funny thing about Kriker. You wouldn't think a man who wore hides and who shunned civilized things would have such patience or sweetness or gentleness, but he did. Those qualities glowed in his eyes and gentled his tongue, and she had learned quickly enough not to be afraid of him.

But still she couldn't talk.

Green summers and white winters came and went, and she found herself becoming part of the settlement itself, doing chores and picking wild flowers and learning how squirrels and raccoons were skinned for stew meat and how milk snakes were ugly but could not hurt you and how rattlesnakes were pretty in their way but could kill you.

Her hair grew long and her limbs grew longer. One day Kriker brought from town a doll that resembled Estelle not in the least, but a doll she loved in as peculiar a way as she loved Kriker.

But still she could not talk.

The granny woman spent hours with her, fumbling with herbs and mice bones and rabbit pelts, but still she could not talk.

The priest spent hours with her, fumbling with holy water and incense and fine blue swaths of cloth, but still she could not talk.

Kriker spent hours with her, holding her in his lap there in the rocker as birds sang softly in the purple dusk, but still she could not talk.

She wanted to talk, of course, and tried to talk, and sounds welled in her throat and filled her mouth, but they were not words, just sounds, and so she did not, no matter how she tried, talk.

And the settlement people came to accept this, shaping the air with gestures that said "Thank you" or "Isn't it a beautiful day?" or "Would you like to run in the woods?" or "Is it time to fill your belly?"

There had been a time when she could talk—when, indeed, Father at the Sunday table filled with roast beef and chocolate cake had called her his "little chatterbox"—but words now were some secret lost seemingly forever.

Forever.

She dreamed of these things as she lay in the corner of the line shack where the two men who'd taken her from the village had placed her.

She dreamed of these things and of a visit to St. Loo and of a train trip east to New York and of how her mother had said that someday Maundy would have her own children and of how Father smelled after shaving, clean and spicy, and how her cat had stretched so gray and beautiful in the sunlight on the white spread of her bed.

She dreamed of these things as she lay there dying.

"He won't kill you."

"He sure will."

"We've got the girl."

"You know what he's like."

"I know what he's like, but I also know we got the girl." Thomas Bruckner paused. "You put a piece of that white sheet on your carbine and you ride into that settlement and you ask to see Kriker."

"I wouldn't even get that far."

"I wouldn't send you if I thought he'd kill you."

James Bruckner shook his head. "You can just imagine what he'll be like now."

"I can also imagine that robbery money. It's part ours, anyway."

James Bruckner looked around the line shack. When the railroads had cut through the timber paralleling the frozen river below, they'd needed temporary facilities for materials and bosses. Shacks such as these were dotted all over the Territory. They smelled of wood and creosote and damp earth. The grave probably would not smell much different. In the summer dogs and rats and cats and snakes slept in them, and termites and worms feasted on them. But now it was too cold for anything except human beings.

When the girl moaned, James Bruckner looked over at her. He'd set a match to a kerosene lantern twenty minutes ago, and now the lantern light showed that her lips were so dry from fever they'd started to crack and bleed.

James said, "She better not die."

"She won't die."

"I could barely feel her pulse."

"She won't die."

"He'd hunt us down if she did. There wouldn't be anyplace we could go without him findin' us."

"You just take that piece of sheet and the carbine and the horse and you ride into that settlement and you tell him if he gives us the money, then an hour later he's got the girl."

"I still say he'll kill me."

"You're just like Ma."

"Don't say nothin' against Ma."

"I ain't," Thomas Bruckner said, knowing how sensitive a subject Ma was with James. "I just mean you always look on the dark side."

"Sometimes that seems like the only side there is."

"I look on the bright side."

"You don't have my face."

"You know that woman in St. Loo. She liked you that time."

"That's 'cause she was crippled and she knew what it was like havin' people stare at you all the time."

"She said she wanted to marry you, didn't she?"

"Yeah, but I saw how she always looked at those other guys. The ones without faces like mine. I saw how she looked at them."

The girl moaned again.

"You better be headin' out, James. You better be headin' out right away."

"He's gonna shoot me, Thomas. He's gonna shoot me for sure."

But Thomas wasn't listening. He went over and tore off a piece of the soiled sheet on which the girl lay on the rusted springs that had once been a bed. He took the white rag and tied it to the cold steel barrel of the carbine and then he handed it back to James.

"I love you, James. I surely do."

Thomas leaned over and kissed him on the cheek. The burned cheek. "I'm sorry for the way I am sometimes. But I do try to be a good brother, James. A true one."

Thomas always did this whenever James wavered about doing a particularly dangerous job. A brotherly kiss and then kind words.

But he sent James out anyway, of course, and without hesitation at all.

Just the way that day, so long ago now yet so perfectly frozen in James's mind, when Thomas had splashed the kerosene on him and then tossed the match.

Just the same way.

16

THREE HAD DIED in the past half hour. The cholera, as cholera always did, struck swiftly. You got stomach cramps that literally threw you around and then you began vomiting and then your fever shot up and then you were dead. Sometimes all this could transpire within three hours, start to finish, and you'd be dead. In the Territory there was nothing like it. Nothing.

Guild sat in the cabin where the girl had been. Kriker, still cuffed, sat in the chair across from him. Guild had his double 10-gauge in his lap.

He said to Kriker, "Why not take the drink I offered?"

"I need my mind clear."

"I'm going to handle the Bruckners, Kriker. Not you."

Kriker, curiously reserved the past twenty minutes, said, "You owe me that at least. For the little girl's sake."

They stared at each other and then Guild said, "Maybe you're right, Kriker. Maybe I do owe you that."

"I don't know many men who'd steal a little girl."

"I guess I don't, either."

"You should have seen her with this blue hair ribbon I bought her last spring."

"Pretty, I'll bet."

"Real pretty." Pause. "She could die, she's so sick."

"She won't die, Kriker. We'll get her back. Just have some whiskey. We'll hear from them soon."

Kriker said, his eyes tearing up again, "You ever have children?"

"No."

"Then you don't know what I mean."

"I know what you mean, Kriker. I know just what you mean." Guild thought about the little girl. He'd been tracking a man to a cabin and he'd seen a rifle glint inside the door and he'd raised his gun instinctively and fired. Then he'd seen that the person with the rifle had been a little girl. The wanted man had been her father, who had left her behind. The girl died right in front of Guild, right in the doorway. All he could do was watch, the way the blood bloomed on her chest, and then the soft clear childish tears there at the quick last. There'd been great outrage and a trial, but he had been found innocent although not once had he ever felt innocent. Which was why, even as a Lutheran, he so often went to Catholic church and confession. To rid his mind of her image, the little girl dying there before the cabin, the scent of pines ridiculously sweet that day, the sky ridiculously blue.

"You aren't going to have that whiskey, I am," Guild said and got up and crossed the cabin floor and poured himself some bourbon. He had had maybe two fingers when the cabin door swung open and with it came icy snow and wind that cut knife sharp.

Father Healy stood there, dazed. "Half the settlement's down with cholera. Half the settlement." He nodded to Guild. "You have any idea what we can do?"

"All we can do is wait till the girl gets back with the doc."

Father Healy said, almost to himself, "Maybe this is my fault."

"What?" Guild said.

Then Father Healy shook the thought away and said, "You haven't heard from the Bruckners yet?"

"No."

The priest nodded to Kriker. "How's he?"

"Not much better."

The priest went over to Kriker and said, "The girl's going to be all right. I'm sure she is."

Kriker's rage was back. "You ain't no priest so don't go around makin' like one! Just get out of this cabin and leave me alone!"

Guild put his hand on the priest's shoulder and pulled him away from Kriker, leading him to the door and outside.

They stood in the wind and the ice and the silver roaring night. It was like being on a very high mountain in the blizzard season.

Guild said, "What'd you mean back there when you said it was your fault?"

Father Healy, exhausted looking, said, "Because I don't have faith. Because, like Kriker said, I'm not really a priest. And that's what we need now. A real doc and a real priest. Otherwise—" He shook his head again, talking loud into the voice-taking wind. "You see, Mr. Guild, back in Chicago I—"

Guild stopped him. "I remember the poster on you."

"Poster?"

"Wanted poster. In all the law offices. A bounty man has to have a good memory for such things. You're wanted for killing another sharp."

"I didn't kill him. My partner did. I wasn't even there. I just came out into the alley later and saw him on the ground there and then somebody else came and saw me and started shouting and—and I got blamed. So I ran and eventually I came here." He pointed to the semicircle of cabins seen through the haze of snow. "They're good people, Guild. They've started life over and they're raising families and—and now this." He stared at Guild again. "They need a doc and a priest."

"There's a lot of different ways to be a priest, Healy," Guild said. "Best one I ever knew smelled of beer half the time and had wooden teeth and couldn't pronounce his Latin. But he was damn good when you needed comfort, and that's all these people need now. Comfort. That's what being a priest is, Healy, and that's all it is."

He had just finished speaking when he saw a lone rider on a grulla coming down the perilous slope from the north. The grulla slipped every few steps. The rider held his carbine high, like an Indian lance. Attached to it was a piece of white cloth. The rider was James Bruckner.

He kept shouting, "Don't shoot! Don't shoot!"

Guild had never wanted to kill a man so badly in his life.

17

HE PUT THE double 10-gauge directly into James Bruckner's face and said, "Get down."

Bruckner said, "You're not going to kill me, are you, Mr. Guild?"

"I said get down."

With the wind, you could scarcely hear their voices. You could see how the grulla was exhausted and frightened from the trip. Snow as light as dust blew over them.

James Bruckner said, "Please don't kill me, Mr. Guild."

Guild slammed the barrel of the double 10-gauge against Bruckner's temple. Bruckner jolted and screamed. Guild had hit him very hard.

Bruckner's own weapon looked like a toy with the white rag tied to its end. He climbed down from the grulla.

Guild switched hands with the double 10-gauge. He wanted his right free.

He hit James Bruckner in the mouth and then in the ribs and then in the mouth again. When Bruckner dropped to his knees, Guild kicked him in the jaw.

Bruckner tumbled over backward and lay sprawled on the ice.

Father Healy came up from behind Guild and said, "Is there any call for that?"

"I need to be alone with him, Father." Then, hearing how harsh his voice was, he turned sideways to the priest and said, "Please."

"I'm asking you not to hit him anymore."

Guild looked at the priest for a long moment and then nodded. "I won't hit him anymore."

The priest nodded and went away.

Guild dropped to his knees and scooped up handfuls of snow and threw them on James Bruckner's burned face.

When Bruckner came to, Guild slapped him once viciously, then remembered what he'd promised the priest.

Bruckner looked almost surprised that Guild had stopped with just a slap.

Then Guild jerked the other man to his feet by the lapels and dragged him into the central cabin where the meeting had been.

He did not want Bruckner in the same cabin with Kriker. He knew what that would do to Kriker.

He said, "Where's the girl?"

"He just wants the money."

"You didn't answer my question."

James Bruckner, bruised badly from Guild's fist and foot, shook his burned face sorrowfully. "Either way I turn, Mr. Guild, somebody's gonna be out for me. If I tell you where he is, he'll kill me. If I don't tell you where he is, you're gonna be mad."

"She all right?"

Bruckner dropped his eyes. "Thomas says she is."

"You don't think so?"

"She's real sick."

"What's Thomas want to do?"

"He wants me to go with you and get the money and then he wants you to give me the money and then we'll turn over the girl."

"I want the girl first."

"He says no, Thomas does."

"You really think I'd trust you or your brother to turn her over?"

"What would we want with her?"

"Why'd you kill Rig and Tolliver?"

"We didn't."

"You're a liar."

He forgot about his agreement with the priest. He caught James Bruckner on the side of the head, where the right sort of punch would daze him and make him nauseated. Then he kicked him twice quickly in the shins and then he slapped him again.

James Bruckner started crying.

"Why'd you kill Rig and Tolliver?"

"I didn't. Thomas did."

"Why did Thomas kill Rig and Tolliver?"

"He wanted all the shares of the money plus he was afraid they'd tell."

"Tell Decker?"

"Yes. The Territory's gettin' smaller. You get a rep for doublin' as a lawman and a bank robber and—" He shook his head sorrowfully again.

Guild took his double 10-gauge and said, "I'm going back with you."

"What?"

"We're not going to get the money. We're going to get the girl and your brother."

"You don't know Thomas."

"What's that mean?"

"He'd kill her. He'd kill that little girl."

Guild stared at him. "You know what you're saying about your own brother?"

"I know."

"That he'd kill a little child."

"Yes."

"Your own brother?"

"It's how he is, Mr. Guild."

Guild, sensing James Bruckner was probably telling the truth, said, "Son of a bitch."

"What?"

"Don't talk."

"What?"

Guild, whirling on him, said, "I said don't talk. You understand? Don't talk."

James Bruckner dropped his head the way a chastised child would.

Guild paced and thought through things well as he could. He was tired and cold, and he kept thinking of the little girl. By now, of course, he was thinking crazy thoughts. If he could save the life of this little girl, then that would somehow lessen the terrible thing he had done to the other little girl.

He had to save this little girl. Had to.

He said, "We're going to go get the money, you and me, and then you're going to take it back to your brother."

James Bruckner said, "It's the best way, Mr. Guild. Given how Thomas is and all. I don't want no little girl to be hurt, either."

"If you're so different from your brother, why do you stay with him?"

"Look at my face," James Bruckner said. "Who else'd have me?"

Ten minutes later, Guild stood in Kriker's cabin. The man lay on the cot staring at the ceiling. He had a rosary entwined in his fingers. The hand-cuffs were still on him. Now Guild handcuffed his ankles as well. He didn't want Kriker getting crazy and spoiling Guild's plan. Kriker hardly seemed to notice the cuffs on his hands. His fingers just kept working the rosary and his wet mouth kept praying big silent words and his eyes kept staring with a certain fixated madness at the cabin ceiling.

Guild said, "What's the easiest way to get to that cave?"

Kriker said, "There was gunfire a while ago. Who was that?"

"Just me. I thought I saw something."

"There any word on Maundy yet?"

"No."

"You haven't heard from the Bruckners?"

Guild considered telling him, then decided he wouldn't be doing Kriker any favors. "No."

"God." Kriker sounded on the verge of tears again.

"It helps, doesn't it, to pray?"

"Yes."

"You just keep praying."

Kriker had gone back to staring at the ceiling. He didn't say anything now. He looked utterly beyond words.

Guild went back to the cabin where he'd tied James Bruckner to a chair.

On the way the priest stopped him. "Two more."

"Dead?"

"Yes."

Guild said, "In St. Loo four hundred died in one afternoon." Then he nodded to the semicircle of cabins. "You know what they need, Father. Comfort."

The priest nodded and hurried on to the next cabin.

18

GUILD TOOK STRIPS of hide and lashed James Bruckner to his saddlehorn, and then Guild swung up on his own horse and they set off to find the cave.

Both men wore bandannas over their faces and both men kept their heads down. Guild estimated the temperature now at close to zero. Purchase anywhere was difficult for the horses. If there was a trail it had been covered by drifting snow hours earlier. Despite gloves he felt the cold in his fingers especially and in his toes even though he wore $5.50-a-dozen lumberman's socks from a Sears store in Yankton.

As they rode, Guild tried to ease his mind from the girl by thinking of a tent-show speech he'd heard once about the Ice Age, how more than a quarter of the planet had been covered with impenetrable sheets of ice, and how two million years later glaciers formed such places as Yosemite Valley, and how right here in the Territory itself there had been an immense glacial lake called Lake Agassiz. When he thought of the things the professor had said that day in his fine, barking politician's voice, it was easy enough to imagine that another such age had befallen the planet and that the only two people left were himself and Bruckner, tight-reining their ice-flanked horses through the eternal night.

He thought of these things as the wind whipped and the plains before them resembled a white tundra with silver dust demons and a sudden moon gazing down on them like the callous eye of a pitiless god. Everywhere you saw small black dots and knew they were animals—squirrels and raccoons and possums—that had frozen in the remorseless night. The only touch of ugly splendor anywhere was in the branches of the dead trees, silvered with ice and glinting like jewelry.

Twice Bruckner's horse slipped and pitched, and both times Bruckner, lashed to the saddlehorn, slammed his head against the unyielding ground. The second time blood began to trickle from his nose. Guild blotted at it with the man's bandanna but he did not cut him free. The second time, getting the horse up was especially difficult, the animal biting Guild's hand hard enough to draw a line of blood beneath the fabric of the glove. After a quick curse at the animal, Guild then reached over and patted the horse. Guild did not blame him for resenting the task they'd set for him. Guild would have bitten his captor, too.

So finally they continued on their way, three hours after leaving the settlement, the wind, if anything, fiercer, the cold more unremitting.

There would be no end to this night, Guild thought, and during it they would fall to the white ground beneath the silver dust devils and the pitiless eye of the moon and become stiff and black like the dead possums and squirrels strewn across the tundra.

A few times Father Healy wondered if he wasn't feeling feverish himself, but then he decided, no, it was only his imagination. His mother in Chicago had always said he'd been blessed with two things: "a face the girls will love and an imagination that'll someday sure and get you in trouble."

Father Healy had spent the last two hours isolating those who showed any symptoms of the disease in the big central cabin. There were not enough cots to go around so the priest and the granny woman, who had reluctantly agreed to help him (she having no more faith in the God he espoused than he did in her remedies), spread out woolen blankets and pillows on the floor and then began to minister to the people one by one.

The smells of vomit and sweat were overpowering. Stomach cramps got so bad in people that they jerked about on the floor as if possessed. Every few moments somebody called out for water. But the eyes were worst. Newspaper accounts invariably described choleric eyes as "sinking." What they meant was that the eyes became those of dead people—a milky white without expression.

Outside the cabin door, huddled under the overhang, family members of the sick people waited word, which too often now came when a pair of burly men would be quietly summoned by Father Healy. The men would come in, wrap the corpse in its woolen blanket, and then take it outside, to put it in the communal barn. Their trek would be accompanied by the cries and screams of the children and spouses who had loved the man or woman. Twice the burly men had carried out small children wrapped in the coarse woolen blankets, and that was the worst, of course, children. The men put them in a special place in the barn, away from the others, and one of the men, after the second child, went over to a wall and began kicking it savagely, until a huge hole was rent into the side of the barn. This calmed him and he went back to waiting another summons from the priest. All he could hope was that the next summons would not be for a child.

At one point Father Healy had to go to the cabin of a couple whose child had just died. The boy had been their only child.

When he entered, he found them sitting apart from each other, some terrible isolation imposed on them, as if the grief of their loss could not be shared any more than their own deaths would be shared in the final moments. They were alone, utterly and irretrievably alone.

He went in, beads in his soft hands, and said, "He's with the Lord now."

"Stan, he has his gun," the woman said, and at first Father Healy did not understand her meaning.

Then he saw that the husband sat on the edge of the cot with his Sharps positioned in such a way that he could easily put it in his mouth. This certainly was not unheard of in the Territory. Disease, drought, hard luck in the hills when gold had been promised but never appeared—man was the only animal who resorted to taking his own life, and this seemed at different times to Father Healy both a blessing and a curse.

"He don't want to live," the woman said. The cabin was in shadows

because of the low-turned kerosene lamp, and the woman's words filled
the priest's ears and he knew what she was saying—in effect, he doesn't
want to live and it's up to you to change his mind.

As always, Healy turned almost instinctively to some sense of order and
justice in the universe—to what others called God. How many nights had
he lain in his solitary bed trying to summon up faith in such a deity, but
always there was just the darkness and the silence. It seemed the most
you could hope for was song in the wine and laughter in the dungeon, and
that it was a world of utter chance, and when chance came against you,
you were obliterated, literally, becoming an element of the cosmic darkness itself.

But then he remembered what the bounty man Guild had said about
people needing comfort, and he knew then that Guild was right. Even if it
was all a fake, this pretense of order and meaning, then it was a necessary
fake and an ennobling one.

He said to Stan, gently as he could, "Next summer would be a good
time for a child, Stan."

Stan said nothing.

"You told me once how you were planning on having another one," the
priest said.

Still, Stan said nothing.

"Think of when the grass is green again and the sky is blue and there's
trout in the stream where we fished that time. Mae here would love to
have you another child, wouldn't you, Mae?"

And Mae flew to her husband then, seeing the opportunity the priest
had given her, huddling against her husband, crying and helping him to
cry, too, at the bitter death of their six-year-old.

"She's been a good wife to you, Stan," Father Healy said. "If you killed
yourself, think what you'd be doing to Mae."

And as he began to cry full now, the hard and racking and reluctant
way a man cries, the priest who was not after all a priest stepped forward
softly in the shadows and took from the aggrieved man the Sharps.

Stan's fingers held the gun only briefly, then released it.

"She loves you, Stan," said the priest who was not after all a priest.
"She loves you."

And then Father Healy left, going back to the cabin to find the two
burly men, and he passed a sobbing group of women and children carrying out another wool-wrapped corpse.

Near dawn they found it.

The place was just as Kriker had described—the trees in the exact formation, though bent now from wind and ice, the cave mouth oval-shaped with a jagged overhang that dipped down.

When he dismounted, Guild saw that his horse was beginning to shudder from exertion and the cold. From his jacket pocket, Guild took a handful of oats and held them up to the animal's mouth. Then he went over and fed Bruckner's grulla.

He said, "I'm going in the cave and get the money." He waved the double 10-gauge at the tundra before them. Faint down the sky came ragged streaks of yellow and pink dawn. The round moon now had a flat look the darker sky had given dimension. "You can take off if you want to, Bruckner, but if anything happens to your horse, he'll take you down with him."

For emphasis, Guild rapped the handcuffs attached to the saddlehorn.

Bruckner said, "I won't be goin' nowhere." He sounded sullen and young, and even though Guild felt sorry for the man and what his burned face must have done to him, he also hated him for going along with his brother's blackmail plan.

Guild walked up to the cave entrance, his boots crunching through snow that snapped like glass.

He had just ducked under the overhang and started inside when he heard the unmistakable low rumble of a timber wolf.

He saw the wolf's eyes glowing there in the darkness and then he took a very deep breath.

He sensed that the animal—frozen and afraid—might do what very few wolves ever did, despite the stories surrounding them.

The wolf might attack.

"You don't talk much."

Nothing.

"You scared?"

Nothing.

"I got no reason to hurt you. There's no reason to be scared."

She had come awake so abruptly, color coming back to her cheeks and eyes, that it had been like a dead person resurrecting. Thomas Bruckner thought of his Bible lesson about Lazarus.

He said, "You want some water?"

She nodded. Her face had an eerie luminous quality, especially her gaze. It made Bruckner uncomfortable and he wanted to tell her to quit looking at him, but he realized it would only make him sound crazy—or somehow afraid of her—and it wouldn't do to have a small girl think you were afraid of her.

He got her water from the canteen and held her head up and helped her drink and then eased her back on her blankets.

He put a hand to her cheek. "Whoo," he said. Then he stared at her. "Ain't you curious what I was sayin' 'Whoo' about?"

She fell into her unnerving silence again.

"I was sayin' 'Whoo' about your cheek. You're still burnin' up."

He plunked himself down next to her cot and huddled into his clothes. The windows rattled and the roof was like to tear off the way it sounded in the wind. Flame fluttered in the kerosene lamp and far distant you could hear animals—cows most likely—down along the rough line of barbed wire.

He did not like the feeling of isolation that had suddenly overtaken him. He felt vulnerable. He needed to talk.

If only to a small girl who couldn't, or wouldn't, talk back.

"I suppose you think I'm a real baddie."

Nothing.

"What with me stealin' you and all."

Nothing.

"But I only done it 'cause I figured Kriker'd give us the money and then we could leave." He paused and thought about rolling a cigarette and then thought, no, he would have to take off his gloves and dig deep in the shirt beneath his sweater and sheepskin and—

"You seen my brother's face?" By now he no longer expected the girl to say anything. He just wanted to hear his own voice here above the wind. "I did that to him. When we was kids. It was only a joke, but I don't think deep down he believes that." He paused once more to look back at the girl. Her eyes were open, but they were beginning to take on the same faded quality as before. He glanced around at the line shack. In the summer, after a hard ten hours' work in the sun, it probably would have been nice to come back here and roll cigarettes and drink local wine and listen to the summer night. He had begun thinking about summer now. It helped cut down the wind and the sound of isolation. "We get the money now, I'm takin' my brother to California, and I'm gonna buy him new clothes and give him a right nice time." Pause. "You know, sort of make things up to him. Then—" He shook his head, about to say something he'd needed to say for years. "Then I'm gonna tell him good-bye. He's got to find his own life and I got to find mine. With his face and all—" He shook his head again. "Well, he ain't real easy to find friends for and I guess I kind of resent it and I take advantage of him and—" He exhaled as if he had just finished some very difficult task. "He'll be all right. On his own, I mean. I'll give him a good share of the money—ten percent, I figure—and buy him a fresh horse in addition to the clothes and"—he shrugged—"and then I won't have to worry about him no more."

He sounded very satisfied suddenly, as if the problem that had been so long burdening him had resolved itself with an ease so miraculous he could not quite believe it.

He said, "You want some more water?"

But he was turned away from her and then he remembered that the girl didn't speak. Or wouldn't.

So he turned around and looked at her and said, "You want some water?"

And the wind—it had never sounded more like alien song.

And the fragile line shack—it had never sounded more like it was being ripped apart.

And Thomas William Bruckner, he had never felt more like all the men he'd killed had come back for him. He'd had dreams of that many times, and now he could see the men as in the stories of Edgar Allan Poe the chautauqua speakers so liked to read—dead and coming back for him.

"You want some more water?" he said again.

But then the wind was up again, and as he gazed down on her he realized that there had been some subtle shift in the angle of her repose and that she looked—poor little girl who reminded him suddenly of one of his many sisters back on the farm—she looked different somehow.

He lifted the canteen and started to bring it close to her parched mouth.

And then he realized why she struck him as having changed, realized why she did not look to be exactly the same little girl his brother had earlier taken from the settlement.

Because she was no longer the same little girl.

In fact, she was no little girl at all.

She was nothing.

She was dead.

19

GUILD HAD JUST struck a Telegraph sulfur match against a dry jut of rock on the roof of the cave when the wolf lunged.

Two quick impressions: the cave was shallow and narrow. Near the back was a pile of small rocks, once more just as Kriker had described, beneath which he would find the bank robbery money.

The second impression was that of the wolf itself. In addition to the powerful teeth revealed as the mouth pulled back in a growl, in addition to the bushy tail and the enormous round pupils of the eyes, in addition to the yellow-gray fur and the white markings on the feet—in addition to all these he saw the dried blood on the side of the wolf, exposing a white glimpse of rib cage.

Something had attacked the wolf earlier and the wolf had crawled here to the cave, using it as a lair in the frozen night, and now intruders had come and—

Which explained why a creature who rarely attacked anything other than small prairie animals and birds—except in packs, when they were then bold enough to go after sheep and bison—would lunge at him now.

Guild had just time to drop to one knee and level the double 10-gauge.

But the wolf surprised him by diving over Guild's shoulder and going straight out of the cave and then jumping up on the grulla holding James Bruckner.

The wolf moved with a blind savagery that Guild could not quite grasp.

Before Guild had time to respond, the wolf had dug its powerful teeth into the side of the grulla and had ripped away a large chunk of bloody flesh.

The animal reared up, crying out above the wind as the wolf continued to leap and rend, even managing to tear away more flesh as the grulla was up on its rears.

Now James Bruckner's screams joined the grulla's. Handcuffed to the saddlehorn, Bruckner clung helplessly to the back of the grulla, the wolf beginning now to snap at Bruckner's legs.

Guild dropped to one knee again and fired.

He got the wolf in the side of the head, a large hole appearing where there had been an eye and the beginnings of a snout.

Then, just to be safe, he sent another one through the wolf's chest.

The yellow-gray animal flopped over on the snow. A silver dust devil whirling up off the tundra began immediately to cover it in white.

The grulla, bleeding badly from the wolf's attack, had now fallen over on its side, its legs kicking uselessly in pain, as if it were going somewhere.

James Bruckner was crying.

Guild got down and took out his handcuff key and got Bruckner separated from the saddle and then yanked the man away from the grulla.

Bruckner said, "What you gonna do, Mr. Guild?" But he saw very well what Guild was going to do.

Guild got the double 10-gauge ready.

"You got to do it, Mr. Guild?"

"Look at him," Guild said. "You think I like it any better than you do?"

"Can I turn around?"

"I don't care."

"Thomas, he says I'm a coward."

"You want me to tell you what Thomas is?"

"I guess I already know that." Pause. The grulla was shrieking, writhing, massive and dying on the white. Red snow formed an ever-widening pool.

"You don't mind, then?" James asked.

"I want to do it fast. For the horse's sake." He stared at James. James stared at the animal. You could see James was scared and heartsick for the horse. Guild said softly, "You can turn around, James. No sense in you watchin'."

"You gonna watch?"

"I'm gonna close my eyes. Otherwise I couldn't do it."

"Poor goddamn thing."

"Yes," Guild said softly. "Poor goddamned thing."

James Bruckner turned around and Guild shot the grulla in the head.

When he turned back to Bruckner, Guild saw that the man was crying again. Guild went over and stood in front of him in the wind, hearing its mordant eternal sound.

James Bruckner tried to hide the fact that he was crying, but he wasn't doing a very good job of it. He said, "Sometimes I like horses a lot better than I do people."

Guild smiled. "You know something, Bruckner?"

"What?"

"So do I."

Then Guild got Bruckner up on his horse and handcuffed him to the saddlehorn, and then Guild went in and got the bank robbery money.

There were two satchels of it and there was plenty enough, green and crisp as it was, to kill people over if that was your inclination.

He went back out and took the reins of the horse and started the trek back to the settlement, James Bruckner snuffling from what had happened to the horse.

Kriker sat in the corner of the cabin, watching as the granny woman poured him coffee from a tin pot. The priest had asked her to stop in and see how Kriker was doing.

Kriker said, "Any more die?"

"Not in the last two hours." She nodded to the window. A light blue sky filled the windows. "The father says maybe the worst of it's over."

"He doesn't know nothin' about it."

The granny woman handed him the coffee. "You shouldn't hate him so much, Kriker. He ain't no better or no worse than anybody else in this settlement."

"He ain't a priest."

She glared at him. "Who's to say who is a priest and who ain't a priest?

Just 'cause you got a piece of paper don't mean nothin'. That ain't what bein' a priest is about."

Even to himself, Kriker smelled. Ordinarily, at such times, he would haul water, heat it, fill a tub, and then sit in there with a cigar while somebody sat nearby to read a newspaper to him. Reading was beyond Kriker, but listening wasn't. He had always imagined the day when the girl would read to him.

Kriker said, "I need your help, granny woman."

"With what?"

"I think you know."

She averted his eyes. "I told Father Healy I'd come in and look in on you. I better be leavin'."

"They took the girl."

"I know."

"I want to go get her."

"The bounty man's goin' to do that."

Kriker paused. "You and me, we been friends a long time."

"I'll grant you that, Kriker. But the settlement's—changed."

"That why you're so trustin' of the priest?"

"You keep your tongue off him, Kriker."

Kriker sighed, held up his hands. The handcuffs had bit into his flesh enough that small tears of blood had appeared along the bone of his wrists.

"There's a saw in the shed out back," he said.

"He'd know who done it, the bounty man would. Then I'd be in trouble."

"I jus' want to go get the girl from the Bruckners and then I want to light out of here." He paused. "You know what's gonna happen to me if the bounty man gets the girl and the money back, don't you?"

"What?"

"He's gonna take me in and they're gonna hang me."

"You didn't kill nobody in that robbery."

"No, but I had to kill people before and they're gonna extradite me and then they're gonna hang me."

"I can't do it, Kriker."

"Her and me, you don't know how good we could have it livin' in California. I could get her the schoolin' she needs, and I'd get me a job in some factory somewhere, and it could be real good for both of us. Then you and the priest, you'd have the settlement here and you could run it any way you wanted to."

Obviously the granny woman was being swept up in his words. Despite her age lines, she had the look of a child fascinated by a clever uncle.

The granny woman said, "She's your curse."

"Who?"

"The girl."

"My curse?"

"Sure. If it wasn't for her, you could do just what I told you yesterday—ride out of here clean and fast."

"She's my daughter."

"She ain't your daughter."

"As good as."

"As good as don't make her your daughter."

"You don't like her?"

The granny woman shrugged. "You was a good leader for the settlement till you brought her here. Then you started to change. It was gradual, but you started to changed. All you cared about was her. The priest, he's been helpin' people more'n you have."

"I'm sick of hearin' about the priest."

She looked at his handcuffs. "I can't help you, Kriker."

"Maybe they're hurtin' her."

"I know you love her, Kriker, but you got to calm down for your own sake. You look wild. Crazy." She went over and picked up a bottle of cheap whiskey. "Why don't you have some of this in your coffee?"

"I need a clear head."

Gently, the granny woman went over and put a hand on Kriker's shoulder. "They ain't hurtin' her, Kriker."

"You sure?"

"I'm sure. They wouldn't have no call to."

"They took her, didn't they?"

"They took her, but they ain't got no call to hurt her."

He raised his head to her, his usual ferocity lessened somewhat by his worry and the fact that he had not slept. "You could go get the saw, granny woman."

"No," she said, "no, I couldn't."

20

TEN MINUTES AFTER he finished listening to the girl, Sheriff Decker picked up his favorite shotgun, pulled on his sheepskin, and then began walking up and down the board sidewalks of the town, handpicking the men he wanted to form the posse.

It took half an hour for the liveryman to get the eight horses ready, half an hour to kiss eight wives and twenty-three children good-bye, and half an hour to make sure that an adequate supply of warm clothing and ammunition was being brought along.

Posses were still an exciting sight in the Territory, so by the time the
nine men left, a crowd had gathered in front of McBride's General Store,
standing in the very sunny day in the very white snow, waving good-bye to
the nine men as if they were marching off to a grand and romantic war.

None of the men's wives or children had any such notions, of course.
They knew better. They knew exactly what their husbands and fathers
were getting into because they were not lawmen or mean men or even
men particularly adept with firearms. They were instead men from the
mercantile and men from the insurance company and men from the telegraph company and men from the bicycle shop and men from the barber-
shop. Several of them hadn't wanted to go at all but knew what young and
well-educated Sheriff Decker could be like when he started in on such
topics as civic responsibility (it must have been those law courses he'd
taken up in Yankton that had caused him to carry on so) and how a
Territory town must show the world the measure of its civilization by
defending that civilization at gunpoint if necessary.

Decker rode in front on a fast sleek roan. It was beautiful as its muscles
pulled and rippled in the sunlight. Not a man had mentioned the fact that
what they were really doing this morning was making up for Decker's
mistaken faith in the Bruckner brothers. He had spent many hours arguing to the city council that such men were needed and that, within limits,
they could be trusted. Now the bounty man Guild had proved otherwise,
but if the lawman Decker was the least bit ashamed, he certainly didn't
show it.

Next to Decker rode the doc, a tall slender man bundled up in an
Alaska-style parka with his black bag lashed to his saddle. Burmeister, his
name was. He'd been one of the city councilmen Decker had always
argued with over the Bruckner brothers. You had to know Burmeister
well enough to notice the faint satisfied smile on his thin pale lips this
morning. The Territory was becoming infested with smart-aleck young
people who studied all sorts of things up in Yankton, including law and
medicine, and then swaggered around the Territory acting as if they knew
something you didn't. Dr. Herman Burmeister was never unhappy to see
such upstarts proved wrong.

There was no snow and the sky was blue as a painting and there was no
wind at all, and so they rode on fast as they could, nine men from town in
the blinding white beauty of the day.

She had started to smell, so Thomas Bruckner took the little girl and
wrapped her tight in the blanket and then carried her outside and placed
her next to the cabin.

He was just religious enough that he considered it only fitting to say a prayer over her, and so he said a few proper words, or at least burial words, as he remembered them from all the tough Territory towns where he and his brother had roamed over the years. Then he took a shovel and covered her with enough snow so that wandering animals would leave her alone.

Because he still needed the girl.

She was dead, but in one way her part in all this had just begun.

Then he went back in the cabin and fell to cleaning his rifle and his pistol.

He kept checking his watch.

His brother should be along anytime now. Anytime.

The man grabbed at Father Healy's hand and said, "Back in Ohio, Father, I used to be a Catholic."

"I see."

"I want you to hear my confession."

"I—"

Father Healy had been going to say, "I can't do that. I'm not a priest." But the man before him on the cot in the big central cabin would most likely be dead in the next twenty minutes, and what choice did Healy have?

All these years Healy had avoided performing any of the real Catholic rituals—communion and confession especially—but now . . .

"It'd make me feel a lot better," the man said.

Healy glanced around the cabin. For the most part, the dying seemed to be over. That was how cholera generally worked. There was a siege and many died right away, and if you were lucky enough to survive the first siege then you had good chances of living.

There was sunlight now, and you could see on the faces of those lying on blankets across the cabin that their fevers had lessened somewhat and their knotting stomachs had calmed some and they did not call out for water quite so often.

Except for this man Hamilton.

He was in and out of consciousness—in and out of delirium, really— and you could see the color of his eyes fading.

He said now, "Please, Father. Hear my confession. I want to be ready."

Healy said, holding the man's hand, "I'm not really a priest, Hamilton. Not really."

But Hamilton grinned and said, "You're good enough priest for the likes of me, Father."

So Healy heard Hamilton's confession and granted him absolution, and two minutes later, there on the blanket, Hamilton died.

* * *

Guild and James Bruckner reached the settlement early in the afternoon.

They went immediately to Kriker's cabin, and it was there they found the handcuffs.

They had been sawed in half and there was no sign whatsoever of Kriker.

They heard footsteps in the doorway, and there stood Father Healy.

In a quiet voice, he said, "I let him go, Mr. Guild. I let him go."

21

FIVE MINUTES LATER, Guild, Bruckner, and Father Healy sat around the stove, sipping coffee and talking.

Healy said, "I owed him that, at least."

"Owed him what?" Guild said.

"One more chance at freedom. After all he did for those of us here in the settlement."

"You let an escaped murderer go."

"You much in the way of redemption, Mr. Guild?"

"Not a whole lot."

"I feel he's been redeemed."

"Half the killers in the Territory have got half the priests and ministers convinced of exactly that."

"And you don't believe them?"

"Not for a minute."

"You're mad, I take it?"

"You think I shouldn't be?"

"We're different people, Mr. Guild. My feelings aren't yours." The priest smiled without any joy evident anywhere on his face. "Besides, you were the one who told me about comforting people."

"I don't see where that's got much to do with this."

"It's got everything to do with this, Mr. Guild."

"Like what?"

"His only solace will be in seeing the girl again. Alive and well. Then they'll have the chance to take off for California. He can live a good life there, Mr. Guild. I believe that sincerely."

Guild said to Bruckner, "You better pray your brother didn't hurt that girl." Guild sighed. He put his wet socks near the stove and said, "Christ."

"What?" said Bruckner.

"Now we've got to double back the way we came."

"What for?"

"Because that's where he'll go."

"Kriker?"

"Yeah."

Bruckner shook his head. "Sure hope he don't hurt Thomas."

Guild glanced at Healy and then at Bruckner. "Guess that's one thing I'll never understand."

"What's that?"

"After all the things your brother did to you, you still worry about him."

"He's my brother."

"He's also the man who threw kerosene on you and the man who sends you on every dirty job he needs doing."

"We all got our ways, Mr. Guild."

Guild sipped some more coffee and then glanced back at the priest. "How much of a head start he got on us?"

"Maybe an hour."

"Damn," Guild says. "He knows these hills a lot better than we do. He can beat us to the cabin."

Bruckner said, "There's a way through the pass."

"You know it?"

"I sort of know it."

Guild said, "That isn't exactly reassuring. You 'sort of' know it."

The man with the burned face looked as if he'd been slapped. "I'm tryin' to help, Mr. Guild."

Guild sighed. "Ah, Christ, kid," he said. "I know you are."

Then to the priest, Guild said, "Next time you want to let somebody go free, make sure it's somebody who doesn't know the mountains as well as Kriker does."

Then Guild and James Bruckner set off.

There had been no way to cut the cuffs themselves from his hands and ankles—only the chain that bound the cuffs together—so now as he pushed his calico through the heavy snow, Kriker's wrists sparkled in the afternoon sunlight. In the scabbard of the saddle rested the Sharps and in his holster sat a .44 of recent vintage.

All he could think of was the little girl. He saw her face that day of the robbery, when he'd taken her, and he saw her face all the times he tried to coax words from her, and he saw her face there at the last, on the cot when the cholera had come down on her.

Then he thought of California. He recalled a painting he'd seen of a bay up in the northern region, a beautiful schooner ship so elegant against the blue ocean sky, the trees in the surrounding cove impossibly lush and green. There was where the two of them belonged, he and his daughter. He would come to see her grow to womanhood and take a man worthy of her as a husband, and they would bear children and Kriker would finish his days with the gunfire of his early life faded in the distance of time, just an average citizen sitting in a rocker on a porch sweet with breezes and the tang of pipe smoke. He would be an old man in the best way to be an old man—at peace in his heart—and she would be a young woman in the best way to be a young woman—with peace in her heart and children like wild flowers dancing round her and a husband judge-sober and heart-peaceful as her companion and protector.

But then the sun angling off the snow blinded him and brought his mind back to the task at hand.

Without the money as trade, he would have to figure out how to get to the line shack and get the girl out without getting her killed.

He would kill Bruckner, of course.

About that there could be no doubt.

No doubt at all.

He rode on.

One of the posse men's horses stepped in a hole and snapped its leg twig-sharp.

The man put a gun to the horse's head and pulled the trigger twice.

The horse rolled over on its side and twitched only once, a great bloody shudder going through it there on the very white afternoon snow.

Then the man climbed on the back of another horse and the posse set off again.

Decker was still not saying much, his thoughts centered on the Bruckner brothers and how he had so smugly told the bounty man Guild that the Territory needed men like them. He had felt that he'd had the Bruckner brothers under control, that they might take the occasional bribe, that they might beat up the occasional whore after taking advantage of her services for free, but that they would not do anything so uncivic as to rob a bank or murder people.

He just hoped that the other young Territory lawmen who had taken those courses up in Yankton did not hear about all this. There would be a reunion of the men someday, and he did not want this tale told over tin buckets of beer, with the scorn of others who had taken the same courses but applied them with more success.

Decker dug his spurs into his mount.

* * *

James Bruckner turned out to be a better guide than Guild had figured. He took them up through steep pine, and he took them around a narrow treacherous ledge that saved them a long ride over a seemingly limitless stretch of plain, and he showed them how to cross a narrow stretch of river where the ice seemed to invite the laughter of children and the click of iron skates on the silver surface.

They stopped for a rest only once during the afternoon.

Guild watched Bruckner carefully. He could see that Bruckner had changed ever since the prospect of his brother being shot had become a distinct likelihood. He wondered if the man with the burned face might now try to make a break for it, get away and warn his brother somehow. It was a very long shot, James Bruckner being neither particularly intelligent nor particularly brave, but as the man went over by a naked black elm tree to put a yellow steaming stream into the snow, Guild kept his double 10-gauge pointed directly at the man's back. There had been a time when he had felt sorry for James Bruckner, and he supposed he still did. But this was before the little girl was taken. Now Guild did not care much at all about anything except getting her back safely.

Bruckner turned around and saw that the double 10-gauge was pointed directly at him.

"You gonna shoot me or somethin', Mr. Guild?"

Guild sighed, looking at the man's poor burned face. He lowered the gun and said, "Just get back up on your horse, Bruckner. We've got to make better time than we have so far."

Bruckner had some difficulty getting mounted. Guild said, "Let's go."

Thomas Bruckner sat in the cabin knowing that something had gone wrong for sure.

By even the safest estimate, James should have been back with the money five hours ago.

But when he looked out the window, all Thomas Bruckner saw were the steep hills leading up to the cabin, and the timber to the north.

The timber would be a perfect place for a man to sneak up on the cabin and perhaps overwhelm the man inside. It would be much easier to fire from inside the timber than to fire from inside the cabin up to the timber.

Much easier.

He went back outside without being quite sure why. He stood under the cabin overhang and looked out at the vast white hills stretching before him. The late afternoon shadows were a soft blue. It was very beautiful and almost windless. The little wind there was whirled up snow like fine silt against his face, which reminded him of when he'd been a boy back on the farm and playing outdoors.

He wondered if James had gone and gotten himself killed. While James had become too much of a responsibility, and while Thomas had certainly planned to part company with his brother as soon as he got the money in hand, he did not want his brother to die, even if a part of him knew that James would probably be happier dead. Then no one could point to his face or snicker at it.

He went around the side of the cabin and checked on the little girl. She was still covered with enough snow that wandering animals would leave her alone. At least during the daylight hours. Night would be another matter. He considered the possibility of taking her inside tonight if James did not come back by then, but then he decided that would be just too eerie, sitting inside with a little dead girl wrapped in the blanket. He hoped for her sake the animals did not get her, but he guessed in the long run it didn't matter much at all. He did not like to think of himself as mean, but he was adamant about thinking of himself as practical.

He went back and stood under the overhang and let the fine cold silty snow cover his face and make his cheeks rosy and make him feel wide awake. He wished he had some good whiskey and a good woman, and he wished he had the bank money. He wished he'd had a clean friendly parting with his brother, and he wished he were on a transcontinental train, one where black porters waited on your every whim, and where you could sit in a private room and look out at the rolling plains and smoke a cigar and have not a worry about anything at all.

He was wishing for all these things when the first bullet sliced into the frame of the door next to him.

22

THERE WERE SOME small granite hills that provided a windbreak. Guild stopped to talk, since the horses needed a rest.

"You're going down to that cabin and you're going to tell your brother that he won't get out alive unless he hands the girl over. You understand?"

James Bruckner gulped. "Yessir."

"Then you're going to bring the girl straight up here, and then I'm going to go in and take your brother just as peaceful as he'll let me. You understand?"

"Yessir."

"That is, if Kriker doesn't kill him first."

"Oh, Jesus."

Guild saw how scared he'd made James Bruckner. "I didn't say Kriker would do that. I only said it was a possibility."

"Yessir."

Night was black in the sky and blue on the ground. The granite cliffs were without detail now, just looming black shapes. The horses shit steaming sweet road apples. Guild pulled on beef jerky. Bruckner, too upset, declined to join them.

Guild said, "You going to do exactly what I say, James?"

"Yes."

"Your brother's going to hang. You know that, don't you?"

"Yessir."

"I'll testify in your behalf. I think I can convince the judge that you didn't kill Rig or Tolliver."

"I don't want him to die, Mr. Guild. He's taken care of me all my life. He really has."

"He hasn't done a real good job of it, son."

"He's not a bad man, sir. Not a real bad one. Just sort of—rambunctious. That's what Pa always called him. Rambunctious."

"How many men you suppose he's killed?"

"None he didn't have to."

"I see," Guild said. He swung back up on his horse. The wind was coming up. Guild thought of Rig and young Tolliver and how Thomas Bruckner had killed them so effortlessly. "Rambunctious, huh?" he said to James Bruckner. "Rambunctious."

They set off again. The night, despite its beauty, was starting to get bitter.

23

HE KNEW MANY things about the pine trees, Kriker did. He knew the white pine and the jack pine and bristlecone pine and the ponderosa pine. He knew that some pine needles were soft and could be used as mattresses when you were camping out, and he knew that some pine needles were hard and could be used in making roofs. He liked the clean sweet high perfume of pines, especially at cold dusk such as now, and he knew few sights so beautiful as a sloping valley of pines, green tops vivid against a pure white sweep of snow beneath. He had lived in these hills four decades now, and the sight of pines—like a cub bear or pink squirming infant born to a settlement woman—still had the power to move him deeply.

But for now such thoughts were beyond Kriker as he positioned himself behind an especially wide pine trunk and looked down the hill at the line shack where Thomas Bruckner held the girl.

Next to Kriker were two large canvas sacks weighted down with rocks. They would suffice from a distance to convince Bruckner that Kriker had the money and was willing to make the trade.

Dusk was now a deep purple. Stars stretched from horizon to horizon, sharp and brilliant against the streaked dark sky. The moon was full and silver.

Kriker, hefting his rifle, walked up to the edge of the clearing and shouted down to the cabin. He let go two shots.

"Bruckner! Can you hear me!" he shouted.

He knew it would be a while before Bruckner responded.

Bruckner knew the voice at once. The whiskey and tobacco rasp of it was unmistakable even from this distance. All he could wonder was what Kriker himself was doing here. Where was James? Where was the money?

Then the worst realization of all struck him.

He had been going to carry the dead body of the girl to a point near the settlement, then drop her off in exchange for the money. By the time they learned the girl was dead, he and James would be gone.

But now—

Being on the side of the law, being the pursuer instead of the pursued, had kept Thomas Bruckner unfamiliar with panic. The authority of the law was very good for steadying your nerves.

But out here—the wilderness at night—the authority of the law did not matter.

Especially when a man such as Kriker—a man who'd vaguely frightened Thomas Bruckner even when they'd been working together—obviously meant to kill him.

Kriker shouted, "I have the money with me, Bruckner! I want the girl!"

In the endless blue-shadowed night, Kriker's voice was as imposing as an Old Testament prophet's.

The next time Kriker shouted, "I want the girl!" Thomas Bruckner had the clear impression that the man had crept much closer to the cabin.

Beneath his heavy clothing, Bruckner's body was soaked with sweat. His eyes scanned the pines and the foothills beneath but found no sign of Kriker.

Given the mountain man's ability to track and hunt, he could be anywhere.

* * *

Kriker swung wide east, in an arc that took him down a deep valley and back up a hill slick with ice. He had to lift his feet high and bring them down heavily for purchase. Then another deep valley and another ice-slick rise awaited him. His intent was to come up from behind the cabin. He was panting and short of breath when he reached the top of the second rise. The satchels of rocks were thrown over his shoulder. His rifle dangled from his right hand. He was thinking about the time he'd brought the girl the store-bought shoes and how he'd had to put them on her himself and how for the first time she'd smiled on that sunny May morning.

Sheriff Decker and the posse reached the settlement just at the time when Father Healy and the granny woman were trying to help the people who'd survived the cholera go back to their cabins and take up their normal lives. There would be long days of nourishment no more substantial than beef broth, and there would be long nights of faint but not fatal nausea, and there would be the grief resulting from the deaths of seventeen people they'd known as friends and neighbors here in the settlement.

The posse came down the hill, their horses kicking up a dust storm of snow in the silver moonlight.

When they came into the settlement proper, they smelled of hard riding and the cold. Their mounts smelled of heat and manure.

Sheriff Decker found Father Healy waiting for him in front of the main cabin.

For most of his life, having grown up scruffy on the streets of Chicago, Healy had always feared lawmen of any sort. Now he found himself facing Decker with a certain self-confidence. He was not sure why, but when he nodded and introduced himself as "Father Healy," he felt for the first time as if this were a fact—he really was a priest now—and not merely a ruse to hide behind.

"I want the Bruckner brothers," Decker said. He sounded exhausted.

"We were just preparing a meal. Why don't you join us?"

Decker glanced back at the men behind him. It had been a hard, fast ride. A break would probably be good for them.

He nodded and let the priest lead him and the others inside the cabin where, five minutes later, the granny woman ladled out beef broth. She also handed out big chunks of fresh wheat bread.

Sheriff Decker was a dunker. He dunked his bread so deep and so long in his soup he could scarcely lift the bread up again. Yet he managed to do so each time. As he dunked and ate, he said, "I want the Bruckners and I want Kriker."

"Kriker is gone, too."

"The girl who rode in told me that the bounty man had Kriker handcuffed and under arrest. How'd he get away?"

Some of Father Healy's old fear of lawmen returned. He could not bring himself to tell Decker that he had let Kriker go. "He just got away."

"I assume he went to the line shack to find the little girl?"

"I assume."

"You don't sound disturbed by that?"

"By what?"

"By a man like Kriker getting away."

"Kriker's a very complicated man."

"He's a killer."

"He didn't kill Rig or Tolliver."

"Maybe not," Decker said. "But he's killed other people."

"The girl has changed him. She's made him gentle."

"Is that why he robbed the bank? Because he's so gentle? Is that why he escaped?"

"There are different ways of being gentle."

"If you know anything about him that can help me, Father, I'd appreciate it if you'd tell me."

The priest shrugged. "I know what you know. Nothing more."

Decker fixed him with a cynical eye. "I have a cousin who's a priest."

"I see."

"He was ordained in St. Louis. Bishop Morgan ordained him."

"Ah, Bishop Morgan."

"Who ordained you, Father?"

He knew there was panic in his face, and then a rush of blood from embarrassment. In his way Decker was a subtle and devious man. Healy stammered, "Bishop Wright."

"Bishop Wright? I don't believe I've ever heard of him."

"Chicago."

"Bishop O'Keefe is in Chicago."

"Bishop Wright served before Bishop O'Keefe."

Decker's eyes had not left Healy's. Something like a smirk was beginning to tug on his lips. "Bishop Wright. I see."

A tall woman in soiled clothes appeared in the doorway. She seemed intimidated by the posse. But she drew herself up and came over to Healy and Decker.

"Hello, Mary," the priest said.

Then the woman smiled. "She's fine now, Father. Our daughter."

"I'm happy for you, Mary." He took her hand and held it gently.

"It was your prayin', Father. It was your prayin'."

"No, Mary, it was God's will."

"I just wanted to thank you, Father."

Father Healy smiled. "Thank God, Mary. He's the one who should be thanked."

She leaned over and gave him a tender kiss on the forehead, all the more tender for the roughness of her life and manner. "We all want you to know how much we appreciate what you done for us, Father."

Then she left.

When he turned back around to look at Decker, he saw something peculiar had happened to the sheriff's hard flat gaze. It had softened considerably.

Decker said, "They seem to appreciate you here."

"They're very kind people, really."

"I've often been told that a lot of them have criminal pasts." He did not say this nearly as harshly as he might have.

"People change, Sheriff."

Decker stared at the empty doorway through which Mary had just come and gone. "They're raising families now, eh?"

"Yes."

"And working the land?"

"Yes."

Decker paused now. "And obeying the law now, Father?"

"Oh, definitely," Father Healy said. "Definitely obeying the law."

Decker stood up and pushed out his hand. "Bishop Wright must train his priests well. You did a good job with the cholera outbreak."

"Thank you."

Decker tugged on his hat. His brown eyes were a lawman's eyes again. "I'm going to have to take them all in, Father. The Bruckners and Kriker."

"You'll bring the little girl back here?"

Decker stared at him a moment. "Is she kin of someone here?"

Father Healy smiled. He seemed both proud and sad at the same time. "That's the nice thing about this settlement, Sheriff."

"What's that?"

"We're all kin here. Just the way God planned for us."

Decker shrugged into his sheepskin coat and put out his hand and shook with the priest. "You give my best to Bishop Wright."

Their eyes held on each other steadily.

"Yes," Father Healy said. "Yes, I'll be sure to do that."

Warmed now, and ready again for the last and most dangerous part of their trek, the posse went outdoors and mounted up.

The horses streamed silver from their nostrils, and the night seemed vast with brilliant yellow stars and the far lonely cry of a barn owl.

Father Healy stood watching the men depart. Then he surprised himself by doing something he had never been able to before. He said a prayer. It was a ragged and informal prayer and not at all the sort of thing a true church man would pray. But it was a prayer, and it did imply, however fragilely, that he had come to believe in some power larger than man's. If not God then some sort of hope that made the night less dark. Perhaps it would be all he would ever have and enough at that.

He was praying for Harry Kriker.

24

THOMAS BRUCKNER OPENED the cabin door and shouted out, "I want you to listen to something, Kriker."

His voice echoed in the deep blue shadows of the winter night.

"I want you to listen to how you're going to get the girl back."

He could hear a distant coyote. He could hear a distant moose. He could hear a distant dog. But in the stillness that lay thick as snow on the hills surrounding the cabin, he could not hear Harry Kriker.

"I'm going to walk the girl and my horse down the hill a ways. Then I'm going to walk the girl back to the cabin. While I'm in the cabin, I want you to put the money on my horse. Then I'll mount up and leave the girl about a mile away. You understand?"

But there was just the silence of the vast blue night again. Just the silence.

Thomas Bruckner had the terrible feeling that somehow Kriker knew the girl was dead and was now merely closing in.

But no.

There was no way that could have happened.

Bruckner went back inside the cabin. He worked quickly. He took a blanket and bundled soft pillows inside it until it looked to be about the size the girl would be, and then he took his carbine and went outside to his horse. Ice had formed on the animal's nostrils. Bruckner chipped it away with the edge of his hand.

Then he mounted up. He was careful with the blanket that was supposed to be the girl. If Kriker was watching—as was very likely—then he would expect Bruckner to be careful with the bundle.

Bruckner rode down the hill. Twice the horse got scared, slipping on ice. Its teeth gnashed and it made a moaning sound. Bruckner made a very similar sound. He wanted it to be over. He knew how crazy a man Kriker was. He'd always known.

He led the horse down to a flat next to a twisted oak tree. It wasn't quite an eighth of a mile from the cabin. The moonlight on the ice around the tree was silver. Silty snow made Bruckner's face red and cold again. He ground-tied the horse, then hefted the bundle that was supposed to be the girl and he put his Colt right against where the girl's head would be in the bundle. He just assumed Kriker was watching. From somewhere. Nobody knew how to hide—even in snow—as well as a man raised in the mountains.

He kept the gun pointed good and direct and hard at the head of the bundle, and then he started making his way back to the cabin.

Wind came and with it dust devils again, white and whirling across the blue shadows on the snow. There was no sound except the wind. He smelled his own sweat and felt how badly he needed a shave and felt suddenly an almost violent need to take a leak, and he thought of his brother and of how he should not treat him the way he sometimes did.

But mostly he thought of Kriker. Where he could be. What he planned to do.

When Bruckner finally pushed open the door to the cabin, he found out what he'd been wondering about.

Just what he'd been wondering about.

Kriker stepped from behind the door and jammed the barrel of his rifle right into the back of Bruckner's head.

Bruckner dropped his Colt to the floor. It sounded very loud dropping just there just then.

Kriker said, "Now you put that little girl down real easy on that cot over there. Then you and me are going to have us a talk."

Thomas Bruckner did not get frightened or angry or sad. He simply sighed, sighed and walked with his Texas boots loud against the wooden floor across the cabin and laid down his bundle on the cot.

"Now," Kriker said, "get her unbundled so I can get a look at her."

"Jesus," Thomas Bruckner said to himself. "Jesus." It was as much a prayer as a curse.

He leaned down and unbundled the girl.

Then he paused.

"I said get her unbundled," Kriker said.

But a curious paralysis had come over Thomas Bruckner. He felt like the time his father had caught him stealing change from his father's overall trousers in the closet. His father had said, "Thomas William, why do you have your hand in my pocket?" "I don't know." "You don't know why you have your hand in my pocket?" "No, Pa, I don't." "Well, Thomas, you're not only a thief, you're a liar." Then his father had really given it to him and given it to him good.

Only this was going to be worse.

Much, much worse.

"You unbundle her so I can look at her," Kriker said. But he had started to sound suspicious.

"I can't," Thomas Bruckner said.

"Why not?"

"Because she ain't."

"She ain't what?"

"She ain't in there."

There was a terrible silence. "She ain't in there?"

"No, she ain't."

"Where is she then?"

"She's . . ."

"She's where?"

"She's . . ."

"Where?"

"Outside."

"Outside?"

"Harry, I didn't do nothin' to her."

"Jesus Christ, you sonofabitch."

Bruckner could feel Harry Kriker ready to go. He had been violated in the worst way possible, and when he let himself go it was going to be just unimaginable.

But Kriker surprised Thomas Bruckner by saying, "She's out in the snow?"

"I didn't want her to smell."

Kriker didn't say anything.

"It was the cholera, Harry. I didn't do nothin' to her. You know I wouldn't do nothin' to a little kid like that, Harry."

Kriker still didn't say anything.

"I got her back here and I laid her out on the cot and I put a couple of good warm blankets over her and I gave her water and I asked her if she needed anything. I kept her just as comfortable as I could, and then she just . . ."

Kriker pulled back the hammer on his rifle.

"Then she just . . ." Thomas Bruckner said.

He didn't need to finish his sentence, and he didn't in fact finish his sentence.

In a voice quieter than Bruckner could ever have imagined, Harry Kriker said, "She speak?"

"What?"

"She talk to you?"

"No."

"Not a word?"

"No."

"Not no kind of sound at all?"

"Not no kind of sound."

Kriker pulled the trigger four times. The first bullet tore away Thomas Bruckner's nose and part of his forehead; the second bullet took away his jaw; the third bullet tore a big red hole in his neck, and the fourth bullet made a soft explosion of Thomas Bruckner's chest from a side angle.

There was a great deal of noise and a great deal of smoke. Then there was just the silence again.

After a time of just standing there and looking down at Thomas Bruckner's body, Kriker went outside the cabin into the chill night. He wanted to find the girl, and it did not take him long at all to find her. It was obvious by the mound of snow to the east of the cabin.

He got down on his hands and knees and scooped her out. It took ten minutes.

She was already discolored, and she was already frozen solid.

He knelt there and stared at her.

He wished she'd talked to him, said just one word, at least once.

He wondered what that word would have been.

And then it fell over him, an animal grief that took the form of a kind of baying sound and a shuddering accompanied by soft silent tears as his rough hands traced the cold lines of her tiny beautiful face.

He wanted to cry and needed to cry, but he could not cry. There were just those few tears. All he could do was kneel beside her body and make that baying sound and rock back and forth as if the swaying relieved the grief that gripped him.

He just wished that she had uttered a single word to him in their years together.

He just wished he knew what that word would have been.

He was wondering about this when he heard the horses on the rise to the west.

He turned and saw two riders silhouetted against the moon and the ink-blue sky.

25

GUILD SAID, "You want to call out to him?"

"Thomas?"

"Yeah."

"Okay."

"I don't want him taking any shots at me. I want you to tell him I've got a gun on you and I plan to use it."

"Thomas won't want me to die."

"Good," Guild said. "Then I won't have to kill you." He was tired and he was cold. In weather like this it was easy for the infirmities of age to begin their tireless work on you, sinus trouble in the nose and constipation in the bowels. He wanted in this wind and this night to get the little girl and the robbery money and take them back to their rightful places.

As they came down the hill, the deep shadows of the trees playing gamely across the blue snow, Guild said, "Call out."

Still shackled to the saddlehorn, James Bruckner couldn't cup his hands to shout, so he merely threw back his head and began bellowing.

"You don't shoot now, hear, Thomas? 'Cause Mr. Guild's got a gun on me. Hear?"

Even in the gloom Guild could see his burned face. The poor bastard, Guild thought. Even in the shadows he didn't look like other people.

They made earnest progress through the deep snow, the horses tiring easily, and as they drew even closer, Guild said again, "Call out one more time."

"Wind takes your voice right away, don't it?" James Bruckner said.

Guild nodded for him to yell again.

They were maybe thirty yards away from the cabin when the door burst open, and silhouetted there in the lamplight was the unmistakable form of Harry Kriker.

He had his rifle, and he said only one thing: "You and your brother killed the little girl!"

"Killed her?" James Bruckner started to say.

But Kriker didn't give him any time, no time at all.

Kriker charged through the snow right toward the horses, and he shot James Bruckner clean in the face.

Bruckner's body wanted to fall off the saddle, but the cuffs kept him hanging there.

Kriker went over and started kicking Bruckner in the ribs.

Guild came around the horse and brought the butt of his rifle down hard on the back of Kriker's head.

He was amazed that the blow merely staggered Kriker, didn't knock him out at all.

Kriker spun, his rifle ready.

"They killed the girl."

"I'm sorry, Kriker."

"They took the girl and they killed her."

He was shouting, he was crying, he was crazy.

He pumped another bullet into the dead man.

"He's dead already, Kriker."

Kriker sobbed, then turned back to Guild.

"They killed the girl," he said.

"I doubt they meant to. They didn't seem the kind. Not really."

Kriker's eyes were something Guild could not bear to see.

"You defendin' them?"

"No. I'm just sayin' it was probably an accident is all." He paused. "You'll have to go back along with the money."

"What?" Kriker said.

"I'm afraid so."

Kriker cocked the rifle. "You try to take me in, bounty man, and we're both gonna die. Right here and right now."

"I don't want to have to kill you," Guild said.

"You can't kill me."

"You haven't been keeping track of your bullets."

"The hell."

"You haven't."

"I got two rounds left."

"You got no rounds left."

Kriker hesitated just long enough for Guild to raise the butt of his rifle and bring it down again on the side of Kriker's face.

This time Guild got a pure clean shot at Kriker's temple, and that made a good deal of difference.

Kriker collapsed on the ground.

Guild took the horses around the back of the cabin where they'd be out of the woods, and then he went to the side of the cabin and looked at the dead girl, and then he dragged Kriker inside the cabin. He had taken his last pair of handcuffs from his saddlebag. He cuffed Kriker to the chair. Guild figured Decker and his men would soon be here.

Kriker came awake ten minutes later. Blood was matted in his hair. He looked like an old animal that was dying out his time in confusion and some inexplicable despair.

They sat in the cabin and Guild read a Yankton newspaper from three years ago detailing the Territory's plans to start a mandatory educational system, an idea that was not meeting with a great deal of favor.

Kriker said, "I want to go see the girl."

A thin wind came up, swirling the snow like topsoil. The wind was musical. In Indian legend it was said that this particular kind of music could only be heard over cursed soil or death ground. Given all the people who had died in the past two days, the notion seemed to have a particular relevance.

"I want to go see her."

"Wouldn't be a good idea."

"I don't give a damn she's dead, Guild. I just want to see her."

Guild sighed and put down his paper. "You believe in God?"

"No."

"Then I can't help you much, I guess."

"You gonna tell me about the angels?"

"I was gonna tell you to calm down."

"You don't know how much I loved her."

"I think I can guess."

"I just want to go see her."

"I just want you to stay put."

He started crying then, and Guild had to look away. The sound Kriker made was harsh, and Guild would remember it for a long time.

"You really gonna take me in?"

"I got to, Kriker."

"They'll just hang me."

"That isn't up to me."

"I didn't kill Rig or Tolliver."

"No, but you killed other people before."

"I don't want to die that way."

"What way?"

"In public and all. Them ladies in their fancy hats standin' down there and glarin' up at you."

"I don't have any choice, Kriker."

"You could let me go."

"No."

"You could say I escaped."

"No."

He didn't say anything then for a long time, and Guild rattled the newspaper back into reading shape and put an unlit cigar in his mouth and went back to reading.

Kriker said, "I got a Colt inside my sheepskin pocket. Belonged to Thomas Bruckner."

Guild put down the paper, curious. "Why would you tell me that? Why wouldn't you try to use it to escape?"

"Because I don't want to escape."

"You want me to take the gun?"

"No, not that either."

"Then what?"

Kriker sighed. "Some ways, we're alike."

"I suspect that's true."

"You had some learnin', didn't you?"

"Some. Not a lot."

"You speak fine."

"Worked for a marshal once who was real high on books."

"He real high on dignity?"

"Meaning?"

"Meaning them ladies in their fancy hats lookin' up at you."

Guild was just starting to catch on. He did not feel so bright. It had taken him a long and laborious time to catch on.

Just at dawn Guild went outside the cabin and peed in the snow. There was just enough light that the urine was yellow in the white snow.

The shot came just after.

26

GUILD WENT IN and took the cuffs off Kriker, and then he heaved Kriker up on his shoulders and carried him outside and laid him out next to the girl. In the morning now you could hear dogs and you could hear distant bawling cattle.

Kriker had done a good clean job of it. There was a hole, a messy one, in the back of his head. Guild wondered if he had been afraid. Guild would have been afraid.

Without quite knowing why, Guild knelt down next to Kriker and took the dead man's hand and placed it over the heart of the little girl.

Then he started digging snow up with both his hands, and he covered them good, the two of them, and then he stood up and looked out on the unfurling white land. There was blue sky and a full yellow sun. Warmer now, there was even that kind of sweetness that comes on sunny winter days. It made him think of pretty women on ice skates, their cheeks touched perfect red by the cold, their eyes daring and blue.

He did not look back at Kriker and the girl. They were done, and Guild had enough ghosts inside him. He did not need more.

He had to pee again—he always got this way after terrible things—and then he went to his saddlebags and got some jerky and then he went inside and picked up the paper again and finally lit up the cigar.

Decker and his men came and, of course being parents themselves, made much of the little girl. One man got sick and one man started to cry.

What Decker mostly wanted to know about, standing there inside the cabin with Guild, was how something like this could have happened.

"How the hell'd he get a gun and kill himself that way?"
All Guild said was, "Damned if I know."

Ten minutes later they packed the little girl across the rump of one horse
and Kriker across the rump of another, and then they set out the long
white distance back to the town.

27

WHEN THEY GOT in, Decker told Guild to come around in the morning for
the reward money. He still did not sound happy that the town had been
cheated out of a hanging. In Yankton, Guild thought, in those law courses
Decker had taken, they'd probably taught him that folks just naturally
liked a hanging every now and then, and here Guild had gone and robbed
him of it.

Guild went over to the house he'd been at the other night. He asked for
the straw-haired girl. She came out from behind the blue chenille curtains
downstairs wearing the same gingham dress and the shoes one size too
big. The way they forced her to walk, with sort of a girlish but fetching
lack of grace, made him think she was even more of a kid than she was.
    The madam put a hand on Guild's arm and led him off to the side. She
was a skinny woman who wore hard pink mascara like a death mask. "She
ain't real reliable, truth to tell." She nodded to a woman who looked
much as the madam must have looked twenty years earlier. "Whyn't you
taken Aberdeen over there?"
    Guild shrugged. "Straw-haired one's fine."

Upstairs he said, "Mind if I blow out that kerosene lamp?"
    "I done it twice last night, but I don't feel like doin' it tonight. That's
why Patty's so mad at me."
    "You didn't answer my question."
    "About the lamp?"
    "About the lamp."
    "I don't care if you blow it out."
    So he blew it out and then he went over and sat in the rocking chair
that faced the street below. You could see stars, and closer to the glass of
the window you could see snow. The wind came in torrents and the glass

rattled, and through the cracks you could feel cold. There was laughter in the next room but it sounded sad.

He said, "Would you sit on my lap?"

She said, "Mister, you really should've taken Aberdeen."

"You ever answer a question directly?"

"I sit on your lap?"

"Yes."

"That's all you want me to do?"

"Yes."

"I won't charge you, then."

"One other thing, too."

"I figured."

"Don't talk."

"What?"

"Don't say anything. Just sit on my lap and don't say anything. Don't say anything at all."

"Okay." For the first time, she sounded hesitant, maybe even a little afraid.

But she came over and sat on his lap. Guild kept his word. He did not touch her. He just let her sit there on his knee the way he'd once held a daughter and sometimes a wife. That had been long, long ago. Sitting there in the darkness he thought again of the little girl he'd killed that time, and then he thought of the little girl who'd died of cholera. He thought of James Bruckner's burned face, and he thought of the way the bullet had sounded, so sharp, the one from Kriker's gun when Kriker'd put the Colt in his mouth and pulled the trigger.

Then the wind came again and the window shook and he could feel the cold clean draft.

He sighed, and it was a very deep sigh, and she said, there in the darkness with her perfume and her sweet farm-girl face, "You all right, mister?"

And he sighed again and just stared out the window at the distant meaningless stars and said, "No, I don't suppose I am."

To that, she said nothing at all.

Permissions